Néstor Ponce de León

The Spanish Civil Code

In force in Spain, Cuba, Puerto Rico, and the Philippines

Néstor Ponce de León

The Spanish Civil Code
In force in Spain, Cuba, Puerto Rico, and the Philippines

ISBN/EAN: 9783337378158

Printed in Europe, USA, Canada, Australia, Japan

Cover: Foto ©Andreas Hilbeck / pixelio.de

More available books at **www.hansebooks.com**

THE SPANISH CIVIL CODE

IN FORCE IN

SPAIN, CUBA, PUERTO RICO,

AND THE PHILIPPINES

TRANSLATED BY

Licenciados Clifford S. Walton and Nestor Ponce de Leon.

PUBLISHED UNDER AUTHORITY OF

MAJOR-GENERAL WILLIAM LUDLOW

MILITARY GOVERNOR OF HAVANA.

EDITED BY

MAJOR CLIFFORD S. WALTON,

Member of the College of Lawyers of Havana and of the Washington, D. C. Bar.

HAVANA.
—
LA PROPAGANDA LITERARIA
PRINTING HOUSE.
1899.

HEADQUARTERS DEPARTMENT OF HAVANA

<table>
<tr><td>SPECIAL ORDERS,
No. 68.</td><td>March 21, 1899.</td></tr>
</table>

1. Major *C. S. Walton*, C. P. M., Department of Havana, in addition to his other duties, is hereby directed to arrange for the making of a translation into English of the Spanish Civil Code, with a view to its subsequent publication for general use and information; the particulars of the arrangements proposed and the estimate of cost will be submitted for approval.

* * * * * * *

By command of Major General Ludlow.

H. L. SCOTT.

Adjutant General.

ROYAL DECREE.

Upon the proposal of the Minister of Colonies (Ultramar), approved by the Council of Ministers;

In the name of my August Son, the King D. Alfonso XIII, and as Queen Regent of the Kingdom,—

I decree the following:—

Article 1. The Civil Code in force in the Peninsula, enacted in conformity with the provisions of the law of May 11, 1888, and approved by Royal Decree of the 24th. instant, is hereby extended to the Islands of Cuba, Puerto Rico, and the Philippines.

Art. 2. This Code will go into effect in the aforesaid Islands twenty days after its publication in the official papers of the same.

Art. 3. In harmony with the provisions of art. 1 of the same Code, the laws shall go in force in the Colonial provinces, twenty days after their promulgation, it being understood that this shall be considered as made the day on which their insertions in the official papers of the Islands terminate.

Given at San Ildefonso, the thirty first day of July 1889.

MARIA CHRISTINA.

The Minister of the Colonies,
MANUEL BECERRA.

CIVIL CODE

PRELIMINARY TITLE.

LAWS, THEIR EFFECT, AND GENERAL RULES FOR THEIR APPLICATION.

Article 1. Laws shall be binding in the Peninsula, the adjacent Islands, the Canaries, and African territory, subject to Peninsular legislation, twenty days after their promulgation, if it is not otherwise provided in them.

The promulgation is understood to be made upon the day of the termination of the insertion of the law in the (Official) Gazette.

2. Ignorance of the law does not excuse from compliance with the same.

3. Laws shall not have a retroactive effect, unless the contrary is provided in them.

4. Acts executed against provisions of law are null, except in the cases in which the same law orders their validity.

Rights conceded by the laws may be renounced, provided they are not contrary to public interest or order or prejudicial to a third person.

5. Laws are abrogated only by other subsequent laws, and the disuse or any custom or practice to the contrary shall not prevail against their observance.

6. Any tribunal which refuses to give sentence on the pretext of silence, obscurity, or insufficiency of the laws shall incur responsibility therefor.

When there is no law exactly applicable to the point in controversy, the custom of the place shall be applied, and, in default thereof, the general principles of law.

7. If, in the laws, months, days or nights are referred to, it will be understood that months have thirty days, days twenty four hours, and nights from the setting to the rising of the sun.

If the months are designated by their names, the number of days which they respectively contain shall be computed.

8. Penal laws, police laws, and those of public security are binding on all those who reside in Spanish territory.

9. Laws relating to family rights and obligations, or to the status, condition, and legal capacity of persons are binding on Spaniards, even when residing in a foreign country.

10. Personal property is subject to the laws of the nation of the owner; real property to the laws of the country in which it is situated.

Nevertheless, legal and testamentary successions, in respect to the order of succeeding as well as to the amount of the successional rights and the intrinsic validity of their provisions shall be regulated by the laws of the nation of the person whose succession is considered, whatever may be the nature of the property and the country in which it may be found.

Biscayanes, although they may reside in towns, shall continue to submit, in respect to the property they possess in the level lands, to law 15, title 20 of the Fuero of Vizcaya.

11. The forms and solemnities of contracts, wills, and other public instruments are governed by the laws of the country in which they are executed.

When such instruments are authorized by diplomatic or consular officials of Spain in a foreign land, the solemnities required for their execution by Spanish laws shall be observed.

Notwithstanding the provisions of this and the preceding article, prohibitive laws concerning persons, their acts or property, and those which have for their object the public order and good morals, shall ot become ineffective by laws or sentences dictated or by regulations or conventions agreed upon in a foreign country.

12. Provisions under this title in as far as they determine

the effects of the laws, statutes, and general rules for their application are binding in every province of the Kingdom. The provisions contained in title 4, book 1, are similarly binding.

In all other matters, the provinces and territories, in which local law *(derecho foral)* is in force, shall preserve it, for the present, in its entirety without suffering any alteration in its existing juridical *regime*, whether written or customary, by the publication of this Code which shall be enforced only as supplementary law in default of that which may be considered as such supplementary law by their special laws.

13. Notwithstanding the provisions of the preceding article, this Code shall go into effect in Aragón and in the Balearic Islands at the same time as in the provinces, not under local law, in so far as it may not oppose those provisions, local or customary, which are actually in force.

14. In accordance with the provision of art. 12, what is established in arts. 9. 10, and 11, respecting persons, acts, and property of Spaniards in a foreign land, and that of foreigners in Spain, is applicable to persons, acts, and property of Spaniards in territories or provinces having different civil legislation.

15. Family rights and obligations, those relating to the status, condition, and legal capacity of persons, and those of testamentary or intestate succession, declared in this Code, are applicable:

1. To persons born in common law *(derecho comun)* provinces or territories of parents subject to local law, if the latter, during the minority of the children, or the same children within the year following their majority or emancipation, declare it is their will to subject themselves to the Civil Code.

2. To the children of a father, and, if he does not exist or is unknown, of the mother belonging to provinces or territories subject to common law, even when born in provinces or territories where local law is in force.

3. To those who, proceeding from provinces or territories having local law, should have gained a residence in places subject to common law.

For the effects of this article, a residence will be gained; by a residence of ten years in provinces or territories subject to common law, unless the interested party, before the termination of this period, manifests his will to the contrary; or by a residence of two years, whenever the interested party manifests this to be his will.

Both manifestations should be made before a municipal judge for the corresponding inscription in the Civil Registry.

In every case, the wife shall follow the condition of the husband; and the children, not emancipated, that of their father, and, in his default, that of their mother.

The provisions of this article are of reciprocal application to Spanish provinces and territories having different civil legislation.

16.   In matters which are governed by special laws, the deficiency thereof shall he supplied by the provisions of this Code.

BOOK FIRST

PERSONS.

TITLE I.

SPANIARDS AND FOREIGNERS.

Article **17.** The following are Spaniards:—

1. Persons born in Spanish territory.

2. Children of a Spanish father or mother, although they may have been born out of Spain.

3. Foreigners who may have obtained letters of naturalization.

4. Those who, without them, may have gained a residence in any place in the Monarchy.

18. Children, while they remain under the parental power (*patria potestad*), have the nationality of their parents.

In order that those born of foreign parents in Spanish territory may enjoy the benefits granted to them by no. 1 of art. 17, it shall be an indispensable requisite that the parents declare, in the manner and before the officials specified in art. 19, that they choose, in the name of their children, Spanish nationality, renouncing any other.

19. Children of a foreigner, born in Spanish dominion, should declare, within the year following their majority or emancipation, if they desire to enjoy the quality of Spaniards which art. 17 concedes to them.

Those who are in the Kingdom shall make this declaration before the official in charge of the Civil Registry of the town in which they reside; those who reside in a foreign land, before one of the consular or diplomatic agents of the Spanish government; and those who are in a country in which the government has no agent shall address the Spanish Minister of State.

20. The quality of a Spaniard is lost by acquiring naturalization in a foreign country, or by accepting employment from another government, or by entering the armed service of a foreign power without permission of the King.

21. A Spaniard who loses this quality by acquiring naturalization in a foreign country can recover it, upon returning to the Kingdom, by declaring before an official in charge of the Civil Registry of the domicil which he elects that such is his will, in order that the official may make the corresponding inscription therein, and by renouncing the protection of the flag of such country.

22. A married woman follows the condition and nationality of her husband.

A Spanish woman who marries a foreigner, shall, upon dissolution of the marriage, recover Spanish nationality by fulfilling the requisites expressed in the previous article.

23. Any Spaniard, who loses this quality by accepting employment of any other government, or by entering the armed service of a foreign power without the King's permission, shall not recover Spanish nationality without previously obtaining the royal authorization.

24. Any person, born in a foreign country of a Spanish father or mother, who may have lost Spanish nationality on account of the parents having lost it, may also recover it by complying with the conditions prescribed by art. 19.

25. In order that foreigners who have obtained letters of naturalization or gained a residence in any place in the Monarchy may enjoy Spanish nationality, they have to previously renounce their former nationality, swear to the Constitution of the Monarchy, and inscribe themselves as Spaniards in the Civil Registry.

26. Spaniards who change their domicil to a foreign country, where they may be considered as natives without other conditions than that of residence in it, in order to [preserve their

Spanish nationality, shall be required to manifest that such is their will before the Spanish diplomatic or consular agent who shall inscribe them in the Registry of Spanish residents, as well as their consorts, if they are married, and any children which they may have.

27.   Foreigners enjoy in Spain the rights which the civil laws concede to Spaniards with the exception of what is provided in art. 2 of the Constitution of the State or in international treaties.

28.   Corporations, institutions, and associations recognized by law and domiciled in Spain shall enjoy Spanish nationality, provided they possess the character of juridical persons in accordance with the provisions of the present Code.

Associations domiciled in a foreign land shall have in Spain the consideration and rights which treaties or special laws may determine.

TITLE II.

BIRTH AND EXTINCTION OF CIVIL PERSONALITY.

CHAPTER FIRST.

NATURAL PERSONS.

Article 29.   Birth determines personality; but the conceived child is considered as born for all the effects favorable to it, provided that it be born with the conditions which are expressed in the following article.

30.   For civil effects, the foetus shall only be considered as born when it may have a human figure and shall live twenty four hours entirely separated from the mother *(seno materno)*.

31.   Priority of birth, in case of double parturition, gives to the first born the rights which the law recognizes in primogeniture.

32.   Civil personality is extinguished by the death of a person.

Minority, insanity or imbecility, state of being deaf and dumb, prodigality, and civil interdiction are only restrictions upon juridical personality.   Those who are in any of these conditions are susceptible of rights and even obligations when such rights or obligations arise from the facts or the relations between the property of the incapacitated and a third person.

33.   If there is doubt, between two or more persons called to succeed each other, which of them has died first, he, who alleges the prior death of one or the other, shall be obliged to prove it; in default of proof, it will be presumed that they both died at the same time, and the transmission of rights from one to the other will not take place.

34.   In respect to the presumption of the death of an absent person and its effects, the provisions of title 8 of this book shall rule.

CHAPTER II.

JURIDICAL PERSONS.

Article 35.   The following are juridical persons:

1.   Corporations, associations, and institutions of public interest recognized by law.

Their personality begins from the very moment in which, in accordance with law, they shall have become validly constituted.

2   Associations of private interests, whether they may be civil, mercantile or industrial, to which the law concedes proper personality, independent of that of each one of the associates.

36.   The associations, to which no. 2 of the previous article refers, shall be governed by the provisions relative to the contract of association, according to the nature of the same.

37.   The civil capacity of corporations shall be regulated by the laws which have created or recognized them, those of associations by their statutes; and those of institutions by the rules of their establishment, duly approved by administrative authority, when such requirement is necessary.

38.   Juridical persons can acquire and possess property of every class, as well as contract obligations and enforce civil and criminal actions, in conformity with the laws and rules of their constitution.

The Church shall be governed, in this particular, by what has been agreed between both powers; and the establishments of instruction and beneficence by the provisions of the special laws.

39. When corporations, associations, and institutions have ceased to act, because of the expiration of the periods during which they should legally exist, or by having realized the ends for which they were constituted, or because it has become impossible to apply to such ends the activity and the means at their disposal, their property shall receive the application which the laws or their statutes or the clauses of their foundation have assigned to them in anticipation of such cases.

When nothing has been previously established, the property shall be applied to the realization of similar purposes in the interests of the region, province, or municipal district which should have principally reaped the benefits of the extinguished institutions.

TITLE III.
DOMICIL.

Article 40. For the enforcement of the rights and the fulfillment of civil obligations, the domicil of natural persons is the place of their usual residence; and, in certain cases, that determined by the Law of Civil Procedure.

The domicil of diplomatic residents, who by reason of their duties in a foreign land enjoy the rights of extra-territoriality, shall be the last domicil which they had when in Spanish territory.

41. When neither the law which has created or recognized them, nor the statutes or rules of their foundation shall fix the domicil of juridical persons, it shall be understood that they have it at the place where their legal representation is established or where they exercise the principal functions for which they were established.

TITLE IV.
MARRIAGE.

CHAPTER FIRST.
GENERAL PROVISION.

SECTION FIRST.
FORMS OF MARRIAGE.

Article 42. The law recognizes two forms of marriage, the canonical, which all who profess the Catholic religion should contract, and the civil, which shall be celebrated in the manner provided in this Code.

SECTION SECOND.

PROVISIONS COMMON TO BOTHS FORMS OF MARRIAGE.

Article **43**. Future espousals do not cause obligation to contract marriage. No tribunal shall entertain a complaint in which their fulfillment is claimed.

44. When the promise has been made in a public or private document by a person of age, or by a minor, assisted by the person whose consent is necessary in order to celebrate the marriage, or when the banns have been published, the one who refuses to marry, without just cause, shall be obliged to indemnify the other party for the expenses which he or she may have incurred by reason of the promised marriage.

An action in order to recover the indemnity for expenses, to which the previous paragraph refers, can be exercised only within a year, counted from the day of the refusal to celebrate the marriage.

45. Marriage is forbidden:

1. To the minor who has not obtained consent and to a person of age who has not asked the advice of the persons to whom it pertains to authorize one or the other, in the cases provided for by law.

2. To the widow, during the three hundred and one days following the death of her husband, or before child birth if she should have been left pregnant, and to the woman whose marriage may have been declared null, under the same circumstances and limitations, to be counted from her legal separation.

3. To the guardian and his or her descendants with respect to persons whom such guardian may have or may have had under charge, until the guardianship has terminated and the accounts of the same have been approved, except in the cases where the father of the person, subject to guardianship, has authorized the marriage in a will or in a public instrument.

46. The consent, referred to in no. 1 of the preceding article, ought to be granted to the legitimate children by the father; in his default, or where he is impeded, the power to grant it devolves, in this order; upon the mother, the paternal and maternal grandparents, and, in default of all of them, upon the family council.

Recognized natural children or children legitimated by royal concession should ask such consent of those who have recognized or legitimated them, of their ascendants, and of the family council, in the order stated in the preceding paragraph.

Adopted children shall ask such consent of the adopting father, and, in his default, of the persons of the natural family upon whom it may devolve.

Other illegitimate children should obtain the consent of their mother, when she is lawfully known, that of the maternal grandparents, in similar cases, and, in default of the above, that of the family council.

It pertains to the heads of foundling institutions to give consent for marriage to those educated therein.

47. Children of age are obliged to ask the advice of the father, and, in his default, of the mother. If they should not have obtained it, or it should be unfavorable, the marriage cannot be celebrated until three months after the petition is made.

48. The consent and the favorable advice for the celebration of a marriage should be proven, upon the latter being asked, by a document authorized by a civil or ecclesiastical Notary or the Municipal Judge of the petitioner's domicil.

When the consent has been asked in vain, the lapse of time, to which the preceding article refers, shall be proven in the same manner.

49. None of those called to give their consent or advice is obliged to make known the reasons for granting or denying it, nor is there any remedy against such dissent.

50. When, notwithstanding the prohibition of art. 45, the persons comprehended within it get married, their marriage shall be valid; but the contracting parties, without prejudice to the provisions of the Penal Code, shall remain subject to the following rules:

1. The marriage shall be understood as contracted with the absolute separation of property, and each consort shall retain the dominion and administration of that which belong to

him or her, making as his or her own all the fruits, although with the obligation of proportionally contributing to the support of the marriage charges.

2.　Neither one of the consorts shall receive from the other anything by donation or by will.

The provisions of the two preceding rules shall not apply in the cases of no. 2 of art. 45, when dispensation has been obtained.

3.　When one of the consorts is a minor, not emancipated, he shall not receive the administration of his property until he attains majority.

In the meantime, he shall only have a right to support which shall not exceed the net income from his property.

4.　In the cases of no. 3 of art. 45, the guardian shall, besides, lose the administration of the property of the ward during her minority.

51.　Civil or canonical marriage shall produce no civil effects, when either one of the consorts is already lawfully married.

52.　Matrimony is dissolved by the death of one of the consorts.

SECTION THIRD.

PROOF OF MARRIAGE.

Article 53.　Marriages celebrated before this Code went into effect shall be proven in the manner established by the former laws. Those contracted afterwards shall be proven only by the certification of the record of the Civil Registry, unless the books thereof have not existed or have disappeared or a question is pending before the courts, in which cases all kinds of proof are admissible.

54.　In the cases referred to in paragraph second of the previous article, the constant possession of the status of the parents, united to the certifications of the births of their children as legitimate ones, shall be one of the means of proof of the marriage of the parents, if it is not shown that one of the two was bound by another previous marriage.

55.　A marriage contracted in a foreign country, where

such acts are not subject to a regular or authenticate registration, may be proven by any of the means of proof admitted by law.

SECTION FOURTH.

RIGHTS AND OBLIGATIONS BETWEEN HUSBAND ANE WIFE.

Article **56.** The consorts are obliged to live together, to be faithful to and mutually help each other.

57. The husband is obliged to protect the wife and the latter to obey the husband.

58. The wife is obliged to follow her husband wherever he may establish his residence. The tribunals, nevertheless, may, with just cause, exempt her from this obligation when the husband changes his residence beyond the seas or to a foreign country.

59. The husband is the administrator of the property of the conjugal society, except when stipulated to the contrary, and that provided in art. 1384.

When he is under eighteen years of age, he cannot administer without consent of his father and, in his default, without that of the mother, and, in default of both, without that of his guardian.

Neither can he appear in a suit in court without the assistance of said persons.

In no case, until he has attained majority, can the husband, without the consent of the persons, mentioned in the preceding paragraph, borrow money, burden nor alienate the real property.

60. The husband is the representative of his wife. She cannot, without his permission, appear in a suit by herself or through an attorney.

Nevertheless, she does not require such permission to defend herself in a criminal proceeding or for bringing suit or defending herself in suits with her husband, or when she may have obtained habilitation in conformity with what the law of Civil Procedure may provide.

61. Neither can the wife without the permission or power of her husband acquire (property) by an onerous or lucrative title, alienate her property or bind herself, except in the cases and with the limitation established by law.

62.　Acts, executed by the wife, contrary to the provisions of the preceding articles, are null and void, except when they involve things which by their nature are destined for the ordinary consumption of the family, in which case, purchases made by the wife shall be valid.

Purchases of jewels, furniture and precious objects, made, without the permission of the husband, shall only be confirmed when he may have consented that his wife should have the use and enjoyment of such objects.

63.　The wife, without permission of the husband, can:—

1.　Execute a will.

2.　Exercise the rights and fulfill the duties which pertain to her in respect to legitimate and recognized natural children whom she may have had by another, and in respect to the property of the same.

64.　The wife shall share the honors of the husband, except those which may be strictly and exclusively personal, and shall retain them as long as she does not contract a new marriage.

65.　Only the husband and his heirs can claim the nullity of the acts executed by the wife without competent permission or authorization.

66.　What is established in this section is understood without prejudice to the provisions of the present Code, about absence, incapacity, prodigality, and interdiction of the husband.

SECTION FIFTH.

EFFECTS OF NULLITY OF MARRIAGE AND DIVORCE.

Article 67.　The civil effects of petitions and decrees about the nullity of marriage and about divorce can only be obtained before the ordinary tribunals.

68.　After the petitions, which are referred to in the preceding article, are interposed and admitted, the following provisions shall be adopted during the pendency of the suit:

1.　To separate the consorts in every case.

2.   To place the wife under protection in the cases and in the form provided by the Law of Civil Procedure.

3.   To place the children under the care of one or both of the consorts, as may be proper.

4.   To provide for the support of the wife and the children who do not remain under the power of the father.

5.   To decree the necessary measures to prevent the husband, who may have given cause for the divorce, or against whom the petition for nullity of the marriage has been instituted, from causing injury to the wife in the administration of her property.

69.   Marriage contracted in good faith produces civil effects, although it may be declared null and void.

When good faith has existed on the part of one of the consorts alone, it shall produce civil effects only as to this one and the children.

Good faith is presumed, if the contrary is not shown.

When bad faith has existed on the part of both consorts, the marriage shall only produce civil effects in respect to the children.

70.   Wen the nullity of the marriage has been finally decreed, the sons over three years of age shall remain under the care of the father, and the daughters under the care of the mother, if there should have been good faith on the part of both consorts.

When good faith may have existed on the part of only one of the consorts, the children of both sexes shall remain under this one's power and care.

When both are guilty of bad faith, the court shall decide as to the disposition of the children in the form provided for in paragraph second of no. 2 of art. 73.

The sons and daughters, under three years of age, shall remain under the care of the mother, in every case, until they complete this age, unless on account of special reasons the sentence has disposed otherwise.

71.   The provisions of the first and second paragraphs of the preceding article shall not be effective, if the parents, by common agreement, shall provide otherwise for the care of the children.

72. The final decree of nullity shall produce, in respect to the property of the marriage, the same effects as the dissolution by death; but the consort who has acted in bad faith shall have no rights to the profits of the conjugal society *(gananciales)*.

When both have acted in bad faith, that shown by one shall be a set off agsinst the other.

73. A decree of divorce shall produce the following effects:

1.   The separation of the consorts.

2.   The children to remain or be put under the power and protection of the innocent consort.

When both are guilty, a guardian shall be provided for the children in conformity with the provisions of this Code.

Nevertheless, when the decree has not provided otherwise, the mother, in every case, shall have in her care the children under three years of age.

Upon the death of the innocent consort, the guilty one shall recover the parental power and his or her rights, when the cause which gave origin for the divorce should have been adultery, violence to the person, or grave acts of contumely *(injurias graves)*.

When the causes are different, a guardian shall be appointed for the children.

The deprivation of the parental power and of its rights shall not exempt the guilty consort from the fulfillment of the obligations which this Code imposes upon him or her in respect to the children.

3.   The guilty consort shall lose all that may have been given or promised him or her by the innocent one or by any other person in consideration for such one; and the innocent consort shall keep all that he has received from the guilty one, being able, besides, to claim forthwith all that may have been promised by the guilty one.

4.   The separation of the property of the conjugal society, and the loss of the administration of that of the wife, if the husband should possess it, and is the one who gave cause for the divorce.

The retention by the innocent husband of the administration, if he should have it, of the property of the wife who shall only have the right to be supported.

74. Reconciliation determines the suit for divorce and leaves, without subsequent effects, the decree dictated in respect thereto; but the consorts must give notice of it to the tribunal who has or may have cognizance of the suit.

The effects of the decree shall subsist in respect to the children, without prejudice to the provision of the preceding article, when it is founded on the attempt or connivance of the husban or of the wife to corrupt the sons or to prostitute their daughters, in which case, if the sons and daughters still continue under the parental power, the tribunals shall adopt convenient measures in order to protect them from corruption or prostitution.

CHAPTER SECOND.
CANONICAL MARRIAGE.

Article 75. The requisites, form, and solemnities for the celebration of canonical marriage shall be governed by the provisions of the Catholic Church and of the Holy Council of Trent, accepted as laws of the Kingdom.

76. Canonical marriage shall produce all the civil effects in respect to the persons and property of the consorts and their descendants.

77. A municipal judge or other state official shall be present at the act of celebration of the canonical marriage with the sole object of verifying the immediate inscription of it in the Civil Registry.

For this object, the contracting parties are obliged to give notice in writing to the respective Municipal Judge, twenty four hours, at least, before the day, hour, and place where the marriage is to be celebrated, incurring, if they do not do so, a fine of from five to eighty pesetas.

The Municipal Judge shall give a receipt for the notice from the contracting parties. Should he decline to give it, he shall incur a fine, which shall not be less than twenty nor exceed one hundred pesetas.

The celebration of the canonical marriage shall not be proceeded with without the presentation of said receipt to the parochial priest.

If the marriage is celebrated without the presence of the Municipal Judge or his representative, notwithstanding that the contracting parties may have advised him of it, the transcription of the certificate of the canonical marriage to the Civil Registry shall be done at his expense, besides he shall pay a fine which shall not be less than twenty nor exceed one hundred pesetas. In this case, the marriage shall produce all its civil effects from the moment of its celebration.

If the contracting parties should be to blame for not having given notice to the Municipal Judge, they can remedy the defect, asking for the inscription of the marriage in the Civil Registry.

In this case, the marriage shall produce no civil effects, except from its inscription.

78. Those who contract canonical marriage *in articulo mortis* shall give notice to the official in charge of the Civil Registry, at any time whatever prior to its celebration, and prove, in any manner whatever, that they have fulfilled this duty.

The penalties imposed upon contracting parties who omit this requisite shall not be applicable to the case of marriage *in articulo mortis* when it is shown that it was impossible to give timely notice.

In every case, in order that the marriage may produce civil effects from the date of its celebration, the sacramental certificate shall be inscribed in the Registry within ten days next following.

79. The secret marriage of conscience, celebrated before the church, is not subject to any formality of the civil order, neither shall it produce civil effects, except from the moment of its publication by virtue of its inscription in the Registry. This marriage, shall, nevertheless, produce civil effects from its celebration, if both contracting parties, of common accord, shall ask the bishop who may have authorized it for a copy of the entry made in the secret Registry of the bishopric, and shall directly send it, with the proper secrecy to the *Dirección General* of the Civil Registry asking for its inscription.

For this purpose the *Dirección General* shall keep a special and secret Registry with the necessary precautions that the contents of such inscriptions may not be known, until the interested parties ask that they may be given publicity by transferring the same to the Municipal Registry of their domicil.

80. The cognizance of suits for nullity and divorce, in case of canonical marriages, belong to the ecclesiastical tribunals.

81. When a suit for divorce or nullity of marriage is commenced before the ecclesiastical tribunal, it belongs to the civil tribunal to dictate, upon the petition of the party interested, the dispositions referred to in art. 68.

82. A final decree for nullity or divorce of canonical marriage shall be inscribed in the Civil Registry, and shall be presented to the ordinary tribunal in order to ask for its execution as to the part relating to civil effects.

CHAPTER THIRD.
CIVIL MARRIAGE.

SECTION FIRST.
CAPACITY OF CONTRACTING PARTIES.

Article 83. The following cannot contract marriage:

1. Males, until they have attained the full age of fourteen, and females until they have attained the full age of twelve.

Marriage contracted by person under puberty, shall, nevertheless, be *ipso facto* validated, without the necessity of an express declaration, if a day after having arrived at the legal age of puberty, they should have lived together without having brought suit against its validity, or if the woman should have conceived before the legal age of puberty or before having established such suit.

2. Those who were not in the full exercise of their reason at the time of contracting marriage.

3. Those who suffered from physical, absolute or relative impotency for the purposes of generation, prior to the celebration of the marriage, in a patent, perpetual or incurable manner.

4. Those ordained *in sacris* and those professed in an

approved religious canonical order, bound by a solemn pledge of chastity, except those who may have obtained the corresponding canonical dispensation.

5.   Those that are already lawfully married.

84.   Neither can the following contract marriage between themselves:

1.   The ascendants or descendants by legitimate or natural consanguinity or affinity.

2.   Collaterals by legitimate consanguinity up to and including the fourth degree.

3.   Collaterals by legitimate affinity up to and including the fourth degree.

4.   Collaterals by natural consanguinity or affinity up to and including the second degree.

5.   The adopting father and mother and the adopted; the latter and the surviving consort of the adopters, and the adopters and the surviving consort of the adopted.

6.   The legitimate descendants of the adopter with the adopted, while the relation of adoption lasts.

7.   Adulterers who have been condemned by a final sentence.

Those who have been condemned as authors or author and accomplice of the death of the consort of any of the parties.

85.   The goverment, with just cause, can, on petition of a party, dispense the inpediment included in no. 2 of art. 45; the third and fourth degrees of collateral relationship by legitimate consanguinity; the impediments growing out of legitimate or natural affinity between collaterals, and those referring to the descendants of the adopter.

SECTION SECOND.
CELEBRATION OF MARRIAGE.

Article **86.**   Those who, in conformity with art. 42, desire to contract marriage in the manner detemined in this Code, shall present to the Municipal Judge of their domicil a declaration signed by both contracting parties, in which appears:

1.   The names, surnames, ages, professions, domicils or residences of the contracting parties.

2.   The names, surnames, professions, domicils or residences of the parents.

Certificates of birth and of the status of the contracting parties, the consent or advice, if required, and dispensations, when necessary, shall accompany this declaration.

87. Marriages shall be celebrated personally or by a proxy to whom a special power has been granted; but the presence of the contracting party who is domiciled or resides in the district of the Judge who is to authorize the marriage shall always be necessary.

The name of the person with whom the marriage is to be celebrated shall be expressed in the special power, and such power shall be valid if, before its celebration, the person so authorized should not have been notified in an authentic form of the revocation of the power.

88. When the Municipal Judge, selected for the celebration of the marriage, should not be at the time (of the district) of both contracting parties, two declarations shall be presented, one before the Municipal Judge of each contracting party, expressing which of the two Judges they have chosen for the celebrations of the marriage, and, in both courts, the proceedings which are established in the following articles shall be observed.

89.   After the petition has been ratified by both parties, the Municipal Judge shall order that edicts or proclamations shall be posted for fifteen days announcing the pretention with all the details, indicated in art. 86 and requiring those who have information of any impediment thereto to denounce it.

Similar edicts shall be sent to the Municipal Judges of the towns in which the interested parties may have lived or been domiciled, during the last two years, requiring that they be posted in the place of the holding of their public court for the period of fifteen days, and that, after the lapse of this time, they should be returned with a certification of said requisite have been fulfilled and whether or not any impediment has been denounced.

90. Soldiers in active service who may intend to contract marriage shall be dispensed from publishing such edicts out-. side of the place where they reside, if they present certificates

that they are unmarried, issued by the commandig officer of the military body to which they belong.

91. When the interested parties are foreigners, and have not resided two years in Spain, they shall prove, by a certificate in due form given by competent authority, that in the territory where they have had their domicil or residence, during the last two years, publication has been made of the marriage which they intend to contract with all the solemnities which are required in said place.

92. In all other cases, the government can dispense with the publication of the banns on account of serious causes, properly approved.

93. Notwithstanding what is provided in the preceding articles, the Municipal Judge shall authorize the marriage of a person who is in imminent danger of death, whether he is domiciled in the place or is a transient.

This marriage shall be considered as conditional, until the previous single status of the contracting parties be legally established.

94. Paymasters of war vessels and captains of merchantmen shall authorize marriages which are celebrated on board (ship) in imminent danger of death.

These marriages shall also be considered as conditional.

95. The provision of the preceding article is applicable to the commanders of military bodies in the field in default of a municipal judge, respecting members of the same who intend to celebrated marriage, *in artículo mortis.*

96. When the fifteen days, which are referred to in art. 89, have elapsed without any impediment having been denounced, and the Municipal Judge.has no knowledge of any such, he shall proceed with the celebration of the marriage in the manner and form prescribed in the Code.

When a year elapses from the publication of the banns without the marriage taking place, the marriage shall not be celebrated without a new publication.

97. When, before the celebration of the marriage, any person should appear opposing it and alleging a lawful impediment, or the Municipal Judge should have knownedge of any

such, he shall suspend the celebration of the marriage, until the truth or falseness of the impediment is established in a final sentence.

98. All those who have knowledge of a pretention of a marriage are obliged to denounce any impediment known to them.

Such denouncement having been made, it shall be transmitted to the Public Attorney, who, if he finds any legal foundation therefor, shall establish opposition to the marriage.

Only private parties who may have an interest in preventing the marriage shall by themselves formalize the opposition and in both cases such opposition shall be followed in conformity with the Law of Civil Procedure, giving it the form of an incidental question *(tramitación de los incidentes)*.

99. When, by a final sentence, the alleged impediments are declared false, he, who taking them as a basis formalized in his name the opposition to the marriage, remains obliged to make indemnity for damages and injuries.

100 The marriage shall be celebrated by the contracting parties appearing before the Municipal Judge, or one of them and the person to whom the absentee may have granted a special power to represent him, accompanied by two witnesses of lawful age and without legal impediments.

Forthwith, the Municipal Judge, after reading arts. 56 and 57 of this Code, shall ask each one of the contracting parties if they persist in the resolution to celebrate the marriage, and if he must actually perform it; and, if both reply affirmatively, he shall drawn up the act of marriage with all the circumstances necessary to make it appear that the requirements, provided in this section, have been complied with.

The act shall be signed by the Judge, the contracting parties, the witnesses and the Secretary (clerk) of the Court.

Consuls and vice-consuls shall exercise the functions of municipal judges in marriages of Spaniards, celebrated in foreign countries.

SECTION THIRD.
NULLITY OF MARRIAGE.

Article 101.   The following marriages are null:—

1.   Those celebrated between persons to whom arts. 83 and 84 refer, except in cases of dispensation.

2.   Those contracted by error as to the person, or by compulsion or serious fear which avoids the consent.

3.   Those contracted by the abductor with the abducted, while the latter is in the former's power.

4.   Those which are celebrated without the intervention of a competent municipal judge or of the person who must authorize it in his place, and without the presence of the witnesses, required by art. 100.

102.   The action to ask for the nullity of the marriage belongs to the consorts, to the Public Attorney, and to any persons whatever who may have interest in it.

The cases of abduction, error, force or fear are excepted, in which cases only the consort, who may have suffered from it, can exercise it; and that of impotency, in which the action belongs to one or the other consort and to the persons who may have an interest in the nullity.

The action lapses, and the marriage shall be confirmed, in their respective cases, when the consorts having lived together during six month after the error has disappeared or after the force or the cause of the fear has ceased, or if, after the abducted party having recovered liberty, he or she should not have interposed a demand for nullity during said term.

103.   The civil tribunals shall take cognizance of the suits for nullity of marriages, celebrated in conformity with the provisions of this chapter, shall adopt the measures, indicated in art. 68, and shall give sentence definitely.

SECTION FOURTH.
DIVORCE.

Article 104.   Divorce only produces the suspension of the life in common of the consorts.

105.   The legitimate causes for divorce are:

1. Adultery on the part of the wife, in every case, and on the part of the husband, when public scandal or disgrace of the wife results from it.

2. Personal violence actually inflicted or grave acts of contumely *(injurias graves)*.

3. Violence exercised by the husband over the wife in order to oblige her to change her religion.

4. The proposal of the husband to prostitute his wife.

5. The atempts of the husband or wife to corrupt their sons or to prostitute their daughters, and the connivance in their corruption or prostitution.

6. The condemnation of a consort to *cadena perpetua* (1) or to *reclusion perpetua* (2).

106. Only the innocent consort can petition for divorce.

107. The provision of art. 103 shall be applicable to suits for divorce and their incidents.

TITLE V.
PATERNITY AND FILIATION.

CHAPTER FIRST.
LEGITIMATE CHILDREN·

Article **108.** Children, born after one hundred and eighty days next following the celebration of marriage and before three hundred days next following its dissolution or the separation of the consorts, shall be presumed legitimate children.

Against this presumption no other proof shall be admitted than that of the physical impossibility of the husband to have had access to his wife, during the first one hundred and twenty days of these three hundred next preceding the birth of the child.

109. A child shall be presumed to be legitimate, even though the mother should have declared against its legitimacy, or should have been condemned as an adulteress.

110. The child, born within one hundred and eighty days

---

(1) To perpetually wear chains and be confined outside of the Islands of Cuba and Porto Rico (P. C. 104).

(2) To be perpetually imprisoned at forced labor within or without the Islands of Cuba and Porto Rico (P. C. 108).

next following the celebration of a marriage, shall be presumed to be legitimate, if any of the following circumstances exist:

1.   If the husband knew, proviously to the marriage, that his wife was pregnant.

2.   If he, being present, has consented that in the record of the birth his name should be given to the child, delivered by his wife.

3.   If he has expressly or tacitly recognized the child as his own.

111.   The husband or his heirs can disavow the legitimacy of the child, born after the expiration of three hundred days next following the dissolution of the marriage or the actual legal separation of the consorts; but both the son and the mother shall also have a right to verify, in such cases, the paternity of the husband.

112.   The heirs can contest the legitimacy of the child only in the following cases:

1.   If the husband has died before the expiration of the term fixed for instituting his action in court.

2.   If he dies after presenting the complaint and without having withdrawn it.

3.   If the child was born after the death of the husband.

113.   The action to contest the legitimacy of the child shall be instituted within two months next following the inscription of the birth in the Registry, should the husband be in the same place, or, in certain cases, (if) any one of his heirs (should be present).

When they are absent, the term shall be three months if they reside in Spain, and six (months) if without Spain.   When the birth of the child has been concealed, the term shall commence to be counted from the date of the discovery of the fraud.

114.   Legitimate children have the right:

1.   To bear the family names of the father and the mother.

2.   To receive support from the same, from their ascendants, and, in certain cases, from his brothers in accordance with art. 143.

3.   To *legitime* the and other suecessional rights recognized in them by this Code.

CHAPTER SECOND.

PROOFS OF THE FILIATION OF LEGITIMATE CHILDREN.

Article 115.   The filiation of legitimate children is proven by the record of the birth, inscribed in the Civil Registry, or by an authentic instrument, or a final sentence in the cases to which arts. 110 to 113 of the preceding chapter refer.

116.   In default of the documents, stated in the preceding article, filiation shall be proven by the constant posession of the status of a legitimate child.

117.   In default of the records of birth, authentic docu-, ments, a final sentence, or posession of status, legitimate filiation may be proven by any other means, provided there is a commencement of proof in writing coming from both parents, either conjointly or severally.

118.   The action to claim its legitimacy belongs to the child during all his life and shall be transmitted to its heirs, should he die during minority or be a lunatic. In such cases, the heirs shall have a term of five years for instituting the action.

The action already instituted by the child is transmitted by its death to the heirs, if it has not before then become void.

CHAPTER THIRD.

LEGITIMATED CHILDREN.

Article 119.   Only natural children can be legitimated.

Natural children are those born out of marriage of parents who, at the date of the conception of the child, could have married with or without dispensation.

120.   Legitimation may be obtained:

1.   By the subsequent marriage of the parents.

2.   By Royal Concession.

121.   Children can only be considered as legitimated by a subsequent marriage, when they have been recognized by the parents before or after the celebration of such marriage.

122.   Those legitimated by subsequent marriage shall enjoy the same rights as legitimate children.

123.   Legitimation shall produce its effects in any case from the date of the marriage.

124. The legitimation of the children who have died before the celebration of the marriage shall benefit their descendants.

125. For the legitimation by Royal Concession the following requirements are necessary:

1. That legitimatiom by subsequent marriage may not be possible.

2. That it may be asked by the parents or by one of them.

3. That the father or mother asking for it has no legitimate children, nor children legitimated by subsequent marriage, nor descendants of the same.

4. That if the party asking for it is married, he has to obtain the consent of the other consort.

126. Legitimation. by Royal Concession may also be obtained by the child whose deceased father or mother has shown in his or her will or in a public instrument a desire to legitimate it, provided the condition stated in no. 3 of the preceding article is complied with.

127. Legitimation by Royal Concession entitles the legitimated child.

1. To bear the name of the father or mother who has asked for it.

2. To receive support from the same in the form expressed in art. 143.

3. To the hereditary share prescribed in this Code.

128. The legitimation may be contested by those believing that their rights may be injured when it may be granted to persons not having the legal status of natural children, or when the requirements set forth in this chapter do not exist.

CHAPTER TOURTH.

ILLEGITIMATE CHILDREN.

SECTION FIRST.

RECOGNITION OF NATURAL CHILDREN.

Article **129.** A natural child may be recognized by the father and mother conjointly or by only one of them.

130. In case the recognition is made by only one of the parents, it shall be presumed that the child is a natural one, if the party recognizing it had, at the time of the conception, legal capacity to contract marriage.

131. The recognition of a natural child shall be made in the record of birth, by will, or by any other public instrument.

132. When the father or mother alone shall make the recognition, he or she shall not reveal the name of the person, the other parent of the child, nor express any circumstance by which it may be discovered. Public officials shall not authorize any document infringing such a prescription. If notwithstanding this prohibition, they should make it, they will incur a fine of 125 to 500 pesetas, and besides the words containing such revelation shall be stricken out.

133. A child of age cannot be recognized without his consent. When the recognition of the minor is not made in the record of birth or in a will, the judicial approval, after a hearing of the Public Attorney, shall be required.

The minor may, in any case, contest the recognition within four years next following is majority.

134. The recognized natural child has rights:

1, To bear the name of the person recognizing him.

2. To receive support from the same in accordance with art. 143.

3. To receive, in the proper case, the hereditary share provided for in this Code.

135. The father is obliged to recognize the natural child in the following cases:

1. When an incontrovertible paper written by him, expressly recognizing his paternity, is in existence.

2. When the chid is in continuous possession of the status of a natural child of the defendant father, justified by direct act of the same father or his family.

In cases of violation, ravishing or rape, the provisions prescribed in the Penal Code shall be followed in what refers to the recognition of the issue.

136. The mother shall be obliged to recognize the natural child:

1. When the child is, in relation to the mother, included in any of the cases set forth in the preceding article.

2. When the fact of the delivery and the identity of the child are fully proven.

137. The actions for the recognitsion of natural children can be instituted only during the life of the presumed parents, except in the following cases:

1. If the father or mother have died during the minority of the child, in which case, it may commence the action before the expiration of the first four years after its majority.

2. If, after the death of the father or mother, some document, before unknown, should be discovered in which the child is expressly recognized.

In this case the action should be commenced within six months next following the discovery of such document.

138. The recognition made in favor of a child which does not reunite the condition of the second paragraph of art. 119, or in which the prescriptions of this section have not been complied with may be contested by those to whom it may cause injury.

SECTION SECOND.

OTHER ILLEGITIMATE CHILDREN.

Article 139. Illegitimate children not having the legal status of natural children shall only have the right to claim support from their parents in accordance with art. 143.

140. The right to support, referred to in the preceeding article, can only be claimed:

1. If the paternity or maternity is inferred from the final sentence rendered in a criminal or civil proceeding.

2. If the paternity or maternity is shown in an incontrovertible document, from the father or mother, in which the filiation is expressly recognized.

3. In reference to the mother, whenever the fact of the delivery and the identity of the child are fully proven.

141. With exception of the cases expressed in nos. 1 and 2 of the preceding article, no complaint shall be admitted in court the purpose of which may be to investigate either directly or indirectly the paternity of illegitimate children who have not the legal status of natural children.

TITLE VI.
THE SUPPORT OF RELATIONS.

Article **142**. It is understood by support all that is indispensable for maintenance, residence, clothing and medical assistance, according to the social standing of the family.

Support includes also the education and instruction of the party receiving it when he is a minor.

143. The following are obliged to support each other reciprocally to the whole extent specified in the preceding article:

1. The consorts.
2. Legitimate ascendants and descendants.
3. Parents and children legitimated by Royal Concession and the legitimate descendants of the same.
4. Parents and the recognized natural children, and the legitimate descendants of such children.

Parents and illegitimate children not having the legal condition of natural children, owe each other, as support, all the help required for their subsistence. Parents, besides, are bound to bear the expenses of the elementary instruction of the children and of teaching them a profession, art, or office.

Brothers also owe to legitimate brothers, even when only on the mother's or fahter's side, the necessary help for living, when by a physical or moral defect or for any other cause not chargeable to the recipient, he may not be able te procure his maintenance. In this help is comprised, in proper cases, the indispensable expenses for paying the elementary instruction and for the learning of a profession, art, or office.

144. The claim for support, when proper, and two or more are obliged to give it, shall be made in the following order:

1. To the consort.
2. To the descendants in the nearest degree.
3. Tho the ascendants in the nearest degree also.
4. To the brothers.

Between descendants and ascendants, the graduation shall be regulated by the order in which they are called to the legitimate succession of the person entitled to support.

145. Whenever the obligation of giving support falls on two or more persons, the payment of the pension shall be divided among them at a rate in proportion to their respective capitals.

However, in case of urgent necessity and in special circumstances, the Judge may oblige only one of them to pay it provisionally, without prejudice to his right to claim from the other obligated parties the shares that correspond to them.

When two or more persons entitled to it claim suppot, at the same time, from the same person legally bound to give it and such person has not sufficient means to bear the expense of all, the order established in the preceding article shall be observed, unless the persons claiming the support are the consort and a child subject to the parental power, in which case, the latter shall be preferred to the former.

146. The amount of support, in the cases included in the four classes of art. 143, is to be proportioned to the capital or means of the person giving it and to the necessities of the recipient.

147. Support, in the cases to which the preceding article refers, shall be increased or reduced according to the increase or decrease suffered by the necessities of the recipient and the fortune of the person obliged to give it.

148. The obligation to give support shall be binding from the moment that the person having right to claim it may require it for his maintenance, but it shall be paid only from the date of the claim.

Payment shall be made monthly, in advance, and, when the recipient dies, his heirs shall not be obligad to refund whatever shall have been received in advance.

149. The person obliged to give support may, at his option, satisfy it, either by paying the pension that may be fixed or by receiving and maintaining in his own home the person having the right to the same.

150. The obligation to support ceases with the death of the person obliged to give it, even if he pays it in compliance with a final sentence.

151. The right to support can not be renounced or transferred to a third party. Neither can it be set off against what the recipient owes to the party obliged to give it. .

But pensions in arrears for support may be set off and renounced and the right to claim them may be transferred by a title with or without consideration. .

152. The obligation to give support shall cease:

1. By the death of the recipient.

2. When the fortune of the person obliged to pay it is reduced to the state where he cannot pay it without disregarding his own necessities and those of his family.

3. When the recipient is able to exercise an office, profession or industry or has obtained employment or improved his fortune in such a manner that the pension for support may not be necessary for his maintenance.

4. When the recipient, be he a forced heir or not, commits any offence which may cause disinheritance.

5. When the recipient is a descendant of the person obliged to give support, and such necessity is caused by bad conduct or by want of attention to work, while such cause exists.

153. The preceding dispositions are applicable to all other cases in which, by this Code, by testament or by stipulation, a right to support may arise, with the exception of what is stipulated, ordered bi the testator, or prescribed by law for the special case under consideration.

TITLE VII.

THE PARENTAL POWER (*Patria Potestad*).

CHAPTER FIRST.
GENERAL PROVISION.

Article 154. The father, and, in his default, the mother has power over their legitimate children, not emancipated, and the children are bound to obey the parents while they remain under such power and always pay them respect and reverence.

Recognized natural children and adopted minors are under the power of the father or the mother who recognizes or adopts them, and are under the same obligations that are referred to in the preceding paragraph.

CHAPTER SECOND.

EFFECTS OF PARENTAL POWER IN RESPECT TO THE PERSONS OF THE CHILDREN.

Article 155. The father, and, in his default, the mother has, in respect to their children, not emancipated:

1. The duty of maintaining them, to keep them in their company, educate and instruct them in proportion to their means, and represent them in the exercise of all actions that may contribute to their benefit.

2. The right to correct and punish them moderately.

156. The father, and, in his default, the mother may ask for the help of the gubernative authorities which must be given to them in support of their own authority over children, not emancipated, either in the interior of the home or for the detention and even for the retention of the same in establishments for instruction or in institutions legally authorized to receive them.

They can also claim the interference of the Municipal Judge for imposing on their children, up to one month of detention in an institution for correctional purposes; the order of the father or mother with the *visé* of the judge shall be sufficient for carrying into effect such detention.

The provisions of the two preceding paragraphs include children, either legitimate, legitimated, natural recognized or adopted.

157. When the father or mother have contracted a second marriage, and the child has been begotten in a former marriage, they shall be bound to state to the Judge the causes on which they base their decision to punish him and the Judge shall hear the child in a personal appearance and decree or deny the detention without any further remedy. The same thing shall be observed when the child, not emancipated, exercises any charge or office, even when the parents have not contracted a second marriage.

158. The father, and, in his default, the mother shall pay for the maintenance of the detained child but they shall have no intervention in the conduct of the institution where he is

detained; they can only have him released when they deem it proper.

CHAPTER THIRD.

EFFECT OF PARENTAL POWER IN RESPECT TO THE PROPERTY OF THE CHILDREN.

Article 159. The father, or, in his default, the mother is the legal administrator of the property of the children who are under their power.

160. The property which the child, not emancipated, has acquired, or may acquired by his work or industry or by any lucrative title belongs to the child in ownership, and in usufruct to the father or mother who has him in his or her power and company, but if the child with the consent of the parents lives independently of them, he shall be considered as emancipated for all effects in respect to said property and shall hold the domain, usufruct, and administration of it.

161. The ownership and usufruct of what the child acquires with the captial of his parents belong to the latter. But should the parents expressly assign to him the whole or a part of the benefits which he may obtain, such benefits shall not be chargeable to him as (a part of) the inheritance.

162. The property or rents donated or left by will to the child, not emancipated, for the expense of his education and instruction belong to him in ownership and usufruct, but the father or the mother shall have the administration thereof, if no other proviso has been made in the donation or bequest in which case the will of the donors shall be strictly complied with.

163. The parents have, in respect to the property of the children, the usufruct or administration of which belongs to them, the obligations of every usufructuary or administrator, and the special obligations established by section third, title third of the Law of Mortgage.

An inventory shall be made with the intervention of the Public Attorney of all property of the children in which the parents have the administration only, and on petition of the same attorney, the Judge may decree the deposit of the stocks, bonds, etc., *(valores mobiliarios)* belonging to the child.

164. The father or the mother, in proper cases, shall not alienate the real property belonging to the child, the usufruct or administration of which belongs to the parents, nor incumber the same, unless for justified causes of utility or necessity and with previous authorization of the Judge of the domicil, upon consultation with the Public Attorney, without prejudice to the provisions which, in reference to the effects of transmission, are established by the Law of Mortgage.

165. Whenever, in any matter, the father or mother may have an interest in opposition to that of the children, not emancipated, a next friend (*defensor*) shall be appointed for the children who is to represent them in or out of court.

The Judge, on petition of the father or the mother or the minor himself, or the Public Attorney, or of any other person capable of appearing in court, shall appoint, as the next friend, the relative of the minor to whom the legitimate guardianship should belong in such cases, and, in default of the above, to another relative or any other person.

166. The parents who recognize or adopt do not acquire the usufruct of the property of the children, recognized or adopted, neither shall they have the administration of such property, unless they give bond for security of it to the satisfaction of the Judge of the domicile of the minor or of such persons who must concur in the adoption.

CHAPTER FOURTH.

MEANS OF DETERMINING THE PARENTAL POWER.

Article **167.** Parental Power is determined:
1. By the death of the parents or of the child.
2. By emancipation.
3. By the adoption of the child.

168. The mother who contracts a second marriage, loses her parental power over her children, unless her deceased husband, father of them, should have in his will expressly anticipated that his widow could remarry and had ordered that, in such a case, she was to keep and exercise the parental power over his children.

169. The father, and, in similar cases, the' mother loses the power over the children:

1. When, by a final sentence in criminal cases, the deprivement of said right is imposed on him as a penalty.

2. When, by a final sentence in a suit for divorce, such a declaration is made, and during the time that the effects of the same are in force.

170. The parental power is suspended by incapacity or absence of the father or, in similar cases, of the mother, when such causes are judicially declared, and also by civil interdiction.

171. The court can deprive the parent of the parental power or suspend the exercise of the same, when they treat their children with excessive cruelty, or if they give them corrupting orders, advice, or examples. In these cases they can also deprive the parents, either totally or partially of the usufruct of the property of the child, or adopt such measures as they may deem convenient for the interests of the same.

172. If the widowed mo ther, who has remarried becomes once more a widow, she will recover from that moment her power over all the children, not emancipated.

CHAPTER TIFTH.

ADOPTION.

Article **173.** Persons who are in the full exercise of their civil rights and over forty five years of age can adopt. The adopter must be at least fifteen years older than the adopted.

174. Adoption is forbidden:

1. To clergmen.

2. To those having legitimate or legitimated descendants.

3. To the guardaín respecting his ward, until his accounts have been finally approved.

4. To the consort without the consent of the other consort. Consorts may adopt conjointly, and, with the exception of this case, nobody can be adopted by more than one person.

175. The adopted may bear together with the name of his family that of the adopter by so stating it in the deed of adoption.

176. The adopter and the adopted owe support to each other. Thi obligation is understood without injury to the preference right of the recognized natural children and of the ascendants of the adopter to be supported by the same.

177. The adopter acquires no right to inherit from the adopted. Neither does the adopted acquire any right to inherit from the adopter, unless by will, excepting when the adopter in the deed of adoption has obliged himself to institute him as an heir. This obligation shall produce no effect when the adopted dies before the adopter. The adopted retains all the rights belonging to him in his original (natural) familly excepting those referring to the parental power.

178. The adoption shall be made with judicial authorization and it must necessarily state the conset of the adopted, when of age; when a minor, that of the persons who must give consent to the minor's marriage, and, when incapable, that of the guardian. The Public Attorney is to be heard about this matter and the Judge, after taking the steps he may consider necessary, shall approve the adoption, if according to law, and he believes it beneficial for the adopted.

179. After the adoption is finally approved by the Judge, a deed is to be executed, and in it shall be stated the condition under which it has been done, and it shall be inscribed in the corresponding Civil Registry.

180. The minor or the incapable, who has be en adopted may contest the adoption within four years next following his majority or the date from which his incapacity has disappeared.

TITLE VIII.

ABSENCE.

CHAPTER FIRST.

PROVISIONAL MEASURES IN CASE OF ABSENCE.

Article 181. When a person has disappeared from his domicil and his whereabouts is unknown and he has not left any attorney to manage his property, the Judge, on petition of a lawful party or the Public Attorney, may appoint some person to represent him in whatever may be necessary.

The same thing shall be done, when under similar circumstances, the power conferred by the absentee becomes void.

182. After the appointment referred to in the preceding chapter has been made, the Judge shall take the necessary measures to secure the rights and interests of the absentee and shall determine the powers, duties, and remuneration of the appointee, regulating them, according to circumstances, by the provisions established about guardians.

183. The consort who absents himself shall be represented by the one present, whenever they are not legally separated.

If the consort is a minor, a guardian shall be appointed in the usual form.

In default of the consort, the absentee shall be represented by the parents, children or grandparents, in the order established in art. 220.

CHAPTER SECOND.
DECLARATION OF ABSENCE.

Article **184.** When two years have elapsed without any news having been received about the absentee, or from the receipt of the last news, and five years, in case the absentee has left a person in charge of the administration of his property, then the absence may be declared.

185. The declaration of absence may be demanded by:

1. The consort who is present.

2. The heirs instituted in his testament and who present a trustworthy copy of the same.

3. The relations who are to inherit in case of intestacy.

4. Those having in the property of the absentee some right subordinate to the condition of his death.

186. The judicial declaration of absence shall produce no effect until six months after its publication in the official papers.

CHAPTER THIRD.
ADMINISTRATION OF PROPERTY OF THE ABSENTEE.

Article **187.** The administration of the property of the absentee is to be granted, according to the order established in art. 220, to the persons specified therein.

188. The wife of the absentee, if of age, can freely dispose of any property belonging to her; but she cannot alienate, barter or mortgage the husband's own property, neither that of the conjugal society, unless under judicial authorization.

189. When the administration belongs to the children of the absentee and they are minors, a guardian shall be provided for them who shall take charge of the property with legal formalities.

190. The administration shall cease in any of the following cases:

1. When the absentee may appear, either personally or through an attorney.

2. When the death of the absentee is proved and his testamentary heirs or the heirs of the intestate appear.

3. When a third party appears provingby proper instruments that he has acquired by purchase or by any other title the property of the absentee.

In these cases the administrator shall cease in the discharge of his duties and the property shall be placed at the disposal of those having a right to it.

CHAPTER TOURTH.

Article **191.** After thirty years have elapsed from the disappearance of the absentee or since the last news was received about him, or ninety years from his birth, the Judge, on petition of an interested party, shall declare the presumption of his death.

192. The sentence declaring the presumption of death of an absentee shall not go into effect until after six month, to be counted from its publication in the official papers.

193. After the sentence of the presumption of death has been declared final, succession to the estate of the absentee shall be opened and its distribution shall be made with the formalities of testamentary or intestate proceedings, according to the case.

194. Should the absentee appear, or, if without appearance, his existance be proven, then he shall recover his property in the condition in which it is found and the value of that sold, or that acquired with such value; but he can claim neither the fruits nor the rents.

CHAPTER FIFTH.

EFFECTS OF ABSENCE UPON THE EVENTUAL RIGHTS OF THE ABSENTEE.

Article **195.** The person claiming a right belonging to another person, whose existence is not recognized, is bound to prove that such other person existed at the time in which his existence was necessary to acquire such right.

196. Notwithstanding what is prescribed in the preceding article, when a succession has been opened, and an absentee is called to it, the share of the absentee shall accrue to his co-heirs, unless there is some person having rights of his own to claim it. · Both the former and the latter in such cases must make an inventory of said property with the intervention of the Public Attorney.

197. The prescription of the preceding article is to be understood as not impairing the actions of petition of inheritance or other rights belonging to the absentee, his representatives, and persons holding rights under him. Such rights shall not be extinguished, except by the lapse of time fixed for prescription. In the inscription to be made in the Registry of real property, which may accrue to the co-heirs, it shall be expressly stated that they are to remain subject to the provisions of this article.

198. Those who have taken possession of the estate shall become owners of the fruits received by them in good faith, while the absentee does not appear and his rights are not claimed by his representatives or holders of rights under him.

TITLE IX.

GUARDIANSHIP.

CHAPTER FIRST.

GENERAL PROVISIONS.

Article **199.** The object of guardianship is the custody of the person and property or only the property of those who, not being under parental power, are incapable of governing themselves.

200. The following are suject to guardianship:

1. Minors not legally emancipated.

2. Insane and demented persons, though they may have lucid intervals, and the deaf and dumb who do not know how to read and write.

3. Those who have been declared prodigal by a final sentence.

4. Those who are suffering the penalty of civil interdiction.

201. Guardianship shall be exercised by a single guardian under the vigilance of a *protutor* (vigilant guardian) and the family council.

202. The charges of guardian and *protutor* can not to be renounced unless for a lawful cause duly shown.

203. Municipal Judges of the places in which persons subject to guardianship reside shall provide for their custody and for their personal property until a guardian shall be appointed, when there is no other person charged with these duties under the law.

Should they not comply herewith they shall be liable for the damages, accruing on this account, to minors or to incapable persons.

204. Guardianship is conferred:

1. By testament.

2. By law.

3. By the family council.

205. The guardian shall not enter upon the discharge of his duties until his appointment has been inscribed in the Registry of guardianships.

CHAPTER SECOND.

TESTAMENTARY GUARDIANSHIP.

Article 206. The father may appoint a guardian and a *protutor* for his minor children or for those of age who are incapable, be they legitimate or recognized as natural or for some of his illegitimate children whom he is obliged to support, as provided in art. 139.

The mother has similar rights, but if she has contracted a second marriage, the appointment made by her for the children of her first marriage shall not be effective without the approval of the family council.

In any case it shall be necessary that the person appointed guardian or *protutor* shall not be subject to the authority of any other person.

207. A guardian may also be appointed for minors or incapables by the person leaving them an inheritance or an important legacy. The appointment, however, shall produce no effect until the family council has decided to accept the inheritance or legacy.

208. The father as well as the mother may appoint a guardian for each of their children, and make different appointments in order that the appointees may be substituted one for another.

In case of doubt, it shall be understood that a single guardian has been appointed for all the children, and the charge shall be conferred upon the first of these named in the appointment.

209. If different persons shoul have appointed a guardian for the same minor, the charge shall devolve upon:

1. The one chosen by the father or mother.

2. The one appointed by the stranger who has instituted the minor or an incapable as his heir, if the amount of the inheritance is important.

3. The one who has been chosen by the person leaving and important legacy.

If there is more than one guardian in nos. 2 and 3, specified in this article, the familly council shall declare which one is to be preferred.

210. When the guardian is in the discharge of his duties and the one appointed by the father appears, the guardianship is to be inmediately transferred to the latter. If the guardian who appears is the one appointed by a stranger, specified in nos. 2 and 3 of the preceding article, he will limit himself to the administration of the property, which belonged to the person who appointed him, until the incumbent guardian vacates.

CHAPTER THIRD.

LEGITIMATE GUARDIANSHIP.

SECTION FIRST.

GUARDIANSHIP OF MINORS.

Article 211.   Legitimate guardianship of minors, not eman-cipated, belongs solely:

1.   To the paternal grandfather.

2.   To the maternal and grandfather.

3.   To the paternal and maternal grandmothers, in the same order, while they remain in widowhood.

4.   To the eldest of the male brothers of full blood, and, in default of them, to the eldest of the brothers on the paternal or maternal side.

The guardianship, to which this article refers, does not apply to illegitimate children.

212.   Heads of foundling institutions are the guardians of those kept and educated therein.   The representation in court of such officials as guardians shall be assumed by the Public Attorney.

SECTION SECOND.

GUARDIANSHIP OF THE INSANE AND THE DEAF AND DUMB.

Article 213.   No guardians (curators) shall be appointed for insane, demented, and deaf and dumb persons, when of age, without a previous declaration having been made that they are incapable of managing their property.

214.   This declaration may be asked for by the consort and the relatives of the person presumed to be incapable who may have rights to succeed him, in case of intestacy.

215.   The Public Attorney must demand it:

1.   When the person is a raving maniac.

2.   When none of the persons mentioned in the preceding article are in existence, or when they do not make any use of the rights granted to them by it.

3.   When the consort and the heirs of the person presumed to be incapable are minors or have not the personality required to appear in court.

In all these cases, the court shall appoint a next friend (curator) for the person presumed to be incapable who does not wish or is not able to defend himself. In all other cases, the Public Attorney shall be their defender.

216. The courts before declaring the incapacity shall hear the family council and shall personally examine the persons denounced as incapable.

217. The relatives who have solicited the declaration of incapacity shall not be able to give information to the court as members of the family council, but they have the right to be heard by the council when they demand it.

218. The declaration of incapacity shall be made summarily. That which refers to the deaf and dumb shall fix the extent and limits of the guardianship, according to their degree of incapacity.

219. Against the decrees, determining the proceedings for incapacity, the interested parties may interpose a suit in the ordinary form. The next friend of the incapable shall, however, require for it special authorization from the family council.

220. Guardianship of the insane and the deaf and dumb belongs:

1. To the consort not legally separated.
2. To the father, and, in his default, to the mother.
3. To the children.
4. To the grandparents.
5. To the brothers and to the unmarried sisters with due preference to the double relationships stated in no. 4 of art. 211.

If there are children, brothers and sisters, the male shall be preferred to the female, aud the oldest to the youngest.

When there are paternal and maternal grandparents, the male shall also be preferred, and in case they are of the same sex, those of the paternal line.

SECTION THIRD.

GUARDIANSHIP OF PRODIGALS (SPENDTHRIFTS).

Article 221. The declaration of prodigality must be made in a contradictory suit.

The sentence shall determine the acts which are forbidden

to the incapable, the faculties which the guardian (curator) is to exercise in the name of the same, and the cases in which one or the other are bound to consult the family council.

222. The declaration, to which the preceding article refers, can be demanded only by the consort, and the forced heirs of the prodigal, and exceptionally by the Public Attorney, either by himself or on petition of some relative of the former, when they are minors or incapables.

223. When the defendant does not appear at the trial, he shall be represented by the Public Attorney, and, if the latter be a party thereto, by a next friend (curator) appointed by the court, without impairing what the Law of Civil Procedeure prescribes in proceedings in contempt.

224. The declaration of prodigality does not deprive the prodigal of the marital and parental power, nor does it give to the guardian any power over the person of the prodigal.

225. The guardian shall administer the property of the children whom a prodigal may have had from ·a previous marriage.

The wife shall administer her dotal and paraphernal property, the property of the children in common, and that of the conjugal society. She will need a judicial authorization to sell them.

226. The acts of a prodigal, previous to the petition for interdiction, cannot be contested on account of prodigality.

227. The guardianship of the prodigal belongs:

1. To the father, and, in his default, to the mother.
2. To the paternal and maternal grandparents.
3. To the eldest of the emancipated male children.

SECTION FOURTH.

GUARDIANSHIP OT PERSONS SUFFERING INTERDICTION.

Article **228.** When the sentence, in which the penalty of interdiction is interposed, has become final, the Public Attorney shall demand that arts. 203 and 293 shall be complied with. If he fails to do it, he shall be liable for the demages and injuries caused thereby.

The consort and the intestate heirs of one so interdicted may also demand it.

229. Such guardianship shall be limited to the administration of the property and to the representation in court of the interdicted person.

The guardian (curator) of the interdicted person shall be obliged, furthermore, to care for the person and property of the minors or the incapables, who are under the power of the person subject to interdiction, until another guardian is provided for them.

The wife of the interdicted person shall have parental power over their common children while the interdiction lasts.

If she is a minor she shall act under the direction of her father and, in his default that of her mother, and in default of both, that of her guardian.

230. The guardianship of those suffering interdiction is granted in accordance with the order established in art. 220.

CHAPTER FOURTH.
GUARDIANSHIP BY APPOINTMENT.

Article 231. When there are neither testamentary guardian, nor persons called by law to the exercise of a vacant guardianship, it is the duty of the family council to elect the guardian in all the cases mentioned in art. 200.

232. A municipal judge, who may neglect calling a family council in any case in which a guardian ought to be provided for minors or incapables, shall be liable for the damage or injury caused by his negligence.

CHAPTER FIFTH.
Protutors (VIGILANT GUARDIANS).

Article 233. The family council is entitled to appoint a *protutor* when he has not been appointed by those who have a right to elect a guardian for minors.

234. The guardian can not begin to exercise guardianship, until a *protutor* has been appointed. If he fails to apply for this appointment, he shall be removed from the guardianship and shall be liable for the damages suffered by the minor.

235. The appointment of a *protutor* shall not be given to a relative of the same line as the guardian.

236. The *protutor* is obliged:

1. To supervise the inventory of the property of the minor and the constitution of the bond of the guardian, when it must be given.

2. To maintain the rights of the minor in and out of court whenever they are opposed to the interests of the guardian.

3. To call the attention of the family council to the management of the guardian, whenever he may consider it injurious to the person or interests of the minor.

4. To promote the meeting of the family council for the appointment of a new guardian when the guardianship may become vacant or abandoned.

5. To discharge all further duties provided by law. The *protutor* shall be liable for the damages and injuries caused to the minor by his omission or neglect to comply with such duties.

The *protutor* may attend the deliberations of the family council and take part in them, but he has no right to vote.

CHAPTER SIXTH.

PERSONS UNABLE TO BE GUARDIANS AND *Protutors*, AND THE REMOVAL OF THE SAME.

Article **237.** The following cannot be guardians or *protutors:*

1. Persons subject to guardianship.

2. Those who have been punished for the crimes of robbery, theft, fraud, forgery, corruption of minors, or public scandal.

3. Those condemned to any corporal punishment, until the sentence expires.

4. Those who have been legally removed from a former guardianship.

5. Persons of bad conduct, or having no visible means of support.

6. Bankrupts and insolvents, not discharged.

7. Women, with the exception of the cases in which they are expressly called by law.

8.   Those who, at the time of taking charge of the guardianship, have a law suit pending with the minor in regard to his civil status.

9.   Those in litigation with the minor in regard to the ownership of his property, unless the father and, in his default, the mother, being aware of it, have disposed otherwise.

10.   Those indebted to the minor in large sums, unless they have been appointed by the father and, in his default, by the mother with knowledge of the debt.

11.   The relatives mentioned in the second paragraph of art. 293, and the testamentary guardian when they have not complied with the duties imposed on them by said article.

12.   Professed members of monastic orders.

13.   Foreigners not residing in Spain.

238.   The following shall be removed from guardianship:

1.   Those, who after having quaiified, come under one of the classes of incapacity mentioned in nos. 1, 2, 3, 4, 5, 6, 8, 12, and 13, of the preceding article.

2.   Those who have assumed the administration of the guardianship without having the family council convened nor having asked for the appointment of a *protutor* or without having given bonds, in cases in which they are required to give them, and having omitted to inscribe the mortgage bond.

3.   Those who have not made the inventory within the term and in the manner prescribed by law or have not made it faithfully.

4.   Those who have not behaved properly in the discharge of the guardianship.

239.   The family council shall not declare the incapacity of guardians and *protutors* or resolve upon their removal, without summoning and hearing them if they appear.

240.   After the incapacity has been declared or the removal has been agreed on by the family council, such decision shall be considered final and the vacant guardianship shall be filled, if the guardian does not present his claims before the court within fifteen days next following the day on which the resolution has been communicated to him.

241.   When the guardian institutes a judicial contention, the council shall litigate it, at the expense of the minor; but the members thereof may be personally condemned to pay the costs, if they have acted with notorious malice.

242.　When the resolution of the family council is favorable to the guardian, and has been unanimously adopted, there shall be no remedy against it.

243.　If by causes of incapacity, the guardian does not enter upon the discharge of his duties, the family council shall attend to the duties of the guardianship, until a final resolution is agreed upon about the impediment.

When the guardian has already entered upon the discharge of his duties and the family council has declared his incapacity and resolved to remove him, the decision which they may take to provided for the care of the guardianship, in case a law suit should be instituted, shall not be executed without a previous judicial approval.

CHAPTER SEVENTH.

EXCUSES FOR NOT ACCEPTING GUARDIANSHIP AND *Protutorship.*

Article 244.　The following may be excused from guardianship and protutorship.

1.　Ministers of the crown.

2.　Presidents of the Co-legislative Houses, of the Council of State, of the Supreme Court, of the Supreme Council of War and Navy, and of the Court of Accounts of the Kingdom.

3.　Archbishops and bishops.

4.　Magistrates, Judges and officials of the Public Attorney's office.

5.　Those who exercise authority immediately depending on the government.

6.　Those in active military service.

7.　Clergymen with curate charges.

8.　Those having under their power five legitimate children.

9.　Those that are so poor that they cannot attend to the guardianship without impairing their livelihood.

10.　Those who in consequence of continuous ill health or

because of inability to read or write cannot well fulfill the duties of the charge.

11. Persons over sixty years of age.

12. Those who are already guardians or *protutors* of another person.

245. Persons, not relatives of the minor or incapable, are not bound to accept the guardianship, if, within the territory of the court appointing the guardian, there are relatives within the sixth degree who may fulfil the charge.

246. The person excused, on petition of the guardian or *protutor*, may be compelled to accept the guardianship as soon as the cause of the exemption has ceased.

247. An excuse, which has not been alleged before the family council in meeting held for the purpose of deciding upon the guardianship, shall not be aceptable.

If the guardian has not been present at the meeting of the council, nor has previously been made aware of his appointment, he must allege the excuse within the ten days next following the date on which he has been notified of it.

248. If the causes of exemption are subsequent to the acceptance of the guardianship, the term for alleging them shall begin to be counted from the day on which the guardian may have become aware of the same.

249. The resolution on which the family council rejects the excuse may be contested before the court within the term of fifteen days.

The resolutions of the family council shall be maintained by the same, at the expense of the minor; but if they should be affirmed, the person promoting the suit shall be condemned to the payment of the costs.

250. During the suit on account of excuses, the one presenting them shall be bound to exercise the guardianship. If he does not do so, the family council shall appoint some person to substitute him, and the substituted shall be liable for the action of the former in case the excuses are not sustained.

251. The testamentary guardian who may excuse himself from the guardianship shall lose whatever may have been left to him by the person who voluntarily appointed him.

CHAPTER EIGHT.

BONDS OF GUARDIANS.

Article **252.** The guardian before he assumes the guardianship shall give bond as security for the performance of his duties.

253. The bond must be secured either by mortgage or by pledge.

Personal bond shall be accepted only when it is impossible to give bond, as above stated. The security given by the bondsmen shall not prevent the adoption of any decision proper for the good keeping of the property of the minor or incapable.

254. The bond shall secure:

1. The value of any personal property which may come into the posession of the guardian.

2. The rents or profits which the property of the minor or incapable may produce during one year.

3. The profits which the minor may receive from mercantile or industrial undertakings during one year.

255. The guardian may have recourse to the courts against any resolution of the family council fixing the amount or qualifying the bond, but he shall not enter upon the discharge of his duties without having given the bond required.

256. Whilst the bond is being executed the *protutor* shall perform the acts of administration which the family council may consider indispensable for the safe keeping of the property and the collection of its proceeds.

257. The mortgage bond shall be inscribed in the Registry of Property. The pledge bond shall be made by the deposit of effects or values in one of the public institutions authotized for this purpose.

258. The inscription or deposit shall be demanded:

1. By the guardian.

2. By the *protutor*.

3. By any of the members of the family council.

Those omitting to do it shall be liable for the damage and injury resulting therefrom.

259.   The bond may be increased or reduced, during the exercise of the guardianship, according to the changes which may occur in the capital of the minor or the incapable and in the values upon which the bond is based.

The bond shall not be totally cancelled until after the accounts of the guardianship are approved and the guardian has extinguished all the liabilities of his management.

260.   The following are exempted from giving bond for guardianship:

1.   The father, the mother, and the grandparents, when called upon to be the guardian of their descendants.

2.   The testamentary guardian, released by the father or, in his default, by the mother from such duty. This exception shall cease, when, subsequently to his appointment, causes unknown to the testator may arise which render the bond indispensable in the judgment of the family council.

3.   The guardian, appointed without bonds, by strangers who may have instituted the minor or incapable as his heir or left him a legacy for a large amount. In this case the exemption shall be limited to the property or rents of which the inheritance or legacy consists.

CHAPTER NINTH.
EXERCISE OF THE GUARDIANSHIP.

Article 261.   The family council shall place the guardian and the *protutor* in posession.

262.   The guardian represents the minor or incapable in all civil acts with the exception of those which the latter can execute by himself alone by express provision of law.

263.   Minors and incapables, subject to guardianship, owe respect and obedience to the guardian. He may punish them moderately.

264.   The guardian is obliged:

1   To maintain and educate the minor or incapable in accordance with his condition and in strict subjection to the dispositions of his parents or, in default of these, with those adopted by the family council.

2.   To endeavor that the insane, demented, or deaf or

dumb may acquire or recover their capacity, by whatever means their capital may furnish.

3.   To make an inventory of the property which the guardianship may cover within the terms fixed for this purpose by the family council.

4.   To administer the estate of the minor or incapable with all the diligence of a good father of a family.

5.   To ask in due time the authorization of the family council for everything that he may not do without such authorization.

6.   To solicit the intervention of the *protutor* in all the cases which the law may deem it necessary.

265.   The inventory shall be made with the intervention of the *protutor* and with the assistance of two witnesses chosen by the family council.   The council shall decide, considering the importance of the capital, if the inventory is, in addition, to be authorized by a Notary.

266.   The jewelry, valuable furniture, publict effects, and merchantile and industrial values, which in the judgement of the family council are not to remain in posession of the guardian, shall be deposited in an institution established for this purpose.

All other personal and self-moving *(semovientes)* property, if it is not appraised, shall be appraised by experts appointed by the family council.

267.   The guardian, who having been summoned for this purpose through a Notary by the *protutor* or by the witnesses, should not enter in the inventory the credits he holds against the minor, shall be understood as renouncing them.

268.   When the will of the person who made the appoitment of the guardian provides nothing about the alimentary pension to be allotted to the minor or incapable, the family council, after inspecting the inventory, shall decide the part of the rents or proceeds which shall be allotted for such purpose.

This resolution may be modified in proportion to the increase or decrease of the inheritance of the minors or incapables or the change their condition may suffer.

269.   The guardian requires to be autorized by the family council:

1. To impose on the minor the punishment referred to in no. 2, art. 155, and in art. 156.

2. To give to the minor a profession or particular avocation when that has not been decideds by the parents, and to modify any disposition that they had made in this respect.

3. To place the incapable in a sanitarium, unless the guardianship is exercised by the father, mother or a son.

4. To follow the commercial or industrial calling to which the incapable, or his ascendants or the ascendants of the minor had pursued.

5. To alienate or encumber any property constituting the capital of the minor or incapable or to make contracts or act subject to inscription.

6. To invest any balance of money remaining each year, after meeting the obligations of the gardianship.

7. To cause the distribution of the inheritance or of any other thing which the minor or incapable may hold in common.

8. To withdrawn from investment any sums producing interest.

9. To loan and borrow money.

10. To accept without the benefit inventory any inheritance or to repudiate such inheritance or donations.

11. To incur extraordinary expenses in connection with tenements, the administration of which is included under the guardianship.

12. To compromise and submit to arbitration the questions in which the minor or incapable may be interested.

13. To institute suits in the name of persons subject to guardianship, and to maintain the remedies of appeal and nullity *(casación)* against the sentences in which they may have been condemned. Demands or remedies in verbal suits are excepted.

270. The family council cannot empower the guardian to sell or encumber the property of the minor or incapable, unless it be for causes of necessity or utility which the guardian has to duly prove.

This power shall be exercised in regard to specified things.

271. The family council before granting authorization to encumber real property or constitute real rights in favor of third persons, may previously hear the opinion of experts about the conditions of the encumbrances and possibilities of bettering them.

272. In respect to real property, rights to be inscribed, jewelry or furniture, the value of which is over 4000 *pesetas*, any sale thereof is to be made at public auction with the intervention of the guardian or *protutor*.

Stock listed on exchanges, either public, commercial or industrial shall be sold by a stock agent or a commercial broker.

273. The guardian is liable for the legal interest on the capital of the minor, when by his omission or negligence, it shall remain unproductive or without investment.

274. The authorization to settle or compromise through arbitrators shall be requested in writing and therein the guardian shall explain all the conditions and advantages of the settlement.

The family council may hear the opinion of one or more lawyers, according to the importance of the matter, and may grant or deny such authorization. In case of granting it, it shall be so stated in the minutes.

275. Guardians are forbidden:

1. To donate or renounce things or rights belonging to minors or incapables.

The donations made on account of marriage by minors, with the approval of the persons who are to give their consent to the marriage, shall be valid, provided they do not exceed the limits fixed by law.

2. To collect from the debtor of the minor or incapable, without the intervention of the *protutor*, sums over 5,000 *pesetas*, unlees they are interests, rents, or fruits.

Payments made without complying with this requirement shall be profitable to the debtors, only when they can prove that the money received has been invested for the benefit of the minor or incapable.

3. To pay themselves, without the intervention of the *protutor*, any sums due them.

4. To buy himself, or through another person, the property of the minor or incapable, unless he has been expressly authorized to do so by the family council.

276.   The guardian is entitled to compensation from the property of the minor or incapable:

When it has not been fixed by those who appointed the testamentary guardian; or when the guardians are legitimate or appointed by court, the family council shall fix it, taking in consideration the importance of the estate and the work to be undertaken in its administration.

In no case shall the compensation be less than 4% nor more than 10% of the net rents or proceeds of the estate.

The guardian may ask a remedy from the courts against the resolution fixing his compensation.

277.   Should the family council maintain its resolution, the council shall then litigate at the expense of the minor or incapable.

278.   The guardianship is determined:

1.   By the minor attaining the age of twenty-three years, by habilitation as to age, and by adoption.

2.   By the cessation of the causes originating the same in cases of persons incapable, subject to interdiction, or prodigals.

CHAPTER TENTH.

ACCOUNTS OF THE GUARDIANSHIP.

Article **279.**   Collateral relatives of the minor or incapable, and strangers, who have not obtained the charge of guardian, with the assignment of proceeds for support, shall render to the family council yearly accounts of their administration.

The accounts, after being examined by the *protutor* and audited by the council, shall be deposited with the clerk of the court where the guardianship has been registered.

In case the guardian does not agree to the resolution of the council, he may apply to the courts before which the interests of the minor or incapable shall be defended by the *protutor*.

280.   The guardian, who may be replaced by another, as well as his heirs, shall be obliged to render a general account of his guardianship to the one taking his place; such account shall be examined and audited in the form prescribed in the preceding article.   The new guardian shall be liable for the damages and injuries to the minor, if he does not claim and examine the accounts of his predecessor.

281. When the guardianship terminates, the guardian or his heirs are obliged to render account of his administration to the person who has been under his guardianship or to his representatives or those holding rights under him.

282. The general accounts of the guardianship shall be audited and reported upon by the family council within a term not exceeding six months, (after the receipt of the same).

283. The accounts are to be accompanied by their vouchers. The only expenses which need not be vouched for are the petty expenses for which a diligent father of a family does not generally ask a receipt.

284. The expensesof rendering the accounts shall be borne by the minor or incapable.

285. Until fifteen days after the rendering of the accounts with the vouchers, the persons holding rights under the minor or the minor himself, if of age, cannot enter into any agreement with the guardian which may have relation to the administration of the guardianship.

The family council without detriment to the agreement which the interested parties may make between themselves, after the expiration of this term, shall denounce to the courts any wrongful act which may have been committed by the guardian in the exercise of the guardianship.

286. The balance shown by the general account, either in favor of or against the guardian, shall bear legal interest. In the first case, from the time the minor is asked for the payment of the balance, after the delivery of his property.

In the second case, from the date of rendering the accounts, if they have been presented within the legal term, and, if not, from the expiration of such term.

287. The actions, reciprocally belonging to the guardian and the minor on account of the exercise of the guardianship, are extinguished five years after the termination of the same.

CHAPTER ELEVENTH.
REGISTRATION OF GUARDIANSHIP.

Article **288.** There shall be in the courts of the First Instance one or several books in which entries shall be made of the guardianships, constituted within the year, within their respective territories.

289. These books shall be in the custody of a judicial clerk who shall make the entries free of cost.

290. The registration of each guardianship shall contain:

1. The name, family name, age, and domicil of the minor or incapable, and the extent and limit of the guardianship, when the incapacity has been judicially declared.

2. The name, family name, profession, and domicil of the guardian, and the statement of whether he is a testamentary or legitimate guardian or is appointed by court.

3. The date on which the guardianship has been conferred, and the day on which the bond, required from the guardian, has been constituted, stating, in such cases, the kind of property on which it has been based.

4. The alimentary pension which has been assigned to the minor or incapable or the declaration of the compensation of proceeds for support.

291. At the foot ot each inscription, at the beginning of the judicial year, it shall be recorded whether the guardian has rendered an account of his administration, if he is obliged to do so.

292. The judges shall examine every year such registries and shall take the necessary steps in each case to defend the interests of the person subject to guardianship.

TITLE X.
THE FAMILY COUNCIL.

SECTION FIRST.
MANNER OF CONSTITUTING.

Article **293.** If the Public Attorney or Municipal Judge should become informed that in the territory within their jurisdiction are found any of the persons to which art. 200 refers, the first shall ask, and the second shall order of his own motion, or upon the petition of the Public Attorney, as the case may be, the constitution of a family council.

The following persons are obliged to notify the Municipal Judge of any fact which give cause for a guardianship, as soon as they have knowledge of it: the testamentary guardian, the relatives who are called to the legitimate guardianship, and those that, according to law, are members of the council; and they are liable, should they not do so, to an indemnity for damages and injuries (caused thereby).

The Municipal Judge shall summon the persons who should compose the family council, stating to them the object of the meeting, and the day, hour, and place in which it shall be held.

294.   The family council shall be composed of the persons whom the father, or, in proper cases, the mother may have appointed in the testament, and, in default of them, of the male ascendants and descendants, and the brothers and husbands of the living sisters of the minor or incapable, whatever their number may be. If they are less than five, this number shall be completed with the nearest male relatives of both the paternal and maternal lines, and, in the event that they do not exist or that they are not bound to form part of the council, the Municipal Judge shall appoint, instead, honest persons, preferring the friends of the parents of the minor or incapable.

If there be no ascendants, descendants, brothers or husbands of living sisters, the Municipal Judge shall constitute the council with the five nearest male relatives of the minor or incapable, and, when there are no relatives in part or at all, he will substitute them with honest persons, preferring always the friends of the parents.

295.   In equal degrees, preference shall be given to the eldest relatives in forming the family council.

296.   The courts may remedy the nullity which may be caused by the non-observance of the preceding articles, if not due to fraud nor causing damage to the person or property of the person subject to guardianship, but taking care to amend the error committed in the formation of the council.

297. The relatives of the minor or incapable, called by law, who do not reside within 30 kilometres of the court having jurisdiction over the guardianship, shall not be obliged to form a part of the council but they may be members of the council, if they willingly accept the charge, for which purpose they shall be summoned by the Municipal Judge.

298. The causes which excuse, disable, and give reason for the removal of guardians and *protutors* apply to the members of the family council. Neither can persons excluded from this charge by the father or, in his default, by the mother in their wills, be members of it.

299. The guardian and *protutor* shall not be, at the same time, members of the family council.

300. The meeting for the formation of the family council shall be presided over by the Municipal Judge. The parties summoned are obliged to appear in person or by a special attorney who shall never represent more than one person. If they de not appear, the Judge may impose on them a fine not exceeding 50 pesetas.

301. After the family council has been costituted by the Municipal Judge, it shall proceed to prescribe all the measures required for the custody of the person and property of the minor or incapable and to constitute the guardianship.

302. The family council for natural children shall be constituted, under the same rules as that for legitimate children but members thereof shall be appointed from the relatives of the father or mother who have recognized them.

The council for illegitimate children shall be constituted by the Municipal Attorney, who shall be the president, and four honest neighbors.

303. The administration of every Institute of Beneficence shall have over the orphans, under its care, all the faculties belonging to the guardian and to the family council.

SECTION SECOND.
MANNER OF PROCEEDING OF THE FAMILY COUNCIL.

Article 304. The member elected by the other members shall be president of the council:

To the president belongs:

1.   To convoke the council, whenever he thinks it convenient or on petition of the members, of the gardian, or of the *protutor*, and to preside over its deliberations.

2.   To draw up and to state the basis of the resolutions, giving therein the opinion of each of the members who shall authorize the minutes by signing the same.

3.   To execute the resolutions.

305.   The family council shall not adopt resolutions about matters submitted to it, unless, at least, three members are present.

Resolutions shall always be adopted by a majority of the voters.   The vote of the president shall decide in case of a tie.

306.   The members of the family council are obliged to attend the meetings of the same for which they may be summoned.   Should they not attend, nor present any lawful excuse, the president of the council shall give notice to the Municipal Judge who may impose on them a fine not exceeding 50 pesetas.

307.   No member of the family council shall attend its meetings nor vote when it has to deal with a matter in which he, his ascendants, descendants, or consort has any interest, but he may be heard, if the council deems it proper.

308.   The guardian and the *protutor* are bound to attend the meetings of the family council, whenever convoked, but have no vote.   They may also attend whenever the council meets on their petition.

The person subject to guardianship, who is over fourteen years of age, has a right to be present and to be heard.

309.   The family council shall take cognizance of the affairs for which they are competent, in accordance with the provisions of this Code.

310.   The members, who have dissented from the majority in voting on any resolution, may appeal to the Judge of the First Instance, as also may the guardian or *protutor* or any relative of the minor or other party interested in the decision, with the exception of the case in art. 242.

311.   On the determination of the guardianship, and the

consequent dissolution of the family council, the latter shall deliver the minutes of its sessions to the person who has been subject to guardianship or to the person who represents his rights.

312. The members of the family council are liable for the damages which the person subject to guardianship may suffer on account of their malice or culpable neglect.

The members dissenting from the resolution, causing such injury, shall be exempted from this liability.

313. The family council shall be dissolved in the same cases in which the guardianship is extinguished.

TITLE XI.

EMANCIPATION AND MAJORITY.

CHAPTER FIRST.

EMANCIPATION.

Article 314. Emancipation takes place:

1. By the marriage of the minor.

2. By majority.

3. By concession of the father or mother exercising the parental power.

315. Marriage produces lawful emancipation with the limitations contained in art. 59 and in rule third of art. 50.

316. Emancipation, referred to in no. 3 of art. 314, shall be granted by public deed or by appearance before the Municipal Judge which appearance is to be inscribed in the Civil Registry and, meanwhile, shall not produce any effect against third parties.

317. Emancipation enables the minor to control his person and property, as if of age, but, until he attains his majority, he cannot borrow money on loan, neither encumber nor sell real property without the consent of the father, and, in his default, of the mother, and, in default of both, without that of a guardian. Neither can he appear in court without the assistance of said persons.

318. In order that emancipation may take place by con-

cession of the father or mother, it is required that the minor be over eighteen years of age and consent to it.

319. Emancipation once granted cannot be revoked.

CHAPTER SECOND.

MAJORITY.

Article 320. Majority commences after attaining twenty three years of age. A person of age is qualified for all acts of civil life, with the exceptions established by this Code in special cases.

321. Notwithstanding what is prescribed in the preceding article, unmarried daughters of age, but under twenty-five years, cannot leave the parental home without permission of the father or mother in whose company they live, unless on account of marriage or when the father or mother have contracted another marriage.

322. The minor, orphan of both parents, may obtain the benefit of majority by the consent of the family council, approved by the President of the territorial Audiencia of the district, after the Public Attorney has been heard.

323. For (granting) the concession and approval stated in the preceding article, it is required:

1. That the minor be over eighteen years of age.
2. That he consents thereto.
3. That it is considered advantageous to the minor.

The authorization (*habilitación*) shall be inscribed in the Registry of guardianships and entered in the Civil Registry.

324. The provisions of art. 317 apply to the minor who has obtained authorization of majority.

TITLE XII.

REGISTRY OF CIVIL STATUS.

Article 325. Acts, relating to the civil status of persons, shall be inscribed in the registry designated for such purpose.

326. The registry of civil status shall contain the inscriptions or entries of births, marriages, emancipations, recognitions, and legitimations, deaths, naturalizations, and

residences *(vecindad)*, and shall be under the charge of municipal judges or other officials of the civil order in Spain, and, in foreign countries, of consular or diplomatic agents.

327. The minutes of the registry shall be evidence of the civil status and any other evidence can be admitted only when such minutes have never existed or the books of registry have disappeared or when a contention arises in court.

328. It is not necessary that a newly born child should be presented to the official in charge of the registry for inscription of birth; the declaration of the person obliged to make it shall be sufficient.

This declaration shall embrace all the requirements of law and shall be subscribed to by the deponent or two witnesses, at his request, if he cannot sign.

329. In canonical marriages, it shall be the duty of the contracting parties to furnish to the official representing the State, who attends the celebration, all the data required for its inscription in the Civil Registry.

Those referring to banns, impediments and their disposition are excepted and not required to be entered in the Registry.

330. Naturalization shall have no legal effects, until it is inscribed in the Registry, whatever the evidence proving it and the date on which it has been granted may be.

331. Municipal Judges and those of the First Instance, in proper cases, may punish the infractions of the provisions about the Civil Rigistry with a fine of 20 to 100 pesetas, when they do not constitute a crime or a misdemeanor.

332. The law of June 17, 1870, shall continue in force in so far as it is not modified by the preceding articles.

BOOK SECOND.

PROPERTY, OWNERSHIP, AND ITS MODIFICATIONS.

TITLE I.

CLASSIFICATION OF PROPERTY.

PRELIMINARY PROVISION.

Article **333.**   All things which are or may be an object of appropriation are considered, either as personal or real property.

CHAPTER FIRST.
REAL PROPERTY.

Article **334.**   Real property consists of.

1.   Lands, buildings, roads, and constructions of every kind adherent to the soil.

2.   Trees, and plants, and ungathered fruits, while they are not separated from the land and form an integral part of the real property.

3.   All that is attached to real property, in a fixed manner, in such a way that it cannot be separated from it without breaking the matter or causing injury to the object.

4.   Statues, reliefs, paintings or other objects of use or ornament placed in a building and on lands or tenements by the owner of the same in such a manner as to reveal the intent of attaching them in a permanent way to the tenement.

5.   Machinery, vessels, instruments, or implements, intended by the owner of the tenement for the industry or works that he may carry on in a building or tenement and which directly tend to meet the necessities of the same industry or works.

6. Vivaries for animals, pigeon-houses, beehives, fish-ponds or beds for similar purposes, when the owner has placed or kept them with the intent of maintaining the same attached to the tenement and forming a permanent part thereof.

7. Manures intended for the cultivation of lands when they are on the place where they are to be employed.

8. Mines, quarries, and slag lands, while the matter forms part of the beds, and waters, either running or stagnant.

9. Docks, and constructions, which, though floating, are intended by their purposes and conditions to remain at a fixed place in a river, lake or on a coast.

10. Administrative concessions for public works, and easements, and other real rights attached to real property.

CHAPTER SECOND.
PERSONAL PROPERTY.

Article **335.** Personal property is considered anything susceptible of appropriation and not contained in the preceding chapter, and, in general, any thing which can be carried from place to place without impairing the real property to which it may be attached.

336. As personal property are also considered; rents or pensions, either for life or hereditary, in favor of a person or family, provided they do not encumber real property with a rea charge, also purchased public offices, contracts for public services, and bonds and certificates representing mortgage loans.

337. Personal property is either consumable *(fungibles)* or non-consumable *(no fungibles)*.

To the first ceass belongs those which can not be used, in a manner appropriate to their nature, without consuming them; all others belong to the second class.

CHAPTER THIRD.
PROPERTY IN RESPECT TO OWNERSHIP.

Article **338.** Things pertain to public domain or to private ownership.

339. To public domain belong:

1.　Those intended for public use, as roads, canals, rivers, torrents, ports, and bridges, constructed by the State, and banks, shores, roadsteads, and others of a similar character.

2.　Those belonging exclusively to the State, not for common use, and which are designed for some public service, or the developement of the national wealth, as walls, fortresses, and other works for the defence of the territorry, and mines, whilst their concession has not yet been granted.

340.　All other property belonging to the State which has not the conditions, stated in the preceding article, is considered as private property.

341.　Property of the public domain, when it is no longer dedicated to general uses or to the necessities of the defence of the territory, shall become a part of the property of the State.

342.　Property of the Royal Patrimony is governed by its special law, and in all matters, not prescribed there in for it, by the general provisions established by this Code about private property.

343.　The property of provinces and of towns is divided into property of public use and patrimonial property.

344.　Property for public use in provinces, and towns, comprises the provincial and town roads, the squares, streets, fountains, and public waters, the walks, and public works for general service, paid for by the same towns or provinces.

All other property, possessed by either of them, are patrimonial, and shall be governed by the prescriptions of this Code, unless otherwise ordered by special laws.

345.　Besides the patrimonial property of the State, of the provinces, and of the towns, cohich belonging to private parties, either individually or collectively, is property of private ownership.

PROVISIONS COMMON TO THE THREE
PRECEDING CHAPTERS.

Article 346.　Whenever by provision of the laws or by an individual declaration, the expression "real things or real property" is used, or "personal things or personal property," it shall be understood as comprised in them, respectively, those enumerated in chapter first and in chapter second.

Whenever the word personal (*muebles*), alone, is used, then, it shall not be understood as including: money, credits, commercial effects, values, jewels, scientific or artistic collections, books, medals, arms, clothing, riding beasts, or carriages and their harnesses, breadstuffs, liquids *(caldos)* and merchandise or other tings, the principal employment of which is to furnish or ornament rooms, with the exception of the cases in which, by the contexture of the law or of the individual disposition, the contrary clearly appears.

347. Whenever, in a sale, legacy or donation or any other disposition in which reference is made to personal or real things, their possession or ownership is transferred with every thing they may contain, there shall not be understood as comprised in the transfer; money values, credits, and actions, the titles to which are contained in the thing transferred, unless the intention is clearly shown of including such values and rights in the transfer.

TITLE II.

OWNERSHIP.

CHAPTER FIRST.

OWNERSHIP IN GENERAL.

Article 348. Ownership is the right to enjoy and dispose of a thing, without further limitations than those established by the laws.

The owner has actions against the holder and the possessor of the thing to recover it.

349. No one shall be deprived of his property, unless it be by competent authority and with justified cause for public utility, and never until he has previously been properly indemnified.

If this requirement has not been complied with, the judges shall protect, and in proper cases, replace the condemned party in posession.

350. The owner of a parcel of ground is owner of its

surface and everything under it, and he can make thereon any works, plantations, and excavations which may be convenient for him, without injury to the easements and subject to what is prescribed by the laws about mines and waters and by Police Regulations.

351. Hidden treasures belong to the owner of the land on which they are found.

However, when the discovery is made on property belonging to a stranger or to the State and by chance, one half of it shall be adjudged to the finder.

If the thing discovered is of interest to the sciences or arts, the State can acquire it at its just value which shall be distributed in accordance with what has been prescribed.

352. By treasure is understood, in its legal effects, hidden or unknown deposits of money, jewelry, or other precious objects, the lawful ownership of which is not proven.

CHAPTER SECOND.
RIGHT OF ACCESSION.

GENERAL PROVISION.

Article 353. Ownership of property gives a right by accession to everything which is produced by it or which is either naturally or artificially united to or incorporated with it.

SECTION FIRST.
RIGHT OF ACCESSION IN RESPECT TO WHAT IS PRODUCED
BY PROPERTY.

Article 354. To the owner belong:
1. Natural fruits.
2. Industrial fruits.
3. Civil fruits.

355. Naturaly fruits are the spontaneous products of the soil, and the brood, and all other produce of animals.

Industrial fruits are those produced by land of any kind through cultivation or labor.

Civil fruits are rents of buildings, receipts for leases of lands, and the amount of perpetual or life rents, and other similar returns.

356. The receiver of fruits is obliged to pay the expenses incurred by a third party in their production, gathering, and preservation.

357. Only those which are in sight or appearing are considered as natural or industrial fruits.

As to animals, it is sufficient if they are in the womb of the mother, though yet unborn.

SECTION SECOND.

RIGHTS OF ACCESSION IN RESPECT TO REAL PROPERTY.

Article 358. Whatever is built, planted or sown on another's land, and the improvements or repairs made on it belong to the owner of the land, subject to what is prescribed in the following articles.

359. All works, sown grounds, and plantings are presumed to be made by the owner, and, at his expense, unless the contrary is proven.

360. The owner of the land who shall make on it, by himself or through another person, plantings, constructions or works, with material belonging to another person, is bound to pay for their value; and should he have acted in bad faith, he shall also be obliged to indemnify said person for damages and injuries caused thereby. The owner of the materials shall have a right to remove them, only in case he can do it without injury to the work contructed, and, when by doing it, the plantings, constructions, and work done, shall not be destroyed.

361. The owner of the land on which somebody has built, sown, or planted, in good faith, is entitled to appropriate, as his own, the work, sowing or planting by previonsly paying the indemnity specified in arts. 453 and 454 or to oblige the person who has huilt or planted the same to pay to him the value of the land and to oblige him, who sowed, to pay the corresponding rents.

362. He, who builds, plants, or sows, in bad faith, on

another's land, loses what he has built, planted, or sown without right to any indemnity.

363. The owner of the land on which any one has built, planted, or sown, in bad faith, may exact the demolition of the work or the removal of the planting or sowing, and the replacing of everything in its former condition, at the expense of him who built, planted or sowed.

364. When there has been bad faith, not only on the part of him who built, sowed or planted on another's land, but also on the part of the owner of such land, the right of both shall be the same as though both had acted in good faith.

Bad faith on the part of the owner is understood, whenever the act has been executed in his 'presence with his knowledge and forebearance and without opposition.

365. If the materials, plants or seed belong to a third party, who has not acted in bad faith, the owner of the land shall be liable subsidiarily for their value, but only in the event that the person who used them has no means to pay for the same.

This prescription shall have no force, if the owner make use of the rights given him by art. 363.

366. The augmentation which the banks of a river gradually receive from the effects of currents of waters, belongs to the owner of the land adjacent to such banks.

367. The owners of tenements, adjacent to ponds or lakes, do not acquire the land left dry by the natural decrease of waters, nor lose those inundated by them in extraordinary floods.

368. When the current of a river, rivulet or torrent cuts off from the tenement on its bank a known portion of land and transfers it to another tenement, the owner of the tenement to which the cut off part belong retaines the ownership of the same.

369. Trees, uprooted and carried away by currents of waters, belong to the owner of the land upon which they are carried, if the former owners do not claimed them within the term of a month.

If such owner claims them, then they must pay all the

expenses caused by the collecting and securing them in a safe place.

370. The beds of rivers, which remain abandoned because the course of the water has naturally changed, belong to the owners of the riparian lands , throughout their respective extents. If the abandoned bed has divided tenements belonging to different owners, the new dividing line shall be run at equal distance therefrom.

371. Islands formed in the sea, adjacent to the coast of Spain, and in navigable or floatable rivers belong to the State.

372. When in a navigable and floatable river, which changes its course by natural causes, a new bed is opened through a private tenement, this bed shall become public domain. The owner of the tenement shall recover it, in the event of the waters leaving it again dry, naturally or through work legally authorized for this purpose.

373. Islands which, through successive accumulations of descending alluviums, are slowly formed in rivers, belong to the owners of the banks or shores nearest to each of them or to those of both shores, if the island is in the middle of the river, and then shall be divided longitudinally in halves. If only one island thus formed be more distant from one bank than from the other, then the owner of the nearest bank shall be the sole owner of it.

374. When the current of a river divides itself into branches, leaving a tenement or a part of it isolated, the owner of the same retains his property. He also retains it, if a portion of the land is rendered isolated by the current.

SECTION THIRD.

RIGHTS OF ACCESSION IN RESPECT TO PERSONAL PROPERTY.

Article 375. When two personal things, belonging to different owners, are united in such a way that they become a unit without bad faith on the part of either owner, the owner of the principal thing acquires the accessory one upon indemnifying its former owner for its value.

376. When two things are incorporated, the principal

shall be considered the one to which the other had been united as an ornament or for its use and perfection.

377. When it is not possible by following the rules of the preceding article to determine which of the two incorporated things is the principal one, the thing of the greater value shall be considered as such, and between two things of equal value, that of the greater volume.

In paintings and sculptures, in writings, printed matter, prints, engravings, and lithographs, the board, metal, stone, canvass, paper or the parchment shall be considered as accessory things.

378. When things united can be separated without injury, their respective owners may claim their separation.

However, when the thing adjoined for the use, embellishment or perfection of another is much more precious than the principal thing, the owner of the first may demand their separation, though the thing to which it is joined may suffer some damage.

379. When the owner of the accessory thing has made the incorporation, in bad faith, he shall lose the thing incorporated and shall be obliged to indemnify the owner of the principal thing for the damages he may have suffered.

When the one acting in bad faith is the owner of the principal thing, the owner of the accessory shall have the right to choose between being paid by the first for the value for the thing or to have the thing, belonging to him, separated, though it may be necessary for such purpose to destroy the principal one, and besides, in both cases, an indemnity for damages and injury may be recovered.

If any of the owners have made the incorporation in the presence, with the knowledge and forbearance and without opposition from the other, their respective rights shall be determined in the manner provided for such cases where both had acted in good faith.

380. Whenever the owner of materials, used without his consent, has a right to an indemnity, he may exact that such indemnity consist in the delivery to him, either of a thing equal in quality and value and in all respects to the one employed or in its price, according to appraisement by experts.

381.   When by the will of their owners, two things of equal or different kinds are mixed, or if the mixture is made by chance, and, in this last case, are not separable without injury, each owner shall acquire a right proportional to the part belonging to him with consideration as to the values of the things mixed or confounded.

382.   When by the will of only one of the owners, but, in good faith, two things of equal or different kinds are mixed or confounded, the rights of the owners shall be determined by the provisions of the preceding article.

When the one making the mixture or confusion acted, in bad faith, he will lose the thing belonging to him, mixed or confounded, besides being obliged to indemnify the owner of the thing with which he made the mixture for the damage caused thereby.

383.   He who, in good faith, wholly or partially used material belonging to another party in making a work of a new kind, may make the work his own upon indemnifying the owner of the material for the value of the same.

When this (material) is more precious than the work on which it was used or superior in value, the owner of it may at his option become owner of the new thing by paying the price of the labor or claiming an indemnity for the material.

When in the making of the new work, there has been bad faith, the owner of the material has the right, either to keep the work without paying any thing to the author or claiming from him an indemnity for the value of the material and the damages he may have suffered.

CHAPTER THIRD.

FIXING BOUNDARIES AND PLACING LAND MARKS.

Article 384.   Every owner has the right to fix the boundaries of his property by giving notice thereof to the owners of adjoining tenements.

The same right belongs to those having real rights.

385.   The demarkation shall be made in accordance with the titles of each owner, and, when in default of sufficient title,

from what may appear from the possession held by the contiguous owners.

386. When the titles do not specify the boundary or area belonging to each owner, and the question cannot be determined by the possession or by other means of proof, the demarkation shall be made by dividing the land in dispute in equal shares.

387. When the titles of the contiguous owners show an area, larger or smaller than that comprised in the total of said land, the increase or decrease shall be distributed in proportion.

CHAPTFR FOURTH.
RIGHT OF ENCLOSING AGRICULTURAL LANDS.

Article 388. Every owner may close or fence his tenements with walls, ditches, live or dead hedges or in any other manner without injury to the easements existing thereon.

CHAPTER FIFTH.
UNSTABLE BUILDINGS AND TREES AEOUT TO FALL.

Article 389. When a building, wall, column or any other construction is in danger of falling, the owner is obliged to demolish it or to do whatever is necessary to prevent its falling.

Should the owner of the ruinous work not do it, the authorities may have it demolished at the expense of the owner.

390. When a large tree threatens to fall in such a way as to cause damage to another person's tenement or to persons passing through a public or private way, the owner of the tree shall be obliged to pull it down and take it away; should he not do so, it shall be done at his expense by order of the authorities.

391. In the cases of the two preceding articles, should the tree or building fall, the provisions of arts. 1907 and 1908 shall be enforced.

TITLE III.
COMMUNITY OF PROPERTY.

Article 392. There is community of property when the ownership of a thing or of a right belongs to different persons undividedly.

In default of contracts or of special provisions, communities shall be governed by the provisions of this title.

393. The share of the participants in the benefits, as well as in the charges, shall be proportionate to their respective interests.

The interests belonging to the participants shall be presumed equal until the contrary is proven.

394. Every participant may use the things, held in common, provided he uses them in accordance with their office and in such a way as not to injure the interests of the community nor prevent the co-participants from utilizing them according to their rights.

395. Every participant shall have a right to oblige a co-participant to contribute to the expenses of keeping the thing or right held in common; only the party renouncing the share belonging to him in the ownership can exempt himself from this obligation.

396. When the different stories of a house belong to different owners, if the titles do not specify the conditions under which they must contribute to the necessary expenses thereof, and there is no stipulation about it, the following provisions shall be observed:

1. The main and party walls, the roof, and other things of use in common shall be preserved at the expense of all the owners in proportion to the value of their stories.

2. Every owner shall pay the cost of maintaining the floor of his story. The floor of the porch, front door, common yard, and hygienic works, common to all, shall be paid pro rata by all the owners.

3. The stairs from the porch to the first story shall be paid for pro rata by all the owners, with the exception of the owner of the ground floor; the stairs from the first to the second story shall be paid for by all, excepting the owners of the ground floor and first story, and successively so on.

397. None of the owners shall, without consent of the others, make any change in the common property though benefits for all may accrue thereby.

398. The resolution of the majority of the part-owners as

to the management and better enjoyment of the thing held in common shall be binding (on all).

There shall be no majority, unless the resolution has been made by the part-owners representing a majority of the interests which constitutes the object of the community.

If there is no majority or the resolution of the same is seriously injurious to the parties interested in the thing held in common, the Judge, on petition of any part-owner, shall decree what may be proper including the appointment of an administrator.

When a part of the things privately belong to one or to some of the part-owners and the remainder in common, the preceding prescription shall only apply to the latter.

399. Each one of the part-owners shall have absolute ownership of his part and in the fruits and benefits belonging to it, and he, therefore, may sell, assign, or mortgage it, and even substitute another person in its enjoyment, unless personal rights are involved. But the effect of the sale or mortgage, in what refers to the part-owner, shall be limited to the share which may be allotted to him in the distribution on the determination of the community.

400. No part-owner shall be obliged to remain a party to the community. Each of them may ask, at any time, the division of the thing held in common.

However, the stipulation of keeping the thing undivided for a stated period of time, not exceeding ten years, shall be valid. This term may be extended by a new agreement.

401. Notwithstanding what is provided in the preceding article, the part-owners cannot compel a division of the thing held in common to be made when by so doing they may render it unserviceable for the use for which it was intented.

402. The division of a thing held in common may be made by the parties in interest or by arbitrators or compromisers appointed at the will of the part-owners.

In case it is made by arbitrators or compromisers, they shall divide it into parts proportional to the rights of each part-owner endeavoring to avoid payments of balances in cash as far as possible.

403. The creditors or assignees of the part-owners may concur in the division of the property, held in common, and object to any division made without their concurrence. But they cannot object to the division already made, except in the cases of fraud or when they have made it, notwithstanding the opposition formally interposed in order to prevent it, but they shall always leave the rights of the debtor or assignee intact to maintain its validity.

404. When the thing is essentially indivisable and the part-owners cannot agree that it be adjudged to one of them who shall indemnify the others, then it shall be sold and the proceeds be distributed.

405. The division of property held in common shall not cause injury to a third party who shall retain the rights of mortgage, easements, or any other real rights belonging to him before the division was made. The personal rights belonging to a third party against the community shall also remain in force notwithstanding the division.

406. The rules, relating to the division of estates, shall apply to the divisions among the part-owners.

TITLE IV.

SOME SPECIAL PROPERTIES.

CHAPTER FIRST.

WATERS.

SECTION FIRST.

OWNERSHIP OF WATERS.

Article **407.** To the public domain belong:

1. Rivers and their natural beds.

2. Continuous or intermittent waters from sources or brooks running in their natural beds and the beds themselves.

3. Waters rising continuously or intermittently in lands on the same public domain.

4. Lakes and ponds formed by nature on public lands, and also their beds.

5. Rain water running through ravines or sandy beaches with their beds also belong to the public domain.

6. Subterranean waters existing on public lands.

7. Waters found within the zone of operation of public works, even when they are made by a grantee.

8. Waters flowing continuously or intermittently from tenements belonging to private parties, to the State, to the provinces or to towns from the moment they leave such tenements.

9. The waste waters of fountains, sewers, and public institutions.

408. To private dominion belong:

1. Waters, either continuous or intermittent, rising on private tenements as far as they run through them.

2. Lakes and ponds and their beds, when formed by nature on said tenements.

3. Subterranean waters found on the same.

4. Rain waters falling on private tenements as long as they remain within boundaries of the same.

5. The beds of flowing waters, continuous or intermittent, formed by rain water, and those of brooks crossing tenements which do not belong to the public domain. In every drain or acqueduct the water, the bed, the sloping bank, and the side-ways are considered as an integral part of the tenement or building for which the waters are intended. The owners of tenements, through which or along the boundaries of which the acqueduct passes, can allege no ownership over it, nor any right to profit by their beds or side-ways, unless they base their claim on title deeds, specifying the right or the ownership claimed by them.

SECTION SECOND.

PROFITABLE USE OF PUBLIC WATERS.

Article **409.** The use of public waters is acquired:

1. By administrative concession.

2. By prescription of twenty years.

The limits of the rights and obligations of their uses shall be those shown, in the first case, by the terms of the concession;

and, in the second, by the manner and form in which the waters have been used.

410. Every concession of use of waters is understood to be without injury to third parties.

411. The right to make use of public waters is extinguished by the forfeiture of the concession, and by the non-usage during twenty years.

SECTION THIRD.

THE USE OF WATERS OF PRIVATE OWNERSHIP.

Article 412. The owner of a tenement which contains the source from which a brook rises, be it continuous or intermittent, may use its waters as far as they run through the tenement; after it leaves the tenement, it becomes public and its use is governed by the special law of waters.

413. Private ownership of the beds of rain waters does not give a right to make works and constructions which may divert the course of such waters with injury to a third party nor those, the destruction of which by the force of floods, may cause such injury.

414. No one may enter private property in search of waters or make use of them without permission from its owner.

415. The dominion which the propietor of a tenement has over waters rising on his land cannot be exercised so as to interfere with the rights which the owner of an inferior tenement may have legally acquired to its use.

416. Every owner of a tenement has a right to construct on his property receptacles for rain water, provided he does no damage thereby to the public or a third party.

SECTION FOURTH.

SUBTERRANEAN WATERS.

Article 417. Only the owner of a tenement or another person, with his permission, may search for subterranean waters thereon.

The search for subterranean water on lands of the public

domain can only be made with the permission of the administration.

418.   Artesian waters, according to the special law of
waters, belong to the persons who discovers the same.

419.   When the owner of artesian wells abandons the
same to their natural course, they become public domain.

SECTION FOURTH.

GENERAL PROVISIONS.

Article 420.   The owner of a tenement on which there
are defensive works to check waters or on which, by the
variation of their course, it may be necessary to reconstruct
them, is bound, at his option, to make the necessary repairs or
constructions or to permit that, without damage to him, the
owners of the tenements, who suffer or are clearly exposed to
suffer damages, should make such works.

421.   The provisions of the preceding article apply to the
cases in which it may be necessary to clear a tenement from
the material, the accumulation or fall of which may obstruct
the course of waters with injury or danger to a third party.

422.   All the proprietors who participate in the benefits
arising from the works, to which the preceding articles refer,
shall be bound to contribute to the expenses of their construction in proportion to their interests.   Those, who by their own
fault may have caused the damages, shall be responsible for
such expenses.

423.   The ownership and use of waters belonging to
corporations or private parties are subject to the law of
expropriation for causes of public utility.

424.   The provisions of this title shall not cause injury to
rights previously acquired nor to the private ownership which
the proprietor of waters, drains, fountains or sources have to
use, sell or to barter, as private property.

425.   Anything not expressly determined by the provisions of this chapter shall be governed by the special law of
waters.

CHAPTER SECOND.
MINERAL ORES.

Article **426**. Any Spaniard or foreigner may freely make prospect pits or excavations, not exceeding ten metres in length or depth, for the purpose of discovering ores on land belonging to the public demain; but they must previously give notice thereof to the local authorities. On land belonging to private parties no prospect pits can be sunk unless the permission of the owner or the party representing him has been previously obtained.

427. The limits of the rights mentioned in the preceding article, the previous formalities, and the conditions for their exercise, the designation of the matters which are to be considered as ores, and the determination of the rights belonging to the owner of the land and to the discoverer of the ores, in case of grants, shall be governed by the special law of mines.

CHAPTER THIRD.
INTELLECTUAL PROPERTY.

Article **428**. The author of any literary, scientific or artistic work has the right to profit by it and dispose of it at h is will.

429. The law of intellectual property determines the persons to whom such right belongs, the manner of exercising it, and the period of its duration. In cases not provided for nor determined by such special law, the general rules about ownership, established by this Code, shall govern.

TITLE V.
POSSESSION.

CHAPTER FIRST.
POSSESSION AND ITS KINDS.

Article **430**. Natural possession is the holding of a thing or the enjoyment of a right by some person. Civil possession is the same holding or enjoyment joined to the intent of having the thing or right as his own.

431.   Possession of things or rights is exercised, either by the same person who holds and enjoys them or by another in his behalf.

432.   Possession in things and rights may be held in one of two different ways, either as that of the owner or as that of the holder of the things or rights to keep and enjoy them when the ownership belongs to another person.

433.   Any person who is not aware that there is in his title or in the manner of acquiring it any flaw, invalidating the same, shall be considered a possessor in good faith.

Possessors to the contrary are considered as possessors in bad faith.

434.   Good faith is always presumed and any person averring bad faith on the part of the possessor is bound to prove it.

435.   Possession, when acquired in good faith, does not lose such character, except in the cases and from the moment in which some act exists proving that the possessor is aware that he possesses the thing unlawfully.

436.   It is presumed that the enjoyment of the possession is continued under the same understanding with which it was acquired, until the contrary is proven.

437.   Only things and rights susceptible of being appropriated can be the objects of possession.

CHAPTER SECOND.
ACQUISITION OF POSSESSION.

Article **438.**   Possession is acquired, either by the material occupation of the thing or right possessed, or by the fact that the same remains subject to the action of our will, or by the proper act and legal formalities established for acquiring such a right.

439.   Possession may be acquired by the same person who is to enjoy it, by his legal representative, by his attorney or by a third person, without any power therefor, but, in this last case, possession shall not be considered as acquired, until the person, in whose name the act of possession has been executed, has ratified the same.

440. He who repudiates an inheritance in a valid manner is understood as not having possessed it for a single moment.

The possession of hereditary property is understood as transferred to the heir without interruption and from the moment of the death of the testator, in case the inheritance be accepted.

441. In no case can possession be forcebly acquired while there is a possessor contesting it. The person, believing that he has a right or action to deprive any other of the holding of a thing, should ask help of competent authority, whenever the holder refuses to deliver it up.

442. The successor, by an heriditary title, shall not suffer the consequences of a faulty possession of his testator, unless it is proven that he was informed of the flaws affecting it; however, the effects of the possession in good faith shall not benefit him, but from the death of the testator.

443. Minors and incapables can acquire the possession of things, but they shall require the assistance of their lawful representatives to make use of the rights in their favor arising from the possession.

444. Acts merely tolerated and those clandestinely executed, and without knowledge of the possessor of a thing or with violence, do not affect the possession.

445. Possession, as a fact, cannot be recognized in two different personalities, unless in cases of indivision. Should a question arise about the fact of the possesion, the actual possessor shall be preferred, the oldest, when two appear; if the date of the possession is the same, the one presenting a title; and when all these conditions are equal, the thing shall be placed in deposit or judicial keeping, until a decision is rendered through proper prcceedings about the possession or the ownership thereof.

CHAPTER THIRD.

EFFECT OF POSSESSION.

Article **446.** Every possessor has the right to be respected in his possesion, and should he be disturbed in it, he shall be protected or possession be restored to him by the means established in the laws of procedure.

447. Only the possession acquired and enjoyed in the belief of being owner can serve as a title to acquire ownership.

448. The possessor who believes himself owner has in his favor the legal presumption that he possesses under a just title and he shall not the obliged to show it.

449. The possession of a real tenement is also a presumption of possession of the furniture and objects within it, as long as it is not show or proven that they ought to be excluded.

450. Each one of the participants, in a thing held in common, is considered as having exclusively possessed the part which may be allotted to him on the distribution, during all the time that the indivision lasted.

The interruption of the possession of the whole or of a part of the thing held in common shall injure all possessors equally.

451. The fruits collected in good faith by the possessor become his own while the possession has not been lawfully interrupted.

Natural and industrial fruits are considered as collectep from the moment they are gather or separated.

Civil fruits are considered as daily proceeds and in this proportion belong to the possessor in good faith.

452. If, at the date on which good faith ceases, some natural or industrial fruits are ungathered, the possessor shall have a right to recover the expenses incurred by him for their production and besides to a part of the net proceeds of the crop in proportion to the time of his possession.

The charges shall be distributed pro rata, in the same manner, between both the possessors.

The owner of a thing may, if he desires, grant to the possessor, in good faith, the right of finishing the cultivation and collecting the pending fruits as an indemnity for the parts of the expenses of cultivation and net proceeds belonging to him; the possessor in good faith, who, for any reason, may not desire to accept such a concession, shall lose the right to be indemnified in any other manner.

453. Necessary expenses are refunded to every possessor; but only those in good faith may retain the thing until they are repaid.

Useful expenses are refunded to the possessor in good faith under the same right of retention and he who has defeated him in his possession has the option, either of refunding the amount of the expenses, or paying him the increase of value which the thing has acquired in consequence of such expenses.

454. The expenses purely for ostentation or mere pleasure are not to be refunded to the possessor in good faith, but he may carry away the ornaments with which he has embellished the principal thing, if it suffers no injury and if the successor in the possession does not prefer to refund the amount expended thereon.

455. A possessor in bad faith shall refund the fruits collected, and those which the lawful possessor could have received, and shall only have a right to be reimbursed for the necessary expenses made for the maintenance of the thing. The expenses incurred in improvements for ostentation and pleasure shall not be refunded to the possessor in bad faith, but he can take away the object for which such expenses have been incurred, provided the (principal) thing suffers no injury and the lawful possessor does not prefer to retain them, paying the value they have at the moment of his entering into possession.

456. The improvements caused by nature or time always pass to the benefit of the one who has won in the possession.

457. The possessor in good faith is not liable for the impairments or loss of the thing possessed, excepting the cases in which it may be proved that he has acted with deceit *(dolo)*. The possessor in bad faith is liable for the impairment or loss in any case, even in those caused by main force, when he maliciously has delayed the delivery of the thing to its lawful possessor.

458. The person obtaining possession is not bound to pay for improvements which have ceased to exist, at the time of acquiring the thing.

459. The actual possessor who shows his possession, during a prior time, is presumed to have had possession also during the intermediate period, until the contrary is proven.

460.   The possessor may lose his possession:

1.   By the abandonment of the thing.

2.   By assignment made to another party under an onerous or gratuitous title.

3.   By the destruction or total loss of the thing or by the thing becoming not (lawfully) marketable.

4.   By the possession of another, even against the will of a former possessor, if the new possession has lasted over a year.

461.   The possession of personal property is not considered as lost while it is under the control of the possessor, though he may accidently not know its whereabouts.

462.   The possession of real property and real rights is not considered as lost, nor transmitted for the effects of prescription to the injury of a third party, except with submission to the provisions of the Law of Mortgage.

463.   The acts relating to possession, either executed or consented to by the person possessing another person's thing as a mere holder for enjoying or retaining it for any cause, neither bind nor cause injury to the owner, unless he should have granted to the holder express powers to execute them or he ratifies them afterwards.

464.   The possession of personal property, acquired in good faith, is equivalent to a title thereto. However, the person, who has lost the personal thing or has been unlawfully deprived of it, may recover it from whoever possesses it.

If the possessor of a personal thing, lost or stolen, has acquired it in good faith at a public auction, the owner cannot recover it, unless by reimbursing (the possessor) the price paid for it.

Neither can the owner of a thing pledged in the loan offices (*Montes de Piedad*), established under authority of the goverment, obtain the recovery thereof, whoever the person may be who has pledged them, without previously refunding to the institution the amount of the pledge and the interest due.

Things acquired on the exchange, at marts or markets or from a merchant lawfully established and habitually employed in a traffic of analagous objects, shall be governed by the provisions of the Code of Commerce.

465. Wild animals are only possessed while they are under ones control; those domesticated or tamed are considered as tame or domestic as long as they retain the habit of returning to the home of their possessor.

466. A person who lawfully recovers the possession, unduly lost, is considered as having enjoyed it without interruption for all the effects that may be beneficial to him.

TITLE VI.

USUFRUCT, USE AND HABITATION.

CHAPTER FIRST.

USUFRUCT.

SECTION FIRST.

USUFRUCT IN GENERAL.

Article **467.** Usufruct gives a right to enjoy another's property under the obligation of maintaining its form and substance, unless the title constituting it or the law allows otherwise.

468. Usufruct is constituted by law, by wish of private persons specified in acts, *inter vivos*, by last will, and by prescription.

469. Usufruct can be constituted on the whole or on a part of the fruits of a thing, in favor of one or more persons, simultaneously or successively, and in any case from and up to a certain date, purely or under conditions. It can also be constituted on a right, provided the same is not absolutely personal or unassignable.

470. The rights and duties of the usufructuaries shall be those specified in the title constituting the usufruct; in default of this or if it is not sufficient, the provisions contained in the two following sections shall be observed.

SECTION SECOND.

RIGHTS OF THE USUFRUCTUARY.

Article **471**. The usufructuary is entitled to receive all the natural, industrial, and civil fruits of the property in usufruct. As to the treasures which may be found on the tenement, he shall be considered as a stranger.

472. Natural or industrial fruits, ungathered at the time of the beginning of the usufruct, belong to the usufructuary.

Those, pending at the time the usufruct expires, belong to the owner.

In the preceding cases, the usufructuary, at the beginning of the usufruct, is not bound to pay to the owner any of the expenses incurred; but, at the expiration of the usufruct, the owner is bound to pay from the proceeds of the pending fruits, the ordinary expenses of cultivation, for the seed, and other similar ones incurred by the usufructuary.

The provisions of this article shall not injure rights of a third party, acquired at the beginning or the determination of the usufruct.

473. If the usufructuary has leased the lands or tenements given in usufruct, and this should be determined before the lease, he or his heirs shall only receive their proportional parts of the rent, which are to be paid by the lessee.

474. The civil fruits are understood to be paid, day by day, and belong to the usufructuary in proportion to the time that the usufruct may last.

475. When a usufruct is constituted on the right to collect a rent or a periodical pension, consisting either of money or of fruits, or in interest on obligations, or certificates to the bearer, each payment due shall be considered as proceeds or fruits of said right.

When it consists in the enjoyments of the benefits, produced by an interest in any industrial or commercial enterprise, the distribution of which has not a fixed date, such benefits shall have the same consideration.

In either case, they shall be distributed as civil fruits and shall be applied in the manner provided in the preceding article.

476. The usufructuary of a tenement, on which mines are found, is not entitled to the proceeds of the mines denounced, granted, or on which there are workings, at the beginning of the usufruct, unless they are expressly granted to him by the title constituting the usufruct or in case such usufruct is universal.

The usufructuary, however, may remove stones, lime, and chalk from the quarries for repairs or works which he may be bound to make or which may be necessay.

477. Notwithstanding what is provided in the preceding article, the usufructuary, in the legal usufruct, may work the mines denounced, granted or being worked on the tenement, taking, as his own, one hald of the profits which may be obtained, after deducting the expenses which shall be equally shared by him and the owner.

478. The status of usufructuary does not deprive the person possessing it of the rights granted to every one, by the Law of Mines, to denounce and obtain the grant of mines existing on the tenement in usufruct, in the form and under the conditions established by said law.

479. The usufructuary shall have a right to enjoy the increase, which the thing in usufruct may receive by accession, of the easements existing in its favor, and in general of all the benefits inherent in the same.

480. The usufructuary may personally enjoy the thing in usufruct, may lease it to another person, or may alienate his rights to the usufruct, even under a gratuitous title; but all the contracts into which he may enter, as such usufructuary, shall terminate, at the expiration of the usufruct, except that of lease of rural tenements which shall be considered as subsisting during the agricultural year.

481. When the usufruct embraces things, which without being destroyed, are slowly deteriorated by usage, the usufructuary shall have the right to make use of them in a proper way, and shall not be bound to return them at the determination of the usufruct, except in the condition in which they may be found; but he shall be obliged to indemnify the owner for the wear they may have received on account of his malice or neglect.

482. When the usufruct embraces things which cannot be used without being destroyed, the usufructuary shall have a right to use them, under the obligation of paying the appraised value on the determination of the usufruct, if they were appraised when given to him. When they have not been appraised, he shall have the right to return them by giving the same amount and quality or paying their market price at the time of the determination of the usufruct.

483. The usufructuary of vinyards, olive orchards, and other trees or shrubs may use for his benefit the dead trunks and even those cut or torn off by accident, under the obligation of replacing them with others.

484. When in consequence of an act of God, or by an extraordinary event, the vines, olive trees, or other trees or shrubs are destroyed, in such a considerable number that the replanting of them should not be practicable, or be too onerous, the usufructuary may leave the dead, fallen, or broken trunks at the disposal of the owner and oblige him to remove them and leave the land clear.

485. The usufructuary of wood land may enjoy all the profits which it may produce according to its nature.

If the wood land is a copse or of timber for building, the usufructuary may cut trees on it or make ordinary felling such as the owner was in the habit of doing, and, in default of this, he shall make them in accordance with the usage of the place as to manner, amount, and season.

In any case, he shall make the cutting or felling of trees in such a manner that it will not damage the preservation of the tenement.

In the nurseries of trees, the usufructuary may make the thinnings required in order that the remaining trees may properly develope.

Besides what is provided in the preceding paragraphs, the usufructuary shall not cut the lower part of the trunk of any trees, unless it be for replacing or improving some of the things held in usufruct, and, in this case, he must give previous notice to the owner about the necessity of the work.

486. The usufructuary of an action to recover a tenement or a real right, or personal property has a right to enforce it, and to oblige the owner of the action to assign him for this purpose, his proper power and to provide him with any elements of evidence which he may have. When, in consequence of the enforcement of such action, he acquires the thing claimed, the usufruct shall be limited to the fruits only and the ownership shall go to the proprietor.

487. The usufructuary may make on the property held in usufruct any improvements, either useful or for recreation, which he may deem proper, provided he does not change the form or substance of the same; but he shall have no right to be indemnified for it. He may, however, remove said improvements, if it is possible to do so without damage to the property.

488. The usufructuary can set off any damages to the property with the improvements he may have made thereon.

489. The owner of property, the usufruct of which is held by another, may alienate it, but cannot change its form or substance nor do anything to the injure of the usufructuary.

490. The usufructuary of a part of a thing, held in common, shall exercise all the rights belonging to the owner of it in respect to the administration and collection of fruits and interests. Should the community cease on account of the division of the thing held in common, the usufruct of the part allotted to the owner or part—owner shall belong to the usufructuary.

SECTION THIRD.

OBLIGATION OF THE USUFRUCTUARY.

Article 491. The usufructuary, before entering upon the enjoyment of the property, shall be obliged:

1. To make, after summoning the owner or his lawful representation, an inventory of all the property, to have the personal property appraised, and to make a description of the condition of the real property.

2. To give bond binding himself to comply with the duties imposed on him by this section.

492. The provision of paragraph 2, of the preceding

article, is not to be applied to the vendor or donor, who has reserved to himself the usufruct of a thing sold or donated, neither to the parent who enjoyed the usufruct of the property of their children, nor to the surviving consort as to the hereditary share granted to him or her by arts. 834, 836, and 837, except in the cases in which the parents or consort contract a second marriage.

493. The usufructuary, whatever the title for his usufruct be, may be excused from the obligation of making an inventory or of giving bond when no one will be injured thereby.

494. When the usufructuary has not given bond, in the cases in which he ought to have given it, the owner may require that the real property be placed under administration, the personal property sold, that public effects, and bonds, notes, stocks, &c. (*valores*), either to order or to bearer, be converted into certificates or be deposited in a bank or public institution, and any capital or sums in cash and money received from sales of personal property, be invested in safe securities.

Interest on money received from the sale of personal property, interest on public effects, and bonds, notes, stocks, shares, &c. (*valores*), and the proceeds of property, placed under administration, belong to the usufructuary.

Furthermore, the owner may, if he so prefers, while the usufructuary gives no bond or is released from it, retain in his possession the property of the usufruct, as administrator under the obligation of delivering the net proceeds to the usufructuary, after deducting the sums which may be agreed upon or may be judicially fixed for his services during such administration.

495. When the usufructuary, who has not given bond, claims, under security given by oath *(caución juratoria)*, the delivery of furniture required for his use, also a dwelling be given to him and his family in a house comprised in the usufruct, the Judge may assent to his petition, after due consideration of the facts in the case.

The same shall be understood about the instruments, implements, and other personal property, required for the industry in which it is employed.

When the owner should not wish that some pieces of

furniture be sold, either on account of their artistic merit or because they have a special value in his eyes *(precio de afección)*, he may require their delivery to him upon giving security for the payment of the legal interest on their appraised value.

496. After the bonps are given by the usufructuary, he shall have a right to all the proceeds from the date on which he ought to have begun to receive them, in accordance with the title constituting the usufruct.

497. The usufructuary is bound to take care of the property given in usufruct as any good father of a family would do.

498. The usufructuary, who alienates or leases his right to the usufruct, shall be liable for the damages suffered by the property in usufruct by the fault or neglect of the person who substitutes him.

499. Should the usufruct be constituted over a flock or herd of cattle, the usufructuary shall be bound to replace, with the young thereof, the animal dying annually or ordinarily and those carried away by the rapacity of preying animals.

Should the herd on which the usufruct is constituted wholly perish without fault of the usufructuary, in consequence of contagious diseases or any other uncommon event, the usufructuary shall fulfill his duty by delivering to the owner the remains saved from this misfortune.

Should the herd partially perish, also by accident and without the fault of the usufructuary, the usufruct shall continue in respect to the part saved.

Should the usufruct be of a sterile herd, it shall be considered for all its effects as constituted over things perishable *(fungibles)*.

500. The usufructuary is bound to make the ordinary repairs, required by the things given in usufruct. Ordinary repairs shall be considered those required by the wear and tear produced by the natural use of things, and which are indispensable for their preservation. Should he not make them, after receiving an intimation from the owner, the latter may make them at the expense of the usufructuary.

501. Extraordinary repairs shall be made on the account

of the owner. The usufructuary is bound to notify him, when the necessity of making them is urgent.

502. When the owner makes extraordinary repairs, he shall be entitled to reclaim from the usufructuary the legal interest on the sum invested in them, during the existence of the usufruct.

Should he not make repairs when they are indispensable for the preservation of the thing, the usufructuary may make them; but he shall have a right to claim from the owner, on the determination of the usufruct, the increase in value which the tenement may have acquired on that account.

Should the owner refuse to refund such amounts, the usufructuary is entitled to retain the thing, until he reimburses himself from the proceeds thereof.

503. The owner may make works and improvements which may be appropriate for the tenement in usufruct, and new plantations on it, if it is rural property, provided the value of the usufruct is not diminished by such acts, nor the rights of the usufructuary impaired.

504. The payment of charges and annual taxes and of those considered as a lien on the fruits, shall be at the expense *(de cuenta)* of the usufructuary, during all the time that the usufruct lasts.

505. The taxes which may be imposed directly upon the capital, during the usufruct, shall be paid by the owner.

When the owner has paid them, the usufructuary is bound to pay him the legal interest upon any sums he may have disbursed for such causes, and when the usufructuary advances the amounts of such taxes, he shall recover such amounts, on the determination of the usufruct.

506. Should the usufruct be constituted upon the whole of a patrimony, and if, at the time of its constitution, the owner has debts, the provisions of arts. 642 and 643 about donations shall be applied to the maintenance of the usufruct as well as for the obligations of the usufructuary to pay such debts.

The same provisions are applicable in case the owner, at the time of the constitution of the usufruct, was obliged to pay periodical sums, even when there is no known principal *(aunque no tuvieran capital conocido).*

507. The usufructuary may personally claim the credits due which form a part of the usufruct, if he has given or gives the appropriate bond. If he has been released from giving bond or if he cannot give it, or if the one given is not sufficient, he shall require the authorization of the owner or, in his default, of the Judge to collect said credits.

The usufructuary under bond can invest the capital in any manner he may deem fit. The usufructuary without bond must invest said capital at interest, upon agreement with the owner, in default of such an agreement, under judicial authorization, and, in every case, with security sufficient to preserve the integrity of the capital in usufruct.

508. The universal usufructuary shall pay in full the legacy of life annuities or the pension for support.

The usufructuary of an aliquot part of the estate shall pay it in proportion to his share.

In neither of the two cases shall the owner be bound to make any reimbursements. The usufructuary of one or more specified things shall pay the legacy only when the rent or pension is expressly constituted upon them.

509. The usufructuary of a mortgaged tenement shall not be obliged the pay the debt for the security of which the mortgage was given.

When the tenement is seized or sold for the payment of the debt, the owner shall be liable to the usufructuary for what he may lose on that account.

510. When the usufruct be for the whole or for an aliquot part of an inheritance, the usufructuary may advance the sums which may belong to the property in usufruct for the payment of the debts of the estate and shall be entitled to claim from the owner its restoration, without interest, on the expiration of the usufruct.

When the usufructuary refuses to make this advance, the owner may ask for the sale of the part of the property in usufruct which may be necessary for the payment of such sums, or pay them with his own money with a right, in this last case, to claim from the usufructuary the corresponding interest.

511. The usufructuary is obliged to notify the owner of any act of a third party, coming to his knowledge, which may injure the rights of ownership, and shall be liable, should he not do so, for the damages and injuries as if they were caused by his own fault.

512. The expenses, costs, and condemnations of the suits, maintained about the usufruct, shall be charged to the usufructuary.

SECTION FOURTH.
MANNER OF EXTINGUISHING THE USUFRUCT.

Article 513. The usufruct is extinguished:

1. By the death of the usufructuary.

2. By the expiration of the term for which it was constituted or by the fulfillment of the resolutory condition stated in the constituting title.

3. By the merger of usufruct and ownership in the same person.

4. By renunciation of the usufructuary.

5. By total loss of the property in usufruct.

6. By determination of the right of the constituent.

7. By prescription.

514. If the thing given in usufruct should suffer a partial loss, the right shall continue as to the remaining part.

515. The usufruct cannot be constituted for over thirty years in favor of a town, a corporation or a society. Should it have been so constituted, and, before that time, the town becomes deserted or the corporation or society be dissolved, the usufruct shall be extinguished by such facts.

516. The usufruct granted for such a time, until a third party becomes of certain age, shall subsist during the number of years specified, even if the third party dies before, unless the usufruct has been expressaly granted only because of the existence of such person.

517. When the usufruct is constituted on a tenement of which a building may form a part, and the building should be destroyed, in any manner whatever, the usufructuary shall have a right to enjoy the use of the land and materials.

The same thing shall happen when the usufruct is constituted only upon the building and it should be destroyed. But, in such a case, if the owner wants to construct another building, he shall have a right to the use of the ground and of the materials, under the obligation of paying to the usufructuary, during the time the usufruct lasts, the interest upon the sum equivalant to the value of the ground and of the materials.

518. When the owner joined with the usufructuary in the insurance of the tenement, given in usufruct, he shall continue, in the case of loss, in the enjoyment of the new building, if constructed, or shall receive the interest on the amount insured, if rebuilding is not convenient to the owner.

When the owner has refused to contribute towards the insurance of the tenement and the usufructuary alone is the insurer, the latter shall acquire the right, in case of loss, to collect in full the amount of the insurance, but under the obligation of investing it in rebuilding the tenement.

Should the usufructuary refuse to contribute to the insurance and the owner be the sole insurer, the latter shall receive, in case of loss, the full amount of insurance, but the usufructuary shall always have the right granted to him in the preceding article.

519. When the thing in usufruct should be condemned for causes of public utility, the owner shall be obliged, either to replace it with another of the same value, and having similar conditions, or to pay to the usufructuary the legal interest on the amount of the indemnity, during all the time the usufruct is to last. If the owner chooses the second manner, he is bound to give security for the payment of the interest.

520. The usufruct is not extinguished by the bad use of the thing in usufruct; but if such abuse causes considerable damage to the owner, the latter may ask that the thing be delivered to him, binding himself to pay annually to the usufructuary the net proceeds of the same, after deducting the expenses and the compensation which may be allowed to him for the administration thereof.

521. The usufruct constituted in favor of several persons in existence, at the time of its constitution, shall not be

extinguished until the death of the last survivor of them.

522. Upon the determination thereof, the thing held in usufruct shall be delivered to the owner, unless the right of retention belonging to the usufructuary or to his heirs, for expenses which they should recover, is enforced. After the delivery is made, the bond or the mortgage shall be cancelled.

CHAPTER SECOND.

USE AND HABITATION.

Article **523.** The rights and duties of the persons enjoying the use and of him who has the right of habitation shall be regulated by the title constituting such rights, and, in default thereof, by the following provisions.

524. Use gives a right to receive, out of the fruits of another person's property, whatever may be needed to provide for the necessities of the person, enjoying the use, and his family, even when such family increases.

Habitation gives the person, having such a right, that of occupying in another person's house the apartments necessary for him and the members of his family.

525. The rights of use and habitation cannot be leased, nor transferred to another person by any title whatever.

526. He, who has the use of a flock or a herd of cattle, may profit of the young, milk, and wool thereof, in so far as it may be necessary for the consumption of himself and family, as well as of the dung required for manuring the land cultivated by him.

527. When the person enjoying the use, consumes all the fruits of another person's property, or when he, who has the right of habitation, occupies the whole house, he will be bound to pay all the expenses of cultivation, of ordinary repairs for the preservation thereof, as well as the taxes, in the same manner as the usufructuary.

When the receives only a part of the fruits, or dwells only in a part of the house, he shall make no payments, provided that a part of the fruits or benefits, sufficient to cover the expenses and charges, remain to the owner. If they are not sufficient, the former shall pay the deficiency.

528. The provisions established for usufruct apply to the rights of use and habitation, in so far as they do not conflict with what is provided in this chapter.

529. The rights of use and habitation are extinguished by the same causes as that of usufruct, and besides by serious abuse of the thing or dwelling.

TITLE VII.
EASEMENTS OR SERVITUDES.

CHAPTER FIRST.
EASEMENTS IN GENERAL.

SECTION FIRST.
DIFFERENT CLASSES OF EASEMENTS WHICH MAY BE ESTABLISHED ON TENEMENTS.

Article 530. An easement is a charge imposed upon real property or a tenement for the benefit of another tenement belonging to a different owner.

The tenement in favor of which the easement is constituted is called the dominant tenement, and the one suffering it, the servient tenement.

531. Easements can also be established for the benefit of one or more persons or for a community to whom the encumbered tenement does not belong.

532. Easements may be continuous or discontinuous, apparent or not apparent.

Continuous are those the use of which is or may be incessant without the intervention of any human act.

Discontinuous are those used at short or long intervals and which depend upon human acts.

Apparent are those which are well known and are continually in sight by external signs, revealing their use and benefit.

Not apparent are those which present no external show of their existence.

533. Easements are also either positive or negative.

A positive easement is one which imposes upon the owner of the servient tenement the obligation of allowing something to be done or doing it himself, and a negative easement is one which forbids the owner of the servient tenement doing some thing which should be licit for him to do, if the easement did not exist.

534. Easements are inseparable from the tenement to which they actively or passively belong.

535. Easements' are indivisible. When the servient tenement is divided among two or more persons, the easement is not modified and each of them has to suffer the part corresponding to it.

If the dominant tenemen tis the one so divided, each part-holder may use the easement wholly, provided the place of its use is not changed, nor if it is not aggravated in any form.

536. Easements are established either by law or by the will of the owners. The former are called legal and the latter voluntary easements.

SECTION SECOND.

MANNER OF ACQUIRING EASEMENTS.

Article **537.** Continuous and apparent easements are acquired, either by a title or by prescription of twenty years.

538. In order to acquire by prescription, easements, referred to in the preceding article, the time of the possession shall be counted, in positive easements, from the day on which the owner of the dominant tenement or the one who has made use of the easement, has commenced to exert it over the servient tenement; and in negative easements, from the date on which the owner of the dominant tenement has, in a formal manner, forbidden the owner of the servient one, the execution of the act which might have been licit, had the easement not existed.

539. Continuous and not apparent easements and discontinuous ones, either apparent or not, can only be acquired under a title.

540. The want of constitutive title of easements, which cannot be acquired by prescription, can only be remedied by deed of acknowledgment executed by the owner of the servient tenement or by a final sentence.

541. The existence of apparent sign of an easement, between two tenements, established by the owner of both of them, shall be considered, should one be sold, as a title for the purpose that the easement should continue actively and passively, unless, at the time of the division of the ownership of both tenements, the contrary should be expressed in the deed of conveyance of either of them, or if such sign is taken away before the execution of such deed.

542. Whenever an easement is established, all the rights required for its use are considered as granted.

SECTION THIRD.
RIGHTS AND OBLIGATIONS OF OWNERS OF DOMINANT AND SERVIENT TENEMENTS.

Article **543.** The owner of the dominant tenement may make, at his own expense on the servient tenement, all the works necessary for its use and maintenance of the easement but without changing it or rendering it more grevious.

He must choose for it the most convenient time and form for the purpose of causing the least possible trouble to the owner of the servient tenement.

544. When there are several dominant tenements, the owners of all of them are bound to contribute to the expenses, referred to in the preceding article, in proportion to the benefit, which each may obtain from the work. He, who does not wish to contribute, may exempt himself by renouncing his interest in the easement for the benefit of the others.

If the owner of the servient tenement should, in any manner, profit by the easement, he shall be obliged to contribute to the expenses in the proportion, already stated, unless there is a stipulation to the contrary.

545. The owner of the servient tenement shall not impair, in any manner, the use of a constituted easement.

However, if by reason of the place originally assigned or

by the form established for the use of the easement, this should become too troublesome to the owner of the servient tenement or should prevent him from making works, repairs, or important improvements, it may be changed, at his expense; provided, he offers another place or manner equally convenient, or a way that may not cause any injury to the owner of the dominant tenement or to those who have a right to the use of the easement.

SECTION FOURTH.

MANNER IN WHICH EASEMENTS ARE EXTINGUISHED.

Article **546**. Easement are extinguished:

1. By merger in the same person of the ownership of the servient and dominant tenements.

2. By non-use during twenty years.

In discontinuous easements, this term shall commence to be counted from the day on which it has ceased to be used; and, in respect to continuous ones, from the date on which an act in opposition to the easement may have taken place.

3. When the tenements become in such condition that the easement cannot be used, but this shall revive, if later on, the condition of the tenements permits it to be used, unless, when the use becomes possible, sufficient time has elapsed for the prescription in accordance with the provisions of the preceding article.

4. When the day matures, or when the condition is complied with, in case the easement is temporal or conditional.

5. By the renunciation of the owner of the dominant tenement.

6. By redemption agreed to between the owners of the dominant and servient tenements.

547. The form of using the easement may be prescribed just in the same manner as the easement.

548. When the dominant tenement belongs to several persons in common, the use of the easement made by one of them, prevents the prescription in regard to the others.

CHAPTER SECOND.
LEGAL EASEMENTS.

SECTION FIRST.
GENERAL PROVISIONS.

Article **549.** The object of the easements, established by law, is either public utility or private interest.

550. Anything concerning easements, established for public or for common utility, shall be governed by the special laws and regulations controlling them, and, in default thereof, by the provisions of the present title.

551. Easements, established by law for the interests of private persons or for causes of private utility, shall be controlled by the provisions of the present title, without conflicting with what is established by the general laws, by-rules and ordinances or local ones about city or rural police.

These easements may be modified by agreement among the interested parties, whenever the law does not forbid it, or it causes no damage to a third party.

SECTION SECOND.
EASEMENTS RELATING TO WATERS.

Article **552.** Inferior tenements are obliged to receive the waters, which naturally and without the intervention of man, come down from the superior tenements, as well as the stone or earth which they may drag along in their course.

Neither can the owner of the inferior tenement make works which may prevent such an easement, nor can the owner of the superior one construct works aggravating it.

553. The banks of the rivers, even when they are of private ownership, are subject in all their extent and margins, within a zone of three metres, to the easement of public use for the general interest of navigation, floatation, fishing, and salvage.

Tenements, adjacent to the banks of navigable or floatable rivers, are, besides, subject to the easement of a tow-path for the exclusive service of fluvial navigation and floatation.

Should it be necessary to occupy, for such purpose, lands of private ownership, the corresponding indemnity shall previously be paid.

554. Whenever for the diversion or taking of waters from a river or brook, or for the use of other continuous or discontinuous currents, it should be necessary to construct a dam, and the person who is to do it, is not the owner of the bank or of the land required as a support for it, he may establish the easement for abutment of the dam, by previously paying the proper indemnity (to the owner).

555. Forced easements for taking water and for drinking troughs for animals *(abrevadero)* can be imposed only for causes of public utility in favor of some town or village, indemnity having been previously paid.

556. The easements for taking water and for watering animals carry with them the obligation on the servient tenements of giving passage for the persons and animals up to the place where they can be utilized, and the indemnity must embrace this service.

557. Whoever wishes to make use of waters, of which he can dispose for the use of a tenement belonging to him, has the right of causing it to pass through intermediate tenements, but he is obliged to idemnify the owners, and also those of the inferior tenements, upon which the waters may filter or fall.

558. A person desiring to make use of the rights granted in the preceding article is obliged:

1. To prove that he is entitled to dispose of the water, and that such water is sufficient for the use intended.

2. To show that the passage way which he asks is the most convenient and less onerous to a third party.

3. To indemnify the owner of the servient tenement in the form provided by the laws and regulations.

559. The easement of an aqueduct for purposes of private interest cannot be imposed upon buildings nor their yards or dependencies, nor over gardens or orchards already in existence.

560. The easement of an aqueduct does not prevent the owner of the servient tenement from closing and fencing it, nor from building over the acceduct, in such a manner, that it may suffer no damage nor render impossible the necessary cleanings and repairs.

561. The easement of aqueduct for its legal effects shall be considered as continuous and apparent, even when the passage of the water is not continuous or its use depends on the necessities of the dominant tenement, or, in turn, established by days or hours.

562. He, who for irrigating his tenement or improving it, has need to construct a stop-lock or a sluice-gate in a mill race, through which it is to receive water, may exact that the owners of the banks allow the construction of the same, upon his previously paying all damages and injuries, including those caused by the new easement to the said owners and to all other persons who irrigate.

563. The establishment, extent, form, and conditions of the easements of waters, to which this section refers, shall be governed by the special law on the matter in all that is not provided in this Code.

SECTION THIRD.
EASEMENT OF WAYS.

Article 564. The owner of a tenement or property enclosed by others, belonging to several owners, and having no ingress or egress to public roads, is entitled to exact a way or passage through the adjacent tenements, by previously paying the proper indemnity.

If this easement is constituted in such a manner that its use may be continuous for all the necessities of the dominant tenement, establishing a permanent way, then the indemnity shall comprise the value of the land occupied by it, and the amount of damage caused to the servient tenement.

When it is limited to the way required for the cultivation of the tenement, enclosed by others, and for the transportation of its crops through the servient tenement, without a permanent way, the indemnity shall consist in the payment of the injury caused by such burden.

565. The easement of way is to be located in the place

where it shall cause the least damage to the servient tenement, in so far as consistent with this rule, through the place where the distance from the dominant tenement to the public road may be the shortest.

566. The width of the easement of way shall be that which may be sufficient for the necessities of the dominant tenement.

567. When a tenement, acquired by sale, barter or partition, remains enclosed by other tenements of the vendor, barterer or co-owner, he shall be obliged to grant to it the right of way, without indemnity, unless there is an agreement to the contrary.

568. If the way granted to an enclosed tenement ceases to be necessary because the owner has joined it to another, adjacent to the public road, the owner of the servient tenement may demand the extinguishment of the easement, returning what he has received as an indemnity therefor.

The same thing is to be done in the event of the opening of a new road giving access to the enclosed tenement.

569. When it is indispensable for the construction or repair of some building to carry the materials over another's tenement, or place scaffolding or other things on it for the work, the owner of such tenement is obliged to consent to it, receiving an indemnity in proportion to the injury it may have caused him.

570. Existing easements for the passage of animals, known under the name of sheep-walk (*cañada*), way, foot-path, or any others, and those of watering, and resting places, and sheep-cot shall be governed by the ordinances and regulations on the matter and, in default thereof, by the uses and customs of the place.

In any case a walk shall not exceed in width seventy five metres, a way, thirty seven metres, fifty centimetres, and a path twenty metres, except when they cause damages to rights lawfully acquired.

When it may be necessary to establish a forcible easement of way or that of a drinking trough for cattle, the provisions of this section and of arts. 555 and 556 shall be followed. In this case the width shall not exceed ten metres.

SECTION FOURTH.
EASEMENTS OF PARTY–WALLS AND FENCES.

Article **571**. The easements of party-walls and fences shall be governed by the provisions of this title, and by local ordinances and uses, in so far as they are not in conflict with them and no provisions exist in regard to the same.

572. The easement of party-walls and fences is presumed, whilst there is no title or exterior mark or proof to the contrary:

1. In dividing walls of contiguous buildings up to the point of elevation in common.

2. In dividing walls of gardens or yards, situated in cities or in the country.

3. In fences, enclosures, and live hedges, dividing rural tenements.

573. It is understood that there are exterior signs, contrary to the easement of party-wall, and fences :

1. When, in dividing walls of buildings, there are windows or openings.

2. When the dividing wall is, on one side, straight and vertical in all its facement and is also similar in the upper part of the other side, but in the lower part thereof it is tapering or has steps.

3. When the wall appears built entirely on the land of one of the tenements, and not half and half between the contiguous tenements.

4. When it bears the burden of the binding beams, floors, and roof frame of one of the houses and not of the contiguous one.

5. When the dividing walls between yards, gardens, and rural tenements is so constructed that the coping sheds the waters towards one of the tenements.

6. When the dividing wall, being constructed of stones, shows stepping stones, which, from distance to distance, jut out of the surface only on one side and not on the other.

7. When rural tenements, contiguous to others, included by fences or live hedges, are not closed. In all these cases, the ownership of the walls, enclosures, or hedges shall be understood

to belong exclusively to the owner of the property or tenement who has in his favor the presumption based on any one of the above mentioned signs.

574. Ditches or drains, opened between tenements, are also considered, as common, when there is no title or sign showing the contrary.

There is a sign contrary to part-ownership, when the earth or dirt excavated for opening the ditch or for its cleaning is only on one side thereof, in which case the ownership of the ditch shall belong exclusively to the owner of the tenement, having in its favor this exterior sign.

575. The repairs and construction of party-walls and maintenance of enclosures, live-hedges, ditches, and drains, in common, shall be borne by all the owners of the tenements, who are interested in the same, in proportion to the rights of each one of them.

However, every owner may refuse to contribute to this charge by renouncing the part-ownership, except in the case when the party-wall supports his own building.

576. When the owner of a building, which is supported by a party-wall, desires to demolish it, he may also renounce the part-ownership but he shall also pay for all repairs and works required for preventing, only on such occasion, damages which the demolition may cause to the party-wall.

577. Every owner may construct a party-wall by raising it, at his own expense, and indemnifying (persons) against any damage which may be caused by the work, even when such damage is temporary.

He shall also have to pay for the expenses of maintaining the wall or the part newly raised or for the deepening of its foundations, compared with what they were before, and besides the indemnity for the further expenses which may be required to be incurred to maintain the party—wall by reason of the greater height or depth which has been added to it.

If the party-wall cannot bear the greater height, the owner desiring to raise it, shall be obliged to rebuild, at his own expense, and, if it is necessary to make it thicker, he shall give the extra space for it from his own land.

578. The other owners, who have not contributed in giving greater height, depth or thickness to the wall, may, however, acquire in it the right of party ownership by paying proportionally for the amount of the work and one half of the value of the land appropriated in giving it greater thickness.

579. Each owner of a party-wall may use it in proportion to the right he has in the part-ownership; he may, therefore build, supporting his construction on the party-wall, or introduce joists up to one-half of the thickness thereof, but without impeding the common and respective uses of the other part-owners.

The part-owner, in order to use this right, must previously obtain the consent of the other parties interested in the part-ownership; and, if he cannot obtain it, the conditions required, in order that the new work may not injure the right of the part-owners, shall be fixed by experts.

SECTION FIFTH.

EASEMENT OF LIGHT AND VIEWS.

Article **580.** No part-owner, can, without the consent of the other, make in the party-wall a window or an opening of any kind.

581. The owner of a wall which is not a party-wall, contiguous to the tenement of another person, may make in it windows or openings to receive light, at the height of the ceiling joists or near the ceiling, of the dimensions of 30 centimetres square, and, in any event, with an iron grate imbedded in the wall and a wire netting.

However, the owner of the house or tenement, contiguous to the wall where the openings are made, may close them, if he acquires the part ownership of the wall and if the contrary has not been agreed upon.

He may also obstruct them by building on his land or raising a wall, adjacent to that having such opening or window.

582. It is forbidden to open windows with direct views or balconies or any similar openings jutting out over the property of the neighbor, if there is not a distance of, at least, two metres from the wall on which they are constructed to said property.

Neither can side or oblique views be opened over said property, unless there is (similarly) a distance of sixty centimetres.

583. The distances, to which the preceding article refers, are to be measured where there are direct views, from the exterior line of the wall when the openings do not jut out, and from the line of these openings when they exist, and for slanting views from the dividing line of both tenements.

584. The provisions of art. 582 do not apply to buildings separated by a public way.

585. When, under any title, right has been acquired to have direct views, balconies, or belvederes over contiguous property, the owner of the servient tenement shall not build thereon, at a distance less than three metres, to be measured as stated in art. 583.

SECTION SIXTH
DRAINAGE OF BUILDINGS.

Article **586.** The owner of a building is obliged to construct his roofs or covers in such a manner that rain water may fall on his own land or on the street or a public place, and not on the land of his neighbor. Even if it falls on his own land, the owner is obliged to collect it, in such a way, that it will not cause damage to the neighboring tenement.

587. The owner or the tenement suffering the easement of receiving water, discharged from roofs, may so build as to receive the waters upon his own roof or give them another diversion, in accordance with local ordinances or customs, in such a manner as not to cause any burden or damage whatever to the dominant tenement.

588. When the yard or court of a house is enclosed between others, and it is not possible to give an outlet through the same house to the rain water collected in it, the establishment of an easement of outlet may be claimed to give passage to the waters through the place of the contiguous tenement, where the egress is the easiest, and to establish a conduit for the egress, in such a way, as to cause the least damage to the servient tenement, upon the payment of a proper indemnity.

SECTION SEVENTH.

DISTANCES AND INTERMEDIATE WORKS FOR CERTAIN CONSTRUCTIONS AND PLANTATIONS.

Artitle **589.** It is forbidden to construct buildings or to make plantations near fortified cities or fortresses, without submitting to the prescriptions of the laws, ordinances, and regulations, peculiar to this matter.

590. No one shall construct, near a wall belonging to a third party or a party-wall, wells, sewers, aqueducts, furnaces, forges, chinneys, stables, deposits of corrosive matters, factories driven by steam, or factories which by themselves or by their products are dangerous or noxious, without observing the distances prescribed by the regulations and uses of the place, and without making the necessary protective works, with subjection, as to form, to the conditions prescribed by said regulations.

In default of ordinances, precautions, considered necessary, shall be taken, after expert's inspection, for the purpose of avoiding all injuries to the neighboring tenements or buildings.

591. No trees shall be planted near another man's tenement, unless it is at the distances authorized by the ordinances or customs of the place, and, in default of these, it shall be at a distance of two metres from the dividing line of the tenements, if the planting is made of tall trees, and at fifty centimetres, if the planting is made of shrubs or small trees.

Every owner has a right to ask that trees, which may be planted in the future at a shorter distance from his tenement, shall be uprooted.

592. Should the branches of any tree extend over a neighboring tenement, gardens or yards, the owner of the latter shall have a right to claim that they be cut, in so far as they extend over his property; and should the roots of the neighboring trees extend through the land of another person, the owner of the land which is penetrated may himself cut them, in so far as they are within his tenement.

593. Trees existing in a party live-hedge shall also be

considered as party-trees, and any one of the owners has a right to exact that they be felled.

Trees serving as land-marks are excepted, and they may only be uprooted by mutual agreement amongst the adjoining owners.

CHAPTER THIRD.

VOLUNTARY EASEMENTS.

Article **594**. Every owner of a tenement has a right to burden it with all the easements he may deem fit, and in the manner and form that he may like best, provided he does not violate either the laws or the public order.

595. The owner of a tenement, the usufruct of which belongs to another person, may impose upon it, without the consent of the usufructuary, any easements which may not damage the rights of usufruct.

596. When the direct dominion of a tenement belongs to one person and the beneficial dominion to another, no perpetual voluntary easement can be established upon it, without the consent of both owners.

597. The consent of every part-owner shall be required in order to impose an easement over an undivided tenement.

The concession, made by some of them, shall remain in suspension until every one of the joint or common owners agrees to it.

But the concession, made by one of the part-owners severally, shall bind the grantors and his successors, even if they hold under a particular title, not to prevent the exercise of the right granted.

598. The title, and in some cases, the possession of an easement acquired by prescription, determines the right of the dominant tenement and the obligation of the servient tenement. In default of them, the easement shall be governed by the provisions of the present title which may apply to it.

599. When the owner of the servient tenement has bound himself, at the time of constituting the easement, to pay for the works required for the use and maintenance of the same, he may free himself from this charge, by abandoning his tenement to the owner of the dominant tenement.

600. Pasturage in common shall only be established, in the future, by express concession of the owners, to be proven by a contract or a last will, and shall not be made in favor of a universality of persons or a universality of property, but in favor of specified persons and over tenements also specified and determined.

The easement, established in accordance with this article, shall be governed by the title of its institution.

601. Pasturage in common in public land, whether it belongs to the municipalities or to the State, shall be governed by the administrative laws.

602. When pasturage in common, exists amongst the residents of one or more villages, the owner, who encloses a tenement with a fence or a hedge, shall free the same from the pasturage in common. However, the other easements established over the same, shall remain subsistent.

The owner who closes his tenement shall keep his right to the pasturage in common in the other tenements not enclosed.

603. The owner of land, burdened with the easement of pasturage, may redeem this charge by paying its value to the persons having the rights to the easement.

In default of an agreement, the capital for such redemption shall be fixed upon the basis of 4% of the annual value of the pasturage, regulated by appraisal by experts.

604. The provision of the preceding article applies to easements established for the use of fuel and other products of wood which belong to private property.

TITLE VIII.

REGISTRY OF PROPERTY.

SOLE CHAPTER.

Article 605. The registry of property has for its object the inscription or annotation of the acts and contracts relating to domain and other real rights pertaining to real property.

606. The titles of dominion or of other real rights,

relating to real property which are not duly inscribed or annotated in the Registry of Property, work no injury to third parties.

607. The Registry of Property shall be public for those who have a known interest in investigating the condition of real property or real rights annotated or inscribed therein.

608. The provisions of the Law of Mortage shall control the determination of titles, subject to inscription or annotation, the form, effect, and extinction of the same, and the manner of keeping the Registry and value of the entries in the books thereof.

BOOK THIRD.

DIFFERENT WAYS OF ACQUIRING OWNERSHIP.

PRELIMINARY PROVISION.

Article 609. Ownership is acquired by occupancy.

Ownership and other rights over property are acquired and transmitted by law, by donation, by succession, either testate or intestate, and by tradition in consequence of certain contracts.

They may also be acquired by prescription.

TITLE I.

OCCUPANCY.

Article 610. By occupancy are acquired things appropriable, on account of their nature, which have no owners, as the animals which are objects of hunting and fishing, hidden treasures, and abandoned personal property.

611. The right to hunt and fish is governed by special laws.

612. The owner of a swarm of bees shall have a right to pursue the same on another person's tenement, indemnifying its possessor for the damage caused thereby. Should the tenement be enclosed, he shall need the consent of the owner to enter it.

If the owner has not pursued, or abandons the pursuit of the swarm for two successive days, the possessor of the tenement may occupy or retain the swarm.

The owner of tamed animals may also claim them during the twenty days following their occupation by another. After this term has elapsed, they shall belong to him who has caught and kept them.

613. Pigeons, rabbits, and fish, which from their respective breeding places, should pass to another, belonging to a different owner, shall become the property of the latter, unless they have been enticed away through some trickery or fraud.

614. He, who by chance, finds a treasure, hidden on another man's property, shall have the right granted to him by art. 351 of this Code.

615. He who finds any personal property, not a treasure, must return it to its former possessor. Should the possessor be not known, he must deliver it immediately to the mayor of the town where the finding has been made.

The mayor shall publish (notice of it) in the usual form, for two successive sundays.

If the personal property found cannot be kept without injury or without causing expenses which may greatly reduce its value, it shall be sold at public auction, after eight days have elapsed from the second advertisement, without the owner having appeared, and the proceeds shall be deposited.

After two years have elapsed from the date of the second publication, without the owner having appeared, the thing found or its value shall be adjudged to the finder of it.

He, or the owner as the case may be, shall be obliged to pay the expenses caused.

616. Should the owner appear, in due time, he shall be obliged to pay, as a reward to the person who found the thing, a tenth part of the sum or of the value of the article found. When the value of article exceeds 2,000 *pesetas*, the reward shall be reduced to one twentieth part thereof in respect to any excess over that amount.

617. Rights in respects to flotsam and jetsam, whatever their nature be, or in plants or herbs, grown on sea shore, are regulated by special laws.

TITLE II.
DONATIONS.

CHAPTER FRIST.
NATURE OF DONATIONS.

Article **618.** Donation is an act of liberality by which any person disposes gratuitously of a thing in favor of another who accepts it.

619. What is given to a person, on account of his merits, or for services rendered to the donor, is also a donation, provided it does not constitute a recoverable debt, and a donation is also what imposes upon the donee a burden inferior to the amount donated.

620. Donations which are to become effective upon the death of the donor partake of the nature of dispositions by last will and shall be governed by the laws on testamentary succession.

621. Donations which are to produce effects *inter vivos* shall be governed by the general provisions of contracts and obligations, in whatever is not prescribed in this title.

622. Donations having onerous causes, shall be regulated by the laws of contracts, and remunerative ones, by the provisions of the present title, in respect to the part exceeding the value of the burden imposed.

623. A donation is perfected upon the donor having knowledge of its acceptance by the donee.

CHAPTER SECOND.
PERSONS WHO CAN MAKE OR RECEIVE DONATIONS.

Article **624.** All persons who can contract and dispose of their property may make donations.

625. All persons, who are not especially incapacitated from it by law, may accept donations.

626. Persons, who cannot contract, cannot accept conditional or onerous donations, without the intervention of their lawful representative.

627. Donations made to persons, conceived but yet

unborn, may be accepted by the persons who should lawfully represent them, were they already born.

628. Donations made to incapable persons are null and void, though made in a concealed way, under the appearance of another contract, by intermediate persons.

629. A donation does not bind the donor nor produce any effect until it is accepted.

630. The donee shall accept the donation personally or by a person authorized by a special power for such purpose or having a general and sufficient power of attorney, otherwise it shall be null.

631. Persons accepting a donation, in behalf of others who cannot accept it personally, are obliged to obtain the notification and annotation to which art. 633 refers.

632. Donations of personal property may be made verbally or in writing. Verbal donations require the simultaneous delivery of the thing donated. In default of this requirement, the donation shall produce no effect, unless made in writing and the acceptance is shown in the same form.

633. In order that the donation of real property may be valid, it shall be made in a public deed and have expressed therein, severally, the property donated, and the amount of the encumbrances which the donee is obliged to satisfy.

The acceptance may be made in the same deed of donation or in a distinct one; but it shall produce no effects, unless made during the life of the donor.

When made in a distinct deed, notice of the acceptance shall be given to the donor, in an authentic manner, and this step shall be annotated in both deeds.

CHAPTER THIRD.

EFFECTS AND LIMITATIONS OF DONATIONS.

Article 634. A donation may comprise all the actual property of the donor or a part of it, provided he reserves in fee-simple or in usufruct, what is required for his support in a condition corresponding to his circumstances.

635. A donation cannot embrace future property. As

future property is considered that which the donor cannot dispose of at the time of the donation.

636. Notwithstanding, what is provided in art. 634, no person can give or receive, by donation, more than what he can give or receive by testament.

A donation shall be considered inofficious in all that exceeds such limits.

637. When a donation has been made to several persons conjointly, it shall be understood as in equal shares; and there shall be among them no right of accretion, unless the donor has otherwise ordered.

From these provisions are excepted donations made to husband and wife conjointly, between whom such right shall obtain, unless the donor has disposed to the contrary.

638. The donee is subrogated to all the rights and actions which, in case of eviction, should belong to the donor. The latter on his part shall not be bound to warrant the things donated, unless the donation is onerous, in which case, the donor shall be liable for the eviction to the amount of the encumbrance.

639. The donor can reserve to himself the right to dispose of some of the property donated or of some amount as a lien over it; but should he die without making use of this right, the property or the sum, which the donor reserved, shall belong to the donee.

640. The ownership of a thing can also be donated to a person, and its usufruct to another or others, under the limitations established by art., 781 of this Code.

641. The reversion in favor of the donor only, in any case and under any circumstances, can also be validly established, but not in favor of other persons, except in the same cases and under equal limitations, as provided for in this Code for testamentary substitutions.

The reversion, stipulated by the donor in favor of a third party, against the provisions of the preceding paragraph, is null and void, but it shall not cause an annulment of the donation.

642. When the donation has been made, imposing on

the donee the duty of paying the debts of the donor, if the clause contained no further declaration, it shall be understood that the donee is only bound to pay those contracted before the donation.

643. When there is no stipulation about the payment of debts, the donee shall be liable for them only in case that the donation has been made in fraud of the creditors.

The donation shall always be presumed to be made in fraud of the creditors, when, at the time of making it, the donor has not reserved for himself property sufficient to pay the debts contracted before the donation.

CHAPTER FOURTH.

REVOCATION AND REDUCTION OF DONATIONS.

Article 644. Every donation *inter vivos* made by a person having no legitimate children nor descendants nor legitimated by subsequent marriage, becomes revoked by the mere fact of the occurrence of any of the following cases:

1. When the donor, after the donation, has legitimate or legitimated, or recognized natural children, even if they be posthumous.

2. When the child of the donor, whom he supposed dead when he made the donation, is found to be alive.

645. When the donation is rescinded by the supervention of children, the things donated shall be returned to the donor, or the value thereof, if the donee has sold them.

If they have been mortgaged, the donor may cancel the mortgage, paying the sum secured by it, and having a right to reclaim from the donee the sum paid.

When the things cannot be restored, they shall be appraised at the price they were worth when the donation was made.

646. The action of revocation by supervention of children shall be prescribed upon the lapse of five years, to be counted from the birth of the last child or from the legitimation or recognition, or from the time news was received of the existence of the child believed dead.

This action cannot be renounced and, on the death of the donor, passes to his children and to their legitimate issue.

647. The donation shall be revoked on petition of the donor, when the donee has not complied with some of the conditions imposed upon him by the donor.

In this case, the things donated shall revert to the donor, and all the transfers made by the donee and the mortgages with which he may have burdened them, shall become null and void, with the limitations as to third parties, provided for in the Law of Mortgage.

648. Donations may also be revoked, on petition of the donor, for causes of ingratitude in the following cases:

1. When the donee commits any crime against the person the honor, or the property, of the donor.

2. When the donee charges the donor with any of the crimes which give cause to official proceedings or public accusation, even if he proves it; unless the crime has been committed against the donee himself, his wife, or the children under his authority.

3. When the donee unduly refuses him support.

649. When a donation is revoked for causes of ingratitude, the transfers or mortgages, executed before the annotation of the complaint for revocation in the Registry of Property, shall, howerer, remain valid.

All those made, after this time, shall be null and void.

650. In the cases, to which the first paragraph of the preceding article refers, the donor shall have a right to exact from the donee the value of the things sold, which he cannot recover from third parties, or the sum for which they have been mortgaged.

For the regulation of the value of such things, the time at which the donation was made will be considered.

651. When the donation is revoked by any of the causes, stated in art. 644 or for ingratitude, or when it shall be reduced on account of being inofficious, the donee shall not return the fruits, except from the date of the presentation of the complaint.

When the revocation is based on the failure to comply with any one of the conditions imposed by the donation, the donee shall, besides the property, return the fruits he has collected after the non-compliance with such conditions.

652. The action granted to the donor for causes of ingratitude cannot be renounced in advance. This action is prescribed, after the lapse of one year to be counted from the time the donor has knowledge of the fact and has been able to enforce the action.

653. This action shall not be transmitted to the heirs of the donor, if he did not enforce it when he could have done so.

Neither can it be enforced against the heirs of the donee, unless, at his death, the complaint had already been presented.

654. Donations which, in accordance with the provisions of art. 636, are found to be inofficious, after computing the net value of the property of the donor, at the time of his death, shall be reduced as to the excess, but this reduction shall not prevent them from being effectual during the life of the donor, nor the donee from appropriating fruits to his own use.

The reduction of donations shall be governed by the provisions of this chapter and by arts. 820 and 821 of the present Code.

655. The reduction of donations can be claimed only by the persons who are entitled to *legitime* or an aliquot part of the estate, and their heirs, or persons holding rights under them.

Persons comprised in the preceding article cannot renounce this right during the life of the donor, neither by express declaration nor by giving their consent to the donation.

The donees, the legatees who are not to receive an aliquot part, and the creditors of the decedent, cannot ask for this reduction or be benefitted by it.

656. When there are two or more donations, and all cannot be covered by the free part of the estate, those of later date shall either be cancelled or reduced as to the excessive part.

TITLE III.

SUCCESSIONS

GENERAL PROVISIONS.

Article 657. The rights to the succession of a person are transmitted from the moment of his death.

658. Succession is bestowed, either by the will of a man as expressed in his testament or, in its default, by disposition of law.

The first is called testamentary, the second legitimate succession.

It may also be bestowed partly by will of man and partly by disposition of law.

659. Inheritance embraces all the property, rights, and obligations of a person, which are not extinguished by his death.

660. An heir is a person inheriting under an universal title; and a legatee, one inheriting under a special title.

661. Heirs succeed the decedent in all his rights and obligations by the mere fact of his death.

CHAPTER FIRST.

TESTAMENTS.

SECTION FIRST.

CAPACITY TO DISPOSE BY TESTAMENT.

Article **662.** All persons who are not expressly forbidden by law may make a testament.

663. The following are incapable of making testaments:

1. Minors of both sexes under fourteen years of age.

2. Persons, who customarily or accidentally, are not of sound mind.

664. A testament made before mental alienation is valid.

665. Whenever a lunatic pretends to make a testament, during a lucid interval, the Notary shall appoint two physicians who shall examine him previously, and he shall not execute the testament unless they assume the responsibility for the capacity of the testator, and they shall testify to their opinion in the testament, which shall be subscribed by the physicians besides the witnesses.

666. For the appreciation of the capacity of the testator, attention shall be exclusively given to his condition at the time of the execution of the testament.

SECTION SECOND.

TESTAMENTS IN GENERAL.

Article 667. The act by which a person disposes of all his property or of a part of it, to take effect after his death, is called a testament (or will).

668. The testator can dispose of his property, either under title of inheritance or under that of legacy.

In case of doubt, even if the testator has not actually used the word "heir", if his will appears clearly on this point, his disposition shall be valid as made under a title, either universal or of inheritance.

669. Two or more persons cannot make a testament conjointly or, in the same instrument, either for their reciprocal benefit or for the benefit of a third party.

670. A testament is absolutely a personal act, the making of it, either wholly or partially, cannot be left to the discretion of a third party nor can it be made by a trustee or attorney.

Neither can there be left to the discretion of a third party, the permanency of the appointment of heirs or legatees, nor the designations of the portions they are to take, when they are nominally instituted.

671. The testator may commit to a third party the distribution of the sums which he may leave in general to specified classes, such as relatives, the poor, or beneficent institutions, and also the election of the persons or institutions to which such sums are applied.

672. Any disposition about the institution of heir, bequest, or legacy, made by the testator, referring to memoranda or private papers which after his death may appear in his domicil or out of it, shall be null and void, if such memoranda or papers do not contain all the requirements provided by law for holographic testaments.

673. A testament executed under duress, deceit or fraud shall be null and void.

674. He, who by deceit, fraud, or violence prevents a person, of whom he is the intestate heir, from freely executing

his last will, shall be deprived of his rights to the inheritance and shall besides be criminally liable for such acts.

675. Every testamentary disposition shall be understood in the literal sense of its words, unless it clearly appears that the will of the testator was otherwise. In case of doubt, that which appears nearest in accordance with the intent of the testator, according to the tenor of the same testament, shall be observed.

The testator cannot forbid the contesting of his testament, in the cases in which there exists nullity specified by law.

SECTION THIRD.

FORM OF TESTAMENTS.

Article 676. Testaments are either ordinary or special. Ordinary testaments may be either, holographic, open or secret.

677. Military and maritime testaments and testaments executed in foreign countries are considered as special.

678. A testament is called holographic when the testator writes it in his own hand in the form and with the requisites specified in art. 688.

679. A testament is called open whenever the testator expresses his last will in the presence of the persons who must authorize the act, and when they become informed of its dispositions.

680. A testament is called secret *(cerrado)* when the testator, without revealing his last will, declares that it is contained in the writing which he presents to the persons who are to authorize the act.

681. The following cannot be witnesses to testaments:

1. Women, with the exception of what is provided in art. 701.

2. Males, under age, with the same exception.

3. Persons who are not residents or domiciled in the place of the execution thereof, unless in the cases excepted by law.

4. Blind persons and those totally deaf and dumb.

5. Persons who do not understand the language of the testator.

6. Persons of unsound mind.

7. Persons who have been condemned for the crimes of forgery of public or private documents, for perjury, and those suffering the penality of civil interdiction.

8. Clerks, amanuenses, servants, or relatives within the fourth degree of consanguinity or within the second of affinity of the Notary who authorized the testament.

682. Neither can be witnesses to an open testament, the heirs and legatees instituted in it, nor the relatives of the same, within the fourth degree of consanguinity or second of affinity.

In this prohibition are not comprised the legatees and their relatives, when the legacy is of some pieces of personal property or of a sum of small importance compared with the amount of the estate.

683. In order that a witness may be declared disqualified, it is necessary that the cause of his incapacity should have existed at the time of the execution of the testament.

684. The presence of two interpreters, chosen by the testator to translate his disposition into Spanish, is required for making a testament in a foreign language. Such testament must be written in the two languages.

685. The Notary and two of the witnesses who authorized the testament must personally know the testator, and should they not know him, such person shall be identified by two witnesses who know him and are known to the Notary and to the instrumental witnesses. The Notary and the witnesses shall also assure themselves that in their opinion the testator has the legal capacity required to make a testament.

Witnesses authorizing a testament without the attendance of the Notary, in the cases of arts. 700 and 701, are under the same obligation of personally knowing the testator.

686. When it is not possible to identify the person of the testator, in the manner provided by the preceding article, this circumstance shall be stated by the Notary or, in default thereof, by the witnesses who shall state any details about the documents which the testator may present for such purpose, and give a personal description of the testator.

If the testament is contested for such a cause, the burden

of proof of the identity of the testator shall be borne by the person sustaining its validity.

687. Any testament, in the execution of which, the formalities, respectively established in this chapter, have not been observed, shall be null and void.

SECTION FOURTH.

HOLOGRAPHIC TESTAMENTS.

Article 688. Holographic testaments can only be executed by persons of lawful age.

In order that this testament should be valid, it shall be drawn on stamped paper, corresponding to the year of its execution, and be written all over and signed by the testator with specification of the year, month, and day of its execution.

When it contains words erased, corrected, or between lines, the testator must correct them under his own hand.

Foreigners may execute holographic testaments in their own language.

689. Holographic testaments shall be protocolled by presenting them for this purpose to the Judge of First Instance of the last domicil of the testator, or of the place where he died, within five years to be counted from the day of his death. They shall not be valid without this requisite.

690. The person, in whose hands such testament has been deposited, shall present it to the court, as soon as he receives notice of the death of the testator, and should he not do it within ten days next following, he shall be liable for the damages and injury which may be caused by his delay.

It may also be presented by any person who may have interest in the testament, either as heir, legatee, executor, or in any other way.

691. After the holographic testament has been presented and the death of the testator has been proven, the Judge shall open it, if within a closed cover, and shall rubricate, together with the Notary, all the leaves and shall prove its identity by three witnesses who know the hand-writing and subscription of the testator, and who depose that they have no reasonable doubt

whatever that the testament is written and subscribed by the testator's own hand.

In default of competent witnesses or if those examined have any doubts, and, whenever the Judge may consider it proper, he may employ experts in hand-writing for the purpose of comparison.

692. For the carrying out of the proceedings, stated in the preceding article, and, as soon as possible, shall be summoned: the surviving consort, if any, the legitimate ascendants and descendants of the testator, and, in default of all of these, his brothers.

When these persons do not reside within the district, or their existence is unknown, or if they are minor or incapables, without legitimate representations, the Public Attorney shall be summoned.

Persons summoned may be present at the carrying out of such proceedings and verbally may make, at the time, the proper observations about the genuineness of the testament.

693. When the Judge considers that the identity of the testament has been proven, he shall order that it be protocolled, together with the proceedings taken, in the Registry of the corresponding Notary, who shall give to the interested parties the copies or authenticated copies which may be proper. In all other cases he shall refuse to protocol it.

Whatever the decision of the Judge may be, it shall be carried into effect, notwithstanding any opposition, and it shall not injure the rights of the interested parties to enforce it in any suit which may be proper.

SECTION FIFTH.

OPEN TESTAMENTS.

Article 694. Open testaments shall be executed before a Notary, qualified to act in the place of its execution, and three competent witnesses who can see and understand the testator and of whom one of which, at least, knows how and is able to write.

From this rule shall only be excepted the cases expressly determined in this same section.

695. The testator shall state his last wishes to the Notary and to the witenesses. After the testament is drawn up in accordance with them, specifying the place, year, month, day, and hour of its execution, it shall be read aloud in order that the testator may declare, if it agrees with his will. If so, it shall be subscribed to immediately by the testator and the witnesses who are able to do so.

Should the testator declare that he does not know how or cannot subscribe it, one of the instrumental witnesses or any other person shall do it for him at his request, and the Notary shall certify to it. The same thing shall be done when any one of the witnesses is not able to sign.

The Notary shall always state that in his judgment the testator has the legal capacity required for executing the testament.

696. When the testator, who intends to make an open testament, presents his testamentary dispositions in writing, the Notary shall draw up the testament in accordance with them, and shall read it aloud in the presence of the witnesses, so that the testator may declare if its contents are the expression of his last will.

697. A person, who is absolutely deaf, shall read his testament himself; if he does not know how or cannot, he shall appoint two persons, who shall read it in his name always in the presence of the witnesses and of the Notary.

698. When the testator is blind, the testament shall be read twice, once by the Notary, as provided by art. 695, and the other time in the same manner by one of the witnesses or any other person appointed by the testator.

699. All the formalities, provided in this section, shall be made in a single act, and no interruption shall be allowed, except such a one as may be caused by a momentary incident.

The Notary shall certify, at the end of the testament, that all such formalities have been complied with and that he knows the testator or the witnesses of acquaintance, when they are required.

700. When the testator is in imminent danger of death, the testament may be executed before five competent witnesses without the necessity of a Notary.

701. In case of epidemics, the testament shall also be executed, without intervention of a Notary, before three witnesses, over sixteen years of age, either male or female.

702. In the cases of the two preceding articles, the testament shall be written when possible; when not possible, the testament shall be valid, although the witnesses do not know how to write.

703. The testaments, executed in accordance with the provisions of the three preceding articles, shall become void, if two months have elapsed after the testator is out of danger of death or the epidemic has ceased.

When the testator dies within such term, the testament shall also become void, if, within three months after his demise, such testament is not taken to the competent tribunal, in order that it may be reduced to a public deed, whether it has been executed in writing or verbally.

704. Testaments, executed without the authorization of a Notary, shall be void, if they are not afterwards reduced to a public deed and protocolled in the form prescribed by the Law of Civil Procedure.

705. When an open testament is declared void for causes of non–compliance with the solemnities established for each case, the Notary authorizing it shall be responsible for the damages and injuries which may arise, if the fault is a result of his bad faith or by inexcusable negligence or ignorance.

SECTION SITXH.

SECRET TESTAMENTS.

Article **706.** A secret testament may be written by the testator or by any other person, at his request, on common paper, stating the place, day, month, and year in which it has been written.

When the testator writes it in his own hand, he shall rubricate every sheet and set his signature at the end, after specifying all the words corrected, scratched or written between lines.

Should any other person write it, at his request, the

testator shall put his full subscription on every sheet and at the end of the testament.

When the testator does not know how, or cannot subscribe his name, another person, at his request, shall do it for him, and shall also countersign every sheet, stating the cause of the testator's inability.

707. In the execution of the secret testament, the following solemnities shall be observed:

1. The paper on which the testament is drawn shall be placed within a closed and sealed cover in such a manner that the former cannot be taken out without tearing the latter.

2. The testator shall appear with the testament closed and sealed, or shall close and seal it at the time in the presence of the Notary, who is to authorize it, and of five competent witnesses, of whom three, at least, shall be able to sign.

3. The testator shall declare, in the presence of the Notary and the witnesses, that the cover which he presents contains his testament, stating if it is written, subscribed, and signed by him, or if written in another's hand, and subscribed by him at the end and on all of the leaves, or if, because he does not know how or cannot subcribe it, another person has done it for him, at his request.

4. On the cover of the testament, the Notary shall write the appropriate minutes of its execution, specifying the number and marks of the seals with which it is closed, and shall certify to the compliance with the above mentioned solemnities, to his knowledge of the testator or of the identification of his person, in the manner provided by arts. 685, and 686, and to the testator having, in his judgment, the legal capacity required for executing a testament.

5. After the minutes have been drawn up and read, they shall be subscribed by the testator and the witnesses who know how to sign, and the Notary shall authorize them with his mark and subscription.

If the testator does not know how or cannot subscribe, one of the instrumental witnesses or any other person appointed by the testator, shall subscribe for him.

6. This circumstance shall also be expressed in the min-

utes, besides the place, hour, day, month, and year of its execution.

708. Blind persons, and those who do not know how or cannot read shall not make a secret testament.

709. Deaf and dumb persons and those who cannot speak, but who are able to write, may execute a secret testament, if the following conditions are observed:

1. The testament shall be wholly written and subscribed by the testator, and the place, day, month, and year stated.

2. On presenting it, the testator shall write on the upper part of the cover, in the presence of the Notary and five witnesses, that such envelope contains his testament and that it is written and subscribed by him.

3. After what is written by the testator, the minutes of execution shall be noted and the Notary shall certify to the compliance with the provisions of the preceding number, and of all other provisions of art. 707, in so far as they may apply to the case.

710. After the secret testament is certified to, the Notary shall deliver it to the testator, after filing in the secret protocol a certified copy of the execution.

711. The testator may keep the secret testament in his possession or entrust it to the custody of a person in whom he may have confidence or deposit it in the hands of the authorizing Notary for safe keeping in his archives.

In this last case, the Notary shall give a receipt to the testator, and shall note in his secret protocol, on the margin or at the foot of the minutes of the execution, that the testament remains in his hands. Should the testator afterwards receive it back, he shall sign a receipt at the foot of such a note.

712. The Notary or a person having in his possession a secret testament shall present it to a competent judge as soon as he learns of the death of the testator.

Should he not do so, within the term of ten days, he shall be responsible for the damages and injuries caused by his neglect.

713. He, who, with malice, fails to present the secret testament, which is in his keeping, within the term fixed by the second paragraph of the preceding article, besides the responsi-

bility stated in it, shall lose all right to the inheritance, should he have it as intestate heir, or as heir or legatee by the testament.

The same penalty shall be incurred by those who maliciously abstract the secret testament from the residence of the testator or from that of the person who keeps it in custody or deposit or by him who conceals, tears or renders it useless, in any other way, without being relieved from the proper criminal responsibility.

714. For the opening and protocolling of a secret testament, the provisions of the Law of Civil Procedure shall be observed.

715. The secret testament, in the execution of which, the formalities prescribed in this section have not been observed shall be null and void, and the Notary who authorizes it shall be responsible for the damages and injuries which may be caused, if it is proven that the fault originated in malice, negligence or in inexcusable ignorance on his part. It shall be valid, however, as an holographic will, if it is written and subcribed all over by the testator and has the other conditions required in such testaments.

SECTION SEVENTH.
MILITARY TESTAMENTS.

Article 716. In times of war, soldiers in the field, volunteers, hostages, prisoners, and other persons, employed in the army or following the same, may execute their testaments before any officer, having, at least, the rank of captain.

This provision applies to members of an army who are in a foreign country.

Should the testator be sick or wounded, he may execute it before the chaplain or physician attending him.

If he is with a detachment, before the person commanding, even if he be a non-commissioned officer.

In all the cases specified in this article, the presence of two competent witnesses shall always be necessary.

717. All the persons, mentioned in the preceding articles, may also execute a secret testament before a staff officer

(comisario de guerra), who shall exercise in such cases the functions of a Notary, and then the provisions of art. 706 and the subsequent ones shall be observed.

718. Testaments, executed in accordance with the two preceding articles, shall be forwarded, as soon as possible, to the general headquarters and by the latter to the Secretary of War.

If the testator has died, such Secretary shall forward the testament to the Judge of the last domicil of the decedent, and, if unknown to him, to the Senior Judge of Madrid, in order that he may officially summon the heirs and other persons interested in the succession.

These latter shall request that it be reduced to a public deed, and be protocolled in the form provided by the Code of Civil Procedure.

If the will is a secret one, the Judge shall officially proceed to open it, in the manner provided by said law, after summoning and with the intervention of the Public Attorney, and, after opening it, shall give notice of its contents to the heirs and other persons concerned.

719. Testaments, mentioned in art. 716, shall become null and void four months after the testator has ceased to be in a campaign.

720. During a battle, assault, engagement, and, generally, in every approximate danger of an action of war, a military testament can be made by word of mouth before two witnesses.

But this testament shall become void, if the testator is saved from the danger in view of which it was made.

Even if he does not escape, the testament shall become void, if not formalized by the witnesses before the Auditor of War or a judicial official following the army, and then it shall be acted upon in the form provided in art. 718.

721. When a military testament is secret, the provisions of arts. 706 and 707 shall be observed; but it shall be executed before the officer and two witnesses, required by art. 716 for an open testament, and all of them shall subscribe the minutes of the execution, as well as the testator, if he is able to do so.

SECTION EIGHTH.

MARITIME TESTAMENTS.

Article **722.** Testaments, either open or secret, of persons on board aship during a sea voyage, shall be executed, as follows:

When the vessel is a man-of-war, before the Paymaster or he who exercises his functions, in the presence of two competent witnesses, who can see and understand the testator. The Captain of the ship or the person occupying his place shall besides *visé* it.

On merchant vessels, the Captain or his representative shall authorize the testament with the assistance of two competent witnesses.

In both the first and second cases, the witnesses shall be selected from the passengers, if any; but one of them, at least must be able to sign, and he shall sign it in his own name and in the name of the testator, if the latter does not know how or cannot do it.

When the testament is an open one, what is provided by art. 695 shall besides be observed; and, if a secret one what is ordered by section sixth of this chapter, excluding what refers to the number of witnesses, and the intervention of the Notary.

723. The testament of the Paymaster of a man-of-war and of the Captain of a merchant vessel, shall be authorized by those who are to substitute them in their duties, and what is prescribed in the preceding article shall, furthermore, be observed.

724. Open testaments made on the high seas shall be kept in the custody of the Commander or the Captain and they shall be noted in the log-book.

The same entry shall be made of holographic and secret testaments.

725. Should a ship arrive at a foreign port, where there is a diplomatic or consular agent of Spain, the Commander of the man-of-war or the Captain of the merchant vessel, shall deliver to said agent a copy of the open testament or of the minutes of the execution of the secret one and of the notes entered in the log-book.

The copy of the testament or of the minutes must bear the same signatures as the original, if the persons who signed them are alive and on board; in other cases, they shall be authorized by the Paymaster or Captain who received the testament or the one acting in his place, and those remaining on board who took part in the testament shall also sign it.

The diplomatic or consular Agent shall have the proceedings of the delivery put in writing, and having closed and sealed the copy of the testament or of the minutes of its execution, if secret, he shall forward them with a copy of the entry in the log-book, in the proper way, to the Secretary of the Navy who shall deposit them in the archives of his office.

The Commander or Captain, who shall deliver them, shall obtain from the diplomatic or consular Agent a certificate of having done so, and shall enter it in the log-book.

726.   When the vessel, either a merchantman or a man--of-war, arrives at the first port of the Kingdom, the Commander or Captain shall deliver the original testament, closed and sealed, to the local naval authority, with a copy of the entry made in the log-book, and, if the testator has died, in addition, a certificate proving it.

The delivery shall be proven in the form, provided by the preceding article, and the naval authority shall forward all the papers, without delay, to the Secretary of the Navy.

727.   When the testator has died and the testament is open, the Secretary of the Navy shall act, as provided by art. 718.

728.   When the testament has been executed by a foreigner, on board of a Spanish vessel, the Secretary of the Navy shall forward the testament to the Secretary of State in order that it may be forwarded, in the proper way, through diplomatic channels.

729.   When the testament is holographic and the testator dies during the voyage, the Commander or Captain shall take possession of the testament for the purpose of keeping it in custody, entering this fact in the log-book, and shall deliver the same to the local naval authority, in the form and for the effects provided in the preceding article, when the vessel arrives at the first port of the Kingdom.

The same thing shall be done when the testament is a secret one, if the testator has it in his possession at the time of his death.

730.   Open and secret testaments, executed in accordance with the provisions of this section, shall be void after the laspe of four months from the day on which the testator landed at a place where he could make a testament in ordinary form.

731.   When in danger of shipwreck, the provisions of art. 720 shall apply to the crews and passengers of war or merchant vessels.

SECTION NINTH.

TESTAMENTS MADE IN FOREIGN COUNTRIES.

Article 732.   Spaniards may make testaments out of the national territory, submitting themselves to the forms established by the laws of the country in which they may be.

They may also make testaments on the high seas, during their passage on a foreign vessel, in accordance with the laws of the country to which the ship belongs.

They may also make an holographic testament in accordance with art. 688, omitting the requirement of stamped paper, even in countries where the laws do not recognize such testaments.

733.   Joint testaments, forbidden by art. 669, shall not be valid in Spain when executed by Spaniards in a foreign country, even when the laws of the country, where they have been executed, authorized them.

734.   Spaniards who are in foreign countries may also execute their testaments, either open or secret, before the diplomatic or consular Agent of Spain, residing at the place of their execution.

In such cases, said Agents shall act as Notaries, and all the formalities, established by sections fifth and sixth of this chapter, shall be respectively observed; however, the condition of residence of the witnesses shall not be necessary.

735.   The diplomatic or consular Agent shall forward a copy of the open testament, or of the act of execution of the

secret testament, authorized under his hand and seal, to the Department of State to be deposited in its archives.

736. The diplomatic or consular Agent, in whose hands a Spaniard may have deposited his holographic or secret testament, shall forward it to the Department of State as soon as the testator dies together with the certificate of the death.

The Department of State shall have the notice of the death published in the Gaceta of Madrid, in order that the parties concerned may obtain the testament and proceed to protocol it in the form prescribed.

SECTION TENTH.

REVOCATION AND INEFFICIENCY OF TESTAMENTS.

Article 737. All testamentary dispositions are essentially revocable, even when the testator states in the testament that his wish or resolution shall not be revoked.

All clauses, derogating future dispositions, shall be considered as not existing, as well as those in which the testator may order that the revocation of the testament should be void, unless marked with certain words and signs.

738. A testament cannot be revoked, wholly or in part, unless the same solemnities required for making it are observed in respect thereto.

739. A former testament becomes revoked by law by a later and perfect one, unless the testator states in the latter his wish of leaving the former subsisting in whole or in part.

However, a formor testament recovers its force when the testator afterwards revokes the latter and expressly declares that it is his wish that the former should be valid.

740. The revocation shall be effective, even when the second testament becomes null by the incapacity of the heir or of the legatees appointed in it, or by the renunciation of the former or the latter.

741. The recognition of an illegitimate child does not lose its force, even when the testament in which it was made is revoked.

742. A secret testament, found in the domicil of the

testator with the cover torn or the seals broken or the signatures authorizing it effaced, erased or corrected is presumed revoked.

This testament, however, shall be valid when it may be proven that such damage has been caused without the wish or knowledge of the testator, or when he was in an insane condition, but, if the cover is found torn and the seals broken, it shall be necessary besides to prove the genuineness of the testament in order that it may be valid.

When the testament is found in the hands of another person, it shall be understood that any impairment was caused by such person, and the testament shall not be valid, unless its authenticity is proven, if the cover is torn or the seals broken; and if the former and latter are found intact, but the signatures effaced, erased or corrected, then the testament shall be valid, unless it is proven that it has been delivered in this condition by the testator himself.

743. Testaments shall become void or testamentary provisions ineffective, in whole or in part, only in the cases expressly provided for in this Code.

CHAPTER SECOND.

INHERITANCES.

SECTION FIRST.

CAPACITY FOR SUCCESSION UNDER OR WITHOUT A TESTAMENT.

Article **744.** All persons not incapacitated by law may succeed under or without a testament.

745. The following are incapable of succeeding:

1. Abortive creatures, and as such are understood those who do not combine the conditions stated in art. 30.

2. Associations or corporations not permitted by laws.

746. Church and church chapters, provincial diputations, provinces, city councils, municipalities, institutions for the sick, for beneficence or for public instruction, associations authorized or recognized by law, and all other juridical persons can acquire by testament in accordance with what is provided in art. 38.

747. When the testator disposes of the whole or part of his property for sufferages and pious works for the benefit of his soul and does it in an indeterminate manner and without specifying how it shall be applied, the executors shall sell the property and distribute the proceeds, giving one half of it to the Diocesan to be employed for such sufferages and the care and necessities of the church, and the other half to the corresponding civil governor for the beneficent institutions of the domicil of the decedent, and, in default of such, for those of the province.

748. A designation made in favor of a public institution, under condition or imposing a lien upon it, shall be valid only when approved by the government.

749. Dispositions made in favor of the poor, in general, without designating persons or towns, shall be limited to those of the domicil of the testator at the time of his death, if it is not clearly shown that his will was otherwise.

The classification *(calificación)* of the poor and distribution of the property shall be made by the person appointed by the testator, in default of such person, by the executors, and if there are none, by the curate, the Mayor, and the Municipal Judge, who shall decide by a majority of votes any doubts which may arise.

The same shall be done when the testator has disposed of his property in favor of the poor of a certain parish or town.

750. Every disposition in favor of an uncertain person shall be null and void, unless by some event the person may become certain.

751. A disposition made generically in favor of the relatives of the testator is understood to be made in favor of those who stand in the nearest degree.

752. Testamentary dispositions made by the testator, during his last illness in favor of the priest who confessed him during it, of the relatives of the latter within the fourth degree, or of his church, chapter community or institute shall not be valid.

753. Neither shall be valid the testamentary dispositions of the ward in favor of his guardian, made before the final accounts of the guardian have been approved, even when the testator dies after such approval.

However, the dispositions made by the ward in favor of the guardian when the latter is his or her ascendant, descendant, brother, sister, or consort, shall be valid.

754. The testator cannot dispose of the whole or a part of his estate in favor of the Notary who authorizes his testament, or of the latter's wife and relatives by consanguinity or affinity within the fourth degree, with the exception stated in art. 682.

This prohibition applies to the witnesses of the open testament made with or without a Notary.

The provisions of this article apply also to the witnesses and persons before whom special testaments are executed.

755. A testamentary disposition in favor of an incapable person, though concealed under the form of an onerous contract or made in favor of an intermediate person, shall be null and void.

756. The following are incapable of succeeding on account of unworthiness:

1. Parents who have abandoned their children, or prostituted their daughters, or made attempts against their virtue.

2. Persons condemned in a trial for having made attempts againts the life of the testator, his consort, and his descendants or ascendants.

When the offender is a forced heir, he shall lose his *ligitime*.

3. He who has accused the testator of a crime for which the law imposes an afflictive penalty, when the accusation is declared as calumnious.

4. The heir of full age, who knowing of the violent death of the testator, has not denounced it to the courts within a month, unless proper judicial proceedings have already been taken *ex officio*.

This prohibition shall cease in cases in which, according to law, there is no obligation to make an accusation.

5. A person condemned at a trial for adultery with the wife of the testator.

6. He, who by menaces, fraud or violence forces the testator to make a testament or to alter it.

7. He, who by the same means, prevents another from

making a testament or from revoking one already made, or who forges, conceals or alters a later one.

757.   The causes of indignity shall produce no effect, when the testator knew them at the time of making the testament or, if after having been informed of them, has pardoned the same by a public instrument.

758.   For determining the capacity of the heir or legatee, the time of the death of the person whose succession is questioned shall be taken into consideration.

In cases nos. 2, 3, and 5 of art. 756, it shall be necessary to wait until the final sentence is rendered, and in no. 4, until the month fixed for the accusation has elapsed.

When the institution or legacy is conditional, the time for the fulfillment of the condition shall, besides, be taken into consideration.

759.   The heir or legatee who dies before the condition is complied with, though he may survive the testator, transmits no rights whatever to his heirs.

760.   Any person, incapable of succeeding, who, contrary to the prohibition of the preceding article, has entered into possession of the hereditary property, shall be obliged to return it together with its accessions and with all the rents and fruits he may have collected.

761.   If the person, excluded from inheritance on account of incapacity, is a son or descendant of the testator and he has children or descendants, they shall acquire his rights to the *legitime*.

Persons so excluded shall have no rights to the usufruct and administration of the portion thus inherited by his children.

762.   No action shall be instituted for the declaration of incapacity, after five years have elapsed from the time that the incapable took possession of the inheritance or legacy.

SECTION SECOND

INSTITUTION OF HEIR.

Article **763**.   A person who has no forced heirs may dispose by testament of all his property or part of it in favor of any person having capacity to acquire it.

A person who has forced heirs can dispose of his property, only in the form and with the limitation provided by section fifth of this chapter.

764. A testament shall be valid, even when it does not contain the institution of an heir, or it does not include the whole of the property, and although the person appointed does not accept the inheritance or is incapable of inheriting.

In such cases, the testamentary disposition, made in accordance with the laws, shall be complied with, and the remainder of the estate shall pass to the lawful heirs.

765. The heirs appointed, without designation of shares, shall inherit share and share alike.

766. The voluntary heir, who dies before the testator, the incapable of inheriting, and he who renounces the inheritance, do not transmit any rights to their heirs, unless as provided in arts. 761 and 857.

767. The statement of a false cause for the institution of an heir or of the appointment of legatee shall be considered as not written, unless it may appear from the testament that the testator would not have made such institution or legacy, had he known the falseness of such cause.

The statement of a cause contrary to law, even if true, shall also be considered as not written.

768. An heir to whom a certain and determined thing is left shall be considered as a legatee.

769. When a testator appoints some heirs individually and other collectively, as when he says:—"I institute as my heirs N and N, and the children of N,"—those collectively appointed shall be considered as individually appointed, unless it appears in a clear manner that the will of the testator was otherwise.

770. If the testator institutes his brothers, and he has some of full blood and others on the father's or mother's side only, the inheritance shall be divided as in cases of intestacy.

771. When the testator calls to the succession any person and his children, it shall be understood that all of them are instituted simultaneously and not successively.

772. The testator shall designate the heir, by his name.

and family name; and when there are two having the same names, he must state some circumstances through which the instituted heir may be known.

Even when the testator has omitted the name of the heir, should he designate him in such a manner that no doubt may exist as to what person has been instituted, the institution shall be valid.

773. An error in the name, family name, or qualities of the heir, shall not vitiate the institution when it may be possible, in any other manner, to know with certainty who is the person appointed.

If among persons of the same name and surname there is equality of circumstances, and these are such as do not permit the person who is instituted to be distinguished, none of them shall be an heir.

SECTION THIRD.

SUBSTITUTION.

Article **774.** The testator may substitute one or more persons in the place of the instituted heir or heirs in the cases where they may die before him or do not desire to or cannot accept the inheritance.

Simple substitution, without expressing which case, comprises the three stated in the preceding paragraph, unless the testator has ordered otherwise.

775. Parents and other ascendants may appoint substitutes in place of their descendants of both sexes, under fourteen years of age, for the cases where they may die before attaining such age.

776. The ascendant may appoint a substitute for the descendant over fourteen years of age who has lawfully been declared incapable on account of unsound mind.

The substitution, to which the preceding article refers, shall be voided by the testament of the incapable made during a lucid interval or after he has recovered his reason.

777. The substitutions, to which the two preceding articles refer, in case the substitute has forced heirs, shall only be valid in so far as they do not injure the legitimate rights of such heirs.

778. Two or more persons can be substituted instead of a single one, contrariwise, a single person for two or more heirs.

779. When the heirs are instituted in unequal portions and are reciprocally substituted, they shall have in the substitution the same portions as in the institution, unless it may clearly appear that the will of the testator was otherwise.

780. The substitute shall be subject to the same charges and conditions as imposed upon the instituted, unless the testator has expressly disposed to the contrary or when the burdens or conditions may be merely personal, respecting the heir instituted.

781. Substitutions in trust (*fideicomisarias*), by virtue of which the heir is charged with keeping and transmitting to a third party the whole or a part of the inheritance, shall be valid, and shall be effective, provided, they do not go beyond the second degree or when made in favor of persons living at the time of the death of the testator.

782. Substitutions in trust can never impair the *legitime*. Should they fall upon the third share intended for advantages (*mejora*), they can be made only in favor of the descendants.

783. To be valid, callings to the substitutions in trust, shall be expressly made.

A fiduciary is bound to deliver the inheritance to the fidei–commissary, without any deductions, excepting those falling upon him for lawful expenses, credits, and improvements, except when the testator has disposed otherwise.

784. The fidei–commissary shall acquire rights to the succession upon the death of the testator, even when he dies before the fiduciary. The rights of the former shall pass to his heirs.

785. No effects shall be produced by:

1. Fidei–commissary substitutions not made in an express manner, either by giving them such a name or by imposing upon the substitute the absolute obligation of deliverying the property to a second heir.

2. Dispositions containing perpetual prohibitions of

alienation, and even a temporal one, when not within the limits provided in art. 781.

3.　Those imposing upon the heir the charge of paying a certain rent or pension to various persons in succession, beyond the second degree.

4.　Those, the object of which is to leave to a person the whole or part of the estate, for the purpose of applying or investing the same, according to secret instructions communicated to him by the testator.

786.　The nullity of a fidei–commissary substitution shall not cause injury, either to the validity of the institution or to the heirs first called; the fidei–commissary clause shall simply be considered as not written (in such cases).

787.　The disposition by which the testator leaves the whole or a part of the inheritance to a person, and the usufruct to another, shall be valid.　If various persons are called to the usufruct, not simultaneously, but in succession, the provisions of art. 781 shall be followed.

788.　The disposition imposing upon the heir the duty of periodically investing certain sums for beneficent purposes, as dowers for poor maidens, pensions for students, or in favor of the poor or for any institution of beneficence, or of public instruction, shall be valid under the following conditions:

When the charge is imposed on real property and is temporal, the heir or heirs may dispose of the incumbered property, but the lien shall not cease until its inscription is cancelled.

When the charge is perpetual, the heir can capitalize it and invest the capital at interest, secured by a first and snfficient mortgage.

The capitalization and investment of the capital shall be made with the intervention of the civil governor of the province, and after a hearing of the Public Attorney.

In any event, when the testator has not established an order for the administration and application of the beneficent legacy, the administrative authority, who may be competent according to law, shall do it.

789.　All that is provided in this chapter in respect to heirs shall also apply to legatees.

SECTION FOURTH.

INSTITUTION OF HEIRS; AND LEGACIES CONDITIONAL OR FOR A TERM.

Article **790**. Testamentary dispositions, either by universal or special title, may be made conditionally.

791. Conditions imposed upon heirs and legatees shall be governed by the rules provided for conditional obligations in whatever is not prescribed in this section.

792. Impossible conditions and those contrary to law and good morals shall be considered as not existing and shall in no way injure the heir or legatee, even when the testator disposes otherwise.

793. The absoulte condition of not contracting a first or subsequent marriage shall be considered as not existing, unless such condition has been imposed on the widower or widow by the deceased consort, or by the ascendants or descendants of the same.

However, the usufruct, use, or habitation or a pension or personal service may be bequeathed to anyone for the time during which such a person may remain unmarried or as a widow or widower.

794. A disposition made under condition that the heir or legatee shall make in his testament some disposition in favor of the testator or of a third party shall be void.

795. A purely potestative condition imposed on the heir or legatee shall be complied with by them when, after the death of the testator, they are informed of it.

The case in which the condition has already been complied with and cannot be reiterated is excepted.

796. When the condition is casual or mixed, it shall be sufficient if it be realized or complied with at any time during the life or after the death of the testator, unless he has ordered otherwise.

If it had existed or had been complied with at the time the testament was executed and the testator did not know it, it shall be considered as complied with.

If he knew it, it shall be considered as complied with only when of such a nature that it can no longer exist or be complied with again.

797. The statement of the object of the institution or of the legacy or the application to be given to what the testator has left or the lien imposed by the same shall not be considered as a condition, unlesss it may appear that such was his will.

What has been left in this manner may be immediately claimed and is transmissible to the heirs who may secure the compliance with the orders of the testator and the repayment of what they may have received with fruits and interest, if they fail to comply with this obligation.

798. When, without the fault or a personal act of the heir or legatee, the institution or the legacy, to which the preceding article refers, cannot take place in the very terms ordered by the testator, it shall be complied with in terms as nearly analogous and in conformity with his will as possible.

When the party, having an interest in its compliance or non-compliance, should prevent it, without fault or a personal act of the heir or legatee, the condition shall be considered as complied with.

799. Suspensive conditions do not prevent the heir or legatee from acquiring his or her respective rights and transmitting them to their heirs, even before the fulfillment of such conditions.

800. When the potestative condition, imposed on the heir or legatee, is a negative one, or of not giving or not doing (a certain thing), they shall comply with it by giving bonds that they will not do or will not give what was forbidden by the testator, and, in case of contravention, that they will refund what they have received with the fruits and interest thereon.

801. When the heir is instituted under a suspensive condition, the estate shall be placed in administration until the condition is complied with or until there is a certainty that it cannot be fulfilled.

The same shall be done when the heir or legatee shall not give the security, referred to in the preceding article.

802. The administration, to which the preceding article refers, shall be confided to the heir or heirs, unconditionally instituted, when among them and the conditional heir, the right of accretion exists. The same shall be understood in respect to legatees.

803. When the conditional heir has no co-heirs or when the right of accretion does not exist among them, he shall take charge of the administration upon giving bond.

If he does not give it, the administration shall be conferred upon the presumptive heir, also under bonds; and when neither of them can give bonds, the court shall appoint a third party who shall take charge of it, also under bonds, which shall be given with the intervention of the heir.

804. Administrators shall have the same rights and obligations as those who administer the property of an absentee.

805. The designation of the day or time on which the effect of the institution of heir or legatee shall begin or be determined shall be valid.

In both cases, the lawful successor shall be considered as called, until the time fixed arrives, or until such time expires. But in the first case, he shall not enter into possession of the property, until after having given sufficient bonds and with the intervention of the heir instituted.

SECTION FIFTH.

LEGITIMES.

Article 806. *Legitime* is that part of the property of which the testator cannot dispose because the law has reserved it for certain heirs, called, on that account, forced heirs.

807. Forced heirs are:

1. Legitimate children and descendants in reference to their legitimate parents and ascendants.

2. In default of the preceding, the legitimate parents and ascendants in reference to their legitimate children and descendants.

3. The widower or widow, the natural children legally recognized, and the father or the mother of the same, in the form and proportion established by arts. 834, 835, 836, 837, 840, 841, 842, and 846.

808. The *legitime* of legitimate children and descendants

is constituted by the two third parts of the hereditary estate of the father and of the mother.

However, the parents may dispose of one of the two third parts forming the *legitime* in order to apply it as an advantage to their legitimate children and descendant.

The remaining third part shall be at their free disposal.

809. The *legitime* of the parents or ascendants is constituted by one half of the hereditary estate of the children and descendants. The latter may freely dispose of the other half, with the exception of what is established in art. 836.

810. The *legitime*, reserved for the parents, shall be divided between both of them equally; when one of the parents is dead, the surviving shall take the whole of it.

When the testator leaves neither father nor mother, but ascendants in the same degree in the paternal or maternal line, the estate shall be divided share and share alike between both lines. When the ascendants are of a different degree, the *legitime* shall wholly belong to the nearest ones of either line.

811. The ascendant who inherits from his descendant property, acquired by the latter under gratuitous title from another ascendant or from a brother, shall be obliged to reserved such property, acquired by ministry of the law, in favor of the relatives within the third degree, belonging to the line from which such property came to him.

812. Ascendants succeed, to the exclusion of all other persons, to things given by them to their children or descendants, who died without issue, when the very objects donated are comprised in the estate. If they have been alienated, they shall succeed in all the actions which the donees have in respect to them, and in the value, if they have been sold or in the property substituting them, if they were bartered or exchanged.

813. A testator cannot deprive the heirs of the *legitime*, except in the cases expressly determined by law.

Neither can he impose on it, any burden, condition, or substitution of any kind, with exception of what has been prescribed about the usufruct of the surviving consort.

814. The preterition of one or of all of the forced heirs in the direct line, either living, at the time of the execution of the testament, or born after the death of the testator, shall void the institution of heir. But the legacies and advantages shall be valid, in so far as they are not inofficious.

The preterition of the widower or widow does not annul the institution, but the person omitted shall keep all the rights granted to him by arts. 834, 835, 836 and 837 of this Code.

If the omitted forced heirs die before the testator, the institution shall be valid.

815. The forced heir to whom the testator has left, for any cause whatever, less than the *legitime* pertaining to him may claim the completion of the same.

816. All renunciations or compromises, about the future *legitime*, among the persons owing it and their forced heirs, are null and void, and the latter can claim it upon the death of the former, but they shall bring to collation whatever they have received on account of renunciations or compromises.

817. Testamentary dispositions, diminishing the *legitime* of forced heirs, shall be reduced on petition of the same in so far as they are inofficious or excessive.

818. To determine the *legitime*, consideration shall be given to the value of the property remaining at the death of the testator, after deducting all debts and charges, without comprising in them those imposed by the testament.

To the net value of the testamentary estate shall be added the value of all the collationable donations, made by the same testator at the time at which they were made.

819. Donations made to children, not considered as advantages, shall be imputed to their *legitime*.

Donations made to strangers shall be imputed to the free part of which the testator may dispose by his last testament.

In so far as they be inofficious or may exceed the part disposable, they shall be reduced according to the rules of the following articles.

820. After the *legitime* is fixed, in accordance with the two preceding articles, the reduction shall be made as follows:

1. Donations shall be respected in so far as the *legitime* can be covered, reducing or voiding, if needs be, the legacies made in the testament.

2. Such reductions shall be made pro rata, without any distinction whatever.

When the testator has ordered that a certain legacy should be paid in preference to others, the former shall not suffer any reduction, until after the latter has been applied in full to the payment of the *legitime*.

3. When the legacy consists of an usufruct or annuity for life, the value of which may be considered greater than that of the disposable part, the forced heirs may choose between complying with the testamentary disposition or delivering to the legatee the part of the estate of which the testator could freely dipose.

821. When the legacy, subject to reduction, consists of a tenement, not convenient of division, it shall go to the legatee, if the reduction does not absorb one half of its value, and, in the contrary case, to the forced heirs; but one or the other shall refund to the opposite party the respective balance in cash.

A legatee having a right to a *legitime* may retain all the tenement, provided its value does not exceed the amount of the disposable portion and the quota belonging to him as *legitime*.

822. When the heirs or legatees do not wish to make use of the rights, granted to them by the preceding article, the one of them who has not such right may use it; if he does not wish to do so, the tenement shall be sold at public auction, on petition of any of the interested parties.

SECTION SIXTH.

ADVANTAGES (*mejoras*).

Article **823.** The father or the mother may dispose of one of the two third parts, intended as *legitime*, in favor of one or more of their children or descendants.

This portion is called advantage (*mejora*).

824. No liens shall be imposed upon the advantage other than those in favor of the forced heirs or their descendants.

825. No donation by contract *inter vivos*, either simple or for onerous causes, in favor of children or descendants who are forced heirs shall be considered as an advantage, unless the donor has expussly declared his wish to give an advantage.

826. The promise of giving or not giving an advantage, made in the public deed of a marriage contract (*capitulaciones matrimoniales*) shall be valid.

Any disposition of the testator, contrary to such promise, shall not be effectual.

827. The avantage, even when made with delivery of the property, shall be revokable, unless made in a marriage contract or by an onerous contract entered into with a third party.

828. The bequest or legacy, made by the testator to one of the children or descendants, shall not be considered as an advantage, unless the testator has expressly declared that such is his will or when it cannot be included in the part at his free disposal.

829. An advantage may be given in a specified thing. When the value of it exceeds both the third parts, designed for advantage and the share of the *legitime* belonging to him who receives the advantage, the latter shall pay the difference in cash to the other interested parties.

830. The authority to give advantages cannot be delegated to a third party.

831. Notwithstanding the provisions of the preceding article in marriage contracts, it may be valid to agree that, when one of the consorts dies intestate, the widower or widow, who has not contracted a new marriage, may distribute, according to his or her prudent judgment, the estate of the decedent, and give advantages in it to the children in common, without damage to the *legitimes* and to the advantages given by the decedent while alive.

832. When the advantage has not been granted in specified things, it shall be paid out of the property of the inheritance, observing, in so far as it may be possible the rules established by arts. 1061 and 1052, in order to preserve the equality of the heirs in the distribution of the property.

833. The legitimate son or descendant receiving an advantage may renounce the inheritance and accept the advantage.

SECTION SEVENTH.

RIGHTS OF THE SURVIVING CONSORT.

Article **834**. The widower or widow, who at the death of his or her consort, is not divorced, or should be so by the fault af the decedent consort, shall have a right to a portion in the usufruct, equal to that which may belong as *legitime* to each of the legitimate children or descendants who have received no advantage.

When only one legitimate child or descendant remains, the widower or widow shall have the usufruct of the third part, designated for advantage, and the former shall keep the direct ownership, until by the death of the surviving consort the ownership is consolidated in him.

When the consorts are separated by a suit for divorce, the results of the suit are to be taken into account.

When there has been a pardon or a reconciliation between the divorced consorts, the surviving one shall retain his or her rights.

835. The hereditary portion, allotted in usufruct to the surviving consort, shall be taken from the third part of the estate which is designed for giving advantages to the children.

836. When the testator leaves no descendants, but only ascendants, the surviving consort shall have a right to the third part of the estate in usufruct.

This third part shall be taken out the free half part and the testator can dispose of the ownership of the same.

837. When the testator leaves no legitimate ascendants or descendants, the surviving consort shall be entitled to one half of the estate also in usufruct.

838. The heirs may satisfy the surviving consort for such part of usufruct, assigning to him or her a life annuity or the proceeds of a certain property or a sum in cash, acting by mutual agreement or, in default of it, by virtue of a judicial decree.

Where this has not been done, all the property of inheritance shall be subject to the payment of the part of the usufruct belonging to the surviving consort.

839. In case of concurrence of the children of two or more marriages, the usufruct, belonging to the surviving consort of the second marriage, shall be taken from the one third part at the free disposal of the parents.

SECTION EIGHTH.
RIGHTS OF ILLEGITIMATE CHILDREN.

Article 840. When the testator leaves legitimate children or descendants, and natural children, legally recognized, each one of the latter shall be entitled to one half of the portion which may belong to each of the legitimate children who have received no advantages, provided it may be comprised in the one third part, at free disposal, from which it must be taken out, after deducting the expenses of the burial and funeral.

The legitimate children may satisfy the quota belonging to the natural ones in cash, or in other property belonging to the estate, according to just regulations.

841. When the testator leaves no children or descendants but has legitimate ascendants, the recognized natural children shall be entitled to one half of the part of the estate at the testator's free disposal.

This is understood without injury to the *legitime* of the surviving consort, in accordance with art. 836; therefore, when the consort concurs with the natural recognized children, whatever may be wanting to complete their *legitime* shall be allotted to them only in naked property, while the consort survives.

842. When the testator leaves no legitimate descendants or ascendants, the recognized natural children shall be entitled to one third part of the estate.

843. The rights recognized in natural children, by the preceding article, are transmitted, upon their death, to their legitimate descendants.

844. The hereditary portion of children, legitimated by Royal Concession, shall be equal to that established by law in favor of recognized natural children.

845. Illegitimate children, who have not the condition of natural children, shall only have a right to support.

The obligation of the person who has to support them shall be transmitted to his or her heirs, and shall subsist until such children attain their majority, and in the event of being incapable, while the incapacity lasts.

846. The right of succession which the laws grant to natural children, extends by reciprocity, in similar cases, to the natural father or mother.

847. The donations which the natural child may have received, during his life, from his father or mother, shall be charged to his *legitime*.

Should they exceed the third part at free disposal, they shall be reduced in the form provided by art. 817 and those following it.

SECTION NINTH.
DISINHERITANCE.

Article 848. Disinheritance shall only take place for one of the causes expressly fixed by law.

849. Disinheritance can only be effected by a testament mentioning therein the legal cause on which it is based.

850. The proof of the truth of the cause of disinheritance shall be established by the heirs of the testator, should the desinherited deny it.

851. Disinheritance, made without stating the cause, or for a cause, the truth of which, if contested, should not be proven or which is not one of those stated in the four following articles, shall void the institution of heir, in so far as it injures the disinherited, but the legacies, advantages, and other testamentary dispositions, which cause no damage to said *legitime*, shall be valid.

852. Just causes for disinheritance are, in their respective cases, those of incapacity for succeeding by unworthiness, specified in nos. 1, 2, 3, 5, and 6 of art. 756.

853. Besides the causes specified in nos 2, 3, 5, 6 of art. 756 for disinheriting children and descendants, either legitimate or natural, the following shall be just causes therefor:

1. To have refused, without lawful cause, support to the father or ascendant who disinherits him.

2. Having used personal violence against or greviously offended the testator by words.

3.   If the daughter or granddaughter has prostituted herself.

4.   To have been condemned for a crime carrying with it the penalty of civil interdiction.

854.   Besides the causes mention in nos. 1, 2, 3, 5, and 6 of art. 756, the following are also just causes to disinherit the parents or ascendants, either legitimate or natural:

1.   The loss of the parental power by the causes stated in art. 169.

2.   The refusal of support to the children or descendants without lawful cause.

3.   An attempt of one of the parents against the life of the other, unless there has been a reconciliation between them.

855.   Besides those specified in nos. 2, 3, and 6 of art. 756, the following shall also be just causes for disinheriting the consort:

1.   Those which give cause for divorce under art. 105.

2.   Those which give cause for the loss of the parental power, as stated in art. 169.

3.   The refusal of support to the children or to the other consort.

4.   An attempt against the life of the consort making the testament, unless they were reconciled.

In order that the causes which give reasons for divorce may also be causes for disinheritance, it is required that the consorts should not live under the same roof.

856.   A succeeding reconciliation of the offender and the offended deprives the latter of the right to disinherit and render the disinheritance already made ineffective.

857.   The children of the disinherited shall take his or her place and shall retain the rights of forced heirs in respect to the *legitime*; but the disinherited parent shall have neither the usufruct nor the administration of the property of said *legitime*.

SECTION TENTH.
LEGACIES AND BEQUESTS.

Article **858.**   A testator may burden with legacies and bequests, not only his heir, but also the legatees.

These shall be liable to the burden only to the extent of the value of the legacy.

859.   When the testator burdens one of the heirs with a legacy, he alone shall be obliged to comply with it. If he does not burden any one in particular, all shall be liable for it, in the same proportion in which they may be heirs of the estate.

860.   The person, bound to the delivery of the legacy, shall be responsible, in case of eviction, if the thing is undetermined and is designated only in kind or species.

861.   The legacy of another person's property, when the testator knew, at the time of bequeathing it, that it was not his, is valid.   The heir is bound to acquire the property for its delivery to the legatee; and, when not possible, to pay the latter its just value.

The proof that the testator knew that the thing was not his own falls on the legatee.

862.   When the testator did not know that the thing he bequeathed was not his, the bequest shall be null and void.

But it shall be valid, if he acquires the thing, after the execution of the testament.

863.   A legacy made to a third party of a thing belonging to the heir or to one of the legatees shall be valid, and they, on accepting the succession, shall deliver the thing bequeathed or the just value thereof, under the limitation established in the following article.

The provision of the preceding paragraph is understood without damage to the *legitime* of the forced heirs.

864.   When the testator, heir, or legatee have only a part or a right in the thing bequeathed, the legacy shall be understood as limited to such part or right, unless the testator expressly declares that he bequeathed the thing integrally.

865.   A legacy of things, out of commerce, is null and void.

866.   The legacy of a thing, which at the time of the execution of the testament, belonged already to the legatee, even when another person has some right to it, shall not be effectual.

When the testator expressly orders that such a thing

should be liberated from such right or burden, the bequest shall be valid in that respect.

867. When the testator bequeaths something, pledged or mortgaged, for the security of an exigible (mature) debt, the payment of the same shall fall upon the heir.

If the legatee pays such debt because the heir has not done so, the legatee shall be subrogated in the place and right of the creditor to make claim against the heir therefor.

Any other lien, either perpetual or temporary, with which the thing bequeathed is burdened, passes together with it to the legatee, but, in both cases, the rents and interests or charges due, up to the death of the testator, are a charge upon the inheritance.

868. When the thing bequeathed is subject to the usufruct, use, or habitation, the legatee is obliged to respect such rights, until they are lawfully extinguished.

869. The legacy shall not be effective:

1. When the testator makes such alterations in the thing bequeathed that it does not retain either the form or the denomination that it before had.

2. When the testator alienates, under any title or cause whatever, the thing bequeathed or a part of it, it being understood, in this last case, that the bequest becomes void only in relation to the alienated part. When, after the alienation, the thing reverts to the ownership of the testator, even by nullity of the contract, the bequest shall not be valid, after such fact; unless in the case in which the reacquisition is made under a contract of revertible sale.

3. When the thing bequeathed perishes in whole, during the life of the testator or after his death, without blame on the part of the heir. Nevertheless, the person obliged to pay the legacy shall be liable for the eviction, if the thing bequeathed has not been determined in species, as provided in art. 860.

870. The legacy of a credit against a third party or of the remission or liberation of a debt of the legatee, shall be effectual only in that part of the credit or of the debt, yet existing at the time of the death of the testator.

In the first case, the heir shall fulfill his duty by assigning to the legatee all the actions he may have against the debtor.

In the second, by giving to the legatee the full release, if he asks for it.

In both cases, the legacy shall comprise the interests on the credits or the debts due to the testator, at the time of his death.

871. The legacy, to which the preceding article refers, is made void when the testator, after having made it, judicially demands from the debtor the payment of such debt, even when the payment has not been made at the time of the death.

By the legacy made to the debtor of a thing pledged, it is understood that only the right of pledge is remitted.

872. The generic legacy of liberation or remission of debts comprises those existing at the time of the execution of the testament, and not subsequent ones.

873. A legacy made to a creditor shall not be imputed in payment of his credit, unless the testator so expressly declares.

In such case, the creditor shall have a right either to collect the excess of the credit or of the legacy.

874. In alternative legacies, the provisions made for obligations of the same kind shall be observed, excepting the modifications made by the express will of the testator.

875. A legacy of generic personal property shall be valid, although there may not be things of the same kind in the estate.

A legacy of an undetermined parcel of real property shall be valid, only if there are things of the same kind in the estate.

The heir shall have the option, and may fulfil his duty by giving a thing which may not be either of inferior or superior quality.

876. Whenever the testator expressly leaves an option to the heir or to the legatee, the former may give or the latter may select what he may consider best.

877. When the heir or legatee cannot make the election, in case of it having been granted to him, his right shall pass to the heir, but the choice once made shall be irrevocable.

878. When the thing bequeathed belonged to the legatee at the date of the will, the legacy is void, even when it has been alienated afterwards.

When the legatee has acquired it by lucrative title, after said date, he can claim nothing for it, but when the acquisition has been made by an onerous title, he can claim from the heir an indemnity for what he may have given for acquiring it.

879. A legacy for education subsists until the legatee is of age.

That for support lasts during the life of the legatee, unless the testator has otherwise disposed.

When the testator has not assigned any sum for said legacies, they shall be fixed in accordance with the position and condition of the legatee and the amount of the inheritance.

When the testator was, during his life, in the habit of giving to the legatee a certain sum of money or other things by way of support, the legacy shall be considered of an equal sum, unless it is greatly disproportionate with the amount of the estate.

880. When a periodical pension, or a certain sum, either annual, monthly, or weekly is bequeathed, the legatee may claim that of the first term, as soon as the testator dies, and those of the following, at the beginning of each of them, without any right of reimbursement, even when the legatee dies before the expiration of the term begun.

881. A legatee acquires a right to the pure and simple legacies from the death of the testator, and transmits it to his heirs.

882. When the bequest is of a thing specific and determined, belonging to the testator, the legatee acquires the property thereof upon the death of the testator and makes the pending fruits or rents his own, but not those which were due and unpaid before said death.

The thing bequeathed shall, from the same moment (of said death), be at the risk of the legatee who, therefore, shall bear its loss or impairment, and he shall also be benefitted by any increase or improvement thereof.

883. The thing bequeathed shall be delivered (to the

legatee) with all its accessories and in the condition in which it is at the death of the testator.

884.   When the bequest is not of a specific and determined thing, but generic or of quantity, its fruits and interests shall belong to the legatee from the death of the testator, if the testator expressly so ordered.

885.   The legatee cannot occupy the thing bequeathed of his own authority, but he shall ask the heir or the executor, when the latter is authorized to give it, for its delivery and possession.

886.   The heir shall deliver the same thing bequeathed, if he is able to do so and he does not comply with this duty by paying for its value.

Legacies in cash shall be paid in cash, even if there is none in the estate.

The necessary expenses for the delivery of the thing bequeathed shall be at the charge of the estate, but without injury to the *legitime*.

887.   When the assets of the estate are not sufficient to cover all the legacies, payment shall be made in the following order:

1.   Remuneratory legacies.

2.   Legacies of things, certain and determined, forming a part of the estate.

3.   Legacies declared by the testator as preferred.

4.   Those for support.

5.   Those for education.

6.   All others pro rata.

888.   When the legatee cannot or does not wish to accept the bequest, or for any cause this may not be effectual, it shall be merged into the whole of the estate, excepting in cases of substitution, and rights of accretion.

889.   A legatee cannot accept a part of the legacy and repudiate the other part, when the latter is onerous to him.

If he dies before accepting the legacy, leaving several heirs, one of them can accept and another can repudiate the part belonging to him in the legacy.

890.   A legatee of two legacies, one of which is onerous,

cannot renounce this one and accept the former. When both are onerous or gratuitous, he is free to accept all of them or repudiate any one he wishes.

The heir, who is at the same time a legatee, may renounce the inheritance and accept the legacy or renounce the latter and accept the former.

891. When all the inheritance is distributed in legacies, the debts and burdens of the same shall be charged to the legatees, pro rata according to their shaies, unless the testator has provided otherwise.

SECTION ELEVENTH.

EXECUTORS *(Albaceas ó testamentarios)*.

Article **892.** A testator may appoint one or more executors.

893. A person, who has no capacity to obligate himself, cannot be executor.

A married woman may be an executrix with the permission of her husband; and such permission shall not be necessary when she is legally separated from him.

A minor cannot be executor, even with the authorization of the father or guardian.

894. Executors may be general or special. In any case, executors can be appointed, either severally, successively or conjointly.

895. When the executors are appointed severally, every act shall be made by all of them together in order that it may be valid, and shall be valid also when done by one of them, legally authorized by the others; and, in case of discord, when the act has been agreed to by the majority.

896. In case of extreme urgency, one of the several executors may do, upon his personal responsibility, such acts as may be necessary, giving notice thereof immediately to the others.

897. When a testator does not clearly provide about the appointment of conjoint executors nor determine the order in which they are to discharge their functions, it shall be understood that they have been appointed severally, and they shall discharge their duties in the form prescribed by the two preceding articles.

898. Executorship is a voluntary charge, and it shall be understood as accepted, if the person appointed does not excuse himself within six days next following the one on which he has received notice of his appointment or if he was already aware of it during the six day next following that on which he knew of the death of testator.

899. An executor who accepts this charge is bound to comply with its duties; but he may renounce it alleging a cause which may be just in the prudent judgment of the court.

900. An executor who does not accept the charge or renounces it, without a just cause, shall lose what the testator has left him, but always without prejudice to the right which he has to the *legitime*.

901. Executors shall have all the powers expressly granted to them by the testator and which are not contrary to law.

902. When the testator has not specially determined the powers of the executors, they shall have the following:

1. To dispose and pay the sufferages and funeral expenses of the testator in accordance with the dispositions made by the same in his testament, and, in default of them, according to the custom of the place.

2. To pay, with the knowledge and consent of the heir, the cash legacies.

3. To look carefully after the execution of whatever more has been ordered in the testament, and maintain, when just, its validity in and out of court.

4. To take the necessary precautions for the preservation and custody of the property, with the intervention of the heirs present.

903. When the estate has not cash enough for the payment of funeral (expenses) and legacies, and the heirs do not contribute their own money therefor, the executors shall endeavor to sell the personal property, and, if this is not enough, the real property with the intervention of the heirs.

When a minor, absentee, corporation or public institution

has any interest in the estate, the sale of the property shall be made, under the formalities provided by the laws for such cases.

904. An executor, for whom the testator has not fixed the term, shall comply with his charge within a year, to be counted from his acceptance, or from the determination of the law suit which may be instituted about the validity or the nullity of the testament or of any one of its provisions.

905. If the testator desires to extend the legal term, he shall expressly fix the time for the extension. When he has not done so, it shall be understood that the term is extended for one year.

When, after the expiration of this extension, the will of the testator has not yet been complied with, the Judge may grant another one for the time which may be necessary, in view of the circumstances of the case.

906. The heirs and legatees may, by common agreement, extend the term of the executorship for the time they deem necessary; but, if the agreement is only that of a majority, the extension shall not exceed one year.

907. Executors shall render to the heirs an account of their charge.

When they have been appointed not to deliver the property to specified heirs, but to invest or distribute it in the form provided by the testator in the cases allowed by law, they shall render their accounts to the Judge.

Any disposition of the testator, contrary to this article, shall be null and void.

908. Executorship is a gratuitous charge. However, the testator may designate the executors, the compensation which he may consider convenient; all of this without injury to the rights which they may have to collect whatever may belong to them for their work in the distribution or for any other professional services.

When the testator bequeathes or designates conjointly any compensation for the executors, the shares of those, who do not accept the charge, shall accrue to those who shall discharge it.

909. Executors cannot delegate their charge, unless they have express authority from the testator for so doing.

910. Executorship is determined by the death, impossibility, renunciation, or removal of the executor, and by the lapse of the term fixed by the testator, by law, and, in certain cases, by the parties concerned.

911. In the cases of the preceding article and when the executor has not accepted the charge, the execution of the will of the testator shall devolve upon the heirs.

CHAPTER THIRD.
INTESTATE SUCCESSION.

SECTION FIRST.
GENERAL PROVISIONS.

Article 912. Legitimate succession takes place:

1. When a person dies without a testament, or under a void testament or under one which afterwards has lost its validity.

2. When the testatment does not contain the institution of heir in the whole estate or in a part of it or does not dispose of all that belongs to the testator. In this case the legitimate succession shall take place only in regard to the part of the estate of which the testator has not disposed.

3. When the condition imposed for the institution of heir is not complied with or when the heir dies before the testator or repudiates the inheritance, without having a substitute, and there is no right of accretion.

4. When the heir instituted is incapable to succeed.

913. In default of testamentary heirs, the law gives the inheritance, according to the following rules, to the legitimate and natural relatives of the decedent, to the widower or widow, or to the State.

914. Provisions about incapacity to succeed by testament equally apply to intestate successions.

SECTION SECOND.
RELATIONSHIP.

Article 915. The proximity of relationship is determined by the number of generations. Each generation forms a degree.

916. A series of degrees forms the line which may be either direct or collateral.

A direct line is one constituted by a series of degrees among persons descending one from the other.

A collateral line is that constituted by a series of degrees among persons not descending one from the other, but proceeding from a common trunk.

917. The right line is either descendant or ascendant.

The first joins the head of the family with those descending from him.

The second joins a person to those from whom he descends.

918. In the lines, as many degrees are counted as there are generations or persons, deducting the progenitor.

In the right line the ascent is made only to the trunk, thus the son is one degree distant from the father, two from the grandfather, and three from the great-grandfather.

In the collateral line, the ascent is made up to the common trunk, and then a descent is made down to the person with whom the computation is made. On account of this reason, the brother is two degrees distant from the brother, three from the uncle, brother of his father or mother, four from the first cousins, and so forth.

919. The computation, stated in the preceding article, governs in all matters, except in those which have relation to the impediments to canonical marriage.

920. Double or whole blood relationship is the relation in the father's and mother's line at the same time.

921. In every inheritance, the relative nearest in degree excludes the farther one, except in the cases in which the right of representation takes place.

The relatives, who are in the same degree, shall inherit in equal shares, with exception of what is provided in art. 949 about relationships of whole blood.

922. When there are several relatives in the same degree and one or some of them do not wish or cannot succeed, his portion shall accrue to the others of the same degree, without affecting the right of representation when it takes place.

923. When the inheritance is repudiated by the nearest relative, if he is a single one, or by all the nearest relatives, called by law, if there are several, then those of the following degree shall inherit in their own right, without being able to represent those repudiating the inheritance.

SECTION THIRD.

REPRESENTATION.

Article 924. The right which all the relatives of a person have to succeed him in all the rights which he should have had, if alive, or if he had been able to inherit, is called right of representation.

925. The right of representation shall always take place in the direct descending line, but never in the ascending.

In the collateral line, it shall take place only in favor of the children of brothers, whether they are of the whole or half blood.

926. Whenever the inheritance is taken by representation, the distribution of the estate shall be made *in stirpes:* thus the representative or representatives shall inherit no more than that which the party represented would inherit, if alive.

927. When children of one or more brothers of the decedent survive, they shall succeed the latter by representation, if they concur with their uncles, but if they concur alone, they shall inherit in equal shares.

928. The right of representing a person is not lost by having renounced the inheritance.

929. A living person cannot be represented unless in cases of disinheritance or incapacity.

CHAPTER FOURTH.

ORDER OF SUCCESSION ACCORDING TO DIVERSITY OF LINES.

SECTION FIRST.

DESCENDING DIRECT LINE.

Article 930. Succession goes, in the first place, to the descending direct line.

931. Legitimate children and their descendants succeed

the parents and other ascendants, without distinction of sex or age, and even if they come from different marriages.

932. The children of the decedent shall always inherit from him in their own rights, dividing the inheritance in equal shares.

933. The grandchildren and other descedants shall inherit by right of representation, and if one of them has died leaving several heirs, the portion belonging to him shall be distributed among such heirs in equal shares.

934. If there are children and descendants of other deceased children, the former shall inherit in their own rights, and the latter by right of representation.

SECTION SECOND.
ASCENDING DIRECT LINE.

Article 935. In default of legitimate children and descendants of the decedent, his ascendants shall inherit from him, excluding collaterals.

936. The father and mother, if living, shall inherit share and share alike.

When only one of them survives, this one shall take all the son's inheritance.

937. In default of mother or father, the ascendants, nearest in degree, shall inherit.

If there are some of equal degree belonging to the same line, they shall share the inheritance *in capita*; if they are of different lines but of equal degree, one half shall belong to the paternal, and the other half to the maternal ascendants. In each line the division shall be made *in capita*.

938. The provisions of the two preceding articles are understood without prejudice to what is ordered by arts. 811 and 812, which are applicable to intestate and testamentary successions.

SECTION THIRD.
RECOGNIZED NATURAL CHILDREN.

Article 939. In default of legitimate descendants and ascendants, natural children legally recognized , and those legitimated by Royal Concession shall succeed the decedent in the whole inheritance.

940. When, together with the natural or legitimated children, concur descendants of another deceased natural or legitimated child, the former shall succeed by their own rights and the latter by right of representation.

941. The hereditary rights, granted by the two preceding articles to a natural or legitimated child, shall be transmitted upon its death to its descendants, who shall inherit from their deceased grandfather by right of representation.

942. In case that there are legitimate descendants and ascendants, the natural and legitimate children shall take from the inheritance only the portion granted to them by arts. 840 and 841.

943. Natural and legitimated children have no rights to succeed intestate the legitimate children and relatives of the father or mother who have recognized them ; nor shall such children or relatives inherit from the natural or legitimated child.

944. When the recognized natural or legitimated child dies without leaving issue, either lawful or recognized by it, the father or mother who recognized it shall inherit its whole estate, and if both recognized it and are alive, they shall inherit from it in equal shares.

945. In default of natural ascendants, the natural and legitimated children shall be succeeded by their natural brothers, according to the rules established for legitimate brothers.

SECTION FOURTH.

SUCCESSIONS OF COLLATERALS AND OF CONSORTS.

Article **946.** In default of the persons comprised in the three preceding sections, collateral relations and consorts shall inherit in the order established in the following article.

947. When there are only brothers of the whole blood, they shall inherit in equal shares.

948. When brothers concur with nephews, children of brothers of the whole blood, the former shall inherit *in capita*, and the latter *in stirpes*.

949. When brothers of the whole blood concur with brothers of the half blood, the former shall take a portion in the inheritance double that of the latter.

950. When there are only brothers of the half blood, some on the father's and some on the mothers side, all shall inherit equal portions, whatever the property may be.

951. Children of brothers of the half blood shall take *in capita* or *in stirpes*, according to the rules established for brothers of the whole blood.

952. In default of brothers and of nephews, children of said brothers, be they or not of the whole blood, the surviving consort, not separated by a final sentence of divorce, shall take all the estate of the decedent.

953. When there are brothers or children of brothers, the widow or widower shall have a right to take, in concurrence with the same, the portion of inheritance in usufruct provided in art. 837.

954. When there are neither brothers or children of brothers, nor surviving consort, the other collateral relatives shall succed in the inheritance of the decedent.

They shall take without difference of line, or preference among them on account of the whole blood.

955. The right to inherit in the case of intestacy shal not extend beyond the sixth degree of relationship in the collateral line.

SECTION FIFTH.

INHERITANCE BY THE STATE.

Article 956. In default of persons having a right to succeed in accordance with the provisions of the preceding sections, the State shall inherit, and the property shall be destined for institutions of beneficence or of gratuitous instruction, in the following order:

1. Municipal institutions of beneficence and gratuitous schools of the domicil of the decedent.

2. Those of the same classes in the province of the decedent.

3. Those of beneficence and instruction of a general character.

957. The rights and obligations of institutions of beneficence and instruction, in the cases of the preceding articles, shall be the same that other heirs may have.

958. In order that the State may take possession of the property of the inheritance, a previous judicial declaration has to be made by which the inheritance shall be adjudged to the State, in default of legitimate heirs.

CHAPTER FIFTH.

PROVISIONS COMMON TO INHERITANCE BY TESTAMENT OR WITHOUT IT.

SECTION FIRST.

PRECAUTIONS TO BE ADOPTED WHEN THE WIDOW REMAINS IN
A PREGNANT CONDITION.

Article **959.** When the widow believes that she has been left in a pregnant condition, she must give notice to those having in the inheritance, rights of such a kind that they shall disappear or be diminished by the birth of a posthumous child.

960. Interested persons, to which the preceding article refers, may ask the Municipal Judge or the Judge of the First Instance, when there is one, to take the proper measures in order to prevent the supposition of parturition or to accept the child born as viable, when, in truth, it is not so.

The Judge shall be careful that the measures which he orders to be taken shall not be offensive, either to the modesty or to the liberty of the widow.

961. Whether the notice stated in art. 959 has been given or not, when the time of the parturition approaches, the widow shall give notice of this fact to the parties interested. They shall have a right to appoint a person in whom they have confidence in order that he may aver the reality of the delivery.

When the person appointed is rejected by the widow, one shall be appointed by the Judge, but said person must be a physician or a woman.

962. The omission of these formalities shall not injure the legitimacy of the parturition, which, when contested, may be proven by the mother or the child lawfully represented.

The action to contest, on the part of those having such right, is prescribed, after the terms specified in art. 113.

963. When the husband has recognized by a document, either public or private, the certainty of the pregnancy of his wife, she shall be excused from giving the notice provided in art. 959, but she shall be subject to comply with the provisions of art. 961.

964. A widow who remains pregnant, even when she is rich, shall receive support from the estate, taking into consideration the portion of it which may belong to the posthumous child, if he is born and is viable.

965. During the time intervening, until the parturition arrives, or until certainty is established that it cannot take place, either on account of a miscarriage, or because the maximum time for the gestation has been exceeded, the security and administration of the estate shall be attended to in the form provided in necessary testamentary proceedings.

966. The distribution of the inheritance shall be supended until the parturition or miscarriage takes place, or the lapse of time shows the widow was not pregnant.

An administrator, however, may pay the creditors under a judicial order.

967. After the delivery or miscarriage has taken place or the time of gestation has elapsed, the administrator of the estate shall cease in his charge, and shall render account of his management to the heirs or their lawful representatives.

SECTION SECOND.

PROPERTY SUBJECT TO RESERVATION.

Article **968.** Besides the reservation imposed by art. 811, the widower or widow contracting a second marriage shall be obliged to reserve for the children and descendants of the first, the ownership of all the property acquired from the deceased consort by will, by intestate succession, by donation, or by any other lucrative title; but not his or her half of the conjugal property.

969. The provision of the preceding article applies to property which has been acquired, under the titles already stated, by the widower or widow from any of the children of the first marriage, or that received from the relatives of the decedent on account of personal considerations for the same.

970. The obligation to reserve shall cease, when the children of a marriage, being of legal age and having a right to the estate, have expressly renounced it, or when the things in question have been given or left by the children to their father or mother, knowing that they had married a second time.

971. Reservation shall cease when, at the death of the father or mother who contracted a second marriage, there remains no legitimate children or descendants of the first marriage.

972. Notwithstanding the obligation to reserve, the father or mother, married a second time, may give advantages in the property, subject to reservation (*reservables*), to any of the children or descendants of the first marriage, as provided in art. 823.

973. When the father or mother has not made use in whole or in part of the right granted to them in the preceding article, the legitimate children or descendants of the first marriage shall succeed to the property subject to reservation, in accordance with the rules prescribed for succession in the descending line, even when, by virtue of a testament, he or she should have unequally inherited from the first decedent consort, or should have renounced or repudiated his or her inheritance.

The son, justly disinherited by the father or by the mother, shall lose all right to the reservation, but, if he has legitimate children or descendants, the provisions of art. 857 shall be followed.

974. Conveyances of reserved real property shall be valid when made by the surviving consort, before contracting a second marriage, under the obligation to secure, from the moment of the marriage, the value of such property in favor of the children and descendants of the first marriage.

975.   Conveyances of real property, subject to reservation, made by the widower or widow, after contracting a second marriage, shall subsist only when, at his or her death, there remains no legitimate children or descendants of the former marriage; this without conflict with the provisions of the Law of Mortgage.

976.   Conveyances of personal property, made before or after contracting a second marriage, shall be valid, but always under the obligation of paying an indemnity when proper.

977.   A widower or widow, on contracting a new marriage, shall make an inventory of all the property subject to reservation, and annotate in the Registry of property that such real property is subject to reservation in accordance with the provisions of the Law of Mortgage and shall have the personal property appraised.

978.   A widower or widow, on marrying again, is also bound to secure by mortgage:

1.   The restitution of the personal property, not alienated, in the condition in which it was at the time of the death of the decedent, when it was paraphernalia or the proceeds from an unestimated dowry; or of their value, if they arise from an estimated dowry.

2.   The payment of the damages, caused or which may be caused by his or her fault or neglect.

3.   The return of any sums received for the personal property already sold or the delivery of the value it had, at the time of the alienation, had it been made under a gratuitous title.

4.   The value of the real property validly alienated.

979.   The provisions of the preceding article for the second marriage shall equally control the third and subsequent marriages.

980.   The obligation to reserve, imposed in the preceding, article, shall apply to the widower or widow, who though not having contracted a new marriage, may afterwards have a recognized natural child or one judicially declared as such.

Said obligation shall be effective from the date of the birth of such child.

SECTION THIRD.

RIGHT OF ACORETION.

Article 981.   In legitimate succession, the part of him who repudiated the inheritance shall always accrue to the co-heirs.

982.   In order that in testamentary succession the right of accretion may take place, it is required:

1.   That two or more persons are called to the same inheritance or to the same portion of it, without a special designation of shares.

2.   That one of the appointees dies before the testator or renounces the inheritance, or is incapable to receive it.

983.   It shall be undertood that a designation has been made by portion only in case that the testator may have expressly designated a quota to each heir.

The phrase "one half to each", or "in equal parts" or any other, although specifying aliquot parts, which does not express this numerically or by such marks as may make each of them the owner of an estate severally, does not exclude the right of accretion.

984.   The heirs, to whom the inheritance accrues, shall succeed in all the rights and obligations which would have belonged to the one who did not wish or could not receive it.

985.   Among forced heirs, the right to accrue shall take place only when the part, at free disposal, is left to two or more of them or to any one of them and a stranger.

When the repudiated part is the *legitime*, the other co-heirs shall succeed to it in their own rights, and not by the right of accretion.

986.   In testamentary successions, when the right of accretion cannot take place, the vacant portion of the heir instituted, for whom no substitute has been appointed, passes to the lawful heirs of the testator who shall receive it under the same charges and obligations.

987.   The right of accretion shall also take place between the legatees and the usufructuaries in the same terms established for heirs.

SECTION FOURTH.

ACCEPTANCE AND REPUDIATION OF THE INHERITANCE.

Article **988.**   Acceptance and repudiation of the inheritance are acts entirely voluntary and free.

989.   The effects of the acceptance and repudiation shall always relate back to the moment of the death of the person whose property is inherited.

990.   Acceptance or repudiation of the inheritance cannot be made, either partially, up to a certain term, or conditionally.

991.   No person can accept or repudiate an inheritance, unless he is certain of the death of the person from whom he is to inherit and of his rights to the inheritance.

992.   Any person having free disposal of his property may accept or repudiate an inheritance.

An inheritance left to minors or incapables may be accepted in the form provided by no. 10 of àrt. 259. When the guardian accepts by himself, the acceptance shall be considered as made under benefit of inventory.

Acceptance of an inheritance, left to the poor, shall pertain to the persons appointed by the testator to classify them and distribute the property, and, in default of them, to those designated in art. 749, and it shall also be understood as accepted under benefit of inventory.

993.   The lawful representatives of associations, corporations, and institutions having capacity to acquire can accept the inheritance left to the same; but for repudiating it they require judicial approval, after the Public Attorney has been heard.

994.   Public official institutions can neither accept nor repudiate inheritances without the approval of the government.

995.   A married woman can neither accept nor repudiate an inheritance, unless with permission of her husband, and, in his default, with the approval of the Judge.

In the last case, the property of the conjugal society , already existing, shall not be liable for the debts of the estate.

996.   The deaf and dumb, knowing how to read and

write, shall accept or repudiate the inheritance personally or through an attorney . If they cannot read or write , their guardian shall accept it under benefit of inventory, subject to what is provided in art. 218 in relation to such disability.

997. Acceptance and repudiation of the inheritance, once made, are irrevocable, and can be contested only in case they suffer from any of the vices which annul the consent, or when an unknown testament appears.

998. Inheritances can be accepted purely and simply or under benefit of inventory.

999. Pure and simple inheritances may be either express or tacit. Express is one made in a public or private instrument. Tacit is one made by acts, which necessarily imply a will to accept, or acts which no one should .have a right to execute unless in the capacity of an heir.

Acts of mere preservation, or provisional administration do not imply the acceptance of the inheritance, if, at the same time, the title and qualification of heir have not been assumed.

1000. An inheritance is considered as accepted:

1. When the heir sells, donates or assigns a right to a stranger, to all his co-heirs or to one of them only.

2. When the heir renounces it, even gratuitously, for the benefit of one or more of his co-heirs.

3. When he renounces it for a consideration in favor of all his co-heirs indiscriminately, but when this renunciation is gratuitous and the co-heirs, in whose favor he makes it, are those to whom the share renounced must accrue, the inheritance shall not be considered as accepted.

1001. When the heir repudiates the inheritance to the damage of his own creditors, they may ask the Judge to authorize them to accept it on behalf of the latter.

The acceptance shall be of benefit to the creditors only in so far as it covers the amount of their credits. The excess, if any, shall not belong, in any case, to the renouncer but shall be allotted to the persons to whom, according to the rules of this Code, it may belong.

1002. The heirs, who have subtracted or concealed any effects of the inheritance, lose the right to renounce it, and retain only the character of pure and simply heirs without being released from the penalties which they may have incurred.

1003. By the acceptance, pure and simple, or without benefit of inventory, the heir shall be liable for all the charges of the estate, not only with the properties of the same, but also with his own.

1004. Until nine days have elapsed from the death of the person whose inheritance is dealt with, no action can be instituted against the heir to compel him to accept or repudiate it.

1005. When a third party having an interest, urges in a suit that the heir should accept or repudiate the inheritance, the Judge shall give the latter a term, not exceeding thirty days, within, which he shall declare his intention, warning him that, in case he does not do it,,the inheritance shall be considered as accepted.

1006. Upon the death of the heir, without having accepted or repudiated the inheritance, the same rights he had are transmitted to his heirs.

1007. When there are several heirs called to an inheritance, some of them may accept and some repudiate it. Every one of the heirs shall enjoy the same liberty to accept it purely and simply, or under benefit of inventory.

1008. Repudiation of an inheritance shall be made by a public or authentic instrument or by a writ presented to the Judge, competent to take cognizance of testamentary or intestate proceedings.

1009. Any person called to an inheritance by a testament or by intestacy and who repudiates it under the former title, is considered as having repudiated under both titles.

If he repudiates it as intestate heir and has no knowledge of his testamentary title, he may yet accept it under the latter title.

SECTION FIFTH.

BENEFIT OF IMVENTORY AND RIGHT TO DELIBERATE.

Article 1010. Every heir may accept an inheritance under benefit of inventory, even if the testator has forbidden it.

He may also ask for the making of the inventory, before

accepting or repudiating the inheritance, in order to deliberate on this point.

1011. Acceptance of the inheritance, under the benefit of inventory, may be made before a Notary, or in a writing before any of the judges, competent for taking cognizance of the testamentary or intestate proceedings.

1012. When the heir, to whom the preceding article refers, is in a foreign land, he may make such declaration before a diplomatic or consular Agent of Spain, who may be authorized to exercise the duties of a Notary in the place of such execution.

1013. The declaration, to which the preceding articles refer, shall produce no effect, unless it be preceded or followed by a true and exact inventory of all the property of the estate, made with the formalities and within the term specified in the following articles.

1014. An heir, having in his hands the property of the estate or a part of it, and who wishes to make use of the benefit of inventory or of the right to deliberate shall so state to the Judge, competent to take cognizance of the testamentary or intestate proceedings, within ten days next following that on which he has become aware that he is such an heir, if he resides in the place where the originator of his inheritance dies. If he resides out of the place, the term shall be thirty days.

In both cases, the heir shall ask, at the same time, for the making of an inventory, and that the creditors and legatees be summoned to be present at it, if convenient for them.

1015. When the heir has not in his possession the inheritance or a part of it, or has not executed any act as such heir, the terms, specified in the preceding article, shall be counted from the next day following the one on which shall expire the term fixed by the Judge for accepting or repudiating the inheritance, in accordance with art. 1005, or from the day on which he has accepted it or has acted as heir.

1016. In the cases not provided for by the two preceding articles, if no complaint has been presented against the heir, he may accept, under the benefit of inventory, or with the right to deliberate while the action to claim an inheritance is not prescribed.

1017. An inventory shall be begun within thirty days next following the summoning of the creditors and legatees and shall be finished within sixty days more.

If, because the property is situated at a long distance, or is very valuable, or for any other just cause, said sixty days are considered insufficient, the Judge may extend this term to such a time as he may deem necessary, but it shall not exceed one year.

1018. If by the fault or neglect of the heir, the inventory is not begun or finished within the term, and with the solemnities prescribed in the preceding article, it shall be understood that he accepts the inheritance purely and simply.

1019. An heir, who has reserved to himself the right to deliberate, shall state to the court, within thirty days, counted from the day following that on which the inventory has been finished, whether he accepts or repudiates the inheritance.

After such thirty days have elapsed, if he has not made such a statement, it shall be understood that he accepts it purely and simply.

1020. In any case, the judge may, on petition of any party interested, during the making of the inventory and until the acceptance of the inheritance, provide for the administration and custody of the hereditary estate, in accordance with the provisions of the Law of Civil Procedure about testamentary proceedings.

1021. A person who judicially claims an inheritance, which another has held in his possession for over a year and who wins the suit, shall not be obliged to make an inventory for enjoying such benefit, and he shall be liable for the burdens of the estate only with the property which has been delivered to him.

1022. The inventory made by the heir, who afterwards repudiates the inheritance, shall benefit the substitutes and the intestate heirs, in respect to whom, the thirty days for deliberation and in which to make the statement, provided by art. 1019, shall be counted from the day next following that on which they were made aware of the repudiation.

1023. The benefit of inventory produces the following effects in favor of the heir:

1. The heir shall not be bound to pay the debts and

other charges of the inheritance but up to the amount that the estate may be worth.

2.   He retains against the estate all the rights and actions which he may have had against the decedent.

3.   The private property of the heir shall not anywise be confused, to his injury, with the property belonging to the estate.

1024.   The heir shall lose the benefit of inventory:

1.   When having knowledge of it, he fails to include in the inventory any of the property, rights or actions of the inheritance.

2.   When, before completing the payment of the debts and legacies, he alienates any property of the estate without judicial authorization, or that of all the parties in interest, or, if he does not apply the value of what is sold to what has been ordered, when the authorization was granted to him.

1025.   During the making of the inventory and the term granted for deliberating, the legatees cannot claim the payment of their legacies.

1026.   Until all known creditors and legatees have been paid, it shall be understood that the estate is under administration.

The administrator, whether it is the heir himself or any other person, shall have, as such, the representation of the estate to enforce all actions pertaining to it, and answer all complaints instituted against the same.

1027.   The administrator shall not pay the legacies, until he has paid all the creditors.

1028.   When there is a pending lawsuit among the creditors about the preference of their credits, they shall be paid in the order and according to the degree fixed by the final sentence of graduation.

When there is no pending lawsuit among the creditors, those presenting themselves first shall be paid first; but where it is well established that one of the known credits is preferred, payment shall not be made without previous security being given in favor of the creditor having a better right.

1029.   If, after the legacies are paid, more creditors appear, they shall have a right to make claims against the legatees only in case that the estate may not have property enough to pay them.

1030. When for the payment of credits and legacies, the sale of the property of the estate may be necessary, it shall be made in the form established by the Code of Civil Procedure about intestate and testamentary proceedings, unless all the heirs, creditors, and legatees agree otherwise.

1031. When the hereditary estate is not sufficient for the payment of the debts and legacies, the administrator shall render an account of his administration to the creditors and legatees who have not been paid in full, and he shall be liable for the damages caused to the estate by his fault or negligence.

1032. After the creditors and legatees are paid, the heir shall have the full enjoyment of the remainder of the estate.

If the estate has been administered by another person, he shall render an account of his administration to the heir, under the responsibility imposed by the preceding article.

1033. The cost of the inventory and other expenses, caused by the administration of the inheritance, accepted under the benefit of inventory, and the defense of its rights, shall be paid by the same estate. The cost to which the heir may have been personally condemned, on account of his deceit or bad faith, shall be excepted.

The same thing shall be understood about the cost caused for making use of the right to deliberate, when the heir repudiates the inheritance.

1034. The private creditors of the heir cannot interfere with the operations of the estate, accepted by him under benefit of inventory, until the creditors and legatees of the same have been paid; but they may claim the retention or the seizure of the remainder which may be left in favor of the heirs.

CHAPTER SIXTH.
COLLATION AND DISTRIBUTION.

SECTION FIRST.
COLLATION.

Article 1035. A forced heir, concurring with others of the same character in a succession, shall bring to the estate the properties or values which he may have received from the originator of the inheritance, during the life of the same, as dowry, donation, or under any other lucrative title for the purpose of computing it, the regulation of the *legitimes*, and in the account of the distribution.

1036. Collation shall not take place among forced heirs when the donor has so expressly ordered, or when the donee repudiates the inheritance, unless in the case in which the donation is to be reduced as inofficious.

1037. What is left by will is not subject to collation, unless the testator orders otherwise; but, in any case, the *legitime* shall remain free.

1038. When grandchildren inherit from their grand-parents in representation of their parents, and concur with their uncles or cousins, they shall bring to collation all that their parents, if alive, would have been required to bring, though they may not have inherited it.

They shall also bring to collation whatever they may have received from the testator, during the life of the same, unless the testator has otherwise disposed, in which case, his will shall be respected, if it does no injury to the *legitime* of the co-heirs.

1039. Parents are not obliged to bring to collation in the inheritance of their ascendants what may have been donated by the latter to their children.

1040. Neither shall the donations made to the consort of the child be brought to collation; but if they have been made by the parent to both of them jointly, the child shall be obliged to bring to collation one half of the thing donated.

1041. Expenses for support, education, for sickness, even if extraordinary, apprenticeship, ordinary equipment or the usual presents are not subject to collation.

1042. Expenses, incurred by the parents in giving their children a professional or artistic career, shall not be brought to collation, unless the parent so disposes or they injure the *legitime*, but when it may be lawful to bring them to collation, the sum which the child should have spent, if living in the house and company of the parents, shall be deducted from them.

1043. The sums paid by the parents to redeem the children from the lot of soldiers, pay their debts, obtain for them a title of honor or other similar expenses, shall be brought to collation.

1044. Wedding presents, consisting of jewels, clothing and equipment, shall not be reduced as inofficious but in the amount exceeding one tenth or more of the sum disposable by testament.

1045. The same things, donated or given in dowry, are not to be brought to collation and distribution, but only the value they had at the time of the donation or dowry, though they were not appraised at such time.

The subsequent increase or impairment and even their total loss, either casually or culpably, shall be to the account and risk for the benefit of the donee.

1046. The dowry or donation, made jointly by both censorts, shall be brought to collation in equal parts in the inheritance of each one of them. That made by only one of them shall be brought to collation in his inheritance.

1047. The donee shall take from the funds of the succession a sum so much less than the sum already received by him, and the co-heirs shall receive the equivelant in property of the same nature, class and quality, in so far as possible.

1048. When what has been provided in the preceding article cannot be executed, if the property donated has consisted of real property, the co-heirs shall have a right to be equalized in cash, or in stocks and bonds, at the rate at which they are quoted; and when there are in the estate neither cash nor stocks and bonds, other property shall be sold at public auction up to the amount required.

When the property donated is personal property, the co-heirs shall have only a right to be equalized in other personal property of the estate at its just value and at their free election.

1049. The fruits and interests of the property, subject to collation, are not due to the bulk of the estate, except from the day on which the succession is opened.

In order to regulate them, the rents and interests of the

hereditary property of the same class as those brought to collation shall be taken into consideration.

1050. When a question arises among the heirs about the obligation to bring to collation or about the objects which are to be brought thereto, the distribution shall not be stopped for such a cause, but proper bond shall be given.

SECTION SECOND.

DISTRIBUTION.

Article 1051. No co-heir shall be obliged to continue in the estate in an undivided condition, unless the testator has expressly forbidden the distribution.

But even when it is so forbidden, the distribution shall always be made for any of the causes on account of which partnerships are extinguished.

1052. Every co-heir having the free administration and disposal of his property, may, at any time, ask for the distribution of the estate.

The lawful representatives of incapables and absentees may ask for the distribution on their behalf.

1053. The wife cannot ask for the distribution of the estate without authority of the husband, and, in certain cases, of the Judge. When the husband asks for it, in the name of his wife, he shall do it with her consent.

The co—heirs of the wife cannot ask for the distribution without the institution of a joint suit against her and her husband.

1054. The heirs, under condition, shall not ask for the distribution until the condition is fulfilled. But the other co-heirs may ask for it, by properly securing the rights of the former for the cases in which the condition may be fulfilled, and until it is known that it has failed or can no longer be complied with, the distribution shall be considered as provisional.

1055. When, before the distribution is made, one of the co-heirs dies leaving two or more heirs, a petition by one of them shall be sufficient; but all those who intervene in such capacity shall appear under a single representation.

1056. When the testator makes a distribution of his property by an act *inter vivos* or by a last will, it shall be accepted in so far as it does not injure the *legitime* of the forced heirs.

The father, who for the interest of his family, desires to keep undivided an agricultural, industrial or manufacturing enterprise, may make use of the powers, granted to him by this article, by disposing that the *legitimes* of the other children be paid in cash.

1057. The testator may, by an act *inter vivos* or *mortis causa*, confer the mere power of making the distribution, after his death, to any person who shall not be one of the co-heirs.

The provisions of this and the preceding articles shall be observed, even when there may be found a minor or a person subject to guardianship among the heirs; but the trustee shall, in this case, make an inventory of the property of the inheritance, after summoning the co-heirs, the creditors, and the legatees.

1058. When the testator has not made any distribution nor trusted this power to another person, if the heirs are of age and have the free administration of their property, they may distribute the estate in the manner they may deem fit.

1059. When the heirs of age cannot agree about the manner of making the distribution, they shall be free to enforce their rights in the manner prescribed by the Law of Civil Procedure.

1060. When the minors are subject to the parental power and are represented in the distribution by the father or, in his default, by the mother, neither the intervention nor the approval of the Judge shall be required.

1061. In the distribution of the estate, all possible fairness shall be observed by drawing lots or adjudging to each one of the heirs things of the same nature, quality, or kind.

1062. When a thing is indivisible or loses considerable by being divided, it may be adjudged to one of the heirs, under condition of paying the excess in cash to the others.

But it shall be sufficient if a single one of the heirs ask for its sale at public auction and that strange bidders may take part in the auction in order that this may be so done.

1063. On making the distribution, the co-heirs shall reciprocally compensate one another for the rents and fruits which each of them may have collected from the estate for the useful and necessary expenses made on said property or for the injuries caused to it by malice or neglect.

1064. The expenses of the distribution, made for the common interests of all the co-heirs, shall be deducted from the estate, those made for the particular interest of one of them, shall be borne by the same.

1065. The titles of acquisition or of ownership shall be delivered to the co-heir to whom the tenement or tenements, to which they refer, were adjudged.

1066. When the same title comprises several tenements adjudged to several co-heirs, or one only which may have been divided among two or more, the title shall remain in the possession of the person having a greater interest in the tenement or tenements, and authenticated copies of it shall be furnished to the other parties, at the expense of the estate. Should the interests be equal, the title shall be delivered to the male heir, and, where there are more than one, to the senior of them.

When the title is an original one, the person in whose possession it remains shall besides be obliged to exhibit it to the other interested parties, when they ask him to do so.

1067. When any of the heirs sell their hereditary rights to a stranger, before the distribution, all or any one of the heirs can subrogate himself in the place of the purchaser, reimbursing him for the value of the purchase, provided they do so with in the term of a month, to be counted from the day on which they have been informed of it.

SECTION THIRD.
EFFECTS OF THE DISTRIBUTION.

Article 1068. A distribution lawfully made confers upon each heir the exclusive ownership of the property adjudged to him.

1069. After the distribution is made, the co-heirs are reciprocally bound to warrant and defend *(eviccion y saneamiento)* the property adjudged.

1070. The obligation, to which the preceding article refers, shall cease only in the following cases:

1. When the testator himself has made the distribution, unless it may appear or be reasonably presumed that he desired to do contrary, it always being understood not to conflict with the *legitime*.

2. When it has been expressly stipulated on making the distribution.

3. When the eviction originates from a cause subsequent to the distribution or has been caused by the fault of the person to whom it was adjudged.

1071. The reciprocal obligation of the co-heirs, in the case of eviction, is proportional to their respective hereditary shares; but if any one of them is insolvent, the other co-heirs shall be liable for his part, in the same proportion, deducting the part belonging to the one to be indemnified.

Those paying for the insolvent co-heir shall retain their action against him, until the time when his fortune may improve.

1072. When a credit is allotted as recoverable, the co-heirs shall not be liable for the subsequent insolvency of the debtor of the estate, and shall be responsible only for his insolvency, at the time the distribution is made.

No one shall be responsible for the credits, qualified as unrecoverable, but when collected, in whole or in part, the amount collected shall be proportionally distributed among the heirs.

SECTION FOURTH.

RESCISSION OF DISTRIBUTION.

Article 1073. Distribution may be rescinded for the same causes as obligations.

1074. Distribution may also be rescinded on account of *lesion* exceding the fourth part, taking into consideration the value of the things when they were adjudged.

1075. The distribution made by the testator, cannot be contested on account of *lesion*, excepting in the cases in which it may injure the *legitime* of the forced heirs, or when it may appear or it may be reasonably presumed that the will of the testator was otherwise.

1076. A rescissory action for *lesion* shall be brought within four years, to be counted from the time the distribution was made.

1077. A defendant heir shall have an option between paying an indemnity for the injury, or consent to a new distribution.

The indemnity may be paid in cash or in the same thing in which the damage took place.

If a new distribution is made, it shall not be effectual as to those who were not injured nor to those who did not receive more than was justly due them.

1078. An heir, who has alienated the whole or a considerable part of the real property adjudged to him, cannot enforce the rescissory action for *lesion*.

1079. The omission of one or several objects or values of the estate shall not cause the rescission of the distribution for *lesion*, but only to complete or increase the estate with the objects or values omitted.

1080. A distribution, made with preterition of any of the heirs, shall not be rescinded, unless it is proven that there was bad faith or deceit on the part of the other parties concerned, but the latter shall be obliged to pay to the ommitted person the proportionate share belonging to him.

1081. When in a distribution, a person, who was believed to be an heir, without being so, has been included, it shall be null and void.

SECTION FIFTH.

PAYMENT OF HEREDITARY DEBTS.

Article 1082. Creditors, recognized as such, can object to the distribution of the estate being carried into effect, until they are paid or the amount of their credits is secured.

1083. Creditors of one or more of the co—heirs may intervene, at their own expense, in the distribution, in order to prevent it being made in fraud or to the injury of their rights.

1084. After the distribution is made, the creditors may

exact the payment of the debts, in full, from any of the heirs who have not accepted the inheritance under benefit of inventory, or up to the amount of their hereditary share in case they have accepted it under such benefit.

In both cases the defendant shall have a right to notify and summon his co-heirs, unless by disposition of the testator or in consequence of the distribution, he alone is bound to pay the debt.

1085. The co-heir, who has paid more than corresponds to his share in the estate, may claim from the others his proportionate part.

The same course shall be pursued, when because of the debt being secured by mortgage or consisting in a specified object, he has paid it in full. The person to whom it has been adjudged may, in such case, claim from his co-heirs only the proportional part, even when the creditor has assigned to him his actions and subrogated him in his place.

1086. When one of the tenements belonging to the estate is encumbered with a perpetual rent or real charge, it shall not be extinguished, even when redeemable, unless a majority of the heirs agree to do it.

When not agreed to or if the charge is not redeemable, its value or principal shall be deducted from the value or capital of the tenement, and this shall pass with the burden to the person to whom it is allotted or adjudged.

1087. The co-heir, who, at the same time, is a creditor of the decedent, may claim from the others the payment of his credit, deducting his proportional part, as such heir, and without prejudice to what is established in section fifth, chapter fifth of this title.

BOOK FOURTH.

OBLIGATIONS AND CONTRACTS.

TITLE I.

OBLIGATIONS.

CHAPTER FIRST.

GENERAL PROVISIONS.

Article **1088.** Every obligation consists in giving, doing, or not doing a certain thing.

1089. Obligations are created by law, by contracts, by quasi–contracts, and by illicit acts and omissions or by those in which any kind of fault or neglect intervenes.

1090. Obligations emanating from law are not presumed. Those expressly determined by this Code or by special laws are the only exigible ones, and shall be governed by the provisions of the laws under which they have been established and by the provisions of this book in respect to what has not been provided by such law.

1091. Obligations arising from contracts have the force of law between the contracting parties, and must be complied with according to the tenor of the contracts.

1092. Civil obligations, arising from crimes or misdemeanors, shall be controlled by the provisions of the Penal Code.

1093. Those emanating from acts or omissions, in which faults or neglect, not punished by law, intervenes, shall be subject to the provisions of chapter second of title 16 of this book.

CHAPTER SECOND.

NATURE AND EFFECTS OF OBLIGATIONS.

Article 1094.   A person obliged to give something is also bound to preserve it with the proper diligence of a good father of a family.

1095.   A creditor has a right to the fruits of a thing from the time the obligation of delivering it to him arises.   However, he shall not acquire real rights therein, until it has been delivered to him.

1096.   When the thing to be delivered is a specified one, the creditor, independently of the right granted to him by art. 1001, may compel the debtor to make the delivery.

When the thing is undetermined or generic, he may ask that the obligation be complied with at the expense of the debtor.

When the person obliged is in default or has engaged himself to deliver the same thing to two or more different persons, until the delivery is made, the debtor shall be liable therefor in respect to unforeseen events.

1097.   The obligation of giving a specified thing comprises that of delivering all its accessories, though they may not have been mentioned.

1098.   When a person obliged to do a certain thing should not do it, it shall be ordered to be done at his expense.

The same shall be ordered, when he does it contrariwise to the tenor of the obligation.

Whatever has been badly done may be ordered to be undone.

1099.   The provision of paragraph two of the preceding article shall also be observed when the obligation consists in not doing, and the debtor does what has been forbidden him.

1100.   Persons obliged to deliver or to do something are in default from the moment on which the creditor exacts judicially or extra-judicially the compliance with their obligation.

However, the intimation of the creditor, in order that default may exist, shall not be necessary:

1.   When the obligation or law declares it expressly.

2.   When from its nature and circumstances, it may appear that the fixing of the time on which the thing was to be deliver-

ed or the service was to be done, was a determinate cause to constitute the obligation.

In reciprocal obligations, none of the obliged parties shall incur default, if the other does not comply with or does not submit to duly comply with what he is bound to do. From the moment on which one of the obligated parties complies with his obligation, the default begins for the other party.

1101. Those who, in compliance with their obligations, incur fraud, neglect or delay, and those who, in any way, act in opposition to the tenor of the same, become subject to pay indemnity for the damages and injuries caused thereby.

1102. Liability arising from fraud is exigible in all obligations. The renunciation of the action to enforce it is null and void.

1103. Liability arising from neglect is also exigible in the fulfillment of all kinds of obligations; but it may be mitigated by the court, according to the case.

1104. The fault or negligence of the debtor consists in the omission of such diligence, as may be required by the nature of the obligation, and may correspond to the circumstances of persons, time, and place.

When the obligation does not state what kind of diligence is to be exercised, that usually shown by a good father of a family shall be required.

1105. No one shall be held liable for events which could not be foreseen or those, even when foreseen, were inevitable, aside from the cases expressly stated by law or those in which the obligation so declares.

1106. Indemnity for damages and injuries comprises not only the amount of the loss suffered, but also that of the benefit which the creditor has failed to obtain, with exception of the provisions contained in the following articles.

1107. The damages and injuries, for which the debtor in good faith is liable, are those foreseen or which may have been foreseen, at the time of constituting the obligation, and which are a necessary consequence of the failure to comply with it.

In case of fraud, the debtor shall be liable for all those which clearly may originate from the failure to fulfill the obligation.

1108.   When the obligation consists in the payment of a sum of money, and the debtor is in default, the indemnity for damages and injuries, when there is no stipulation to the contrary, shall consist in the payment of the interest agreed upon, and, when there is no agreement, the legal interest shall be paid.

While another rate is not fixed by the government, interest, at the rate of six per cent per year, shall be considered as legal.

1109.   Interest due shall produce legal interest from the date on which it was judicially demanded, even if the obligation is silent on this point.

In comercial transactions, the provisions of the Code of Commerce shall govern.

Government pledging institutions *(Montes de Piedad)*, and savings banks shall be governed by their special regulations.

1110.   A receipt from the creditor for the principal, without making any reservation about interest, extinguishes the obligation of the debtor as to such interest.

The receipt for the last installment of a debt, when the creditor has made no reservation, shall also extinguish the obligation in respect to the preceding installment.

1111.   Creditors, after having pursued the property, of which the debtor is in possession, for the purpose of collecting all that is due them, may enforce all the rights and actions of the debtor for the same purpose, excepting those inherent in his person; they may also contest the acts which the debtor may have done in fraud of their rights.

1112.   All rights acquired by virtue of an obligation, are transmissible, subject to the laws, when there is no stipulation to the contrary.

CHAPTER THIRD.

DIFFERENT KINDS OF OBLIGATIONS.

SECTION FIRST.

PURE AND CONDITIONAL OBLIGATIONS.

Article 1113.   Every obligation, the compliance with which does not depend upon a future or uncertain event or upon a past event, unknown to the parties concerned, shall be immediately exigible.

Every obligation, containing a resolutory condition, shall also be exigible without prejudice to the effects of the resolution.

1114. In conditional obligations, the acquisition of rights, as well as the extinction or loss of those already acquired, shall depend upon the event constituting the condition.

1115. When the fulfillment of the condition depends upon the exclusive will of the debtor, the conditional obligation shall be null and void. If it depends upon chance or upon the will of a third person, the obligation shall produce all its effects in accordance with the provisions of this Code.

1116. Impossible conditions, those contrary to good morals, and those forbidden by law, shall void the obligation depending upon them. The condition of not doing a thing which is impossible is considered as non-existing.

1117. The condition, that a certain event shall happen within a certain time, shall extinguish the obligation as soon as the time has elapsed or it should be indubitable that the event cannot take place.

1118. The condition that a certain even shall not occur, at a certain time, shall render the obligation binding as soon as the time fixed has elapsed or when it becomes evident that such event cannot happen.

When there is no fixed time, the condition shall be considered as complied with, within the time which should probably have been fixed, considering the nature of the obligation.

1119. The condition shall be considered as complied with when the obligated party voluntarily prevents its compliance.

1120. The effects of the conditional obligation of giving, when the condition is complied with, will be retroactive from the day on which such obligation was constituted. Nevertheless, when the obligation imposes reciprocal prestations on the parties concerned, the fruits and interests for the time during which the condition has been pending, shall be understood as compensating each other. When the obligation is unilateral, the debtor shall become owner of the fruits and interests collected, unless by the nature and circumstances of the obligation, it must be inferred that the will of the person constituting it was otherwise.

In the obligations of doing or of not doing, the courts are to determine, in each case, the retroactive effect of the condition complied with.

1121. The creditor may, before the fulfillment of the conditions, enforce the actions which may be proper for the preservation of his rights.

The debtor may recover what he has paid during the same period.

1122. When the conditions were established with the intent of suspending the efficiency of the obligation of giving, the following rules shall be observed in the cases in which the thing improves, or is lost, or impaired, while the condition is pending:

1. When the thing is lost without fault of the debtor, the obligation shall become extinguished.

2. When the thing was lost by the fault of the debtor, he is obliged to make an indemnity for damages and injuries.

It his understood that the thing is lost whenever it perishes, remains out of market, or disappears in such a manner that its existence is unknown, or it is not possible to recover it.

3. When the thing is impaired without fault of the debtor, the impairment is to be borne by the creditor.

4. When the thing is impaired by fault of the debtor, the creditor may choose between the resolution of the obligation and its fulfillment, with indemnity for damages in both cases.

5. When the thing improves by its nature or by time, the improvements are for the benefit of the creditor.

6. When it improves at the expense of the debtor, the latter shall have no more rights than those granted to the usufructuary.

1123. When the object of the conditions is to resolve the obligation of giving, after they are complied with, the parties in interest shall reciprocally return all that they have collected.

In cases of loss, impairment or improvement of the thing, the provisions in respect to the debtor, contained in the prec eding article, shall be applied to the person bound to make restitution.

As to the óbligation of doing or not doing, the provisions of the second paragraph or art. 1120 shall be observed in regard to the effects of the resolution.

1124. The right to resolve the obligations is considered as implied in reciprocal ones, in the cases in which one of the obligated persons does not comply with his duties.

The injured party may choose between exacting the compliance with the obligation or its resolution with indemnity for damages and payments of interest in both cases. He may also ask for the resolution, even after having asked for the compliance, when the latter may appear impossible.

The court shall decree the resolution petitioned for, unless there are just causes authorizing it for fix a term.

This is understood without prejudice to the rights of third acquirers, in accordance with arts. 1295 and 1298, and with the provisions of the Law of Mortgage.

SECTION SECOND.

OBLIGATIONS DEPENDING ON A TERM.

Article 1125. Obligations, the fulfillment of which has been fixed for a certain day, are exigible only when such day arrives.

By a certain day is understood one which shall necessarily arrive, even when the date of the arrival is unknown.

When the uncertainty consists in the arrival or non-arrival of the day, then the obligation is conditional and shall be controlled by the rules of the preceding section.

1126. In obligations depending on a certain term; what has been paid in advance cannot be recovered.

When he who paid was not aware, when he did it, of the existence of the term, he shall have a right to claim from the creditor the interests or fruits which the latter has received from the thing.

1127. Whenever there is a term fixed in obligations, it is presumed as established for the benefit of both the creditor and debtor, unless from its tenor or from other circumstances, it may appear that it has been established for the benefit of one or the other.

1128. When the obligation does not fix a term, but it can be inferred from its nature and circumstances that there was an intention of granting it to the debtor, the courts shall fix the duration of such a term.

The courts shall also fix the duration of a term when it may have been left at the will of the debtor.

1129. The debtor shall lose all right to profit by the term:

1. When, after the obligation has been contracted, it appears that he is insolvent, unless he gives security for the debt.

2. When he does not give to the creditor the security he is bound to give.

3. When by his own acts, he has reduced such security, after giving it, or when it disappears through an unforeseen event, unless it is immediately substituted by a new one equally safe.

1130. When the term of the obligation is fixed by days, to be counted from a specified one, such day shall be excluded from the computation which shall begin on the following day.

SECTION THIRD.

ALTERNATIVE OBLIGATIONS.

Article 1131. A person, who is alternatively obliged to make different prestations, shall fully comply with one of them.

A creditor cannot be compelled to receive a part of one and a part of another.

1132. The election belongs to the debtor, unless it has been expressly granted to the creditor.

A debtor shall not have the right to select prestations which are impossible, illicit or which could not have been the matter of such obligation.

1133. An election shall not be effectual, until due notice has been given of it.

1134. A debtor shall lose the right to elect when, of the prestations which he is alternatively obliged to fulfill, only one is feasible.

1135. A creditor shall have a right to be indemnified for damages and injuries when, by the fault of the debtor, all the things, which were alternatively the objects of the obligation, have disappeared, or it has become impossible to comply with the same.

The indemnity shall be fixed, taking as a base the price of the last thing which has disappeared or of the last service which has become impossible.

1136. When an election has been expressly given to the creditor, the obligation shall cease to be alternative, from the date on which notice of such election has been given to the debtor.

Until this date, the liability of such debtor shall be governed by the following rules:

1. When any of the things has been lost by an unforeseen event, he will comply by delivering the one which the creditor may select from among those remaining, or the one that remains, if only one exists.

2. When the loss of any of the things has been caused by the fault of the debtor, the creditor may claim any of those which still remain, or the value of the one which has disappeared by the fault of the debtor.

3. When all the things have been lost by the fault of the debtor, the creditor shall have a right to select the value of any one of them.

The same rules shall apply to the obligation of doing or not doing, in case that some or all of the prestations shoul be impossible.

SECTION FOURTH.

SEVERAL AND JOINT OBLIGATIONS.

1137. The concurrence of two or more creditors or of two or more debtors, in a single obligation, does not imply that each one of the former has a right to ask, nor each one of the latter is bound to comply in full with the things which are the objects of such obligation. This shall only take place when the obligation determines it expressly, and is constituted as a joint obligation.

1138. If from the context of the obligation, referred to in the preceding article, any other thing does not appear, the credit or the debt shall be presumed as divided in as many equal parts as there are creditors or debtors, and shall be considered as credits or debts, each one different from the others.

1139. When the division is impossible, the right of the creditors shall only be impaired by the collective acts of the same, and the debts shall only be recoverable by proceedings againts all of the debtors. If any one of them is found to be insolvent, the others shall not be obliged to pay his share.

1140. Solidarity may exist, even when the creditors and debtors are not bound in the same manner, and for the same periods and under the same conditions.

1141. Each one of the joint creditors can do whatever may be profitable, but not what may be injurious to the others.

Actions, enforced against any one of the joint debtors, shall be to the injury of all of them.

1142. A debtor may pay the debt to any one of the joint creditors, but when it has been judicially demanded by any one of them, he must pay to this particular one.

1143. Novation, compensation, confusion or remission of the debt, made by any of the joint creditors, or with any of the debtors of the same class, extinguishes the obligation without prejudice to the provisions of art. 1146.

A creditor who has executed any of these acts, and also the person who collects the debt, shall be responsible to the others for the part pertaining to them in the obligation.

1144. A creditor may sue any of the joint debtors or all of them simultaneously. The claims instituted against one shall not be an obstacle for those that may be later presented against the others, as long as it does not appear that the debt has been collected in full.

1145. A payment made by one of the joint debtors extinguishes the obligation.

A person who has made the payment can only claim from

his co-debtors the shares pertaining to each one with the interest on the amounts advanced.

The failure to comply with the obligation, on account of the insolvency of a joint debtor, shall be made good by the co-debtors in proportion to the debt of each one of them.

1146. The liberation or remission, made by the creditor of the part affecting one of the joint debtors, does not release this one of his liability as to the co-debtors, in case the debt has been fully pay by any one of them.

1147. When the thing has perished, or the prestation has become impossible, without any fault of the joint debtors, the obligation shall be extinguished.

If there has been any fault on the part of any of them, all shall be liable, as to the creditor, for the value and the indemnity for damages and payments of interests, without injury to his action against the culpable or negligent.

1148. A joint debtor may utilize, against the claims of the creditor, all the exceptions derived from the nature of the obligation, and those which are personal to him. Those which personally pertain to the others may be employed by him only as to the share of the debt for which such co-debtors may be responsible.

SECTION FIFTH.
DIVISIBLE AND INDIVISIBLE OBLIGATIONS.

Article 1149. The divisibility or indivisibility of things, objects of obligations, in which there is a single debtor and a single creditor, neither changes nor modifies the provisions of chapter second of this title.

1150. An indivisible several obligation is determined by paying the indemnity for damage and injury, from the moment that any of the debtors fails to comply with his duties. The debtors, who have been ready to comply with their duties, shall only contribute to the indemnity in a sum equivalent to the corresponding portion of the value of the thing or of the service in which the obligation consists.

1151. For the effects of the preceding articles, the obligation of giving specified things, and all those which are not susceptible of partial fulfillment, shall be considered as in-divisible.

The obligations of doing shall be divisible when their object is the prestation of a number of days of work, the execution of work by units of measure, or any other similar things which by their nature are susceptible of partial fulfillment.

In the obligation of not doing, the divisibility or in-divisibility, shall be decided by characteristics of the prestation in each particular case.

SECTION SIXTH.
OBLIGATIONS WITH PENAL CLAUSE.

Article 1152. In obligations with a penal clause, the penalty shall substitute the indemnity for damages and the payment of interest in cause of a failure to comply therewith, if it has not been otherwise stipulated.

This penality can only be made effective, when it is exigible in accordance with the provisions of this Code.

1153. The debtor cannot exempt himself from the fulfillment of the obligation by paying the penalty, unless in case that such right has been expressly reserved to him.

Neither can the creditor jointly exact the fulfillment of the obligation and the payment of the penalty, unless such right has clearly been granted to him.

1154. The Judge shall equitably modify the penalty, when the principal obligation has been partly or irregularly complied with by the debtor.

1155. The nullity of the penal clause does not carry with it that of the principal obligation.

The nullity of the principal obligation carries with it that of the penal clause.

CHAPTER FOURTH.
EXTINCTION OF OBLIGATIONS.

GENERAL PROVISIONS.

Article 1156. Obligations are extinguished:
By their payment or compliance with them.

By the loss of the thing due.

By remission of the debt.

By the merging of the rights of the creditor and debtor.

By compensation.

By novation.

SECTION FIRST.

PAYMENT.

Article 1157. A debt shall not be considered as paid, until the total amount of the thing has been delivered, or the prestation of which the obligation consisted has been made.

1158. Any person, whether he has an interest or not in the compliance with the obligation, and whether the debtor knows it and approves it or is not aware of it, can make the payment.

He who pays the account of another may recover from the debtor what he has paid, unless he has done it against the latter's express will.

In this last case, he can only recover from the debtor in so far as the payment has been useful to him.

1159. He who pays in the name of the debtor, when the latter is not aware of it, cannot compel the creditor to subrogate him in the rights the creditor possesses.

1160. In obligations of giving, the payment made by the person who has not the free disposal of the thing due, and capacity for conveying it, shall not be valid.

However, when the payment has consisted in a sum of money or a thing perishable, no recovery shall be had against the creditor who has spent or consumed it in good faith.

1161. In obligations of doing, the creditor cannot be compelled to receive the prestation or the services from a third party, when the quality and circumstances of the person of the debtor has been taken into account in establishing the obligation.

1162. Payment shall be made to the person in whose favor the obligation is constituted, or to another authorized to receive it in his name.

1163. The payment, made to a person who is incapable

to manage his property, shall be valid, in so far as it may be employed for his benefit.

A payment made to a third party shall also be valid in so far as it may have been beneficial to the creditor.

1164. A payment made, in good faith, to the person who is in possession of the credit shall release the debtor.

1165. A payment made by the debtor to the creditor, after he has been judicially ordered to retain the debt, shall not be valid.

1166. The debtor for a thing cannot oblige his creditor to receive a different one, even when it should be of equal or superior value to the thing due.

Neither in obligations of doing can a prestation be substituted by another against the will of the creditor.

1167. When the obligation consists in the delivery of a thing, not specified or generic, the quality and circumstances of which have not been expressed, the creditor cannot exact one of a superior quality nor can the debtor deliver an inferior one.

1168. Extrajudicial expenses, caused by the payment, shall be charged to the debtor. The court in accordance with the Code of Civil Procedure shall decide about the judicial expenses.

1169. Unless the contract expressly authorizes it, the creditor cannot be compelled to partially receive the prestations of which the obligation consists.

However, when the debt is in part liquid and in part illiquid, the creditor may exact, and the debtor can make payment of the former without awaiting for the liquidation of the latter.

1170. Payments of debts in money shall be made in the class of coins stipulated, and when it is not possible to deliver the same class, in legal silver or gold coin current in Spain.

The delivery of bills to order or drafts or other mercantile paper shall only produce the effects of payment, when collected or when, by the fault of the creditor, they have become dishonored.

Meanwhile, the action, derived from the original obligation, shall remain in suspense.

1171. Payments shall be made at the place designated in the obligation.

When it is not expressed and when a determined thing is to be delivered, the payment shall be made at the place where the thing existed, at the moment of constituting the obligation.

In any other case, the place of payment shall be that of the domicil of the debtor.

IMPUTATION OF PAYMENTS.

Article **1172.** A person having several debts of the same class, in favor of a single creditor, can declare, at the time of making a payment, to which of them it must be applied.

When the debtor accepts a release from the creditor in which the application of the payment is made, he cannot make a claim against it, unless some cause has intervened which may invalidate the contract.

1173. If the debt bears interest, the payment cannot be considered as made on account of the principal, until the interest is covered.

1174. When the payment cannot be imputed, according to the preceding rules, the debt, which is most onerous for the debtor among those which have matured, shall be considered as the one paid.

When they have the same nature and liens, the payment shall be imputed to all pro rata.

PAYMENT BY ASSIGNMENT OF PROPERTY.

Article **1175.** The debtor may assign his property to creditors in payment of his debts. This assignment liberates the former from liability to the net amount of the property assigned, unless there are stipulations to the contrary. Agreements in respect to the effects of an assignment, entered into between the debtor and his creditors, shall be made in accordance with the provisions of title seventeenth of this book, and with what is prescribed in the Code of Civil Procedure.

TENDER OF PAYMENT AND CONSIGNATION.

Article **1176.** When the creditor, to whom the tender of payment has been made, refuses to accept it, without reason, the debtor shall remain free from all liability by the consignation of the thing due.

The same effect shall be produced by the consignation alone when made in the absence of the creditor, or when he is incapacitated from receiving the payment, at the time in which it is due, and when several persons pretend to have a right to collect it, or when the title of the obligation has been mislaid.

1177. In order that the consignation of the thing due may liberate the obligee, notice of it shall previously be given to the persons interested in the fulfillment of the obligation.

Consignation shall be ineffective when not strictly adjusted to the provision regulating payment.

1178. Consignation shall be made by depositing the things due, at the disposal of the judicial authority before whom it shall be proven that, in the proper case, the tender has been made and, in all other cases, that notice has been given of the consignation. After consignation is made, notice thereof shall also be given the parties concerned.

1179. The expenses of consignation, when proper, shall be charged to the creditor.

1180. After the consignation is duly made, the debtor can ask the Judge to order the cancellation of the obligation.

While the creditor has not accepted the consignation or no judicial decision has been rendered that it has been well done, the debtor may withdraw the thing or sum consigned, leaving the obligation subsisting.

1181. If, after the consignation is made, the creditor authorized the debtor to withdraw it, the former shall lose all the (right) of preference which he has in the thing.

The co-debtors and sureties shall become discharged.

SECTION SECOND.

LOSS OF THE THING DUE.

Article 1182. The obligation, which consists in the delivery of a specified thing, shall be extinguished when this thing is lost or destroyed without fault of the debtor and before he has become liable for delay.

1183. Whenever the thing is lost, when in the possession of the debtor, it shall be presumed that the loss has occurred by his fault and not by an unforeseen event, unless there is proof to the contrary and without prejudice to provision of art. 1096.

1184. In obligations of doing, the debtor shall also be liberated when the prestation appears to be legally or physically impossible.

1185. When the debt for a certain and specified thing originates from a crime or fault, the debtor shall not be exempted from the payment of its value, whatever the cause of the loss may be, unless, when after he has offered the thing to the person, who should have received it, this person without reason had refused to accept it.

1186. Whenever the obligation is extinguished by the loss of the thing, all actions which the debtor should have against third persons, on account of it, pass to the creditor.

SECTION THIRD.

REMISSION OF DEBTS.

Article **1187.** A remission may be made either expressly or tacitly.

Both of them shall be governed by the provisions which rule inofficious donations.

An express remission must, besides, be adjusted to the forms of a donation.

1188: A voluntary surrender, made by a creditor to his debtor, of a private document which bears evidence of a credit, implies the renunciation of the action which the former had against the latter.

When, for the purpose of invalidating this renunciation, it is claimed that it is inofficious, the debtor and his heirs may support it by proving that the delivery of the document was made on account of the payment of the debt.

1189. Whenever a private document from which the debt appears is in the possession of the debtor, it shall be presumed that the creditor delivered it by his own will, unless the contrary is proven.

1190. The remission of the principal debt shall extinguish the accessory obligations, but the remission of the latter shall leave the former existing.

1191. The accessory obligation of a pledge shall be considered remitted, when the pledge, after having been delivered to the creditor, is found in the possession of the debtor.

SECTION FOURTH.
CONFUSION OF RIGHTS.

Article 1192. Whenever the capacities of creditor and debtor are merged in the same person, the obligation becomes extinguished.

The case in which this confusion takes place by title of inheritance is excepted, when such inheritance has been accepted under benefit of inventory.

1193. The confusion which takes place in the person of the debtor or of the principal creditor is beneficial to the sureties. The one which takes place in the person of any of such sureties does not extinguish the obligation.

1194. Confusion does not extinguish debts in severalty, except as to the part which corresponds to the creditor or debtor in whom both capacities are merged.

SECTION FIFTH.
COMPENSATION (SET–OFF).

Article 1195. Compensation shall take place when two persons, in their own rights, are reciprocally creditors and debtors of each other.

1196. In order that compensation may be effectual, it is required:

1. That each one of the persons bound may be principally so, and that he may be, at the same time, the principal creditor of the other.

2. That both debts consist in a sum of money or, when the things due are perishable, that they be of the same kind and also of the same quality, when the latter has been stipulated.

3. That both debts are due.

4. That they are liquid and exigible.

5.   That no retention or suit, instituted by a third party and of which due notice has been given to the debtor, affects any of them.

1197.   Notwithstanding the provisions of the preceding article, the sureties may oppose compensation in respect to what the creditor owes to his principal debtor.

1198.   The debtor, who has consented to an assignment of rights, made by a creditor in favor of a third party, cannot oppose, against the assignee, the compensation which should pertain to him against the assignor.

When the creditor gave him notice of the assignment and the debtor did not consent to it, he may oppose compensation for the debts, prior to such assignment, but not for those contracted afterwards.

When the assignment is made without knowledge of the debtor, he can oppose compensation for the credits, prior to it, and for those contracted subsequently, until he has been informed of the assignment.

1199.   Debts payable in different places may be compensated by an indemnity for the expenses of transportation or for the exchange at the place of payment.

1200.   Compensation shall not take place when any of the debts arises from a deposit or from the obligations of the depositary or borrower.

Neither can it be opposed to the creditor for support due under a gratuitous title.

1201.   When a person has against himself different debts, which may be compensated, the provisions referring to imputation of payments shall be observed in the order of compensation.

1202.   The effect of compensation is to extinguish both debts to the concurrent amount, even when the creditors and debtors have no knowledge of it.

SECTION SIXTH.
NOVATION.

Article 1203.   Obligations can be modified :

1.   By change of object or their pricipal conditions.

2. By substituting the person of the debtor.

3. By subrogating a third party in the rights of the creditor.

1204. In order that an obligation may be extinguished by another which substitutes it, it is necessary that it should be so expressly declared, or that the old and new be absolutely incompatible.

1205. Novation, consisting in the substitution of any debtor in the place of the original one, can be made without the knowledge of the latter, but not without the consent of the creditor.

1206. The insolvency of the new debtor, who has been accepted by the creditor, shall not revive the action of the latter against the original debtor, unless said insolvency has been prior, public, and known to the debtor when he transfers his debt.

1207. When the principal obligation is extinguished by effect of the novation, the accessory obligations shall only subsist in so far as they benefit third parties who have not given their consent.

1208. Novation is null and void, if the original obligation is also so, unless the cause of nullity can be claimed by the debtor only or the ratification gives validity to acts which were null in their origin.

1209. The subrogation of a third party in the rights of a creditor cannot be presumed, except in the cases expressly mentioned in this Code.

In other cases, it shall be necessary to prove it clearly in order that it may be effectual.

1210. Subrogation is presumed:

1. When a creditor pays another preferred creditor.

2. When a third party, who is not interested in the obligation, pays with the express or tacit approval of the debtor.

3. When the person, who has interest in the fulfillment of the obligation, pays, without injury to the effect of the confusion in respect to the share belonging to him.

1211. A debtor may make the subrogation, whithout the consent of the creditor, when for paying the debt, he has borrowed money by a public deed, stating therein his intent and setting forth, in the release, the origin of the sum paid.

1212. Subrogation transfers to the subrogated the credit with the rights annexed to it, either against the debtor or against third parties, be they sureties or holders of mortgages.

1213. A creditor, to whom a partial payment has been made, may enforce his right for the balance, with preference to the person subrogated in his stead by virtue of the partial payment of the same credit.

CHAPTER FIFTH.
PROOF OF OBLIGATIONS.

GENERAL PROVISIONS.

Article 1214. Proof of obligations devolves upon the persons claiming their fulfillment, and that of their extinguishment falls upon those who oppose the same.

1215. Proofs can be made by instruments, by confession, by the personal inspection of a Judge, by experts, by witnesses, and by presumptions.

SECTION FIRST.
PUBLIC DOCUMENTS.

Article 1216. Public documents are those authorized by a Notary or by a competent public official, with the solemnities required by law.

1217. Documents in which a Notary Public intervenes shall be governed by the Notarial law.

1218. Public instruments are evidence, even against a third party, of the fact which gave cause for their execution and of the date of the same.

They shall also be evidence against the contracting parties and those holding rights under them, as to the declarations made in them by the former.

1219. Public instruments, made for the purpose of weakening a former deed, between the same parties, shall be effectual against third parties only when their contents have been annotated in the proper public registry or on the margin of the original deed, and on the transcription or copy by virtue of which the third parties have acted.

1220. Copies of public instruments of which there is an original or protocol, when contested by those to whom they cause damage, shall have probatory force only when they have been duly collated.

If there is any difference between the original and the copy, the contents of the former shall govern.

1221. When the original deed, the protocol, and the original file have disappeared, the following shall constitute evidence: ·

1. The first copies taken by the public officer who had authorized them.

2. The subsequent copies, issued by order of a court, after summoning the interested parties.

3. Those which may have been taken in the presence of the interested parties and with their assent, but without judicial order.

In default of the above mentioned copies, any other copies, thirty or more years old, shall be evidence, provided they have been taken from the original by the officer who authorized them or by any other in charge of their custody.

Copies less than thirty years old, or which are authorized by a public official, in which the circumstances, specified in the preceding paragraph do not concur, shall serve only as a beginning of written evidence.

The probatory force of copies of a copy shall be valued by the courts according to circumstances.

1222. The inscription in any public registry of a document which has disappeared shall be valued, according to the rules established in the last two paragraphs of the preceding articles.

1223. An instrument, defective by the incompetency of the Notary, or by any other fault in its form, shall be considered as a private document when signed by the parties who executed the same.

1224. An instrument of recognition of an act or contract proves nothing against the instrument by which the same was executed, when, by excess or omission, they disagree whith it, unless the novation of the former is expressly proven.

PRIVATE DOCUMENTS.

Article **1225**. A private document legally recognized shall have, as to those who executed it and those holding rights under them, the same force as a public instrument.

1226. A person against whom a written obligation, which appears subscribed by him, is set up in court is bound to declare whether the subscription is or is not his own.

The heirs and those holding rights under the person bound may limit themselves to state if they know whether the subscription of the obligation is, or is not that of their principal.

Refusal, without a just cause, to make the declaration mentioned in the preceding paragraph, may be considered by the court as a confession of the genuineness of the document.

·**1227**. The date of a private document shall be considered, in respect to third parties, only from the date on which it has been filed or inscribed in a public registry, from the death of any of the persons who subscribe it, or from the date on which it is delivered to a public official by virtue of his office.

1228. Entries, registries, and private papers shall be evidence only against the person who has written them in all that may appear clearly stated, but the person who wants to be benefited by such is bound to accept them also in the part which is injurious to him.

1229. A note written or signed by a creditor, at the end, in the margin, or on the back of a document held by him, constitutes evidence in all that is favorable to the debtor.

The same thing shall be understood of the notes written or signed by the creditor, on the back, in the margin, or at the foot of the duplicate of a document or receipt which the debtor holds.

In both cases, the debtor, who wishes to avail himself of what is favorable to him, shall have to abide by what is injurious as well.

1230.   Private documents made for the purpose of changing the stipulations made in a public instrument produce no effect against a third party.

SECTION SECOND.

CONFESSION.

Article 1231.   Confession may be made either judicially or extrajudicially.

In both cases, it shall be an indispensable condition for the validity of the confession that it should relate to personal acts of the confessor and that he may have legal capacity for making it.

1232.   Confession is evidence against the author.

Exception is made of the cases in which compliance with the laws may be evaded by such confession.

1233.   The confession cannot be partially used against him who makes it, unless it refers to different facts or when a part of the confession is proven by other means, or when, in any particular, it may be contrary to nature or law.

1234.   Confession loses its effectiveness only when it is proven that on the making of it an error of fact was committed.

1235.   A judicial confession must be made under oath before a competent judge, and when he who may be benefitted by it has actual representation in the proceedings.

1236.   When judicial confession under decisory oath is demanded, the party from whom it is requested may ask the oath to be referred to the adversary, and if the latter refuses to give it, it shall be considered that the person has confessed.

1237.   Decisory oath cannot be demanded about incriminating facts nor on questions about which the parties cannot compromise.

1238.   Confession made under decisory oath, whether deferred or referred, constitutes a proof only in favor or against the parties who submitted to it or their heirs, and persons holding rights under them.

No proof shall be admitted about the falseness of such oath.

1239. Extrajudicial confession shall be considered as an act subject to the appreciation of the courts, according to the rules established about evidence.

SECTION THIRD.

PERSONAL INSPECTION BY THE JUDGE.

Article 1240. Evidence by personal inspection of the Judge shall only be effective in so far as it clearly permits the court to estimate, by the external appearance of the thing inspected, the fact which he tries to ascertain.

1241. The inspection made by a judge may be estimated in the sentence rendered by another judge, provided the former has set forth with perfect clearness, in the proceedings, the details and circumstances of the things inspected.

SECTION FOURTH.

EVIDENCE BY EXPERTS.

Article 1242. This class of evidence can only be used, when, in order to estimate the facts, scientific, artistic or practical knowledge is necessary or convenient.

1243. The value of this evidence and the form in which it must be given are the subjects of the provisions of the Code of Civil Procedure.

SECTION FIFTH.

EVIDENCE BY WITNESSES.

Article 1244. Evidence by witnessess shall be admissible in all cases in which it has not been expressly forbidden.

1245. All persons, of either sex, who are not unable by natural incapacity or by the provisions of law, can be witnesses.

1246. The following cannot be witnesses by natural incapacity:

1. Lunatics or insane persons.

2. The blind and deaf, in those things, knowledge of which depends upon sight and hearing.

3. Minors under fourteen years of age.

1247. The following persons are incapable by provisions of law:

1.   Those who are directly interested in the suit.

2.   The ascendants in the suits of their descendants and the latter in those of the former.

3.   The father-in-law or mother-in-law in the suits of the son-in law or daughter-in-law, and vice versa.

4.   The husband in the suits of his wife and the wife in those of the husband.

5.   Those who, on account of their condition or profession, are bound to keep secrecy in matters relating to their profession or condition.

6.   Those who are especially disqualified to be witnesses in certain acts.

The provisions of nos. 2, 3, and 4 shall not be applied in suits in which it is intended to prove the birth or death of children or any other private family act, which it may not be possible to verify by any other means.

1248.   The probatory force of the depositions of the witnesses shall be valued by the courts in accordance with the provisions of the Law of Civil Procedure, taking care to avoid that, by the simple coincidences of some depositions, unless their truthfulness be evident, the affairs may be finally decided in which are usually employed public deeds, private documents, or any commencement or written evidence.

SECTION SIXTH.

PRESUMPTIONS.

Article 1249.   Presumptions are only admissable when the facts from which they are to be deduced are completely proven.

1250.   Presumptions established by law exempt those favored by them from producing any further evidence.

1251.   Presumptions established by law can be destroyed by evidence to the contrary, except in those cases in which it is expressly prohibited.

Only a sentence obtained in a suit for revision shall be effective against the presumption that a final judgment is true

1252.   In order that the presumption of a final sentence

may be effective in another suit, it is necessary that between the case determined by the sentence and that in which the same is invoked, there shall be the most perfect identity, between the things, the causes, and the persons of the litigants, and the capacity, under which they litigated.

In questions relating to the civil condition of persons and in those about the validity or nullity of testamentary provisions, the presumption of a final sentence shall be effective against third parties, even if they have not litigated.

It is understood that there is identity of persons whenever the litigants of the second suit hold rights under those who. litigated in the preceding suit, or when they are united to them by liens of solidarity, or by those which are established by the indivisibility of prestations among those who have the right to exact them, or those who are bound to satisfy the same.

1253. In order that presumptions, not established by law, may be considered as means of evidence, it is indispensable that between the facts demonstrated and the one that is to be deduced, should exist a precise and direct connection according to the rules of human criterion.

TITLE II.

CONTRACTS.

CHAPTER FIRST.

GENERAL PROVISIONS.

Article **1254**. A contract exists from the moment when one or several persons consent to bind himself or themselves, in respect to another or others, to give some thing or to render some service.

1255. The contracting parties may establish any pacts, clauses, and conditions which they deem convenient, provided they do not conflict with the laws, morals, or public order.

1256. The validity and fulfillment of contracts cannot be left to the will of one of the contracting parties.

1257. Contracts shall only be effectual between the parties by whom they are executed and their heirs, except, with respect to the latter, in the cases where the rights and obligations originating from the contract are not transmissible, either by their nature, or by pact, or by provision of law.

When the contract contains any stipulation in favor of a third party, he can exact its fulfillment, whenever he has given notice of his acceptance to the person bound, before the said stipulation has been revoked.

1258. Contracts are perfected by mere consent and from that time they are binding, not only in respect to the fulfillment of what has been expressly stipulated, but also in all the consequences which, according to their nature, are in accordance with good faith, use, and law.

1259. No one can contract in the name of another without being authorized by him, or without lawfully having his legal representation.

A contract, entered into in the name of another by one who has not either his authorization or legal representation, shall be null and void, unless it is ratified by the person in whose name it was executed, before it is revoked by the other contracting party.

1260. Oaths shall not be admitted in contracts. If admitted, they shall be considered as not existing.

CHAPTER SECOND.

ESSENTIAL REQUIREMENTS FOR THE VALIDITY OF CONTRACTS.

Article **1261.** There is no contract unless the following requirments are present:

1. The consent of the contracting parties.
2. A definite object which may be a matter of contract.
3. A cause for the obligation which is established therein.

SECTION FIRST.

CONSENT.

Article **1262.** Consent is shown by the concurrence of the offer and of the acceptance of the thing and the cause which shall constitute the contract.

Acceptance made by letter only binds the person who made the offer when it came to his notice. The contract, in this case, is presumed as entered into at the place where the offer was made.

1263.　The following persons cannot give their consent:

1.　Minors who are not emancipated.

2.　Lunatics or the insane, and the deaf and dumb who cannot write.

3.　Married women, in the cases specified by law.

1264.　The incapacity, set forth in the preceding article, is subject to the modifications which are determined by law and is to be understood without prejudice to the special incapacities established by such law.

1265.　Consent given by error, under violence, intimidation or by deceit shall be void.

1266.　In order that the error may invalidate the consent, it must refer to the substance of the thing, object of the contract, or to those conditions of the same, which should have been principally the cause of its celebration.

An error as to the person shall invalidate a contract only when the consideration of the person should have been the principal cause of the contract.

A mere error of accounts shall only give cause for its correction.

1267.　Violence exists when, to exact the consent, an irresistable force is used.

Intimidation exists when one of the contracting parties is inspired with a reasonable and well grounded fear of suffering and imminent and serious injury to his person or property, or to the person or property of his consort, descendants or ascendants.

To qualify the intimidation, the age, sex, and status of the person must be considered.

Fear of displeasing the persons to whom obedience and respect is due shall not annul the contract.

1268.　Violence or intimidation shall annul the obligation, even if they have been employed by a third person who did not intervene in the contract.

1269.　There is deceit, when by words or insidious contrivances on the part of one of the contracting parties, the other is induced to enter into a contract which he would not have done without the use of them.

1270. In order that deceit may cause the nullity of a contract, it should be grevious and must not have been employed by both of the contracting parties.

Incidental deceit renders only the party who employed it liable to indemnity for damages and injuries.

SECTION SECOND.
OBJECTS OF CONTRACTS.

Article **1271.** All things, even future ones, which are not out of the commerce of men, can be objects of contracts.

Notwithstanding, no contract can be entered into in respect to future inheritances, other than those whose object is to make a distribution *inter vivos* of the estate, according to art. 1056.

All services not contrary to law or to good morals may also be the object of a contract.

1272. Things or services which are impossible cannot be the object of a contrat.

1273. The object of every contract must be a thing determined as to its kind. The indetermination of the sum cannot be an obstacle to the existence of the contract, provided it may be possible to determine it without necessity of a new agreement between the contracting parties.

SECTION THIRD.
CONSIDERATION (*causa*) FOR CONTRACTS.

Article **1274.** In onerous contracts, the prestation or promise of a thing or services by the other party is understood as a consideration for each contracting party; in remuneratory ones, the services or benefits remunerated, and in those of pure beneficence, the mere liberality of the benefactor.

1275. Contracts without consideration or with an illicit one are not effectual. A consideration is illicit, when it is contrary to law and good morals.

1276. The statement of a false consideration in contracts shall render them void, unless it is proven that they were based on another real and licit one.

1277.	Although the consideration is not expressed in the contract, it is presumed as existing and that it is licit, unless the debtor proves the contrary.

CHAPTER THIRD.

EFFECTIVENESS OF CONTRACTS.

Article 1278.	Contracts shall be binding, whatever the form may be in which they have been entered into, provided the essential conditions required for their validity are present.

1279.	When the law exacts the execution of a deed or other special form for making effectual suitable obligations of a contract, the contracting parties may compel each other to comply with such forms, from the moment in which consent and the other requirements, necessary for their validity, have taken place.

1280.	The following must be executed by a public instrument:

1.	Acts and contracts the object of which is the creation, transmission, modification or extinction of real rights on real property.

2.	The leases of the same property for six or more years, whenever they shall cause damage to third parties.

3.	Marriage contracts, and the constitution and increase of dowries, whenever it is intended to enforce them against third parties.

4.	The assignment, repudiation, and renunciation of hereditary rights or of those of the conjugal society.

5.	The power for contracting marriage, the general one for law suits, and the special ones which are to be presented in a law suit; the power for administering property and any other, the object of which is an act drawn or which is to be drawn in a public instrument, or which may do injury to a third party.

6.	The assignment of actions or rights proceeding from an act specified in a public instrument.

All other contracts, on which the amount of the prestations of one or both of the contracting parties exceed 1500 pesetas, must be drawn in writing , even when a private document.

CHAPTER FOURTH.

INTERPRETATION OF CONTRACTS.

Article 1281.   When the terms of a contract are clear and leave no doubt about the intentions of the contracting parties, the literal sense of its clauses shall rule.

When the words appear contrary to the evident intention of the contracting parties, the intention is to prevail.

1282.   To form a judgment about the intention of the contracting parties, attention must principally be paid to their acts, contemporaneous and subsequent to the contract.

1283.   However general the terms of a contract may be, there should not be understood as comprised in it, things and cases different from those about which the parties interested intended to contract.

1284.   When any of the clauses of a contract admits of different meanings, it should be understood in the sense most suitable to be effective.

1285.   The clauses of a contract should be interpreted in relation to one another giving to those that are doubtful the meaning which may result from the consideration of all of them together.

1286.   Words which may have different meanings shall be taken in the meaning which may be nearest in accordance with the nature and object of the contract.

1287.   The uses or customs of the country shall be taken in consideration in interpreting the ambiguity in contracts, and shall supply in them the omissions of clauses which are usually established therein.

1288.   The interpretation of the obscure clauses of a contract shall not favor the party who caused such obscurity.

1289.   When it is absolutely impossible to resolve the doubts by the rules set forth in the preceding articles, if these deal with incidental circumstances of the contract, and this contract be gratuitous, they shall be resolved in favor of the smallest transmission of rights and interests. If the contract be onerous, the doubt shall be decided in favor of the greatest reciprocity of interests.

When the doubts, a decision about which is referred to in this article, deal about the principal object of the contract, in such a way that the intention or will of the contracting parties cannot be ascertained, the contract shall be null and void.

CHAPTER FIFTH.
RESCISSION OF CONTRACTS.

Article 1290. Contracts validly entered into may be rescinded in the cases provided by law.

1291. The following contracts are rescindable:

1. Those which may be entered into by guardians without the authorization of the family council, whenever the person represented by them has suffered *lesion* of more than one fourth part of the value of the things which have been the object of such contracts.

2. Those entered into in representation of absentees, provided they have suffered the *lesion*, referred to in the preceding paragraph.

3. Those entered into in fraud of the creditors, when they cannot recover, in any other way, what is due them.

4. Contracts which refer to litigious things, when they have been entered into by the defendant without the knowledge and approval of the parties in litigation or of competent judicial authority.

5. Any others specially determined by law.

1292. Payments made, while in the condition of insolvency, by a debtor on account of obligations, the compliance with which at the time of making them the debtor could not be compelled to do, are also rescindable.

1293. No contract shall be rescinded for *lesion*, except those specified in nos. 1 and 2 of art. 1291.

1294. The action for rescission is a subsidiary one and can be enforced only when the injured party has no other legal remedy to obtain the reparation for the injury.

1295.   Rescission obliges the return of the things which were the objects of the contract, together with their fruits and the value with interest, therefore, it can only be carried into effect when the person who claims it can return that which, on his part, he is bound to do.

Neither can rescission take place when the things, objects of the contract, are lawfully in the possession of third parties who have not acted in bad faith.

In this case the indemnity for damages may be claimed from the person who caused the *lesion*.

1296.   The rescission, to which no. 2 of art. 1291 refers, shall not be allowed in contracts made with judicial authorization.

1297.   All contracts by virtue of which the debtor conveys property, under gratuitous title, are presumed to be made in fraud of creditors.

Conveyances, under onerous titles, made by persons against whom a condemnatory sentence, in any instance, has been previously rendered, or a writ of seizure of property has been issued, shall also be presumed fraudulent.

1298.   Any person, who has in bad faith acquired things, alienated in fraud of creditors, shall indemnify the latter for the damages and injuries caused to them by the conveyance, whenever, by any reason, it may be impossible for him to return them.

1299.   The action asking rescission must be brought within four years.

For persons subject to guardianship and for absentees, the four years shall not commence to run, until the incapacity of the former has ceased to exist or the domicil of the latter is known.

CHAPTER SIXTH.

NULLITY OF CONTRACTS.

Article 1300.   Contracts, in which the requirements stated in art. 1261 concur, can be annulled, even when there is no *lesion* to the contracting parties, whenever they are affected by one of the vices which invalidate them according to law.

1301.   The action for nullity shall last only four years.

This term shall commence to run in cases of intimidation or violence from the day on which it has ceased.

In those of error or deceit or falseness of consideration, from the date of the consumation of the contract.

When the object of the action is to invalidate contracts, made by a married woman, without consent or by competent authority, from the date of the dissolution of the marriage.

And when it refers to contracts, entered into by minors or incapables, from the date when they were freed from guardianship.

1302.   The action for nullity of contracts can be exercised by those who are principally or subsidiarily obligated by virtue of them.   Capable persons cannot, however, allege the incapacity of those who contracted with them; neither those who caused the intimidation or violence, or employed deceit, or caused the error, can base their action on such vices of the contract.

1303.   When the nullity of an obligation has been declared, the contracting parties shall restore to each other the things which have been the matter of the contract with their fruits, and the value with its interest, except what is provided by the following articles.

1304.   When the nullity is caused by the incapacity of one of the contracting parties, the incapable is not obliged to make restitution, except to the extent he has profited by the thing or by the value received by him.

1305.   When the nullity arises from the illegality of the consideration or the object of the contract, if the fact constitutes a crime or fault, common to both contracting parties, they shall have no action against each other and proceedings shall be instituted against them, and the things or value which may have been the matter of the contract shall be applied, as provided in the Penal Code in respect to the goods or instruments of the crime or fault.

This provision is applicable to the cases in which there is a crime or fault on the part of only one of the contracting parties, but the one who is not culpable, shall be entitled to recover what he has given, and shall not be bound to comply with what he has promised.

1306. If the fact of which the illicit consideration consists does not constitute either a crime or fault, the following rules shall be observed:

1. When both parties are culpable, neither of them can recover what he has given by virtue of the contract, nor claim the fulfillment of what the other party has offered.

2. When only one of the contracting parties is culpable, this one shall not recover what he has given by virtue of the contract, nor ask for the fulfillment of what has been offered to him. The other party, who has had nothing to do with the illicit consideration, may claim what he has given, without being obliged to comply with what he has offered.

1307. Whenever a person, who is obliged by a declaration of nullity to return a thing, cannot return it because it has been lost, he shall return the fruits collected and the value which the thing had when lost, together with the interest from the same date.

1308. While one of the contracting parties does not return that which he is obliged to deliver by virtue of the declaration of nullity, the other cannot be compelled to comply with what is incumbent on him.

1309. The action of nullity becomes extinguished from the moment in which the validity of the contract has been confirmed.

1310. Only contracts which have all the requirments stated in art. 1261, can be confirmed.

1311. The confirmation can be made either expressly or tacitly. It shall be understood that there is a tacit confirmation, when being aware of the cause of the nullity and such cause having ceased to exist, the person, who has the right to invoke it, executes an act which necessarily implies his will to renounce such a right.

1312. Confirmation does not require the consent of the contracting parties who are not entitled to exercise the action of nullity.

1313. Confirmation cures the contract of all vices which affected it from the moment of its execution.

1314. The action for nullity of a contract shall also be extinguished when the thing, object of the contract, is lost by deceit or blame of the person entitled to enforce the action.

When the cause of the action is the incapacity of one of the contracting parties, the loss of the things shall be no obstacle for the action to prevail, unless it has occurred by deceit or blame on the part of the plaintiff, after having acquired capacity.

TITLE III.

CONTRACTS ABOUT PROPERTY ON ACCOUNT OF MARRIAGE.

CHAPTER FIRST.

GENERAL PROVISIONS.

Article 1315. Persons who are to be united in marriage may, before entering into it, execute contracts, stipulating the conditions for the conjugal society in reference to present and future property without any other limitations than those stated in this Code.

In default of contracts about property, it shall be understood that the marriage has been contracted under the system of legal conjugal community.

1316. In the contracts, to which the preceding article refers, the contracting parties shall not stipulate anything contrary to law or to good morals, nor humiliating to the authority belonging respectively to the future consorts within the family.

All stipulations not conformable to the provisions of this article shall be considered null and void.

1317. Shall also be considered as null and void and as not written in the contracts, mentioned in the two preceding articles, the clauses by which the contracting parties, in a general manner, stipulate that the property of the consorts shall be submitted to the local laws and customs of regions governed by such laws, and not by the general provisions of this Code.

1318. A minor, who can marry in accordance with law, may also execute his marriage contract, but it shall be valid only when in its execution there take part the persons designated by the same law for giving consent to the minor for the purpose of contracting marriage.

In case the marriage contract is null and void, because the concurrence and subscription of the aforesaid persons are wanting and yet the marriage is valid according to law, it shall be understood that the minor has contracted it, under the system of conjugal community.

1319. In order that any change in the marriage contract be valid, this change should be made before the celebration of the marriage and in the presence and with the concurrence of the persons who took part in the contract as executors. The attendance of the same witnesses shall not be necessary.

Any of the persons, whe attended the execution of the original contract, can only be substituted by another, or his attendance may not be required when, by cause of death or any other legal cause, at the time of the execution of the new stipulation or the modification of the preceding one, the attendance is impossible or might not be required according to law.

1320. After the marriage has been celebrated, the marriage contract, executed before the marriage, cannot be changed, whether present or future property is involved.

1321. Marriage contracts and modifications made in them shall be executed in a public instrument before the celebration of the marriage.

Property in the conditions referred to in art. 1324, is an exception to the preceding rule.

1322. Any modification made in the marriage contract shall be legally ineffectual in respect to third persons, if it does not comprise the following conditions:

1. That in the respective protocol and by marginal note, reference be made to the notarial act or instrument which contains the modification of the previous contract.

2. That in case the original contract is inscribable in the Registry of property, the document by which the former has been modified must also be inscribed.

The Notary shall set forth these modifications in the

authenticated copies of the stipulations or original contract which he may issue, under the penalty of indemnifying the parties for any damages and injuries, if he fails to do so.

1323. For the validity of the marriage contract, made by a person against whom a judgment of civil interdiction or incapacity has been rendered or against whom a suit for the same cause has been instituted, the attendance and consent of the guardian shall be indispensable and said guardian shall be appointed, to his end, by the persons who are entitled to do so according to the provisions of this Code, and of the Code of Civil Procedure.

1324. When the property brought by the consorts is not real, and that of the husband and wife together amount to a total sum not exceeding two thousand five hundred pesetas, and no Notary exists in the town of their residence, the marriage contract may be executed in the presence of the Secretary of the Municipal Board and two witnesses, who shall state, on their responsibility, that they know said property has been delivered or that it has been brought to the marriage, as the case may be.

The original contract or contracts shall be kept in custody, under registry, in the archives of the corresponding municipality.

When amongst the property brought to the marriage, whatever its value may be, there are one or more tenements, or the contracts refer to real property, they shall always be executed in a public instrument before a Notary, as provided in art. 1321.

1325. When the marriage is contracted in a foreign country, between a Spaniard and a foreign woman or between a foreigner and a Spanish woman, and the contracting parties do not state or stipulate anything about their property, it shall be understood, when the husband is a Spaniard, that he marries under the system of the legal conjugal community, and when the wife is a Spaniard that she marries under the system of laws which are in force in the husband's country, all without prejudice to what is established in this Code in respect to real property.

1326. All that is agreed to in the stipulations or contracts about which the preceding articles refer, in contemplation of a future marriage, shall be null and ineffectual in case the marriage is not celebrated.

CHAPTER SECOND.

DONATIONS ON ACCOUNT OF MARRIAGE.

Article 1327. Donations on account of marriage are those made, before its celebration, in consideration of the same, and in favor of one or of both intented consorts.

1328. These donations shall be governed by the rules established in title second, book third, in so far as they are not modified by the following articles.

1329. Persons under age may grant and receive donations in their antenuptual contracts, provided they are authorized by persons who must give their consent for contracting marriage.

1330. Acceptance is not required for the validity of such donations.

1331. Affianced persons may give each other in their marriage contract as much as the tenth part of their actual property, and, in regard to future property, they can give to each other, only in case of death, a portion within the limit set forth in the provisions of this Code which refer to succession by testament.

1332. The donor, on account of marriage, must liberate the property donated from mortgages and any other charges burdening them, except ground-rents and easements, unless in the marriage stipulations or contract the contrary has been specified.

1333. A donation made on account of marriage can only be revoked in the following cases:

.   1. When it is conditional and the condition is not fulfilled.

2. When the marriage does not take place.

3. When the persons marry without having obtained the consent according to the provisions of rule 2, art. 50, or when the marriage is annulled and there exists bad faith on the part of one of the consorts, in conformity with no. 3, art. 73 of this Code.

1334. All donations between consorts, made during the marriage, shall be null and void.

Moderate gifts which the consorts make to each other on days of rejoicing of the family are not included in this rule.

1335. All donations made during marriage by one of the consorts to the children, whom the other consort had by a former marriage, or to the persons of whom he or she is a presumptive heir, when the donation is made, shall be null and void.

CHAPTER THIRD.

DOWRY.

SECTION FIRST.

THE CONSTITUTION OF AND GUARANTEE FOR DOWRY.

Article 1336. Dowry is composed of the property and rights brought, as such, by the wife to the marriage, at the time of contracting it, and of those which she acquires during the marriage by donation, inheritance or legacy, as dotal property.

1337. Real property, acquired during the marriage, shall also be considered as dotal in the following cases:

1. When they are exchanged for other dotal property.
2. By right of redemption belonging to the wife.
3. By delivery in payment of the dowry.
4. By purchase with money pertaining to the dowry.

1338. The parents and relatives of the consorts and persons not belonging to the family may constitute the dowry in behalf of the wife, either before or after the celebration of the marriage.

The husband may also constitute it before the marriage but not after it.

1339. The dowry, constituted before, or at the time of the celebration of the marriage, shall be governed, in all that is not provided in this chapter, by the rules of donations made in contemplation of marriage.

Dowry constituted after the marriage shall be governed by the rules of common donations.

1340. The father or the mother or whichever one of them is alive is bound to give a dowry to his or her legitimate daughters, except in the cases in which they need their consent, according to law, to contract marriage and yet marry without obtaining said consent.

1341. The obligatory dowry, to which the preceding article refers, shall consist in a moiety of the presumptive rigorous *legitime*. When the daughter has property equivalent to the moiety of her *legitime*, this obligation shall cease, and if the value of the property does not cover the moiety of the *legitime*, the donor shall supply the balance required to complete it.

In any event, it is prohibited to make investigations about the fortune of the parents, in order to determine the amount of the dowry, and the courts, in an act of voluntary jurisdiction, shall regulate it without any further investigations than the statement of the same parents who are to give the dowry and of the two nearest relatives of the daughter, male and of full age, one of the paternal line and the other of the maternal, residing in the same place or within the judicial district.

In default of relatives of full age, the courts shall decide, in their prudent judgment, only by the statements of tho parents.

1342. The parents may comply with the obligation of giving dowries to their daughters, either by delivering to them the capital of the dowry, or by paying them an annual rent, as fruits or interest of the same.

1343. When the husband alone or both consorts jointly constitute a dowry for their daughters, it shall be paid out of the property of the conjugal community; if there is no property, said dowry shall be paid by halves or in the proportion in which the parents may have respectively bound themselves with the property belonging to each consort. When the wife alone grants the dowry, what she has given or promised should be charged to her own property.

1344. The dowry confessed by the husband, the delivery of which is not proven, or is shown only in a private document, shall produce no other effect than that of a personal obligation.

1345. Notwithstanding the provisions of the preceding

article, the wife in whose behalf a confessed dowry has been constituted by the husband before the celebration of the mariage, or within the first year of such marriage, may require, at any time, that the said husband secure it with a mortgage, provided she judicially proves the existence of the dotal property or of other similar or equivalent property, at the time she instituted her claims.

1346.   Dowry may be either estimated or not estimated.

It shall be estimated, if the property of which it consists was appraised, at the time of the constitution of the dowry, and when the ownership was transferred to the husband who became obliged to return its value.

It shall be not estimated, if the wife retains the ownership of the property, whether appraised or not, and the husband remains bound to return the same property.

When the marriage contract does not state the kind of dowry, it shall be considered as not estimated.

1347.   The increase or the impairment of the estimated dowry shall be on the account of the husband, who shall remain bound only to return the value at which he received it and to guarantee the rights of the wife, in the manner provided in the following articles.

1348.   When the husband who has received the estimated dowry believes himself injured by its appraisal, he may ask that the error or injury be remedied.

1349.   The husband is bound:

1.   To inscribe in his name and to mortgage in behalf of his wife the real property and real rights which he received as estimated dowry, or other sufficient ones to secure the value of the same.

2.   To secure with a sufficient special mortgage all other property which has been delivered to him as estimated dowry.

1350.   The sum which must be secured by reason of the estimated dowry shall not exceed the amount of the valuation, and if that of said dowry be reduced, the mortgage shall be reduced in the same proportion.

1351.   The mortgage, constituted by the husband in behalf of the wife, shall be security for the restitution of the property or of the valuation of the same, in case it should be effected according to the laws and with the limitations therein provided, and it shall become ineffectual and may be cancelled when, for any lawful cause, the husband may be exempted from the obligation of making the restitution.

1352. A married woman of full age may herself exact the constitution of the mortgage and the inscription of the property referred to in art. 1349.

When she has not yet celebrated the marriage, or if having contracted it, she is a minor, said right should be enforced in her name and the qualification of the sufficiency of the mortgage, which is constituted, shall be passed upon by the father, the mother, or the person who has given the dowry or the properties which must be secured.

In defaut of these persons, and when the woman is a minor, whether she be married or not, the guardian, the *protutor*, family council or any of its members, shall require that the same rights be enforced.

1353. When the guardian, *protutor* or the family council do not ask for the constitution of the mortgage, the Public Attorney shall officially, or upon the request of any other party, demand that the husband be compelled to execute the same.

The Municipal Judge shall also be obliged to interest and to urge the Public Attorney to comply with the provisions of the preceding paragraph.

1354. When the husband has no property of his own upon which to constitute the mortgage, stated in art. 1349, he shall remain bound to constitute the same on the first real estate or real rights which he may acquire.

1355. Whenever whole or a part of the property which constitutes the estimated dowry consists in government securities or stocks listed on the exchange *(efectos públicos ó valores cotizables)*, and as long as the value is not secured by the mortgage which the husband is bound to constitute, the titles, inscriptions or documents representing that value, shall be deposited, in the name of the wife and with the knowledge of the husband, in any of the public institutions designated for that purpose.

1356. When the husband is bound so secure, with a mortgage, personal property belonging to not estimated dowry, the provisions of arts. 1349 to 1355, with regard to estimated dowries, shall apply.

SECTION SECOND.

ADMINISTRATION AND USUFRUCT OF THE DOWRY.

Article 1357. The husband is the administrator and usufructuary of the properties which constitute the not estimated dowry with the rights and obligations annexed to the administration and the usufruct, but with the modifications set forth in the following articles.

1358. The husband is not bound to give the bonds required from common usufructuaries, but is obliged to inscribe in the Registry, when they are not registered, in the name of the wife and as not estimated dowry, all the real property and real rights which he may receive as such, and to constitute a sufficient mortgage as security for his administration, usufruct, and restitution of the personal property.

1359. Notwithstanding the provisions of the two preceding articles, the husband who receives bonds, stocks, or values listed on the exchange, or perishable property, as estimated or not estimated dowry, and has not secured them with a mortgage, may, nevertheless, substitute them with others, equivalent to the same, with the consent of the wife, if she is of age or of the persons referred to in art. 1352, if she is a minor.

Said property may also be alienated by the husband with the consent of the wife, and, when proper, with that of the aforesaid persons, under the condition that the amount of its value shall be invested in other property, bonds or rights equally safe.

1360. The wife preserves her dominion over the property which constitutes the not estimated dowry, and, consequently, to her belongs also any increase or decrease the same may have.

The husband is only liable for the impairment which such property may suffer by his fault or neglect.

1361. The wife may alienate, incumber or mortgage the property of the not estimated dowry, when she is of full age, with the license of the husband, and, when she is a minor, with judicial license and with the intervention of the persons stated in art. 1352.

When she alienates said property, the husband shall be bound to constitute a mortgage, in the same manner and under the same conditions as in respect to the property of the estimated dowry.

1362. The property of the not estimated dowry shall be security for the usual daily expenses of the family, incurred by the wife or by her order, under the tacit assent of the husband, but in this case levy *(excusion)* shall first be made on the properties belonging to the conjugal society, and then on that belonging to the husband.

1363. The husband shall not, without the consent of the wife, lease for longer than six years the real property of the not estimated dowry.

In any case, the advancment of the rents or leases, made to the husband for more tham three years, shall be considered void.

1364. When the consorts, by virtue of the provisions of art. 1315, have stipulated that the legal conjugal community shall not exist between them, without stating the rules by which their property is to be governed, or if the wife or her heirs renounce said community, the provisions of this chapter shall be observed and the husband in compliance with the obligations stated in the same chapter, shall receive all the fruits which should be considered as earnings of the community, in case it should exist.

SECTION THIRD.

RESTITUTION OF DOWRY.

Article 1365. Dowry shall be restored to the wife or to her heirs in the following cases:—

1. When the marriage is dissolved or declared null.
2. When the administration of the dowry is transferred to

the wife in the case provided by the second paragraph of art. 225.

3.   When the courts order it, in accordance with the provisions of this Code.

1366.   The restitution of the estimated dowry shall be effected by the husband or his heirs delivering to the wife or her heirs the value at which it was estimated when the husband received the same.

From the value shall be deducted:

1.   The dowry constituted in favor of the daughters, in so far as it can be imputed to the sole property of the wife, in accordance with art. 1343.

2.   The debts contracted by the wife before the marriage and which the husband may have paid.

1367.   The real property of the not estimated dowry shall be restored in the condition in which it may be found; and when it has been alienated, the proceeds of the sale shall be delivered, deducting what may have been applied to the payment of the exclusive obligations of the wife.

1368.   The payments of the expenses and the improvements, made by the husband in the not estimated dotal property, shall be governed by what is provided with regard to the possessor in good faith.

1369.   After the marriage is dissolved or has been declared null, the husband or his heirs may be compelled to the inmediate restitution of the real and personal property of the not estimated dowry.

1370.   Until one year, to be counted from the dissolution of the marriage, has elapsed, neither the husband nor his heirs can be required to return the money, the perishable property and public effects which do not exist totally or in part upon the dissolution of the conjugal society.

1371.   The husband or his heirs shall pay to the wife or to her heirs, from the date of the dissolution of the marriage until the restitution of the dowry, the legal interest on what they are bound to return in money, also that on the amount of the perishable property and what may be produced by public values or credits, in the meantime, according to their condition or nature, without conflict with the provision of art. 1379.

1372. In default of an agreement between the person s interested, or of an express stipulation in the marriage contract, the credit of not estimated dowry or the part of the same which is not restored in the same property which had constituted the dowry or in those which substituted the same, shall be restored and paid in money.

From this rule is excepted the restitution of the value of personal dotal property which does not exist, and said value may be paid with other personal property of the same kind, if there is any such remaining to the conjugal society.

The restitution of the perishable property, not appraised, shall be made with an equal amount of property of the same kind.

1373. In the same manner, as designated in the pre—ceding article, shall be restored the part of the dotal credit consisting:

1. Of marriage donations, legally made by the husband to his wife to be effectual after his death, excepting the provisions in respect to the consort who has acted in bad faith; in the case of the nullity of the marriage, and in that of art. 1440.

2. Of indemnities which the husband may owe to the wife in accordance with this Code.

1374. The daily bed, with whatever constitutes it, and the clothing and dresses for ordinary use of the widow shall be delivered to her without charging them to her dowry.

1375. The credits or rights brought to the marriage as not estimated dowry, or assigned with this character, shall be delivered in the condition in which they are, at the time of the dissolution of the marriage, unless throngh negligence of the husband, said credits have not been collected or have become unrecoverable, in which cases, the wife and her heirs shall have the right of exacting their value.

1376. When two or more dowries are to be restored, at the same time, each of them shall be paid with the property which may exist and originally belonged to them respectively, and, in default of the same, if the estate inventoried is not sufficient to cover both of them, their payment shall be effected according to priority of time.

1377. For the liquidation and restitution of the not estimated dowry, the following items shall be deducted in case they have been paid by the husband:

1. The amount of the judicial costs and expenses incurred for the collection and defence of the dowry.

2. The debts and obligations inherent to or affected by the dowry, which in accordance with the marriage contract or with the provisions of this Code are not chargeable to the conjugal community.

3. The sums for which the wife may be peculiarly liable, in accordance with the provisions of this Code.

1378. At the time of the restitution of the dowry, the marriage donations legally made to the husband by his wife shall be paid to him without conflict with the provisions of this Code for the cases of separation of property, or that of nullity of the marriage in which bad faith has existed on the part of one of the consorts.

1379. When the marriage is dissolved by the death of the wife, the interests or fruits of the dowry which are to be restored shall commence to run in favor of the heirs from the day of the dissolution of the marriage.

When the marriage is dissolved by the death of the husband, the wife may, either demand the interests and fruits of one year of the dowry, or that support be given her from the estate of the inheritance of the husband. In any case, the widow shall receive from the estate the value of the mourning apparel.

1380. After the dissolution of the marriage, the pending fruits or rents shall be divided pro rata among the surviving consort and the theirs of the deceased, in accordance with the rules established for the cases in which the usufruct ceases.

CHAPTER FOURTH.

PARAPHERNA.

Article 1381. Parapherna is the property which the wife brings to the marriage, not included in the dowry, and what she acquires after the constitution of the same and which is not added to such dowry.

1382. The wife retains dominion over the parapherna.

1383. The husband shall not institute actions of any kind, whatever, in regard to the parapherna, without the intervention of the wife or her consent.

1384. The wife shall have the management of the parapherna, unless she has delivered the same to her husband, before a Notary, with the intent that he may administer said property.

In this case, the husband is bound to constitute a mortgage for the value of the personal property which he receives, or to secure said property, in the manner provided for dotal property.

1385. The fruits of the parapherna form a part of the capital of the conjugal community, and are liable for the payment of the expenses of the marriage state.

The property itself also shall be liable, in the case of article 1362, whenever that of the husband and the dotals are insufficient to pay the liabilities set forth in the same.

1386. The personal obligations of the husband shall not be paid out of the fruits of the parapherna, unless it is proven that they were incurred for the benefit of the family.

1387. The wife shall not alienate, incumber or mortgage the parapherna without the permission of the husband, nor appear in court to litigate about the same, unless she has been judicially authorized for that purpose.

1388. When the parapherna, the administration of which has been reserved by the wife, consists in money or public stocks or valuable personal property, the husband shall have a right to require that said property be deposited or invested in such a way that the alienation or pignoration of the same should be impossible without his consent.

1389. The husband, to whom the parapherna has been delivered, shall be governed, with regard to the management of the same, by the provisions in respect to the property of the not estimated dowry.

1390. The alienation of the parapherna entitles the wife to demand the constitution of a mortgage for the amount of the value which the husband may have received. Both the husband and the wife may, in their respective cases, exercise, with regard to the value of the sale, the right granted by arts., 1384 and 1388.

1391. The return of the parapherna, the management of which has been granted to the husband, shall take place in the same cases and in the same manner as that of property belonging to the not estimated dowry.

CHAPTER FIFTH.
CONJUGAL COMMUNITY.

SECTION FIRST.
GENERAL PROVISIONS.

Article 1392. By virtue of the conjugal community, the earnings or profits indiscriminately obtained by either of the consorts, during the marriage, shall belong to the husband and the wife, share and share alike, when the marriage is dissolved.

1393. The conjugal community shall always begin on the same day that the marriage is celebrated.

Any stipulation to the contrary shall be void.

1394. This community cannot be renounced during the marriage, except in case of judicial separation.

When the renunciation takes place on account of a separation, or after the marriage has been dissolved or declared null, said renunciation shall be set forth in a public instrument, and the creditors shall have the right granted them in art. 1001.

1395. The conjungal community shall be governed by the rules of the contract of partnership in all that does not conflict with the express provisions of this chapter.

SECTION SECOND.
PROPERTY BELONGING TO EACH ONE OF THE CONSORTS.

Article 1396. The following is the separate property of each of the consorts:

1. That brought to the marriage as his or her own.

2. That acquired under a lucrative title by either of them, during the marriage.

3.   That acquired by right of redemption or by exchange for other property belonging to only one of the consorts.

4.   That bought with money belonging exclusively to the wife or to the husband.

1397.   A person giving or promising capital to the husband shall not be subject to eviction, except in case of fraud.

1398.   Property, donated or left by will conjointly to the consorts and with designation of specified shares, shall belong as dowry to the wife and as capital to the husband, in the proportion directed by the donor or testator; and, in default of such designation, share and share alike, without conflict with provisions of art. 637.

1399.   When donations are onerous, the amount of the burdens shall be deducted from the dowry, or from the capital of the consort who makes them, provided they have been borne by the conjugal community.

1400.   In case that any credit, payable within a certain number of years, or a pension for life belongs to either of the consorts, the provisions of art. 1402 and 1403 shall be observed for determining what constitutes the dowry, and what forms the capital of the husband.

SECTION THIRD.

PROPERTY OF THE CONJUGAL COMMUNITY.

Article **1401.**   To the conjugal community belong:

1.   Property acquired by onerous title, during the marriage, at the expense of the community property, whether the acquisition is made for the community or for only one of the consorts.

2.   That obtained by the industry, salaries or work of the consorts or of either of them.

3.   The fruits, rents, or interests collected or accrued during the marriage, and which come from the community property, or from that which belongs to either one of the consorts.

1402.   Whenever a sum or credit, payable in a certain

number of years, belongs to one of the consorts, the sums collected for installments due during the marriage shall not be community property, but shall be considered as capital of the husband or of the wife, according to whom the credit belongs.

1403. The right to an usufruct or pension, belonging to one of the consorts, either in perpetuity or for life, shall form part of his or her own property; but the fruits, pensions, and interests due, during the marriage, shall be community property.

In this provision is comprised the usufruct which the consorts have in the property of their children, even when they are of another marriage.

1404. The useful expenses, made on behalf of the private property of either one of the consorts, through advancements made by the community, or by the industry of husband or wife, are community property.

Buildings constructed, during the marriage, on land belonging to one of the consorts, shall also belong to the community, but the value of the land shall be paid to the consort owning the same.

1405. Whenever the dowry or the capital belonging to the husband consists, in whole or in part, of cattle existing at the time of the dissolution of the community, the heads of cattle, exceeding the number which were brought to the marriage, shall be considered as common property.

1406. The earnings obtained by the husband or wife by gambling or proceeding from other causes, exempted from restitution, shall belong to the conjugal community, without conflicting, in certain cases, with the provisions of the Penal Code.

1407. All the property of the marriage shall be considered as community property, until it is proven that it belongs exclusively to the husband or to the wife.

SECTION FOURTH.

CHARGES AND OBLIGATIONS OF THE CONJUGAL COMMUNITY.

Article 1408. The conjugal community shall be responsible for:

1. All the debts and obligations contracted during the

marriage by the husband, and also those contracted by the wife in the cases in which she can legally bind the community.

2.   The arrears or interests, matured during the marriage, of obligations which affect the private property of the consorts as well as the community property.

3.   The minor repairs or of mere preservation, made during the marriage, on the private property of the husband or the wife.   Extensive repairs shall not be chargeable to the community.

4.   Extensive or minor repairs of the property of the community.

5.   The maintenance of the family and the education of the children in common, and of the legitimate children of only one of the consorts.

1409.   The conjugal community shall also bear the amount of what has been donated or promised to the children in common by the husband, only for their establishment or for a professional career, or by both consorts by common consent, when it may not have been stipulated that it should be paid in whole or in part out of the private property of one of them.

1410.   The payment of debts contracted by the husband or by the wife, before the marriage, shall not be borne by the community.

Neither shall it bear the payment of fines or pecuniary condemnations imposed on either of them.

However, the payment of debts contracted by the husband or the wife, prior to the marriage. and that of fines and condemnations imposed on either of them may be claimed against the community property, after covering the erogations, enumerated in art. 1408, when the debtor consort has no private capital, or it be insufficient; but at the time of the liquidation of the community, the payments, made for the specified causes, shall be charged to said consort.

1411.   What has been lost and paid for, during the marriage, by either of the consorts, in any kind of game whatever, shall not diminish his or her respective share in the community.

Whatever has been lost and not paid for by either of the

consorts, in licit games, shall be charged to the conjugal community.

SECTION FIFTH.

ADMINISTRATION OF THE CONJUGAL COMMUNITY.

Article **1412**. The husband is the administrator of the conjugal community, with the exception of what is prescribed in art. 59.

1413. Besides the faculties which the husband has as administrator, he may alienate and burden by onerous title the property of the conjugal community without the consent of the wife.

Notwithstanding, every alienation or agreement which the husband may make, respecting said property in opposition to this Code or in fraud of the wife, shall not cause injury to her or to her heirs.

1414. The husband can dispose of his half of the property of the conjugal community only by testament.

1415. The husband may dispose of the property of the conjugal community for the purposes stated in art. 1409.

· He may also make moderate donations for objects of piety or beneficence, but without reserving to himself the usufruct.

1416. The wife cannot bind the property of the conjugal community without the consent of the husband.

The cases provided in arts. 1362, 1441, and 1442 are excepted from this rule.

SECTION SIXTH.

DISSOLUTION OF THE CONJUGAL COMMUNITY.

Article **1417**. The conjugal community expires on the dissolution of the marriage or when it is declared null.

The consort who, on account of his or her bad faith, caused the nullity, shall not share any part of the property of the community.

The conjugal society shall also terminate in the cases specified in art. 1433.

SECTION SEVENTH.

LIQUIDATION OF THE PROPERTY OF THE CONJUGAL COMMUNITY.

Article 1418. Upon the dissolution of the community, an inventory shall immediately be made, but the same shall not be required for the liquidation:

1. When, after the community is dissolved, one of the consorts or the persons holding rights under him have, in due time, renounced its effects and consequences.

2. When the separation of property has preceded the dissolution of the community.

3. In the case to which paragraph second of the preceding article refers.

In case of renunciation, the rights granted to the creditors by art. 1101 shall always continue in force.

1419. The inventory shall comprise numerically *(numéricamente)* for the purpose of collating them, the sums, which having been paid by the conjugal society, are to be deducted from the dowry or from the capital of the husband, in accordance with arts. 1366, 1377, and 1427.

The amount of the donations and alienations which may be considered illegal or fraudulent, as provided in art. 1413, shall also be brought to collation.

1420. In the inventory shall not be included things constituting the bed and bedding *(lecho)* ordinarily used by the consorts. These things, as well as the clothing and dresses ordinarily used by the deceased consort, shall be delivered to the surviving one.

1421. When the inventory is completed, the dowry of the wife shall first be liquidated and paid, according to the rules, which for its restitution are determined in section third, chapter third of this title, and subject to the provisions of the following articles.

1422. After the dowry and the parapherna of the wife have been paid, the debts, charges, and obligations of the community shall be paid.

When the inventoried estate is not sufficient to satisfy all the provisions of this and the preceding article, the prescriptions of title seventeen of this book shall be observed.

1423. After the debts, charges, and obligations of the community are paid, the capital of the husband shall be liquidated and paid, in so far as the inventoried estate may reach, making the corresponding deductions according to the same rules which are prescribed in art. 1366, in reference to dowry.

1424. After the deductions from the inventoried estate, specified in the three preceding articles, have been made, the remainder of the same estate shall constitute the assests of the conjugal community.

1425. The losses or impairments which any personal property, belonging to either of the consorts, may have suffered even by unforseen events, shall be paid out of the conjugal property, when any remains.

Those suffered by the real property shall not be payable, in any case, except those falling upon the dotal property, and which have been caused by the fault of the husband, when an indemnity shall be paid for them as provided in arts. 1360 and 1373.

1426. The net remainder of the community property shall be divided, share and share alike, between the husband and the wife or their respective heirs.

1427. The mourning apparel of the widow shall be paid out of the estate of the inheritance of the husband, as provided in art. 1379. The heirs of the husband shall pay it according to the standing and means of the decedent.

1428. In regard to making the inventory, rules for the appraisal and sales of the property belonging to the conjugal community, security and bonds for the respective dowries, and all other particulars, not expressly determined in the present chapter, the prescriptions of sections fifth, chapter fifth, title third, book third, and sections second and third, chapter third of this title shall be observed.

1429. When the conjugal community is dissolved by the nullity of the marriage, the provisions of arts. 1373, 1378, 1417 and 1440 shall be observed, and if it is dissolved by reason of the separation of the property of the consorts, what is prescribed in chapter sixth of this title shall be complied with.

1430. Support shall be given out of the property belonging to the community to the surviving consort and his or her children, pending the liquidation of the inventoried estate and until they have received their share; but it shall be deducted from their portion in so far as it exceeds what should have belonged to them as fruits or rents.

1431. Whenever the liquidation of the community properties of two or more marriages, contracted by the same person, has to be simultaneously effected in order to determine the estate of each community, every kind of evidence shall be admitted, in default of inventories; and, in case of doubt, the community property shall be distributed between the different communities in proportion to the time of the duration of the same and to the property belonging to the respective consorts.

CHAPTER SIXTH.

SEPARATION OF THE PROPERTY
OF THE CONSORTS AND ITS ADMINISTRATION BY THE WIFE
DURING THE MARRIAGE.

Article 1432. In default of express declarations in the marriage contract, the separation of the property of the consorts, during the marriage, shall only take place by virtue of a judicial decree, except in the case provided by art. 50.

1433. The husband and the wife may demand the separation of the property, and it shall be decreed, whenever the consort of the plaintiff has been condemned to a penalty to which civil interdiction is annexed, or has been declared an absentee or has given cause for the divorce.

In order that the separation may be decreed, it shall be sufficient to present the final sentence rendered against the culpable or absent consort in each one of the three cases, above stated.

1434. After the separation of property is ordered, the legal conjugal community becomes dissolved, and its liquidation shall be made according to the provisions of this Code.

Husband and wife, however, shall reciprocally attend to their maintenance during the separation, and to the maintenance of the children, as well as the education of the same; each one in proportion to his or her respective means.

1435. The power to administer the property of the marriage, granted to the husband by this Code, shall subsist when the separation has been granted on his petition; but, in such case, the wife shall not have any right to the future profits of the community, and the rights and obligations of the husband shall be governed by the provisions of sections second and third, chapter third of this title.

1436. When the separation has been granted on the petition of the wife by the civil interdiction of the husband, the administration of all the property belonging to the marriage, and the rights to all the future community property, shall be transferred to the wife to the exclusion of the husband.

When the separation is granted because the husband has been declared an absentee, or because he has given cause for divorce, the wife shall enter upon the administration of her dowry, and of all further property which may have been apportioned to her, as a result of the liquidation.

In every case, to which this article refers, the wife shall remain obliged to comply with all that is prescribed in paragraph second of art. 1434.

1437. The demand for separation and the final sentence in which it is declared, when rendered about real property, must be noted and inscribed respectively in the corresponding Registries of property.

1438. Separation of the property shall not injure the rights previously acquired by creditors.

1439. Whenever the separation ceases by reconciliation, in cases of divorce, or, because, in the other cases the causes have disappeared, the property belonging to the marriage shall be governed by the same rules as before the separation, without injury to what may have been lawfully done during the same.

The consorts, at the time of their reuniting, shall specify in a public instrument the property which they bring anew, and such property shall be that forming the private estate of each one of them respectively.

In the case provided in this article, all said property shall always be considered as new property brought to the marriage, even when it is the same, either partially or wholly, as existed before the liquidation made on account of the separation.

1440. Separation shall not entitle the consorts to exercise the rights provided under the presumption of death of one of them, nor those granted to them by art. 1374 and 1420, neither shall it injure them in the exercise of the same, when such case occurs, except as provided in art. 73.

1441. The administration of the property belonging to the marriage shall be transferred to the wife:

1. Whenever she is the guardian of the husband in accordance with art. 220.

2. When ske asks for the declaration of absence of her husband, in acordance with arts. 183 and 185.

3. In the case stated in paragraph first of art. 1436.

The courts shall also confer the administration upon the wife, with such limitations as they may consider convenient, when the husband is a fugitive or has been declared contumacious in a criminal prosecution, or if, when he is absolutely incapacitated for the administration, he has taken no steps in respect thereto.

1442. The wife, upon whom the administration of all the property of the marriage may devolve, shall have, in respect thereto, the identical powers and liabilities as the husband when he exercises it, buy always subject to what is provided in the last paragraph of the preceding article, and in art. 1444.

1443. The administration of her dowry shall be trans—ferred to the wife, in the case provided by art. 225, and when the court orders it by virtue of the provisions of art. 441; but she shall remain subject to what is prescribed in paragraph second of art. 1434.

GENERAL PROVISION.

Article **1444.** During the marriage, the wife can neither alienate nor encumber, without judicial permission , the real property which may have been allotted to her, in case of separation, nor that, the administration of which , has been

Such permission shall be granted whenever the convenience or necessity of the alienation be justified.

When it refers to public bonds or stocks of mercantile enterprises, and companies and cannot be delayed without serious or imminent injury to the estate in administration, the wife, with the intervention of an agent or broker, may sell them placing the proceeds in judicial deposit, until the approval of a competent judge or tribunal is obtained.

The agent or broker shall always be personally responsible for the making of the consignation or deposit to which the preceding paragraph refers.

TITLE IV.
CONTRACT OF PURCHASE AND SALE.

CHAPTER FIRST.
NATURE AND FORM OF THIS CONTRACT.

Article **1445.** By the contract of purchase and sale, one of the contracting parties binds himself to deliver a specified thing and the other (binds himself) to pay a certain price for it, either in money or in something *(signo)* representing the same.

1446. When the price of the sale consists partly in money and partly in something else, the contract shall be qualified by the manifest intention of the contracting parties. When this intention does not appear, the contract shall be considered as a barter, if the value of the thing given as a part of the price exceeds that of the money or its equivelant; and, otherwise, it shall be considered as a sale.

1447. In order that the price may be held as certain, it shall be sufficient that it be certain with reference to another thing also certain, or that the determination of the same be left to the will of a specified person.

When such person cannot or will not fix the price, the contract shall be inoperative.

1448. The price of bonds, grain, liquids, and of other perishable things shall also be held as certain, when the prices fixed are the same as the things, if sold, would have on a certain day on the exchange or market, or when a certain amount is fixed above or below the price of such day, exchange or market, provided said price be certain.

1449. The determination of the price shall never be left to the judgment of one of the contracting parties.

1450. The sale shall be perfected between vendor and vendee and shall be binding on both of them, if they have agreed upon the thing, object of the contract, and as to the price, even when neither one nor the other has been delivered.

1451. A promise to sell or to buy, when there has been an agreement about the thing and the price, gives a right to both the parties reciprocally to claim the compliance with the contract.

Whenever a promise of purchase and sale cannot be complied with, the provisions about obligations and contracts, set forth in this present book, shall govern the vendor and the vendee, according to the case.

1452. The injury to or the profit of the thing sold shall, after the contract is perfected, be governed by the provisions of arts. 1096 and 1182.

This rule shall be applied to the sale of perishable things, made independently and for a single price, or without consideration as to weight, number, or measure.

If the perishable things are sold for a price fixed with relation to weight, number, or measure, the risk shall not be imputed to the vendee, until they have been weighed, counted, or measured, unless the vendee is in default.

1453. A sale, made subject to approval or trial of the things sold, and the sales of things which are customarily tested or tried before being received, shall always be considered as made under suspensive conditions.

1454. When earnest or binding money has beeen given in the contract of purchase and sale, the contract may be rescinded, when the vendee agrees to forfeit the money, or the vendor to return double the amount of it.

1455. The expenses of the execution of a public deed shall be on account of the vendor, and those of the first copy and subsequent omes, after the sale, shall be charged to the vendee, unless the contrary is stipulated.

1456. Forcible expropriation on account of public utility shall be governed by the provisions of special laws.

CHAPTER SECOND.
CAPACITY TO PURCHASE OR SELL.

Article **1457.** The contract of purchase and sale may be entered into by all persons who, according to this Code, are authorized to bind themselves, with the modifications, however, contained in the following articles.

1458. The husband and the wife cannot reciprocally sell any property to each other, except in the cases in which they have stipulated about the separation of their property or when a judicial separation of the same property exists, authorized, under the provisions of chapter sixth, title third, of this book.

1459. The following persons cannot acquire by purchase, even at public or judicial auction, neither in person nor by an intermediate representative:

1. The guardian or *protutor* as to the property of the person or persons who are under their guardianship.

2. The attorneys as to the property of which they have been given charge to administer or sell.

3. Executors as to the property entrusted to their care.

4. Public officials as to the property of the State, municipalities, towns, and also of public institutions, the administration of which has been entrusted to them.

This provision shall apply to judges and experts who, in any way whatever, intervene in the sale.

5. Magistrates, judges, Public Attorney, and, their assistants, clerks of tribunals and courts, and officials of justice as to the property and rights about which litigation is pending before the tribunal in the jurisdiction or territory over which they exercise their respective functions; this prohibition includes the act of acquiring by assignment.

From this rule shall be excepted the cases in which hereditary action among co-heirs are dealt with, or of assignments in payment of debts, or of warranty of the goods they may possess.

The prohibition contained in this number shall comprise the lawyers and attorneys as to the property and rights, matters of the suit, in which they intervene by virtue of their profession or office.

CHAPTER THIRD.

EFFECTS OF THE CONTRACT OF PURCHASE AND SALE WHEN THE THING SOLD HAS BEEN LOST.

Article **1460.** When, at the time of making the sale, the thing, object of the contract, has been wholly lost, the contract shall be ineffectual.

But if the thing is lost only in part, the vendee shall choose either to withdraw from the contract or to claim the existing part, paying its price, in proportion to the total sum agreed upon.

CHAPTER FOURTH.

OBLIGATIONS OF THE VENDOR.

SECTION FIRST.

GENERAL PROVISION.

Article **1461.** A vendor is bound to deliver and warrant the thing, object of the sale.

SECTION SECOND.

DELIVERY OF THE THING SOLD.

Article **1462.** A thing sold shall be considered as delivered, when it is placed in the hands and possession of the vendee.

When the sale is effected by a public instrument, the execution of the same shall be equivalent to the delivery of the thing, object of the contract, provided that in the same instrument the contrary does not appear or may be clearly inferred.

1463. Except in the cases stated in the preceding article, the delivery of personal property shall be made by the delivery of the keys of the place or depository where it is stored or kept, and by the mere consent and agreement of the contracting parties, if the thing sold cannot be transferred to the possession of the vendee, at the time of the sale, or if the latter already held it in his possession for any other cause.

1464. With regard to incorporeal things, the provision of paragraph second of art. 1462 shall govern. In any other case in which this paragraph cannot be applied, the fact of placing the titles of ownership in the possession of the vendee or the use which the vendee may make of his right with the consent of the vendor shall be considered as a delivery.

1465. The expenses of the delivery of the thing sold shall be borne by the vendor, and those of the removal or transportation of the same by the vendee, except in case of special stipulation.

1466. A vendor shall not be bound to deliver the thing sold, when the vendee has not paid the price, or when a term for such payment has not been designated in the contract.

1467. Neither shall the vendor be bound to deliver the thing sold, when a delay or time for payment has been agreed upon, and it is discovered after the sale that the vendee is insolvent to such a degree that the vendor is in imminent danger of losing the price.

From this rule is excepted the case in which the vendee gives security for the payment within the time agreed upon.

1468. A vendor is bound to deliver the thing sold in the condition in which it existed on the completion of the contract.

All the fruits shall belong to the vendee from the day on which the contract was perfected.

1469. The obligation to deliver the thing sold includes that of placing in possession of the vendee all that is set forth in the contract, according to the following rules:

When the sale of real property has been made and its dimensions stated at the rate of a certain price for an unit of measure or number, the vendor shall be bound to deliver to the vendee, if the latter requires it, all that has been mentioned in the contract; but when this is not possible, the vendee may choose between proportional reduction of the price or the rescission of the contract, provided that, in this last case, the decrease of the tenement, is not inferior to the tenth part of the dimensions attributed to it.

The same thing shall be observed, even when the dimensions appear to be the same, if any part of the tenement is not of the quality stated in the contract.

The rescission, in this case, shall only take place, at the will of the vendee, when the inferior value of the thing sold exceeds the tenth part of the price agreed upon.

1470. When, in the case of the preceding article, there are greater dimensions or number in real property, than those stated in the contract, the vendee shall be bound to pay the price of the excess, if the greater dimensions or number does not exeed the one twentieth part of those set forth in the contract; but when it surpasses such one twentieth part, the vendee may choose between paying the greater value of the estate or withdrawing from the contract.

1471. In the sale of a parcel of real estate made for a fixed price and not at the rate of a specified sum for an unity of measure or number, the increase or decrease of the same shall not be considered, even when greater or less dimensions or amount than that stated in the contract may be found.

The same provision shall apply when two or more tenements are sold for a single price, but, if besides mentioning the boundaries, indispensable in every conveyance of real property, their dimensions and number are designated in the contract, the vendor shall be bound to deliver all that is included within such boundaries, even when they exeed the dimensions or number specified in the contract; and, if he is not able to do it, he shall suffer a reduction in the price, in proportion to what is wanting in the dimensions or number, unless the contract be annulled because the vendee does not accept the default of delivery of what had been stipulated.

1472. Actions, arising from the three preceding articles, shall be prescribed after six months, counted from the day of the delivery.

1473. When the same thing has been sold to different vendees, the ownership shall be transferred to the person who firts took possession of it in good faith, if the thing is personal.

When the thing is a piece of real property, it shall belong to the person acquiring it who first inscribed it in the Registry.

When there is no inscription, the property shall belong to the person who first took possession of it in good faith, and, in default of said possession, to the person who presents the oldest title, provided there is good faith.

SECTION THIRD.

WARRANTY.

Article **1474.** By virtue of the warranty to which art. 1461 refers, the vendor shall warrant to the vendee:

1. The lawful and peaceful possession of the thing sold.
2. That there are no hidden vices or defects in said thing.

§ 1º

WARRANTY IN CASE OF EVICTION.

Article **1475.** Eviction shall take place, when by a final sentence and by virtud of a right prior to the sale, the vendee is deprived of the whole or of a part of the thing purchased.

The vendor shall be liable for the eviction even when nothing hes been stipulated about it in the contract.

The contracting parties may, however, increase, decrease, or suppress this legal obligation of the vendor.

1476. Any stipulation exempting the vendor from the obligation of answering for the eviction shall be void, whenever there is bad faith on his part.

1477. When a vendee has renounced the right of warranty in the case of eviction and it occurs, the vendor shall only be bound to deliver the price which the thing had, at the time of the eviction, unless the vendee has made the renunciation, knowing the risk of eviction and submitting himself to the consequences thereof.

1478. When a warranty has been stipulated or when nothing has been agreed upon about this point, if the eviction has been effected, the vendee shall have the right to claim from the vendor:—

1. The restitution of the price which the thing sold had at

the time of the eviction, whether it be greater or less than that of the sale.

2. The fruits or proceeds, when he has been condemned to deliver them to the person who won the suit instituted against such vendee.

3. The costs incurred in the suits which caused the eviction, and, in proper cases, the costs of the suit instituted against the vendor for the warranty.

4. The expenses of the contract, when the vendee has paid them.

5. The damages and interests and the voluntary expenses or of mere recreation or ornamentation, when the sale was made in bad faith.

1479. When the vendee loses, on account of the eviction, a part of the thing sold of such importance, in relation to the whole, that he would not have purchased it without such part, he may claim the rescission of the contract; but under the obligation of returning the thing without other incumbrances than those it had when he acquired it.

The same provision shall be observed when two or more things are conjointly sold for a total price, or a partial price for each one of them, when it clearly appears that the vendee would not have purchased one without the other.

1480. A warranty cannot be claimed until a final sentence has been rendered by which the vendee is condemned to lose the thing acquired or a part of it.

1481. A vendor shall be bound to the corresponding warranty, whenever it is proved that he was given notice of the demand for eviction on petition of the vendee. In default of this notice, the vendor shall not be bound to the warranty.

1482. A defendant vendee shall ask, within the term fixed by the Code of Civil Procedure for answering the demand, that notice thereof be given to the vendor or vendors with the least possible delay.

This notification shall be made in the maner provided by the same law for the summoning of defendants.

The term for answering the complaint granted to the vendee shall be suspended until the expiration of that granted to. the vendor or vendors for appearing and answering the complaint; said terms shall be the same granted to all defendants by the aforesaid law of Civil Procedure, and shall be counted from the notificacion provided by the first paragraph of this article.

When the persons summoned for eviction do not appear, in time and form, the term in which to answer the complaint shall continue with regard to the vendee.

1483. When the tenement sold is encumbered by any non-apparent burden or easement which is not stated in the deed, but is of such a nature that it must be presumed that the vendee would not have acquired it if he was aware of the same, he may ask for the rescission of the contract, unless he prefers the corresponding indemnity.

During a year, to be counted from the date of the execution of the deed, the vendee may either exercise the rescissory action or claim an indemnity,

After the lapse of one year, he can only claim such indemnity within an equal period, te be counted from the date on which the lien or easement was discovered by him.

§ 2º

WARRANTY AGAINST HIDDEN DEFECTS OR BURDENS OF THE THING SOLD.

Article 1484. A vendor is bound to give a warranty against hidden defects in the thing sold, when these defects render it unfit for the use for which it was intended, or when they diminish said use in such a way that had the vendee known them, he would not have acquired it, or would have given a lower price for it; but said vendor shall not be liable for the patent defects or those which may be visible, neither for those which are not in sight, when the vendee is an expert and by reason of his office or profession ought easily to perceive them.

1485. The vendor is responsible to the vendee for the warranty against vices or hidden defects in the thing sold, even when the same were unknown to him.

This provision shall not rule when the contrary has been

stipulated and the vendor was not aware of such vices or hidden defects.

1486. In the cases of the two preceding articles, the vendee may elect, either to withdraw from the contract, the expenses which he incurred being returned to him, or to demand a proportional reduction of the price, according to the judgment of experts.

When the vendor knew the vices or hidden defects in the thing sold, and did not give notice of them to the vendee, the latter shall have the same option, and, furthermore, he shall be indemnified for the damages and injuries, should he choose the rescission.

1487. When the thing sold is lost on account of hidden vices, and the vendor was aware of them, he shall bear the loss, and return the price and pay the expenses of the contract, with damages and injuries. When he was not aware of them, he shall only return the price and pay the expenses of the contract, which may have been paid by the vendee.

1488. When the thing sold has any hidden vice, at the time of the sale, and is lost afterwards by an unforeseen event, or by fault of the vendee, the latter may claim from the vendor the price he paid, deducting the value which the thing had when lost.

When the vendor acted in bad faith, he shall pay damages and interests to the vende.

1489. The liability for damages and injuries shall never take place in judicial sales, but all the other provisions of the preceding articles shall be applied.

1490. Actions growing out of the provisions of the five preceding articles shall be extinguished after six months, to be counted from the delivery of the thing sold.

1491. When two or more animals are sold together, whether it be for a lump sum or by fixing a separate price for each one of them, the redhibitory vice of each one shall only cause the redhibition of the same and not that of the others, unless it appears that the vendee would not have bought the sound one or ones without defective ones.

The latter is presumed when a team, yoke, pair or set is

bought, even when a separate price has been fixed for each one of the animals composing the same.

1492. The provision of the preceding article, with regard to the sale of animals, shall be understood applicable also to the sale of any other things.

1493. Warranty for the hidden vices of animals and cattle shall not take place in the sales made at fairs or public auctions, nor that of riding beasts, sold as condemned, except in the case determined in the following article.

1494. Animals and cattle ·suffering from contagious diseases shall not be objects of a contract of sale. Any contracts made with respect to the same shall be null and void.

A contract of sale of animals and cattle shall also be null and void, when the use or service for which they were acquired is stated, and they are found useless therefor.

1495. When the hidden vice of animals, even if they have been subject to a professional inspection, is of such a nature that the knowledge of experts is not sufficient to discover it, it shall be considered as redhibitory.

But when the veterinarian *(professor)*, through ignorance or bad faith, shall fail to discover or to give notice of it, he shall be liable for damages and injuries.

1496. The redhibitory action, based on the vices or defects of animals, shall be instituted within forty days, to be counted from the delivery of the same to the vendee, unless owing to the usages in each locality, longer or shorter terms are established.

This action, in the sale of animals, shall only be enforced in reference to the vices and defects of the same, determined by law or by local usages.

1497. When the animal dies, within three days after it has been bought, the vendor shall be responsible, provided that the disease that caused the death, according to the judgment of veterinarians *(professors)*, existed before the contract.

1498. When the sale is rescinded, the animal shall be returned in the condition in which it was sold and delivered, and the vendee shall be liable for any injury caused by his negligence and which does not arise from the redhibitory vice or defect.

1499. In the sale of animals and cattle with redhibitory vices, the vendee shall also have the power set forth in art. 1486; but he shall make use of the same within the same term which has been respectively determined for the exercise of the redhibitory action.

CHAPTER FIFTH.

OBLIGATIONS OF THE VENDEE.

Article **1500.** A vendee is bound to pay the price of the thing sold at the time and place stipulated in the contract.

When the time and place have not been fixed, the payment shall be made at the time and place where the thing sold is delivered.

1501. In the three following cases the vendee shall owe interest from the time the thing is delivered, until the payment of the price:

1. When it has been so stipulated.

2. When the thing sold and delivered produces fruits and rents.

3. When he is in default in accordance with art. 1100.

1502. When the vendee is disturbed in the possession or dominion of the thing acquired, or may have reasonable grounds to fear being disturbed by a revindicatory or hypothecary action, he may suspend the payment of the price until the vendor has caused the disturbance or danger to cease, unless the latter gives security for the restitution of the price, if needs be, or when it has been stipulated that, notwithstanding such contingency, the vendee shall be bound to make the payment.

1503. When the vendor has reasonable grounds to fear the loss of the real property sold and the price of the same, he may immediately ask for the resolution of the sale.

When such reasonable grounds do not exist, the provisions of art. 1124 shall be observed.

1504. In the sale of real property, even when it is stipulated that in default of the payment of the price, within the time agred upon, the resolution of the contract shall take place by full right, the vendee may pay, even after the expiration of the term, as long as he has not been summoned either judicially or by a notarial act.

After such summons have been made the Judge shall not grant him a further term.

1505. With regard to personal property, the resolution of the sale shall take place by full right for the benefit of the vendor when the vendee, before the naturity of the term fixed for the delivery of the thing, has not presented himself, to receive it, or when having presented himself, he has not offered the price, at the same time, unless a longer term has been stipulated for the payment of said price.

CHAPTER SIXTH.
RESOLUTION OF THE SALE.

Article 1506. The sale shall be resolved by the same causes as all other obligations, and furthermore those set forth in the preceding chapters and by conventional or legal redemption *(retracto)*.

SECTION FIRST.
CONVENTIONAL REDEMPTION *(Retracto Convencional)*.

Article 1507. Conventional redemption shall exist when the vendor reserves to himself the right to recover the thing sold, binding himself to fulfill that which is stated in art. 1518, and whatever more may have been stipulated.

1508. The right stated in the preceding article, in default of an express stipulation, shall last four years to be counted from the date of the contract.

When a stipulation exists, the term shall not exceed ten years.

1509. When the vendor does not comply with the provisions of art. 1518, the vendee shall irrevocably acquire the ownership of the thing sold.

1510. A vendor may exercise his action against every possessor whose right originates from that of the vendee, even when in the second contract mention has not been made of the conventional redemption; without conflict with the provisions of the Law of Mortgage in respect to third parties.

1511. A vendee substitutes the vendor in all his rights and actions.

1512. The creditors of the vendor shall only be able to make use of the conventional redemption against the vendee, after having levied upon the property of the vendor.

1513. A vendee who has a stipulation for redemption of a part of an undivided estate and who acquires the whole estate, in the case of art. 404, may oblige the vendor to redeem the whole estate, if said vendor pretends to make use of the redemption.

1514. When several persons, conjointly and in one and the same contract, sell an undivided estate under condition of redemption, neither of them shall exercise this right for more than his respective share.

The same rule shall be observed, when the person alone who has sold an estate has left several heirs in which case each one of them may only redeem the part which he may have acquired.

1515. In the cases of the preceding article, the vendee may require all the vendors and co-heirs to agree about the redemption of the whole of the thing sold; and when they do not do so, the vendee shall not be bound to the partial redemption.

1516. Each one of the owners in common of an undivided estate, who has separately sold his share, may independently exercise the right of redemption for his respective share and the vendee can not oblige him to redeem the whole of the estate.

1517. When the vendee leaves several heirs, the action of redemption cannot be exercised against each of them, except for his respective share, whether it be undivided, or whether it has been distributed among them.

But when the inheritance has been divided, and the thing sold has been adjudicated to one of the heirs, the action of redemption may be exercised against him for the whole.

1518. A vendor cannot exercise the right of redemption without returning to the vendee the price of the sale, and furthermore:

I. The expenses of the contract and any other legitimate payments made on account of the sale.

2. The useful and necessary expenses incurred by the thing sold.

1519. When on the execution of the sale, there are on the tenement visible and grown fruits, no indemnity or payment pro rata shall be made for those existing at the time of the redemption.

When there were no fruits, at the time of the sale, but some exist at the time of the redemption, they shall be divided pro rata, between the redemptor and the vendee, giving to the latter the share corresponding to the time he possessed the estate during the last year, counted from the date of the sale.

1520. A vendor, who recovers the thing sold, shall receive it free of all burdens and mortgages, imposed by the vendee, but he shall remain bound to respect the contracts of lease, executed by the latter in good faith and according to the usage of the place, where it is located.

SECTION SECOND.
LEGAL REDEMPTION *(Retracto Legal)*.

Article 1521. Legal redemption is the right to be subrogated, under the same conditions, stipulated in the contract, in the place of the person who acquires a thing by purchase or in payment of a debt.

1522. An owner in common of a thing held in common may exercise the redemption when the shares of all the other owners in common or of any of them are sold to a third party.

When two or more owners in common wish to exercise the right of redemption, they shall only do so pro rata as to the shares they have in the thing held in common.

1523. Proprietors of adjacent lands shall also have the right of redemption, when the rural tenement is sold, the extent of which does not exceed one hectare.

The right, to which the preceding paragraph refers, shall not apply to adjacent lands which are divided by brooks, drains, ravines, roads and other apparent easements for the benefit of other tenements.

When two or more adjacent owners make use of the redemption, at the same time, the one who is owner of the adjacent land of lesser area shall be preferred; and if both are equal in area, the person who first asked for it.

1524. The right of legal redemption cannot be exercised except within nine days to be counted from the inscription in the Registry, and, in default of it, from the time the redemptor has been informed of the same.

The redemption of an owner in common excludes that of adjacent owners.

1525. In legal redemptions, the provisions of articles 1511 and 1518 shall be observed.

CHAPTER SEVENTH.
ASSIGNMENTS OF CREDITS AND OTHER INCORPOREAL RIGHTS.

Article 1526. The assignment of a credit, right or action, shall produce no effect against a third party but from the time when the date is considered certain, in accordance with articles 1218 and 1227.

When said assignment refers to real property, from the date of its inscription in the Registry.

1527. A debtor, who before having been informed of the assignment pays the creditor, shall be free from the obligation.

1528. The sale or assignment of a credit includes that of all the accessory rights, as the security, mortgage, pledge or privilege.

1529. A vendor in good faith shall be responsible for the existence and legitimacy of the credit, at the time of the sale, unless said credit has been sold as doubtful, but said vendor is not responsible for the solvency of the debtor, unless it has been expressly stipulated, or when the insolvency is prior and public.

Even in these cases, he shall only be liable for the price received and for the expenses stated in no. 1 of art. 1518.

The vendor in bad faith shall always be liable for the payment of all the expenses and for the damages and injuries.

1530. When the assignor in good faith has made himself responsible for the solvency of the debtor, and the contracting parties have not stipulated any thing about the duration of such responsibility, it shall only last one year, to be counted from the assignment of the credit, if the term had already matured.

When the credit is payable within a term or period not yet expired, the responsibility shall cease one year after its maturity.

When the credit consists of a perpetual rent, the responsibility shall be extinguished after ten years, to be counted from the date of the assignment.

1531. A person who sells an inheritance, without enumerating the things of which it is composed, shall only be obliged to prove that he is an heir.

1532. A person who sells for a total or lump sum certain rights, rents, or products, as a whole, shall comply by answering for the ligitimacy of the whole in general, but he shall not be bound to warrant each of the parts of which it is composed, unless in the case of eviction of the whole or of the greater part.

1533. When the vendor has profited by some of the fruits, or has received anything from the inheritance which he sells, he must pay the vendee therefor, if the contrary has not been stipulated.

1534. The vendee shall, on his part, pay to the vendor all that the latter has paid for debts or charges on the estate and for the credits which he may have against the same, unless the contrary has been stipulated.

1535. When the litigious credit is sold, the debtor shall have the right to extinguish the same by reimbursing the assignee for the price the latter paid for it, the judicial expenses incurred by him, and the interest on the price, from the day on which the same was paid.

A credit shall be held as litigious from the day on which the demand, relating to the same, has been answered.

The debtor may make use of his right within nine days, counted from the day the assignee claimed the payment from him.

1536. From the provisions of the preceding article are excepted the assigments or sales made:

1. To a co-heir or co-owner of the right assigned.

2.   To a creditor in payment of his credit.

3.   To the possessor of a tenement, subject to the litigious right which has been assigned.

CHAPTER EIGHT.
GENERAL PROVISION.

Article 1537.   All that is prescribed in this title is understood subject to the provisions of the Law of Mortgage in regard to real property.

TITLE V.
BARTER OR EXCHANGE.

Article 1538.   Barter or exchange is a contract by which each of the contracting parties binds himself to give a thing in order to receive another.

1539.   When one of the contracting parties has received the thing promised to him in exchange, and he proves that it did not belong to the person who gave it, he shall not be bound to deliver the one which he offered in exchange, and he shall comply with his duty by returning the one that he received. ·

1540.   A person, who loses by eviction the thing received in exchange, may choose between recovering the one which he gave in exchange or claiming an indemnity for damages and injuries; but he shall only be able to enforce the right of recovering the thing which he delivered in so far as said thing remains in the hands of the other party, and without damage to any rights acquired to such thing, in good faith in the mean time, by a third party.

1541.   Exchange shall be governed by the provisions relating to purchase and sale in all that is not specially determined in this title.

TITLE VI.
CONTRACT OF LEASE.

CHAPTER FIRST.
GENERAL PROVISIONS.

Article 1542.   Leases may be made in respect to things, woks *(obras)*, or services.

1543. In a lease of things, one of the parties thereto binds himself to give to the other the enjoyment or use of a thing for a specified time and at a determined price.

1544. In a lease for works or services, one of the parties binds himself to execute a work or to render a service to the other for a determined price.

1545. Perishable things, which are consumed by use, can not be a matter of this contract.

CHAPTER SECOND.
LEASES OF RURAL AND CITY TENEMENTS.

SECTION FIRST.
GENERAL PROVISIONS.

Article **1546.** A person who binds himself to grant the use of a thing, execute a work, or render a service is called the lessor; and the person, who acquires the use of a thing or a right to the work or service, for which he binds himself to pay, is the lessee.

1547. When the performance of a contract of verbal lease has begun and the evidence of the price is wanting, the lessee shall return to the lessor the thing leased, paying him such price as may be adjudged for the time he has enjoyed such thing.

1548. The husband cannot give, in lease, the property of the wife, the father and guardian, that of the son or minor, and the administrator of property, that for which he has not a special power, for a term exceeding six years.

1549. In regard to third parties, leases of real property, which are not duly recorded in the Registry of property, shall not be effectual.

1550. When it is not expressly forbidden in the contract of lease of things, the lessee may sub-let the whole or a part of the things leased, without lessening his responsibility for the fulfillment of the contract entered into with the lessor.

1551. A sub-lessee, notwithstanding his obligation with regard to the sub-lessor, shall remain bound to the lessor for all the acts which refer to the use and preservation of the thing leased, in the manner agreed upon between the lessor and the lessee.

1552. The sub-lessee shall also remain bound with respect to the lessor for the amount of the price agreed upon in the contract of sub-lease, which said sub-lessee owes, at the time of the summons, considering the payments made in advance as not made, unless he has paid them according to usage.

1553. The provisions respecting warranty, contained under the title of purchase and sale, shall apply to the contract of lease.

In the cases in which restitution of the price is required, a deduction of the price should be made proportional to the time for which the lessee has enjoyed the thing.

SECTION SECOND.

RIGHTS AND OBLIGATIONS OF THE LESSOR AND LESSEE.

Article 1554. The lessor is bound:

1. To deliver to the lessee the thing which is the object of the contract.

2. To make thereon, during the lease, all the necessary repairs with a view of preserving it in condition to serve for the purpose for which it was intended.

3. To maintain the lessee in the peaceful enjoyment of the lease during all the time of the contract.

1555. The lessee is bound:

1. To pay the price of the lease in the terms stipulated.

2. To use the thing leased as a diligent father of a family would do, applying the same to the use agreed upon: and, in default of a stipulation, to the use which may be inferred from the nature of the thing leased according to the custom of the land.

3. To pay the expenses incurred for the deed of contract.

1556. When the lessor or lessee does not comply with the obligations, set forth in the preceding articles, they may ask for the rescission of the contract and the indemnity for damages and injuries, or only for the latter, leaving the contract in force.

1557. The lessor shall not change the form of the thing leased.

1558. When, during the lease, it becomes necessary to make any urgent repairs in the thing leased, which cannot be delayed until the expiration, thereof, the lessee shall be obliged to suffer the execution of the work, even when it is very annoying to him, and even when, during such repairs, he may be deprived of a part of the tenement.

When the repairs last more than forty days, the price of the lease shall be reduced in proportion to the time and the part of the tenement of which the lessee is deprived.

When the work is of such a nature that the part which the lessee and his familly require for a dwelling becomes inhabitable, the lessee may rescind the contract.

1559. The lessee is bound to give notice to the owner; with the least possible delay, of any usurpation or injurious alterations (*novedad*) which any other person may have done or openly is preparing to do to the thing leased.

He is also bound to give notice with the same promptness to the owner of the necessity of all repairs, stated in no. 2, of art. 1554.

In both cases the lessee shall be liable for the damages and injuries, which through his negligence, may be caused to the lessor.

1560. The lessor shall not be obliged to answer for the mere fact of a trespass (*perturbacion de mero hecho*), made by a third party in the use of the tenement leased, but the lessee shall have a direct action against the trespasser.

The fact of trespass does not exist, when the third person, whether it be the administration or a private party, has acted by virtue of a right belonging to the same.

1561. The lessee shall return the tenement at the expiration of the lease, in the same condition in which he received it, exept what may have been destroyed or impaired by time or by inevitable causes.

1562. When, at the time of the lease of the tenement, the condition of the same was not stated, the law presumes that the lessee received it in good condition, unless there be proof to the contrary.

1563. The lessee is liable for the impairment or loss of the thing leased, unless he proves that the same was caused without his fault.

1564. A lessee is liable for the impairment caused by the members of his household.

1565. When the lease has been entered into for a specified time, it shall expire on the day previously fixed without the necessity of any notice.

1566. When, at the expiration of the contract, the lessee continues enjoying the thing leased for fifteen days (longer) with the acquiescence of the lessor, it shall be understood that there is a tacit new lease for the time set forth in arts. 1577 and 1581, unless a notice has previously been given.

1567. In the case of a tacit renewal, the obligations contracted by a third party for the security of the principal contract shall cease in regard thereto.

1568. When the thing leased is lost, or any of the contracting parties do not comply with what has been stipulated, the provisions of arts. 1182, 1183, 1101, and 1124 shall be respectively observed.

1569. The lessor may judicially eject the lessee for any of the following causes:

1. Upon the expiration of the conventional term or the one fixed for the duration of leases by arts. 1577 and 1581.

2. Default in payment of the rent agreed upon.

3. Breach of any of the conditions stipulated in the contract.

4. When the lessee employs the thing leased in uses or services not stipulated and which cause the same to be impaired, or when he does not comply, in respect to its use, with what is prescribed in no. 2 of art. 1555.

1570. Besides the cases mentioned in the preceding article, the lessee shall have the right to avail himself of the terms fixed in arts. 1577 and 1581.

1571. The purchaser of a leased tenement has the right to determine the lease in force at the time of the consumation of the sale, unless there is a stipulation to the contrary, and the provisions of the Law of Mortgage are considered.

When the purchaser exercises this right, the lessee may

require to be allowed to gather the fruits of the crop corresponding to the current agricultural year and to be indemnified by the vendor for the damages and injuries which he may have suffered.

1572. A purchaser with a stipulation of redemption cannot use the power of ejecting the lessee, until the term for the use of the right of redemption has expired.

1573. A lessee shall have, in respect to the useful and voluntary improvements, the same rights granted to the usufructuary.

1574. When no stipulation exists about the place and time of the payment of rent, the provision of art. 1171 shall govern as to place, and the custom of the land in respect to time.

SECTION THIRD.

SPECIAL PROVISIONS FOR LEASES OF RURAL PROPERTY.

Article 1575. A lessee shall not have the right to a reduction of the rent on account of the sterility of the land leased or on account of the loss of the fruits, through usual unforeseen events, but he shall have said right in case of loss of more than half of the fruits through extraordinary unforeseen events, unless there are special stipulations to the contrary.

By extraordinary unforeseen events shall be understood fire, war, pestilence, extraordinary inundations, locusts, earthquakes or any other equally unfrequent events, and which the contracting parties could not have reasonably foreseen.

1576. A lessee shall neither have the right to a reduction of the rent, when the fruits have been lost, after having been separated from their roots or trunks.

1577. The lease of a rural tenement, when its duration has not been fixed, shall be understood as executed for all the time which is necessary for the gathering of the fruits which the whole tenement leased might produce in one year, or all it could produce, at one time, even when two or more years may be required for obtaining such fruits.

That of arable lands, divided into two or more terms (*ho-jas*), shall be considered as executed for as many years as there are terms.

1578.   The outgoing lessee shall permit the incoming one the use of the place and of all other necessary means for the preparatory labor for the following year, and, reciprocally, the latter is bound to permit the outgoing one all that may be necessary for the gathering and enjoyment of the fruits, all according to the custom of the place.

1579.   Leases for partnerships of arable lands, breeding cattle, and for industrial or manufacturing establishments, shall be governed by the provisions, relating to the contract of partnership and by the stipulations of the contracting parties, and, in default of the same, by the customs of the land.

SECTION FOURTH.
SPECIAL PROVISIONS FOR THE LEASE OF URBAN TENEMENTS.

Article 1580.   In default of a special stipulation for the repairs of urban tenements, which should be borne by the owner, the customs of the place shall rule.   In case of doubt, said repairs shall be understood as chargeable to the owner.

1581.   When a term has not been fixed for the lease; it is understood for years, when an annual rent has been fixed, for months, when the rent is monthly, and for days, when it is daily.

In every case, the lease ceases without the necessity of a special notice upon the expiration of the term.

1582.   When the lessor of a house, or of a part of the same, intended as a dwelling for a family, or for a store or storehouse or industrial establishment, leases also the furniture, the lease of the latter shall be understood as executed for a time equal to that of the house leased.

CHAPTER THIRD.
LEASES OF WORKS AND SERVICES.

SECTION FIRST.
SERVICES OF HIRED SERVANTS AND LABORERS.

Article 1583.   This class of services may be contracted, either without a time being specified, for a fixed time, or for a specified work.   A lease made for the whole life is null.

1584.   A domestic servant, hired for a fixed time and to be employed in the personal service of his master or of the family of the latter, may leave the service or be dismissed before the expiration of the term; but when the master dismisses such servant, without a just cause, he shall indemnify him by paying him the salary due and that for fifteen additional days.

The master's (statement) shall be believed, unless there is proof to the contrary:

1.   About the amount of the salary of the domestic servant.

2.   About the payment of the salaries earned during the current year.

1585.   Besides what is prescribed in the preceding articles, with regard to masters and servants, what is determined in the special laws and ordinances shall be observed.

1586.   Field-hands, mechanics, artisans, and other hired laborers, for a certain time and for a certain work, shall not leave nor be dismissed, without just cause, before the fulfillment of the contract.

1587.   The dismissal of servants, mechanics, artisans and other hired laborers, to which the preceding articles refer, gives the right to dispossess them of the working tools and of the buildings which they occupy by reason of their duties.

SECTION SECOND.
WORKS AT A PRICE AGREED UPON OR FOR A LUMP SUM.

Article **1588**.   The execution of a work may be contracted by agreeing that the person, who is to execute the same, shall employ only his labor or industry, or that he shall furnish the materials in addition.

1589.   When the person, who contracted for the work, bound himself to furnish the materials, he shall bear the loss, in case of the destruction of the work before it is delivered, unless, delay has been incurred in receiving the work.

1590.   A person, who has bound himself to provide only his labor or industry, shall not claim any payment, when the work is destroyed before it is delivered , unless delay has been incurred in receiving the same, or when the destruction has been due to the bad quality of the materials, provided that he may have given due notice of this circumstance to the owner.

1591. The contractor of a building, which has been destroyed on account of vices of construction, shall be liable for any damages and injuries, when said building falls down within ten years, to be counted from the completion of the construction; and, during the same time, the same liability shall be incurred by the architect, who directed the work, when the ruin is on account of vices of the ground or of his directions.

When the cause is the non-compliance of the contractor with the conditions of the contract, the action for indemnity can be enforced within fifteen years.

1592. A persons who binds himself to do a work, by piece or by measure, may require from the owner to receive it by parts and to pay for it in proportion. The part paid for shall be presumed approved and received.

1593. An architect or contractor, who for a lump sum, takes charge of the construction of a building, or of any other work by inspection of plans agreed upon, with the owner of the ground, cannot ask for an increase in the price, even when that of the materials or wages have increased, but be may do so when any change which increases the work is made in the plans, provided the owner has given his authorization.

1594. The owner may desist, by his own will, from the construction of the work, even when it has been begun, indemnifying the contractor for all the expenses, labor, and profits which he may have obtained from the same.

1595. When a certain work has been entrusted to a person by reason of his personal qualities, the contract shall be rescinded upon the death of said person.

In this case, the owner shall pay to the heirs of the constructor, in proportion to the price agreed upon, the value of the part of the work which has been executed, and for the prepared materials, provided he may obtain any benefit from such materials.

The same provisions shall apply, when the person who contracted the work cannot finish it on account of any cause independent of his will.

1596. A contractor is responsible for the labor done by the persons he employs on the work.

1597. Those, who furnish their labor and materials in a work agreed upon for a lump sum by a contractor, shall have no action against the owner, except for the sum which the latter may owe to the former when the claim is made.

1598. When it is agreed that the work is to be made to the satisfaction of the owner, in default of his acceptance, such approval shall be understood as reserved for the proper judgment of experts.

When the person who has to approve the work is a third party, his decision shall govern.

1599. When there is no stipulation or custom to the contrary, the price for the work shall be paid upon delivery.

1600. A person, who has performed a work on personal things, has the right to retain the same as a pledge until he is paid therefor.

SECTION THIRD.

TRANSPORTATION BY WATER AND LAND, EITHER OF PERSONS OR OF THINGS.

Article 1601. Carriers of goods by land or by water shall be subjected, as to the keeping and preservation of the things entrusted to them, to the same obligations as prescribed for inn-keepers by arts. 1783 and 1784.

The provision of this article shall be understood without prejudice to what is prescribed by the Code of Commerce, with regard to transportation by sea and land.

1602. Carriers are also responsible for the losses and damages of the things which they receive, unless they prove that the loss or damage has happened on account of an unforeseen event or by main force (*fuerza mayor*).

1603. The provisions of the foregoing articles are understood without conflict with what is prescribed by special laws and regulations.

TITLE VII.
RENTS OF LAND OR GROUND-RENTS *(CENSOS)*.

CHAPTER FIRST.
GENERAL PROVISIONS.

Article **1604.** A ground-rent *(censo)* is constituted when any real property is subjected to the payment of a pension or annual rent in compensation, either for a capital which is received in cash, or for the full or partial ownership of the property which is conveyed.

1605. A ground-rent is called emphyteusis *(enfitéutico)* when a person transfers to another the useful ownership of a tenement, reserving to himself the direct ownership and a right to receive from the *emphyteuta* an annual pension in recognition of such dominion.

1606. A ground-rent is consignative *(consignativo)* when the owner of land imposes upon a tenement belonging to him the burden of a rent or pension which he binds himself to pay to the lender for a sum in cash which he has received from the latter.

1607. A ground-rent is reservative *(reservativo)* when a person transfers to another the complete ownership of a tenement, reserving to himself the right to receive from said tenement an annual pension which is to be paid by the holder of the land.

1608. The nature of a ground-rent requires that the transfer of the capital or of the tenement should be perpetual or for an unlimited time; however, the *censatario* (1) may redeem the ground-rent, at his will, though the contrary is stipulated, and this provision is applicable to ground-rents actually existing.

It may, however, be stipulated, that the redemption of the ground-rent can not be made during the life of the *censualista* (2) or of a specified person, or that it may not be redeemed within a certain number of years, which cannot exceed twenty years,

---

(1) *Censatario,* the person who pays the ground-rent.

(2) *Censualista,* the person to whom the ground-rent is owed.

in consignative ground-rents, nor sixty years in reservative ground-rents and in emphyteusis.

1609. To carry into effect such redemption, the *censatario* must give notice thereof one year in advance to the *censualista*, or must pay to him, in advance, the amount of one year's pension.

1610. Ground-rents cannot be partially redeemed, unless by virtue of an express stipulation.

Neither can they be redeemed against the will of the *censualista*, unless the payment of all the pensions due have been made.

1611. For the redemption of all ground-rents, constituted before the promulgation of this Code, when the capital is unknown, it shall be regulated by the principal which may result, by computing the pension on the basis of three per centum.

When the pension is payable in fruits, for the determination of the capital, they shall be appraised, at the average price which such fruits may have had during the last five years.

The provisions of this title shall not apply to local ground-rents (*foros* and *sub foros*), rights of surface, or any other similar burdens, in which the principles of redemption of dominion shall be regulated by a special law.

1612. The expenses, caused for the redemption and liberation of ground-rents, shall be borne by the *censatario*, except those caused by temerarious opposition which are subject to the discretion of the courts.

1613. The pension or rent of ground-rents shall be agreed to by the parties upon the execution of the contract.

It may consist in money or of fruits.

1614. The pensions shall be paid at the times agreed upon, and, in default of a contract, if they consist in money, by the years, as due, to be counted from the date of the contract; and, if in fruits, at the end of the respective crops.

1615. When the place, at which the pensions are to be paid, has not been designated in the contract, this obligation shall be complied with at the place in which the tenements, encumbered with the ground-rent, are located, provided the *censualista* or his attorney have their domicil in the Municipal district of the same town. When such person has not his domicil in said town, but the *censatario* resides there, the payment shall be made at the domicil of the latter.

1616. The *censualista*, at the time of the delivery of the receipt of any pension, can oblige the *censatario* to give him a written notice in which it may appear that the payment has been made.

1617. Tenements, encumbered with ground–rents, may be conveyed by virtue of an onerous or lucrative title, and the same can be done with the right to receive the pensions.

1618. Tenements, encumbered with ground–rents, shall not be divided among two or more persons without the express consent of the *censualista*, even when acquired by a title of inheritance.

When the *censualista* consents to the division, the part of the ground-rent, with which each portion remains encumbered, shall be designated with his consent, and as many different ground-rents shall be constituted as there are]portions in which the tenement is divided.

1619. When the tenement encumbered with a ground-rent is to be adjudged to several heirs, and the *censualista* does not give his consent to the division, it shall be placed at auction among said heirs.

In default of agreement or when none of the parties in interest offers the price of the appraisement, the tenement shall be sold with the encumbrances and the proceeds shall be distributed among the heirs.

1620. The principal as well as the pension of ground-rents may be prescribed, in accordance with the provisions of title 18 of this book.

1621. Notwithstnading the provisions of art. 1110, the payment of two consecutive pensions shall be necessary to presume that all the preceding ones have been paid.

1622. The *censatario* shall be bound to pay the taxes and all other imposts which effect the tenement burdened with the ground-rent.

At the time the *censatario* pays the pension, he may deduct from the same the part of the imposts which pertains to the *censualista*.

1623. Ground-rents give cause for a real action against the tenement encumbered. Besides the real action, the *censualista* may enforce a personal action for the payment of the pensions in arrears, and when proper for damages and interests.

1624. A *censatario* shall not ask for the remission or reduction of the pension on account of an accidental sterility of the tenement nor on account of the loss of its fruits.

1625. When a tenement encumbered with a ground-rent is totally destroyed or rendered useless by main force or by an unforeseen event, the ground-rent shall be extinguished and the payment of the pension shall also cease.

When it is partially destroyed, the *censatario* shall not be exempt from the payment of the pension, unless he prefers to abandon the tenement to the *censualista*.

When there is fault on the part of the *censatario*, he shall be bound, in both cases, to an indemnity for damages and injuries.

1626. In the case of the first paragraph of the preceding article, when the tenement is insured, the amount of the insurance shall be subject to the payment of the principal of the ground-rent and of the pensions due, unless the *censatario* prefers to invest it in rebuilding the tenement, in which case the ground-rent shall survive with all its effects, including the payment of the unpaid pensions. The *censualista* may exact from the *censatario* that he secure the investment of the amount of the insurance in the rebuilding of the tenement.

1627. When a tenement, encumbered with a ground-rent, is expropriated on account of public utility, the price of the same shall remain liable for the payment of the principal of the ground-rent and of the pensions due, and said ground-rent shall be extinguished.

The preceding provision is also applicable in the case in which the forced expropriation is only of a part of the tenement when its price is sufficient to cover the principal of the ground-rent.

When this price is not sufficient, the ground-rent shall continue to encumber the remainder of the tenement, provided its price be sufficient to cover the principal of the ground-rent and an additional twenty five per centum over and above it.

In any other case the *censatario* shall be bound, either to substitute the part expropriated with another security, or to redeem the ground-rent, at his option, without prejudice to what is provided in art. 1631, in respect to emphyteusis.

CHAPTER SECOND.
EMPHYTEUSIS *(CENSO ENFITÉUTICO)*.

SECTION FIRST.
PROVISIONS REFERRING TO EMPHYTEUSIS.

Article **1628**.   Emphyteusis can only be constituted on real property and by a public deed.

1629.   At the time of the constitution of the emphyteusis, the value of the tenement and the annual pension to be paid shall be fixed in the contract, under the penalty of nullity.

1630.   When the pension consists of a fixed amount of fruits, the kind and quality of the same shall be stated in the contract.

When it consists in an aliquot part of what the tenement may produce, in default of an express stipulation, as to the intervention which the direct owner may exercise, the *emphyteuta* shall give to said owner or his representative previous notice of the day on which he intends to commence the gathering of each kind of fruit, in order that he may be able, either personally or by his representative, to inspect all the operations, until he receives the share belonging to him.

After the notice is given, the *emphyteuta* may gather the crops, even when neither the direct owner nor his representative or intervenor is present.

1631.   In case of forcible expropriation, the provisions of the first paragraph of art. 1627 shall be applied when the whole tenement is expropriated.

When it is expropriated only in part, the price of what has been expropriated shall be distributed between the direct owner and the *emphyteuta*, the former receiving the part of the principal of the ground-rent, which proportionally belongs to the expropriated part, according to the value given to the whole tenement when the ground-rent was constituted, or to that which has served as a basis for the redemption, and the remainder shall belong to the *emphyteuta*.

In this case the ground-rent shall continue on the rest of the tenement, with the proper reduction of the principal and the pension, unless the *emphyteuta* elects between the total redemption or the abandonment in behalf of the direct owner.

When, in accordance with what has been stipulated, *laudemium* is to be paid, the direct owner shall receive that, which for this reason belongs to him, only from the part of the price belonging to the *emphyteuta*.

1632. To the *emphyteuta* belongs the products of the tenement and of its accessions.

He has the same rights which the owner would have in the treasures and mines which may be discovered on the tenement held in emphyteusis.

1633. The *emphyteuta* may dispose of the tenement held in emphyteusis and of its accessions, by acts *inter vivos*, as well as by last will, leaving intact the rights of the direct owner, and subject to the provisions of the following articles.

1634. When the pension consists of an aliquot part of the fruits of the tenement held in emphyteusis, neither an easement nor any other burden which may diminish the proceeds of the same, shall be imposed upon it, without the express consent of the direct owner.

1635. The *emphyteuta* may freely donate or exchange the tenement, giving notice of it to the direct owner.

1636. To the direct owner and to the *emphyteuta* reciprocally belong the right of pre-emption and of redemption, whenever they sell or give in payment their respective ownerships of the tenement held in emphyteusis.

These provisions shall not apply to forcible sales for causes of public utility.

1637. For the effects of the preceding article, the persons who intend to alienate the ownership of a tenement, held in emphyteusis, shall give notice of it to the other owner stating the final price which is offered to him or the one for which he intends to alienate his ownership.

Within twenty days after the notice is given, the other owner may make use of the right of pre-emption by paying the price indicated. When he does not do this, he shall lose such right and the alienation may be carried into effect.

1638. When the direct owner or the *emphyteuta*, in certain cases, has not made use of the right of pre-emption, to which the preceding article refers, he may make use of that of redemption to acquire the tenement for the price at which it has been sold.

In this case, the redemption shall be made use of within nine working days next following the execution of the deed of sale. If this sale is concealed, said term shall be counted from the inscription of the same in the Registry of property.

Concealment is presumed when the deed is not filed in the Registry within the nine days next following its execution.

Besides this presumption, the concealment may be proven by any other lawful means.

1639. When the alienation has been affected without the previous notice, which art. 1637 prescribes, the direct owner, and, in certain cases, the *emphyteuta* may exercise the action of redemption, at any time, until the lapse of a year to be counted from the day the alienation is inscribed in the Registry of property.

1640. In judicial sales of tenements held in emphyteusis, the direct owner and the *emphyteuta*, in their respective cases, may make use of the right of pre-emption, within the term fixed in the notices of the sale at auction, paying the price which served as a basis for the auction, and that of the redemption within the nine working days next following that of the execution of the deed.

In this case, the previous notice, required by art. 1637, shall not be necessary.

1641. When there are several tenements alienated, subject to the same ground-rent, the right of pre-emption or that of redemption cannot be exercised with regard to some of them and to the exclusion of others.

1642. When the direct or useful ownership undividedly belongs to several persons, each one of them may make use of the right of redemption subject to the rules set forth for that of owners in common and preference shall be given to the direct owner, if a part of the useful ownership has been alienated; or to the *emphyteuta*, when the alienation has been of the direct ownership.

1643. When the *emphyteuta* is disturbed in his right by a third party who disputes the direct ownership or the validity of the emphyteusis, he shall not have the right to claim the corresponding indemnity from the direct owner, if he does not summon him for the eviction, in accordance with the provisions of art. 1481.

1644. In alienations under an onerous title of tenements held in emphyteusis, *laudemium* shall be paid to the direct owner only, when it has been expressly stipulated in the contract of emphyteusis.

If when it has been stipulated, a fixed sum has not been determined, this sum shall consist of two per cent of the price of the alienation.

In emphyteusis, prior to the promulgation of this Code, subject to the payment *laudemium*, even when it has not been stipulated, this prestation shall continue in the usual manner, but it shall not exceed two per cent of the price of the alienation, unless a higher one has been expressly contracted.

1645. The obligation to pay *laudemium* corresponds to the person who acquires the tenement, unless there is a stipulation to the contrary.

1646. When the *emphyteuta* has obtained permission from the direct owner for the alienation or has given him the previous notice, prescribed in art. 1637, the direct owner shall not have the right to claim the payment of the *laudemium*, except within a year following the day on which the public deed is inscribed in the Registry of property. Besides said cases, this action shall be subject to ordinary prescription.

1647. The direct owner may, every twenty nine years, exact the recognition of his right by the person who is in possession of the tenement held in emphyteusis.

The expenses of the recognition shall be borne by the *emphyteuta* and no other prestation, whatever, for this reason, shall be required from him.

1648. The tenement shall be forfeited and the direct owner may claim its restitution:

1. By default in the payment of the pension during three consecutive years.

2. When the *emphyteuta* does not comply with the conditions stipulated in the contract or seriously impairs the tenement.

1649. In order that the direct owner may claim the confiscation in the first case of the preceding article, he shall demand payment from the *emphyteuta*, either judicially or through a Notary, and when said *emphyteuta* does not pay within thirty days next following the demand, the right of the owner may be freely excercised.

1650. The *emphyteuta* may free himself from the forfeiture, in every case, by redeeming the ground-rent and paying the pensions due, within thirty days next following the formal demand for the payment or the summons for the suit.

Creditors of the *emphyteuta* may make use of the same right, within thirty days after the one upon which the direct owner has recovered the full domain.

1651. The redemption of the emphyteusis shall consist in a payment of cash in full to the direct owner for the capital which may have been fixed as the value of the tenement, at the time of the constitution of the ground-rent, and no other prestation can be exacted, unless it has been stipulated.

1652. In case of forfeiture, or in that of rescission of the contract of emphyteusis on account of any cause whatever, the direct owner shall pay for the improvements which may have increased the value of the tenement, provided such increase exists at the time of the restitution.

When the tenement has been damaged, through fault or negligence on the part of the *emphyteuta*, the same shall be set off against the improvements, and as to those which these do not cover, the *emphyteuta* shall remain personally bound to pay for them, as well as for the pensions due and not prescribed.

1653. In default of testamentary heirs, descendants, ascendants, the surviving consort and relatives within the sixth degree of the last *emphyteuta*, the tenement shall revert to the direct owner in the condition in which it may exist, unless the *emphyteuta* did not otherwise dispose of it.

1654. The contract of sub-emphyteusis shall not be valid in the future.

SECTION SECOND.

LOCAL GROUND–RENTS (*FOROS*), AND OTHER CONTRACTS ANALOGOUS TO THAT OF EMPHYTEUSIS.

Article **1655**. Local ground–rents *(foros)*, and any other burdens of analogous nature which may be established after the promulgation of this Code, when they are for an unlimited time, shall be governed by the provisions of emphyteusis, set forth in the preceding section.

When they are temporal or for limited times, they shall be considered as leases and shall be governed by the provisions relating to such contracts.

1656. The contract by virtue of which the owner of land grants its use for the plantation of vines, during the time that the first root-stocks may live, the grantee paying him an annual pension or rent in fruits or in money, shall be governed by the following rules:

1. It shall be considered extinguished fifty years after the grant, when no other time has been expressly fixed in the same grant.

2. It shall also be extinguished by the death of the first root-stocks, or when two thirds of those planted have become barren.

3. The grantee or parcenary may make sprigs or shoots from new vines during the time of the contract.

4. This contract does not lose its character by the power of making other plantations on the lands granted, provided its main object is the plantation of vines.

5. The grantee may freely transmit his right under an onerous or gratuitous title, but the use of the tenement shall not be divided, unless the owner expressly consents to it.

6. In the alienations under an onerous title, the grantor and grantee shall reciprocally have the rights of pre-emption and redemption in accordance with the provisions set forth for

emphyteusis, and with the obligation of giving previous notice, as prescribed in art. 1637.

7.   A parcenary or grantee may relinquish or return the tenement to the grantor, when convenient, upon paying for the impairments caused by his fault.

8.   The grantee shall have no right to the improvements existing on the tenement at the time of the expiration of the contract, provided they are necessary or have been made in fulfillment of what has been stipulated.

In respect to the useful and voluntary improvements, said grantee shall not have a right to be paid for the same, unless he made them with the written consent of the owner of the land, who bound himself to pay for them. In this case, said improvements shall be paid for according to the value which they may have when the tenement is returned.

9.   A grantor may make use of the action of ejectment upon the expiration of the term of the contract.

10.   When, after the expiration of the term of fifty years or the one expressly fixed by the persons interested, the grantee continues in the use and enjoyment of the tenement by the implied consent of the grantor, the former cannot be ejected without previous notice which the latter should give him a year in advance to determine the contract.

CHAPTER THIRD.

CONSIGNATIVE GROUND-RENTS *(CENSO CONSIGNATIVO)*.

Article 1657.   When the payment of the pension for the consignative ground-rent is stipulated in fruits, the species, quantity and quality of the same shall be fixed, and it can not consist of an aliquot part of those which the tenement, held in ground-rent, produces.

1658.   The redemption of the consignative ground-rent shall consist in the restitution to the *censualista* in cash and in full of the capital paid for the constitution of the ground-rent.

1659.   When a real action is instituted against a tenement, held under a ground-rent, for the payment of pensions, if what remains of the value of the same is not sufficinet to cover the capital of the ground-rent and twenty five per cent over and above the same, the *censualista* may oblige the *censatario*, at the latter's option, either to redeem the ground-rent or to complete the guarantee or to abandon the remainder of the tenement in behalf of the former.

1660. The *censualista* may also exercise the right, set forth in the preceding article, in all the other cases in which the value of the tenement is not sufficient to cover the capital of the ground-rent and twenty five per cent more, when any of the following circumstances exist:

1. When the value of the tenement has decreased by the fault or negligence of the *censatario*.

In this case the latter shall also be liable for such damages and injuries.

2. When the *censatario* has failed to pay the pensions during two consecutive years.

3. When the *censatario* may have been declared in bankruptcy, in failure (*en concurso*), or in insolvency.

CHAPTER FOURTH.

RESERVATIVE GROUND-RENT (*CENSO RESERVATIVO*).

Article **1661.** Reservative ground-rent cannot be validly constituted, unless preceded by an avaluation of the tenement for a sum agreed to by the parties or upon a just appraisement by experts.

1662. The redemption of this ground-rent shall be effected by the *censatario* delivering to the *censualista*, in cash and in full, the principal which may have been fixed in accordance with the preceding article.

1663. The provisions of art. 1657 are applicable to reservative ground-rent.

1664. In the cases provided in arts. 1659 and 1660, the debtor of the reservative ground–rent can only be bound, either to redeem the ground-rent, or to relinquish the tenement in favor of the *censualista*.

TITLE VIII.
PARNERSHIP.

CHAPTER FIRST.
GENERAL PROVISIONS.

Article 1665. Partnership is a contract by which two or more persons bind themselves to place money, property, or industry, in common, with the intention of dividing the profits among themselves.

1666. Partnerships must have licit objects, and be established for the common interests of the partners.

When the dissolution of an illicit partnership is declared, the profits shall be destined for the institutions of beneficence of the domicil of the partnership, and, in default of the same, to those of the province.

1667. Civil partnerships may be constituted in any form whatever, unless when real property or real rights are brought to the same, in which case a public deed is necessary.

1668. A contract of partnership is null and void, when real property is brought to the same, if an inventory of said property is not made and signed by the partners and annexed to the deed.

1669. Partnerships, the stipulations of which are kept secret among the partners, and in which each one of the partners may contract in his own name with third parties, shall have no juridical personality.

This kind of partnership shall be governed by the provisions referring to property held in common.

1670. Civil partnerships, on account of the objects for which they are destined, may adopt all the forms accepted by the Code of Commerce. In this case, the provisions of the same shall be applicable, in so far as they are not in conflict with those of the present Code.

1671. Partnerships are either general or particular.

1672. General partnerships may consist of all the present property or of all the profits.

1673. Partnerships which comprise all the present

property are those in which the parties place all the property which actually belongs to them, in common, with the intention of dividing the same among themselves, as well as all the profits which they may acquire through said property.

1674.   In general partnerships of all the present property, what belongs to each of the partners becomes common property of all the partners, as well as all the profits which they may acquire through the same.

A general partnership of any other property may also be agreed upon, but the property which the partners acquire, thereafter, by inheritance, legacy or donations shall not be comprised in the same, though the fruits of said property shall be included therein.

1675.   General partnerships for profits comprise all that the partners may acquire by their industry or work, as long as the partnership lasts.

Personal or real property which each of the partners possess, at the time of the celebration of the contract, shall continue to be their private property, and the usufruct only passes to the partnership.

1676.   A contract of general partnership, entered into without specifying its nature, only constitutes a general partnership of profits.

1677.   Persons who are forbidden to reciprocally grant to each other donations or advantages cannot contract a general partnership.

1678.   A particular partnership has for its object only specified things, their uses or profits, or a specified undertaking, or the exercise of a profession or art.

CHAPTER SECOND.

OBLIGATIONS OF PARTNERS.

SETION FIRST.
OBLIGATIONS OF THE PARTNERS AMONG THEMSELVES.

Article 1679.   A partnership begins from the moment of the celebration of the contract, when not otherwise stipulated.

1680.   A partnership lasts, during the time agreed upon;

in default of an agreement, for such time as the business which has been the exclusive object of the partnership may last, if by its nature, it has a limited duration; and, in any other case, during the lives of the partners, without prejudice to the rights reserved to them in art. 1700, and to the provisions of art. 1704.

1681. Each partner is a debtor of the partnership for whatever he has promised to bring to it.

He is also bound to eviction in regard to the specified and determined things brought by him to the partnership, in the same cases and in the same manner as a vendor is bound in respect to the vendee.

1682. A partner who has bound himself to bring to the partnership a sum of money, and fails to do so, is, at law, a debtor for the interest thereon from the day on which he should have brought it, and may also be bound to pay an indemnity for the damages which he may have caused thereby.

The same thing shall be observed with regard to sums which he may have taken from partnership funds, and interest shall be counted from the day on which he took them for his private benefit.

1683. An industrial partner owes to the partnership, the profits which, during its existence, he has earned in a branch of the industry which is the object of the partnership.

1684. When a partner who is authorized as a manager collects an exigible sum, which was owed to him in his own name, from a person who owed to the partnership another sum, also exigible, the sum collected shall be imputed to the two credits in proportion to their amounts, even when he has given a receipt for his own account only, but when he has given it on account of the partnership, it shall all be imputed to the credit of the latter.

It shall be understood that the provisions of this article shall not prevent the debtor using the power granted to him in art. 1172, but only in the case where the personal credit of the partner is more onerous to him.

1685. A partner who has received in full his share of a partnership credit, when the other partners had not collected theirs, remains bound, when the debtor afterwards becomes, insolvent, to bring to the partnership capital what he received, even when he gave the receipt for his part only.

1686. Every partner shall be liable to the partnership for the damages and injuries caused to the same by his fault, and he can not set off against them the benefits which he may have given to the partnership by his industry.

1687. The risk of things, certain and specificied, which are not perishable, brought to the partnership, in order that only their use and fruits be common, shall be borne by the partner owning them.

When the things brought are perishable, or when they cannot be kept without being impaired, or when they were brought to be sold, the risk shall be assumed by the partnership. It shall also be assumed by the same, in default of a special stipulation in respect to the things brought and appraised in the inventory, and, in this case, the claim shall be limited to the value at which they were appraised.

1688. The partnership is liable to each partner for the sums which he may have disbursed on account of the same and for the corresponding interest; it shall also be liable to each partner for the obligations which he may have contracted in good faith on account of the partnership business, and for risks inseparable from its management.

1689. The losses and profits shall be distributed in conformity with what has been stipulated. When a stipulation exists only in respect to the share of each one in the profits, his share in the losses shall be in the same proportion.

In default of a stipulation, the share of each partner in the profits and losses shall be in proportion to what he brought. The partner who contributes only his industry shall have a share equal to the one who has brought less. When besides his industry, he has brought a capital, he shall also receive the proportional share which may belong to him for this capital.

1690. When the partners have agreed to entrust to a third person the designation of the share of each one in the profits and losses, such designation shall be contested only when it has evidently been made contrary to equity. In no case shall the partner, who has commenced to execute the decision of the third party or who has not contested the same within three months, to be counted from when it was known to him, make a claim against it.

The designation of the profits and losses shall not be entrusted to one of the partners.

1691. A stipulation in which one or more of the partners are excluded from any share in the profits or in the losses is void.

Only the industrial partner may be exempted from any liability in the losses.

1692. A partner, who has been appointed manager in a contract of partnership, may execute all administrative acts, notwithstanding the opposition of his partners, unless he acts in bad faith, and his power is irrevocable, unless it be for a legitimate cause.

A power, executed after the contract, without having it stipulated therein that it should be conferred, may be revoked at any time.

1693. When two or more partners have been charged with the management of a partnership without their functions being specified, or when it has not been expressed that one of them shall not act without the consent of the others, each one may severally excercise all acts of administration; but any of them may oppose the acts of the others before the same has produced any legal effect.

1694. When it has been stipulated that some of the managing partners cannot act without the consent of the others, the consent of all shall be necessary for the validity of the acts; and the absence or impossibility of any one of them to act shall not be alleged, unless there is imminent danger of a serious or irreparable damage to the partnership.

1695. When no stipulation has been made about the form of management, the following rules shall be observed:

1. All the partners shall be considered agents, and whatever anyone of them does by himself alone shall bind the partnership; but each one may oppose the operations of the others before the same has produced any legal effect.

2. Each partner may make use of the things which

compose the partnership capital, according to the customs of the land, provided he does not use them against the interest of the partnership or in such a way as to prevent the use of them to which his co-partners are entitled.

3. Every partner can bind the others to bear together with him the expenses necessary for the preservation of the things held in common.

4. None of the partners shall, without the consent of the others, make any alteration in the partnership real property, even when he alleges that it is useful to the partnership.

1696. Each partner may associate another person in his share; but said person shall not enter the partnership without the unanimous consent of the other partners, even when the former is the manager.

SECTION SECOND.
OBLIGATIONS OF PARTNERS IN RESPECT TO THIRD PERSONS.

Article 1697. In order that the partnership may remain liable to a third person for the acts of one of the partners, it is necessary :

1. That the partner may have acted as such and on account of the partnership.

2. That he may have had the power to bind the partnership by virtue of an express or implied power of attorney.

3. That he may have acted within the limits of the power granted to him.

1698. Partners do not remain jointly bound in respect to the debts of the partnership, and none of them can bind the others by a personal act, if a power has not been conferred on him therefor.

A partnership does not remain liable in respect to a third person for the acts which one of the partners has done in his own name and without a power from the partnership therefor, but it remains liable to the partner in so far as said acts have benefitted said partnership.

The provision of this article shall be understood without prejudice to what is set forth in rule first of art. 1695.

1699. Creditors of the partnership shall be preferred to the creditors of each partner as to the partnership property. Notwithstanding this right, the private creditors of each partner may ask for the seizure and sale at auction of the latter's share in the partnership capital.

CHAPTER THIRD.

MANNERS OF EXTINGUISHING PARTNERSHIP.

Article 1700. Partnership is extinguished:

1. When the term for which it was constituted expires.

2. When the thing is lost, or the business for which it was constituted ends.

3. By the natural death, civil interdiction, or insolvency of any of the partners, and in the case provided for in art. 1699.

4. By the will of any of the partners, subject to the provisions of arts. 1705 and 1707.

Partnerships, to which art. 1670 refer, are excepted from provisions of nos. 3 and 4 of this article, in the cases in which they should exist, according to the Code of Commerce.

1701. When a specific thing, which a partner has promised to bring to the partnership, perishes before the delivery has been effected, its loss produces the dissolution of the partnership.

A partnership shall also be dissolved, in every case, by the loss of the thing, when the partner who brings it reserves to himself the ownership thereof and transfers to the partnership only the use or enjoyment of the same.

But the partnership shall not be dissolved by the loss of the thing, when this loss happens after the property thereof has been acquired by the partnership.

1702. A partnership constituted for a specified time may be extended by the consent of all the partners.

Such consent may be express or implied and it may be shown by any ordinary means.

1703. When the partnership is extended, after the expiration of its term, it shall be understood that a new partnership is constituted. When it is extended before the expiration of such term, the original partnership continues.

1704. A stipulation is valid which provides that, on the death of one of the partners, the partnership shall continue among the survivors. In this case, the heir of the decedent shall have only the right to have a distribution made, fixing it on the day of the death of his constituent; and he shall not participate in the successive rights and obligations only in so far as they are a necessary result of what has been done before said day.

When the stipulation is that the partnership shall continue with the heir, it shall be enforced, without prejudice to the provisions of no. 4 of art. 1700.

1705. The dissolution of the partnership by the will or renunciation of one of the partners shall only take place when a term for its duration has not been fixed, or this term does not appear from the nature of the business.

In order that the renunciation may be effectual, it shall be made in good faith and timely; notice thereof shall also be given to the other partners.

1706. A renunciation shall be considered in bad faith when the person who makes it proposes to appropriate to himself alone the benefits which should be common for all. In this case the person who renounces it does not free himself from responsibility to his partners, and they shall have the power to exclude him from the partnership.

A renunciation shall be presumed as not made in time when, the things not being integral, the partnership is interested in delaying its dissolution. In this case the partnership shall continue until the termination of the pending business.

1707. No partner can demand the dissolution of a partnership, which either by a provision of the contract, or by the nature of the business, has been constituted for a specified time, unless there exists a just cause, such as when one of the co-partners fails to comply with his obligations, or when he becomes incapacitated for the partnership business, or any other similar cause, according to the judgement of the courts.

1708. Distribution among the partners shall be governed

by the rules of inheritances, both with regard to its form and to the obligations resulting from the same. To the industrial partner shall not be given any part of the property brought to it, but only its fruits and profits, according to the. provisions of art. 1689, unless the contrary has been expressly stipulated.

TITLE IX.

AGENCY.

NATURE, FORM AND KIND OF AGENCY.

Article 1709. By the contract of agency, a person binds himself to render some service, or to do something in behalf of or at the request of another person.

1710. Agency may be express or tacit.

Express agency may be given by a public or private instrument and even by parol.

The acceptance may also be express or tacit, and the latter may be inferred from the acts of the agent.

1711. In default of a stipulation to the contrary, the agency is presumed to be gratuitous.

Nevertheless, when the agent has for an occupation the performance of services of the kind to which the agency refers, the obligation of giving him a compensation is presumed.

1712. Agency is general or special.

The former embraces all the business of the principal.

The latter, one or more specified businesses.

1713. Agency stated in general terms only comprises acts of administration.

To compromise, alienate, mortgage or to execute any other act of rigorous ownership express authority is required.

The power to compromise does not give authority to place. the matter in the hands of arbitrators or compromisers.

1714. An agent shall not exceed the limits of the authority granted to him.

1715. The limits of the authority shall not be presumed exceeded, when the business is complied with in a manner more advantageous for the principal than that specified.

1716. An emancipated minor can be an agent; but the

principal shall only have an action against him in conformity with the provisions concerning the obligations of minors.

Married women can only accept an agency with authorization of their husbands.

1717. When an agent acts in his own name, the principal shall have no action against the persons with whom the agent has contracted, nor the said persons against the principal.

In this case, the agent remains directly bound to the person with whom he has contracted, as if it were his own personal, business. The case in which the contract refers to things belonging to the principal is excepted.

The provision of this article shall be understood without prejudice to actions between the principal and the agent.

CHAPTER SECOND.

OBLIGATIONS OF THE AGENT.

Article 1718. An agent by his acceptance remains bound to comply with the agency and shall be liable for the damages and injuries caused to the principal for his non-compliance.

Business, which has already been begun at the death of the principal, must be completed by him, when there is any peril in delay.

1719. In compliance with the agency, the agent shall observe the instructions received from the principal.

In default of the same, he shall do all that, which according to the nature of the business, a good father of a family would do.

1720. Every agent is bound to render an account of his operations and to pay to the principal all that he has received by virtue of the agency, even when what he has received is not owed to the principal.

1721. An agent may appoint a substitute, when the principal has not forbidden him to do so, but he shall be liable for the acts of the substitute:

1. When the power to appoint such substitute was not given to him.

2. When such power was granted to him, but without designating the person, and the person appointed by said agent was notoriously incapable or insolvent.

Whatever is done by the substitute , who has been appointed against the prohibition of the principal, shall be null and void.

1722. In the cases stated in the two numbers of the preceding article, the principal shall also have the right to enforce his action against the substitute.

1723. The liability of two or more agents, even when they have been simultaneously appointed, shall not be joint, unless it has been so stated.

1724. An agent shall owe interest for the sums which he has applied to his own use, from the day on which he did so, and of those which he still owes, after the expiration of the agency and from the time of his default.

1725. An agent who acts as such shall not be personally liable towards the persons with whom he contracted, except when he expressly binds himself therefor, or when he exceeds the limits of his authority without giving a sufficient notice of his powers to said person.

1726. An agent shall be liable not only for deceit, but also for his negligence, which shall be judged with more or less severity by the courts, taking into consideration whether the agent has been paid for his services or not.

CHAPTER THIRD.

OBLIGATIONS OF THE PRINCIPAL.

Article 1727. A principal shall comply with all the obligations which the agent has contracted, within the limits of his power.

A principal remains liable, in so far as the agent has exceeded his power, only when he expressly or tacitly ratifies the same.

1728. A principal shall advance to the agent , if the latter asks it, such sums as may be necessary for the execution of the agency.

When the agent has advanced them, the principal shall reimburse him for the same, even when the business has not succeeded, provided the agent be exempt from blame.

The reimbursement shall comprise the interests on the sums advanced, counted from the day on which the advance was made.

1729. A principal shall also indemnify the agent for all damages and injuries caused to him in complying with the agency, when there is no fault or imprudence on the part of said agent.

1730. An agent may retain the things, which are the objects of the agency, in pledge, until the principal pays the indemnity and reimbursement referred to in the two preceding articles.

1731. When two or more persons have appointed an agent for a business in common, they shall remain jointly bound to the latter for all the effects of the agency.

CHAPTER FOURTH.

MANNER OF DETERMINING THE AGENCY.

Article 1732. Agency is determined:

1. By revocation.

2. By renunciation of the agent.

3. By death, interdiction, bankruptcy or insolvency of either the principal or the agent.

1733. A principal may, at his will, revoke the power and compel the agent to return the document in which the authority was given.

1734. When an agency has been granted to contract with determined persons, the revocation of the agency shall not be to the injury of said persons, unless notice was given to them.

1735. The appointment of a new agent for the same business produces a revocation of the preceding power of attorney from the day on which notice was given to the former agent, without prejudice to the provisions of the preceding article.

1736. An agent may renounce the agency by giving notice to the principal. When the latter suffers any injuries by the renunciation, he should be indemnified for the same by the agent, unless the latter bases his renunciation on the impossibility of continuing to act as such without serious detriment to himself.

1737. Even when the agent has renounced the power for a just cause, he should continue acting as such until the principal shall be able to take the necessary steps to provide therefor.

1738. What has been done by the agent, when he was not aware that the principal was dead, or of any other of the causes which terminate the agency, shall be valid and effectual with regard to third persons who have contracted with the agent in good faith.

1739. When the agent dies, his heirs shall give notice of his death to the principal, and, meanwhile, adopt the measures which circumstances may require for the interest of the latter.

TITLE X.

LOANS.

GENERAL PROVISION.

Article 1740. By the contract of loan, one of the parties delivers to the other, either anything not perishable, in order that the latter may use it during a certain time and return it to the former, in which case it is named *commodatum*, or money or any other perishable thing, under the condition to return and equal amount of the same kind and quality, in which case it is merely called a loan.

Commodatum is essentially gratuitous.

A simple loan may be gratuitous, or made under a stipulation to pay interest.

CHAPTER FIRST.
COMMODATUM.

SECTION FIRST.
NATURE OF *COMMODATUM.*

Article 1741. A lender (*comodante*) retains the ownership of the thing loaned. The borrowar (*comodatario*) acquires the use of the same, but not its fruits; when the person who acquires the use has to pay any compensation, the agreement shall cease to be a *commodatum*.

1742. The obligations and rights which grow out of the *commodatum* shall pass to the heirs of both contracting parties, unless the loan has been made in consideration for the person of the borrower, in which case his heirs shall not have the right to continue using the thing loaned.

SECTION SECOND.

OBLIGATIONS OF THE BORROWER *(COMODATARIO)*.

Article 1743. The borrower shall be bound to pay the ordinary expenses which are necessary for the use and preservation of the thing loaned.

1744. When the borrower puts the thing to a different use than that for which it was loaned, or keeps the same in his possession for a longer time than that agreed upon, he shall be liable for its loss, even when said loss occurs by an unforeseen event.

1745. When the thing loaned was delivered under appraisal and is lost, even if it be by an unforeseen event, the borrower shall be liable for its value, unless there is a stipulation in which he is expressly exempted from said liability.

1746. The borrower shall not be liable for the wear and tear caused to the thing loaned only on account of its use and without fault on his part.

1747. A borrower shall not retain the thing loaned under the pretext that the lender owes him something, even if it is on account of expenses.

1748. All the borrowers to whom the thing is jointly loaned shall be jointly liable for the same, according to the provisions of this secion.

SECTION THIRD.

OBLIGATIONS OF THE LENDER *(COMODANTE)*.

Article 1749. A lender cannot claim the thing loaned, exc ept after the termination of the use for which it was loaned.

Nevertheless, when, previous to such term, the lender has an urgent necessity for the same, he may claim its restitution.

1750. When the duration of the *commodatum* has not been stipulated, nor the use to which the thing loaned was to be destined, and the latter does not appear determined by the customs of the land, the lender may claim it at his will.

In case of doubt the burden of proof falls upon the borrower.

1751. The lender shall pay the extraordinary expenses, caused during the contract for the preservation of the thing loaned, provided that the borrower gives notice of the same before making them, unless when they are so urgent that the answer to the notice cannot be waited for without risk.

1752. A lender, who, knowing the vices of the thing loaned, has not given notice thereof to the borrower, shall be liable to the same for the damages which he may have suffered on that account.

CHAPTER SECOND.

SIMPLE LOAN.

Article 1753. A person who receives money or any other perishable thing on loan acquires its ownership, and is bound to return to the creditor an equal amount of the same kind and quality.

1754. The obligations of a person who takes money on loan shall be governed by the provisions of art. 1170 of this Code.

When what has been loaned is some other perishable thing, or a quantity of metal, not in coin, the debtor owes a quantity, equal to the one received, and of the same kind and quality, although it may have suffered a change in its value.

1755. Interests shall only be owed when they have been expressly stipulated.

1756. A borrower, who has paid interests without it being stipulated, cannot claim them nor impute them to the capital.

1757. Pawn shops shall besides be subject to the ordinances relating to them.

TITLE XI.
DEPOSIT.

CHAPTER FIRST.
DEPOSITS IN GENERAL AND DIFFERENT KINDS THEREOF.

Article 1758. A deposit is constituted when a person receives a thing belonging to another under the obligation of keeping and returning the same.

1759. A deposit may be judicially or extrajudicially constituted.

CHAPTER SECOND.
DEPOSITS PROPERLY SPEAKING.

SECTION FIRST.
NATURE AND ESSENCE OF THE CONTRACT OF DEPOSIT.

Article 1760. Deposit is a gratuitous contract, unless the contrary is stipulated.

1761. Personal property only shall be an object of deposit.

1762. Extrajudicial deposit is either necessary or voluntary.

SECTION SECOND.
VOLUNTARY DEPOSIT.

Article 1763. Voluntary deposit is that in which the delivery is made by the will of the depositor. The deposit may be effected by two or more persons who believe themselves to have a right to the thing deposited in the hands of a third person who shall, in proper casse, deliver said thing to the party to whom it belongs.

1764. When a person able to contract accepts the deposit made by another who is an incapable, the former remains bound to all the obligations of a depositary, and may be compelled to return it by the guardian, curator or administrator of the person who made the deposit or by the same person, if he becomes capable.

1765. When the deposit has been made by a capable person, in the hands of another who is incapable, the depositor shall only have the action to revindicate the thing deposited as long as it remains in the hands of the depositary, or to oblige the latter to pay him the sum by which he may have profitted on account of the thing or its price.

SECTION THIRD.

OBLIGATIONS OF THE DEPOSITARY.

Article 1766. A depositary is bound to keep the thing, and, when required, to return it to the depositor or person holding rights under the same, or to the person who has been designated in the contract. His liability, with regard to the keeping and loss of the thing, shall be governed by the provisions of title first of this book.

1767. A depositary shall not make use of the thing deposited without the express permission of the depositor.

Otherwise he shall be liable for damages and injuries.

1768. When the depositary has permission to serve himself or make use of the thing deposited, the contract loses the character of deposit and becomes a loan or a *commodatum*.

Such permission shall not be presumed, and its existence must be proven.

1769. When the deposit is delivered closed and sealed, the depositary shall return it in the same condition and he shall be liable for damages and injuries when the seal or lock has been broken by his fault.

Such depositary is presumed to be culpable, unless the contrary is proven.

With regard to the value of the thing deposited, the statement of the depositor shall be admitted, when the forcible opening is chargeable to the depositary, unless there is proof to the contrary.

1770. The thing deposited shall be returned with all its proceeds and accretions.

When the deposit consists of money, the provisions in regard to agents, set forth in art. 1724, shall be applied to the depositary.

1771. The depositary cannot force the depositor to prove that he is the owner of the thing deposited.

Nevertheless, if he discovers that the thing has been stolen and who is the true owner, be shall give notice of its deposit to the latter.

When the owner, notwithstanding said notice, does not claim it within the term of one month the depositary shall be free from any liability by returning the thing deposited to the person from whon he received it.

1772. When there are two or more depositors and they are not joint and the thing can be divided, each one of them can ask for his part only.

When they are joint depositors or the thing does not admit of division, the provisions of art. 1141 and 1142 of this Code shall rule.

1773. When the depositor loses his capacity to contract after having made the deposit, the latter cannot be returned, except to the persons who have the management of the property and rights of the depositor.

1774. When, on making the deposit, a place is designated for the return of the thing deposited, the depositary should take it to such place, but the expense caused by the conveyance shall be chargeable to the depositor.

When a place has not been designated for the return thereof, it shall be made at the place where the thing deposited is, even when it is not the same place where the deposit was made, provided that malice on the part of the depositary has not intervened.

1775. The deposit shall be restored to the depositor, when he claims it, even though a term or specified time for such return has been fixed in the contract.

This disposition shall not be observed when the deposit has been judicially seized or attached in the hands of the depositary, or when the latter has been notified of the opposition of a third party to the return or to the transfer of the thing deposited.

1776. The depositary, who has just motives for not keeping the deposit, may, even before the term designated, return it to the depositor, and if the latter refuses it, he may obtain its consignation from the Judge.

1777.   The depositary, who has lost the thing deposited through main force and received another in its place, shall be bound to deliver the latter thing to the depositor.

1778.   An heir of the depositor who, in good faith, has sold the thing, which he did not know was deposited, shall only be bound to return the price which he may have received or to assign his actions against the purchaser in case the price has not been paid to him.

SECTION FOURTH.
OBLIGATIONS OF THE DEPOSITOR.

Article 1779.   A depositor is bound to reimburse the depositary for the expenses incurred by the latter in the preservation of the thing deposited, and to indemnity him for all the injuries which may have been caused to him on account of the deposit.

1780.   The depositary may retain the thing deposited in pledge until the total payment of what is due him on account of the deposit.

SECTION FIFTH.
NECESSARY DEPOSIT.

Article 1781.   A deposit shall be necesssary:

1.   When made in compliance with a legal obligation.

2.   When made on account of any calamity, such as fire, ruin, pillage, shipwreck or any other similar cases.

1782.   A deposit, comprised in the first number of the preceding article, shall be governed by the provisions of the law which establishes it, and, default of the same, by those of voluntary deposit.

Those comprised in the second number shall be governed by the rules of voluntary deposit.

1783.   The deposit of effects, made by travelers, in inns or hostelries, shall also be considered a necessary one.

The keepers of inns and hostelries shall be liable for them as such depositaries, provided that notice thereof has been given to them or to their clerks, and that the travelers on their part observe the precautions which said innkeepers or their substitutes may have about the care and watchfulness over such effects.

1784. The liability to which the preceding article refers shall comprise damages to the goods of travelers, caused by servants or clerks of the keepers of inns or hostelries as well as by strangers, but not for those arising from robbery or which may be caused by any other case of main force.

CHAPTER THIRD.

SEQUESTRATION.

Article 1785. A judicial deposit or sequestration takes place when a seizure or placing in security of property in litigation is decreed.

1786. Personal as well as real property may be subject to sequestration.

1787. A depositary of the property or things sequestrated shall not be released from his charge, until the controversy which caused it is ended, unless the Judge orders it on account of the consent of all the persons interested, or for any other lawful cause.

1788. A depositary of property sequestrated is bound in respect to the same to comply with all the obligations of a good father of a family.

1789. Judicial sequestration shall be governed by the provisions of the Law of Civil Procedure in whatever is not provided for in this Code.

TITLE XII.

ALEATORY OR HAZARDOUS (CONTINGENT) CONTRACTS.

CHAPTER FIRST.

GENERAL PROVISION.

Article 1790. By an aleatory contract, one of the parties binds himself, or both reciprocally bind themselves to give or do something as an equivalent for what the other party has to give or to do, in case of the happening of an event which is uncertain or is to happen at an undetermined time.

CHAPTER SECOND.
CONTRACT OF INSURANCE.

Article 1791. A contract of insurance is one by which the insurer is liable for the fortuitous damages which may occur to the personal or real property insured, in consideration of a certain price, which may be freely fixed by the parties.

1792. Two or more proprietors may mutually insure against fortuitous damages which may happen to their respective properties. This contract is called mutual insurance, and, when it has not been otherwise stipulated, it is understood that the indemnity for such damages shall be paid by all the contracting parties in proportion to the value of the property which each one has insured.

1793. A contract of insurance shall be made in a public or private instrument signed by the contracting parties.

1794. Said instrument shall specify:

1. The designation and situation of the things insured and their value.

2. The classes of risks for which indemnification is stipulated.

3. The day and hour on which the effects of the contract commence and end.

4. All the other conditions to which the contracting parties have agreed.

1795. The contract shall not effectual as to the part in which the sum of the insurance exceeds the value of the thing insured, and only one insurance can be collected for the whole value of the same.

When two or more contracts of insurance exist in respect to the same object, each insurer shall be liable for the damage, in proportion to the capital which he has insured, until the total value of the thing insured has been paid in full by them.

1796. When the damage occurs, the insured must give notice of the same to the insurer and all the other persons concerned, within the term agreed to; and, in default of the same, within twenty four hours to be counted from the time the insured had knowledge of the loss. When he fails to do so, he shall have no action against them.

1797. A contract shall be null when, at the time it was made, the insured knew that the damage, which was the object of the same, had occurred, or when the insurer knew that the property insured was already free from said danger.

CHAPTER THIRD.
GAMING AND BETTING.

Article 1798. The law does not give any action to claim what is won in a game of chance, luck or hazard, but the person who loses cannot recover what he has voluntarily paid, unless fraud has intervened, or he is a minor or incapacitated to administer his property.

1799. The provisions of the preceding article in regard to gambling are also applicable to betting.

Bets which have analogy with prohibited games are considered as prohibited.

1800. Games which contribute to the exercise of the body, as those whose object is to acquire skill in the management of arms, and races on foot or horse back, by vehicles, ball games, and others of an analogous nature are not considered prohibited.

1801. A person who loses in a game or a bet which is not prohibited shall be civilly liable therefor.

Nevertheless, judicial authority may, either not consider the claim when the sum which was wagered in the game or bet is excessive, or such authority may reduce the obligation to the extent it exceeds the customs of a good father of a family.

CHAPTER FOURTH.
ANNUITIES FOR LIFE.

Article 1802. An aleatory contract of annuity binds the debtor to pay a pension or annual sum to one or more specified persons, during their lives, for a capital in personal or real property, the ownership of which is at once transferred to such debtor with the liability of paying such pension.

1803. An annuity may be constituted on the life of the person who gives the capital, on that of a third person, or on that of several persons.

It may also be constituted in behalf of the person or persons for whose life it is agreed, or in behalf of another or other different persons.

1804. An annuity constituted on the life of persons dead, at the time of making the contract, or who, at the same time, is suffering from disease which may cause his death, within twenty days next following that date, is null and void.

1805. Default in payment of pensions due does not authorize the receiver of the life annuity to exact the reimbursement of the capital, nor to re-enter the possession of the tenement alienated; he shall only have the right to judicially claim the payment of the pensions in arrears, and security for future ones.

1806. Annuity, corresponding to the year in which the person who enjoys it dies, shall be paid in proportion to the days which he has lived; when it must be paid in installments in advance, the total amount for such a term, which began to run during his life, shall be paid.

1807. A person, who by a gratuitous title constitutes an annuity on his property, may dispose, at the time of the execution of the contract, that said annuity shall not be subject to attachments for debts of the annuitant.

1808. Annuity cannot be claimed without proving the existence of the person on whose life it was constituted.

TITLE XIII.

COMPROMISES AND ARBITRATIONS.

CHAPTER FIRST.

COMPROMISES.

Article 1809. Compromise is a contract by which each one of the parties by giving, promising, or retaining some thing avoids the provocation of a suit, or puts and end to the one that has already been instituted.

1810. A guardian cannot compromise the right of a person who is under guardianship, except in the manner prescribed in no. 12 of art. 269, and in art. 274 of the present Code.

The father, and, in certain cases, the mother, may compromise in regard to the property and rights. of the child who is under their power, but if the value of the object about which the compromise is made exceeds two thousand *pesetas*, it shall not be effective without judicial approval.

1811. Neither the husband nor the wife can compromise in regard to dotal property and rights, except in the cases and with the formalities provided for alienating or encumbering the same.

1812. Corporations which have a juridical personality can only make compromises in the manner and with the requisites necessary for alienating their property.

1813. A civil action arising from a crime may be compromised; but the public action for the imposition of the legal penalty shall not be extinguished thereby.

1814. No compromises can be made in regard to the civil status of persons, neither in regard to matrimonial questions, nor about future support.

1815. A compromise shall only embrace the objects specifically set forth in the same, or those which by a necessary induction from its words must be considered embraced therein.

A general renunciation of rights shall be understood as including only those which have relation with the question about which the compromise has been made.

1816. A compromise has, as among the parties, the same authority as a final judgment, but summary proceedings shall not be taken, except when they are in compliance with a judicial compromise.

1817. A compromise, in which error, deceit, violence, or forgery of documents intervenes, shall be subject to the provisions of art. 1265 of this Code.

Nevertheless, one of the parties shall not oppose an error of fact against the other, when, on account of a compromise, the latter has withdrawn from a suit already begun.

1818. The discovery of new documents is not a cause for annulling or rescinding a compromise, unless bad faith has been shown.

1819. When a suit has been decided by a final sentence

and a compromise about the same has been made, because one of the parties interested did not know about the existence of such a final sentence, said party may ask that the compromise be rescinded.

Ignorance of a revocable sentence is not a cause for contesting a compromise.

CHAPTER SECOND.

ARBITRATION.

Article **1820.** The same persons who can compromise may also submit their contentions to a third party for decision.

1821. The provisions of the preceding chapter about compromises are applicable to arbitrations. With regard to the form of procedure in arbitrations and as to the extent and effects of the same, the provisions of the Law of Civil Procedure shall be observed.

TITLE XIV.

SECURITY.

CHAPTER FIRST.

NATURE AND EXTENT OF SECURITY.

Article **1822.** By security a person binds himself to pay or to comply with some obligation for a third party in case the latter fails to do so.

When the surety binds himself jointly with the principal debtor, the provisions of section fourth, chapter third, title first of this book shall be observsd.

1823. Security may be conventional, legal or judicial, gratuitous, or under an onerous title.

In may also be constituted, not only in behalf of the principal debtor, but in behalf of another surety, either with the consent, ignorance, and even against the opposition of the latter.

1824. Security cannot exist without a valid obligation.

Nevertheless, an obligation, the nullity of which may be claimed by virtue of an exception purely personal on the part of the obligee, as that of minority, may be the subject of security.

From the provisions of the preceding paragraph is excepted the case in which a loan is made to a minor, not emancipated.

1825.   Security may also be given as a guaranty for future debts, the amount of which is not yet known, but no claim shall be instituted against the surety until the debt is liquid.

1826.   A surety may bind himself to less, but not more than the principal debtor, as to quantity as well as to the oppressiveness of the conditions.

When he binds himself for more, his obligation shall be reduced to the same limits as that of the debtor.

1827.   Security shall not be presumed, it must be express and shall not be extended farther than that specified therein.

When it is simple and indefinite, it shall comprise not only the principal obligation, but all its accessories, including the expenses of the suit, it being understood in regard to the latter that the surety shall only be liable for those incurred, after he has been asked to pay.

1828.   A party who is bound to give security shall present a person having capacity to bind himself and with sufficient property to answer for the obligation which he guarantees.   The surety shall be understood as submitting himself to the jurisdiction of the Judge of the place where this obligation is to be fulfilled.

1829.   When the surety becomes insolvent, the creditor may require another who may have all the qualifications set forth in the preceding article.

The case is excepted where the creditor has required and stipulated that a specified person should be the surety.

CHAPTER SECOND.

EFFECTS OF SECURITY.

SECTION FIRST.

EFFECTS OF SECURITY BETWEEN SURETY AND CREDITOR.

Article 1830.   A surety cannot be compelled to pay a creditor, until a levy has been previously made upon all the property of the debtor.

1831. A levy shall not be made:

1. When the surety has expressly renounced it.

2. When he has jointly bound himself with the debtor.

3. In case of bankruptcy or general assignment of the debtor.

4. When the debtor cannot be judicially sued within the Kingdom.

1832. In order that the surety may avail himself of the benefit of a levy, he must set it up against the creditor, as soon as the latter summons the former for payment, and points out the property of the debtor to him, which can be sold within Spanish territory and which is sufficient to cover the amount of the debt.

1833. When the surety has fulfilled all the conditions of the preceding article, the creditor who is negligent in making a levy upon the property, pointed out to him, shall be liable, to the extent of the value of said property, for the insolvency of the debtor, resulting from said negligence.

1834. A creditor may summon the surety, when he institutes the claim against the principal debtor, but the benefit of a levy shall always be effective, even when a sentence is rendered against both of them.

1835. A compromise made by a surety with a creditor shall have no effect in respect to the principal debtor.

That made by the latter shall neither be of any effect in respect to a surety against his will.

1836. A surety of a surety enjoys the benefit of a levy both with respect to the surety and to the principal debtor.

1837. When there are several sureties but only one debtor for the same debt, the obligation to answer for it shall be divided among them all. The creditor can only 'claim from each surety the corresponding portion which he has to pay, unless the solidarity has been expressly stipulated.

The benefit of division against the co-sureties ceases in the same cases and for the same causes as that for levy against the principal debtor.

SECTION SECOND.

EFFECTS OF SECURITY BETWEEN THE DEBTOR AND THE SURETY.

Article **1838.** A surety who pays for a debtor shall be indemnified by the latter.

Such indemnity comprises:

1. The total amount of the debt.

2. Legal interest on the same from the day on which the payment was made known to the debtor, even when it did not produce interest for the creditor.

3. The expenses caused to the surety after the latter has given notice to the debtor that he has been required to pay.

4. Damages and injuries, when proper.

The provision of this article shall be effective, even when the security has been given without knowledge of the debtor.

1839. By virtue of such payment the surety is subrogated in all the rights which the creditor had against the debtor.

When the surety has compromised with the creditor, he shall not ask from the debtor more than that which he has really paid.

1840. When the surety pays without giving notice to the debtor, the latter may make use against the former of all the exceptions which he could have set up against the creditor, at the time of making the payment.

1841. When the debt is for a term and the surety pays before the expiration, he can not require the debtor to reimburse him until such term has expired.

1842. When the surety has paid without giving notice to the debtor, and the latter, not having knowledge of the payment, also pays it, the former has no remedy against the debtor.

1843. The surety, even before paying, may proceed against the principal debtor:

1. When he is judicially sued for the payment.

2. In case of bankruptcy, general assignment of property, or insolvency.

3. When the debtor has bound himself to relieve him from the security within a specified term, and this term has expired.

4. When the debt has become exigible because the term in which it should have been paid has elapsed.

5. At the end of ten years, when the principal obligation has not a fixed term for its expiration, unless it be of such a nature that it cannot be extinguished except in a term longer than ten years.

In all these cases, the action of the surety tends to obtain his release from the security or a guaranty to defend him against any proceedings of the creditor and from the danger of insolvency of the debtor.

SECTION THIRD.

EFFECTS OF SECURITY AMONGST THE CO-SURETIES.

Article **1844**. When there are two or more sureties for the same debtor and for the same debt, the one who has paid it may claim from each of the others the portion which he or they should proportionally have paid.

If any one of them is insolvent, his portion shall be paid by all in the same proportion.

In order that the provision of this article be applicable, the payment must have been made by virtue of a judicial demand, or when the principal debtor has made a general assignment, or is a bankrupt.

1845. In the case of the preceding article, the co-sureties may set up against the one who paid, the same exceptions which would have corresponded to the principal debtor against the creditor, and which are not purely personal on the part of the same debtor.

1846. A surety for a surety *(subfiador)*, in case of the insolvency of the surety for whom he bound himself, remains liable to the co-sureties in the same terms as the surety was bound.

CHAPTER THIRD.

EXTINGUISHMENT OF SECURITY.

Article **1847.** The obligations of a surety shall expire at the same time as that of the debtor, and for the same causes as all other obligations.

1848.　A merger which takes place in the person of the debtor and of the surety, when one of them becomes the heir of the other, does not extinguish the obligation of the surety for the surety.

1849.　A surety shall be released when the creditor voluntarily acepts a tenement, or any other things in payment of a debt, even when he afterwards loses them on account of eviction.

1850.　Liberation, made by a creditor to one of the sureties, without the consent of the others, shall avail all the others to the extent of the portion of the surety to whom it has been granted.

1851.　An extention granted to a debtor by a creditor, without the consent of the surety, extinguishes the security.

1852.　Sureties, even when they are joint, shall be released from their obligation, whenever by any act of the creditor, they cannot remain subrogated in the rights, mortgages, and privileges of the same.

1853.　A surety may set up against the creditor all the exceptions which pertain to the principal debtor and which may be inherent in the debt, but not those which are purely personal in respect to the debtor.

CHAPTER FOURTH.

LEGAL AND JUDICIAL SECURITY.

Article **1854.**　Sureties, who must give bail by provision of law or by a judicial decree, shall possess the qualifications prescribed in art. 1828.

1855.　When a person who is bound to give security, in the cases of the preceding articles, does not obtain it, a pledge or mortgage which may be considered sufficient to cover his obligation shall be accepted in place of it.

1856.　A judicial surety cannot ask for a levy on the property of the principal debtor.

A person who offers security for a surety, in the same case, shall not ask for either a levy on the property of the debtor nor on that of the surety.

TITLE XV.

CONTRACTS OF PLEDGE, MORTGAGE, AND ANTICHRESIS.

CHAPTER FIRST.

PROVISIONS COMMON TO (CONTRACTS OF) PLEDGE AND OF MORTGAGE.

Article **1857**. The following are essential requisites of the contracts of pledge and of mortgage:

1. That they be constituted to secure the fulfillment of a principal obligation.

2. That the ownership of the thing pledged or mortgaged belongs to the person who pledges or mortgages the same.

3. That the persons, who constitute the pledge or mortgage, may have the free disposition of their property, and, in case they do not have the same, it may be lawfully authorized for such purpose.

Third persons, strangers to the principal obligation, may secure the latter by pledging or mortgaging their own property.

1858. It is also essential in these contracts that when the principal obligation is due, the things of which the pledge or mortgage consists may be sold to pay the creditor.

1859. A creditor can not appropriate to himself the things given in pledge or mortgage, nor dispose of the same.

1860. The pledge and the mortgage are indivisible, even when the debt is divided among persons holding rights under the debtor or the creditor.

An heir of the debtor who has paid a part of the debt shall not therefore ask that the pledge or mortgage be proportionally extinguished, as long as the debt has not been paid in full.

Neither can an heir of the creditor, who received his part of the debt, return the pledge nor cancel the mortgage to the prejudice of other heirs who have not been paid.

From these provisions is excepted the case in which there are several things given in mortgage or pledge and each of them secures only a specified portion of the credit.

The debtor, in this case, shall be entitled to have the pledge or mortgage extinguished in proportion as the part of the debt for which each thing is particularly held liable is paid.

1861. A contract of pledge and of mortgage can secure all kinds obligations, either pure or suject to suspensive or resolutory conditions.

1862. A promise to constitute a pledge or mortgage gives rise only to a personal action among the contracting parties, without prejudice to the criminal responsibility which a person incurs who defrauds another in offering in pledge or mortgage, as not encumbered, things which he knew were encumbered, or pretending to be the owner of things which do not belong to him.

CHAPTER SECOND.

PLEDGE.

Article **1863.** Besides the requisites, specified in art. 1857, it is necessary, to constitute the contract of pledge, that the or of a pledged should be placed in possession of the creditor thing third person by common agreement.

1864. All personal things which are in commerce may be given in a pledge, provided they be susceptible of possession.

1865. A pledge shall not be effective against a third person, when evidence of its date does not appear in a public instrument.

1866. A contract of pledge gives a right to the creditor to retain the thing in his possession or in that of the third person to whom it was delivered, until his credit is paid.

If, while the creditor retains the pledge, the debtor contract with him another debt to be paid before the first one has been paid, the creditor may extend the retention until both credits are paid to him, even when it has not been stipulated that the pledge should be subject to the security for the second debt.

1867. A creditor shall take care of the thing given in pledge with the diligence of a good father of a family; he has the right to recover the expenses incurred for the preservation of the same, and is liable for its loss or impairment, in accordance with the provisions of this Code.

1868. When the pledge produces interest, the creditor shall set off that collected by him against that due him; and if none is due to him, or to the extent that it exceeds that legally due, he shall impute it to the principal.

1869. As long as the case of ex-propriation of the thing given in pledge does not happen, the debtor shall continue as owner of the same.

Nevertheless, the creditor may exercise the actions which belong to the owner of the thing pledged in order to reclaim or defend it against a thing person.

1870. A creditor shall not make use of a thing given in pledge without the authorization of the owner, and when he does so or misuses said thing, in any other manner, the latter may ask it to be placed in deposit.

1871. The debtor cannot ask for the restitution of the thing pledged, against the will of the creditor, until he has paid the debt and its interest with the expenses, when proper.

1872. A creditor, to whom the debt has not been paid in due time, may proceed, before a Notary, to sell the pledge. This sale shall in every case be made at public auction and with due notice, in proper cases, to the debtor and to the owner of the thing pledged. When the pledge has not been sold, at the first sale, a second auction with the same formalities may be held, and when no sale is made, the creditor may become owner of the pledge. In this case he shall be bound to give a discharge for the full amount of his credit.

When the pledge consists of stocks, listed on exchange, they shall be sold in the manner provided for in the Code of Commerce.

1873. Government pawnshops (*Montes de Piedad*), and other public institutions, which by their character or special purpose loan money on pledge, shall be governed by the special laws and regulations in respect thereto, and subsidiarily by the provisions of this title.

CHAPTER THIRD.
MORTGAGE.

Article 1874. Only the following property may be the object of the contract or mortgage :

I. Real Property.

2. Real rights which may be alienated according to law, when imposed on real property.

1875. Besides the requisites, specified in art 1857, it is indispensable, in order that the mortgage be validly constituted, that the instrument in which it is constituted be inscribed in the Registry of property.

The persons, in behalf of whom the law establishes a mortgage, shall have no other right than to exact the execution and inscription of the instrument in which the mortgage is formally drawn, without prejudice to what the Law of Mortgage provides in favor of the State, provinces, and towns for the amount of the last year's taxes, and in favor of the insurers for the premium of the insurance.

1876. A mortgage directly and immediately binds the property on which it is imposed, whoever its possessor may be, for the fulfillment of the obligation for the security of which it was given.

1877. A mortgage is extensive to the natural accessions, to the improvements, to the fruits pending and rents un-collected, when the obligation is due, and to the amount of the indemnities granted or owed to the owner by the insurers of the property mortgaged, or by virtue of ex-propriation or on account of public utility, with the declarations, amplifications and limitations established by law, whether in the case in which the tenement continues in the power of the person who mortgaged it, or when it passes to the hands of a third party.

1878. A hypothecary credit may be alienated or assigned to a third party, wholly or partially, under the formalities required by law.

1879. A creditor may claim from a third possessor of the property mortgaged the payment of the portion of the credit secured with what the latter possesses, according to the terms and with the formalities established by law.

1880. The form, extention and effects of the mortgage, and also whatever relates to its constitution, modification, and extinction, and all that has not been comprised in this chapter, shall remain subject to the provisions of the Law of Mortgage which continues in force.

CHAPTER FOURTH.

ANTICHRESIS.

Article **1881**. By antichresis a creditor acquires a right to receive the fruits of certain real property of his debtor, with the obligation to apply them to the payment of interest, when due, and then to the principal of his credit.

1882. A creditor is bound to pay the taxes and charges which burden the tenement, unless there is a stipulation to the contrary.

He shall also be bound to meet the expenses necessary for its preservation and repair.

From the fruits shall be deducted the sums which may be employed for both purposes.

1883. A debtor cannot recover the enjoyment of the real property, unless he has previously paid in full what he owes to his creditor.

But in order to free himself from the obligations imposed on him by the preceding article, the creditor may always oblige the debtor to re-enter upon the enjoyment of the tenement, unless there be a stipulation to the contrary.

1884. A creditor does not acquire ownership of the real property by default in payment of the debt within the term agreed upon.

Any stipulation to the contrary shall be void. But in this case, the creditor may ask, in the manner provided for in the Code of Civil Procedure, either for the payment of the debt, or for the sale of the real property.

1885. The contracting parties may stipulate that the interest of the debt be set off against the fruits of the tenement given in antichresis.

1886. The last paragraph of art. 1857, paragraph second of art. 1866, and arts. 1860, and 1861 shall be applicable to this contract.

TITLE XVI.

OBLIGATIONS CONTRACTED WITHOUT AGREEMENT.

CHAPTER FIRST.

QUASI-CONTRACTS.

Article **1887**.   Quasi-contracts are those lawful and purely voluntary acts by which the author thereof becomes obligated in regard to a third person, and, sometimes, by which there results a reciprocal obligation amongst the parties concerned.

SECTION FIRST.

MANAGEMENT OF A STRANGER'S BUSINESS.

Article **1888**.   A person who voluntarily takes chage of the agency or administration of the business of another, without authorization, is bound to continue managing the same until the end of the business and its incidents, or to notify the interested person in order that the latter may come to substitute him in his management, if such a one is in condition to personally do it.

1889.   An officious manager must discharge his duties with all the diligence of a good father of a family and make an indemnity for injuries which, through his fault or negligence, may be caused to the owner of the property or business which he is managing.

Notwithstanding, the courts may moderate the amount of the indemnity, according to the circumstances of the case.

1890.   When the manager delegates all or some of the duties of his charge to another person, he shall answer for the acts of the delegate, without prejudice to the direct obligation of the latter towards the proprietor of the business.

The responsibility of the managers, when they are two or more, shall be joint.

1891.   A manager of a business shall be liable for unforeseen events, when he undertakes venturesome operations, which the proprietor was not in the habit of doing, or when he has postponed the interests of the latter in favor of his own business.

1892. Ratification of such management by the proprietor of the business produces the effect of an express authorization.

1893. The owner of property or a business who avails himself of the advantages of the administration of another, even when he has not expressly ratified the same, shall be liable for the obligations contracted for his benefit, and he shall indemnify the administrator for the necessary and useful expenses which he may have incurred and for the injuries which he may have suffered in the discharge of his duties.

The same obligations shall be incumbent on said owner, when the object of said administration was to avoid any imminent or manifest damage, even when no profit results therefrom.

1894. When, without knowledge of the person who is bound to give support, a stranger supplies it, the latter shall have the right to claim the same from the former, unless it appears that he gave it out of charity, and without the intention of recovering it.

Funeral expenses, suitable to the status of the person and to the customs of the locality, shall be paid by those who during their life would have had the obligation to support him, even when the deceased has left no property.

SECTION SECOND.

COLLECTION OF WHAT IS NOT DUE.

Article **1895.** When there was no right to claim a thing which was received and which, through an error, has been unduly delivered, there arises an obligation to restore the same.

1896. A person who accepts an undue payment, when he has acted in bad faith, shall pay the legal interest, when a sum of money has been received, or shall pay for the fruits collected or which ought to have been collected, if the thing received produces them.

He shall also be liable for the impairments which the thing may have suffered on account of any cause whatever and for the damages caused to the person who delivered it, until the latter recovers it. He shall not be liable for unforeseen events, when such events may have affected the things, in the same manner, had they been in the possession of the person who delivered them.

1897. A person, who in good faith has accepted an undue payment of a certain and specified thing, shall only be liable for the impairment or loss of the same and its accessories, in so far as he may have enriched himself from it. When he has alienated it, he shall return the price or assign the action to make the same effective.

1898. With regard to the payment for improvements and expenses, made by the person who unduly received the thing, the provision of title fifth of book second shall rule.

1899. A person shall be exempted from the obligation of restitution, who, believing in good faith that the payment was made on the account of a legitimate and subsistent credit, destroys the title or has allowed the action to be prescribed, or has abandoned the pledge or cancelled the warranties of his right. A person who has unduly made a payment can only address himself to the true debtor or to the sureties with regard to whom the action may yet be enforced.

1900. The proof of payment is incumbent upon the person who pretends to have made the same. He shall all also be obliged to prove the error under which he made it, unless the defendant denies having received the thing claimed from him. In this case, when the plaintiff has proven the delivery, he shall be released from any further proof.

This does not limit the right of the defendant to justify that (the thing) which he is supposed to have received was due him.

1901. It is presumed that there has been an error in the payment, when a thing which was never owed or which was already paid for has been delivered, but the person from whom the return is asked may prove that the delivery was made through liberality or for any other just cause.

CHAPTER SECOND.
OBLIGATIONS WHICH ARISE FROM FAULT OR NEGLIGENCE.

Article **1902.** A person who by an act or omission causes damage to another, when blame or negligence intervenes, shall be bound to make an indemnity for the damage so done.

1903.   The obligation imposed by the preceding article is exigible, not only for personal acts and omissions, but also for those of the persons for whom they should be responsible.

The father, and when he is dead or has been incapacitated, the mother is liable for the injuries caused by the minors who live with them.

Guardians are liable for the injuries caused by minors or incapacitated persons who are under their authority and live with them.

Owners or directors of an establishment or enterprise are equally liable for the damages, caused by their clerks in the service of the branches in which the latter are employed, or on account of their duties.

The State is liable, in this sense, when it acts through a special agent, but not when the damage has been caused by the official to whom properly it pertains to do the act already done, in which case the provision of the preceding article shall apply.

Finally, masters or directors of arts and trades are liable for the damages caused by their pupils or apprentices, while they are under their custody.

The responsibility, to which this article refers, shall cease, when the persons mentioned in the same prove that they employed all the diligence of a good father of a family to avoid the danger.

1904.   A person who pays the damage caused by his subordinates may recover from the latter what he has paid.

1905.   The possessor of an animal, or a person who uses the same, shall be liable for the damages which it may cause, even when said animal escaped or becomes strayed.

This liability shall only cease in case that the damage proceeds from main force or from the blame of the person who has suffered the damage.

1906.   The proprietor of a game-preserve shall be liable for the damage caused by the game to the neighboring tene- ments, when what is necessary to avoid the increase of the same has not been done, or when the efforts of the owners of said tenements to preserve the game has been hindered.

1907.   The proprietor of a building is liable for the

damages which may result from the ruin of the whole or a part thereof, when this happens through default of the neccessary repairs.

1908. The owners shall also be liable for the damages caused:

1. By the explosion of machines of which care has not been taken with due diligence, and for inflammation of explosive substances which were not placed in a safe and proper place.

2. By excessive smoke, which may be injurious to persons or properties.

3. Through the fall of trees, located in places of transit, when it has not been caused by main force.

4. By the emanations of sewers or deposits of infectious matters, when constructed without precautions proper for the place where they are located.

1909. When the damages considered in the two preceding articles occur by defects in the construction, a third person who suffers it may claim damages against the architect, or, in proper cases, against the constructor, only within the term prescribed by law.

1910. The head of a family who dwells in a house or in a part of the same is liable for the damages caused by the things which may be thrown or may fall from the same.

TITLE XVII.
CONCURRENCE AND PREFERENCE OF CREDITS.

CHAPTER FIRST.
GENERAL PROVISIONS.

Article 1911. A debtor is liable for the fulfillment of his obligations to the extent of all his present and future property.

1912. A debtor may judicially ask from his creditors a reduction in the amount and an extension of time in the payment of his debts, or either of the two things, but the exercise of this right shall not produce juridical effects, except in the cases and in the manner set forth in the Code of Civil Procedure.

1913. A debtor, whose liabilities are greater than his

assets, and who has failed to meet his current obligations, shall file a petition of bankrupcty *(concurso)* in a competent court, as soon as he is aware of being in such condition.

1914. A declaration in bankrupcty , incapacitates the bankrupt *(concursado)* from administering his property and any other, which by law pertains to him.

He shall be reinstated in his rights, upon the termination of the bankruptcy when no cause preventing it appears in the qualification of bankruptcy.

1915. By the declaration in bankruptcy, all the immature debts of the bankrupt become due.

Should they be paid before the time fixed in the obligation, they shall suffer the discount corresponding to the amount of the legal interest of the money.

1916. From the date of the declaration in bankruptcy, all the debts of the bankrupt shall no longer bear interest, with the exception of mortgage and pledge credits to the amount of their respective guarantees.

When, after the principal of the debt is paid, any sum remains, interest, reduced to the legal rate, unless the one stipulated is less, shall be paid.

1917. Agreements, which the debtor and his creditors judicially enter into, under the formalities of law about reduction of the amount and extention of time, or in bank-ruptcy, shall be binding on all the concurrent parties and on those who, having been summoned and notified in due form, did not protest in time. Those creditors who, having the right to abstain, have duly made use of such right, shall be excepted.

Creditors comprised in arts. 1922, 1923, and 1924 have the right to so abstain.

1918. When an agreement for reduction of amount and extension of time is entered into with creditors of the same class, the lawful agreement of the majority shall be binding on all, without prejudice to the respective preference of creditors.

1919. When the debtor complies with the agreement, his obligations shall be extinghised in accordance with the conditions stipulated in the same; but, when he fails to comply with the whole or a part of said agreement, the right of the creditors shall revive for the sums of their original credits which they have not received, and any of said creditors may ask for a declaration in or continuance of bankruptcy.

1920. When there is no express stipulation to the contrary, between the debtor and the creditors, the latter shall preserve their rights, afther the termination of the bankruptcy, to collect from the property, which the debtor may afterwards acquire, that portion of their credits, which they have not received.

CHAPTER SECOND.
CLASSIFICATION OF CREDITS.

Article **1921.** Credits shall be classified for their graduation and payment according to the order and terms set forth in this chapter.

1922. In respect to the specified personal property of the debtor, the following are preferred :

1. Credits for the construction, repair, preservation or for the amount of the sale of personal property which may be in the possession of the debtor to the extent of the value of such property.

2. Those secured by a pledge which is in the possession of the creditor, in respect to the thing pledged and to the extent of its value.

3. Those guaranteed by a security of goods or negotiable paper, constituted in a public or mercantile establishment in respect to security and for the value of the same.

4. Credits for transportation, in respect to the goods transported, for the amount of said transportation, expenses and rates of carriage and preservation, until the time of the delivery and for a period of thirty days afterwards.

5. Expenses of boarding in respect to the personal property of the debtor remaining in inns.

6. Credits for seeds and expenses of cultivation and harvesting, advanced to the debtor in respect to fruits of the crops for which they were applied.

7. Credits for rents and leases for one year in respect to the personal property of the lessee existing on the tenement leased and on the fruits thereof.

When the personal property, in respect to which the preference is allowed, has been surreptitiously removed, the creditor may claim it from the person who has the same, within the term of thirty days to be counted from the time it was so removed.

1923. In respect to determined real property and real rights of the debtor, the following are preferred:

1. The credits in favor of the State, in respect to property of tax payers for the amounts of the last annual assessments, due and not paid, of the taxes which burden the same.

2. The credit of insurers, in respect to the property insured, for the premiums of insurance for two years, and when the insurance is mutual, for the last two assessments declared.

3. Mortgage, and statutory and agricultural *(refaccionarios)* credits, noted and inscribed in the Registry of property, in respect to property mortgaged, or which has been the object of the advance *(refacción)*.

4. Credits, preventively noted in the Registry of property by virtue of a judicial order, for attachments, seizures, or execution of sentences, in respect to the property noted therein and only in regard to subsequent credits.

5. Statutory agricultural credits, neither annotated nor inscribed, in respect to the real estate to which the advance *(refacción)* refers, and only with regard to other credits different from those stated in the four preceding numbers.

1924. In respect to the other personal and real property of the debtor, the following credits are preferred:

1. Credits in favor of the province or municipality for the taxes of the last year, due and unpaid, not comprised in number one of art. 1923.

2. Those incurred:

A. For judicial expenses and those of administration of the bankruptcy for the common interest of the creditors, made with due authorization or approval.

B. For the funeral expenses of the debtor, acccording to the customs of the place, and also those for his wife and for his children, under parental power, when they have no property of their own.

C. For expenses of the last illness of the same persons,

caused during the last year, counted up to the day of their death.

D. For daily wages and salaries of the clerks and domestic servants, corresponding to the last year.

E. For advances made to the debtor for himself and his family, constituted under his authority, in provisions, clothing or shoes, during the same period of time.

F. For pensions for support during the proceedings in bankruptcy, unless they are based on a title of liberality only.

3. Credits which without a special privilege appear:

A. In a public instrument.

B. In a final judgment, when they have been the object of litigation.

These credits shall have preference among themselves, according to the priority of dates of the instruments and of the judgments.

1925. Credits of any other kind or by any other title, not comprised in the preceding article, shall have no preference.

CHAPTER THIRD.

PRIORITY OF PAYMENT OF CREDITS.

Article **1926.** Credits, which enjoy preference in respect to certain personal property, exclude all others to the extent of the value of the personal property to which the preference refers.

When two or more creditors claim preference in respect to certain personal property, the following rules shall be observed, as to priority of payment:

1. Credits secured by a pledge exclude all others, to the extent of the value of the thing given in pledge.

2. In case there is a security, and if it is lawfully constituted in behalf of more than one creditior, the priority amongst them shall be determined by the order of the dates of the execution of the guarantee.

3. Credits for advances for seeds, expenses of cultivation and gathering, shall be preferred over those for rents and leases, in regard to the fruits of the crop for which they were incurred.

4. In all other cases, the value of the personal property shall be distributed pro rata among the credits which enjoy special preference in regard to the same property.

1927. Credits, which enjoy preference in regard to certain real property or real rights, exclude all others for their full amounts to the extent of the value of the real estate or real rights to which the preference refers.

When two or more credits affecting certain real property or real rights concur, the following rules shall be observed in respect to their priority:

1. Those set forth in nos. 1 and 2 of art. 1923 shall be preferred, according to the order, to those comprised in the other numbers of the same article.

2. Mortgages and statutory agricultural credits, annotated or inscribed and specified in no. 3 of said article, and those comprised in no. 4 of the same, shall enjoy priority among themselves, according to the order of the dates of the respective inscriptions or annotations in the Registry of property.

3. Statutory agricultural credits not annotated or inscribed in the Registry, to which no. 5 of art. 1923 refers, shall enjoy preference among themselves in the inverse order of their dates.

1928. The residue of the estate of a debtor, after the credits which enjoy preference in regard to certain property, personal or real, have been paid, shall become part of the free property which the latter may possess for the payment of the other credits.

Those which enjoy preference in regard to certain property, personal or real, and which have not been totally paid in full with the amount of such property, shall be paid as to the deficit in the order and place pertaining to the same, according to their respective natures.

1929. Credits which have no preference in regard to certain property; those which have preference for the amount not collected; and those which, by prescription, have lost the right of preference, shall be paid according to the following rules:

1. In the order established in art. 1924.

2. Those by priority of dates, according to the order of the same, and those which have a common date, pro rata.

3. Common credits, to which art. 1925 refers, without consideration of their dates.

TITLE XVIII.
PRESCRIPTION.

CHAPTER FIRST.
GENERAL PROVISIONS.

Article **1930**. Ownership and other real rights are acquired by prescription in the manner and under the conditions specified by law. Rights and actions, of whatever kind, also become extinguished by prescription in the same manner.

1931. Persons able to acquire property or rights by other lawful means can also acquire the same by prescription.

1932. Rights and actions shall be extinguished by prescription to the prejudice of all classes of persons, including juridical ones, according to the terms provided by law.

Persons incapacitated to administer their property shall always retain the right to make claim against their lawful representatives whose negligence may have been the cause of the prescription.

1933 Prescription gained by a co-proprietor or owner in common shall be for the benefit of all the others.

1934. Prescription produces its juridical effects in behalf and against the estate of inheritance, before the latter has been accepted, and during the time granted to make an inventory and for deliberation.

1935. Persons with the capacity to alienate may renounce the prescription gained, but not the right to prescription in the future.

Prescription shall be understood as tacitly renounced when the renunciation results from facts which lead to the supposition that the right acquired has been abandoned.

1936. All things which are in commerce are susceptible of prescription.

1937. Creditors and all other persons, interested in

making a prescription valid may profit by the same, notwithstanding the express or tacit renunciation of the debtor or owner.

1938. The provisions of the present title shall be understood without prejudice to what may be established in this Code or in special laws in respect to specified cases of prescription.

1939. Prescription, which began to run before the publication of this Code, shall be governed by the laws then prevailing; but if, after this Code is in force, all the time required in the same for prescription has elapsed, such prescription shall be effectual, even when according to the former laws a longer period of time was required.

CHAPTER SECOND.

PRESCRIPTION OF OWNERSHIP AND OTHER REAL RIGHTS.

Article **1940.** For ordinary prescription of ownership and other real rights, it is necessary to possess things in good faith and under a just title, during the time specified by law.

1941. Possession must be held under belief of ownership, and be public, peaceful, and uninterrupted.

1942. Acts of a possessory character, executed by virtue of permission, or by mere tolerance of the owner, are of no effect for establishing possession.

1943. For the effects of prescription, possession is interrupted either naturally or civilly.

1944. Possession is interrupted naturally, when, for any cause, it ceases for more than one year.

1945. Civil interruption is caused by a judicial summons on the possessor, even when made by order of an incompetent judge.

1946. A judicial summons shall be considered not made and shall fail to cause interruption:

1. When it is null and void by lack of legal solemnities.

2. When the plaintiff withdraws his complaint or fails to prosecute it in due time.

3. When the possessor is discharged from the suit.

1947. Civil interruption shall also be caused by a judgment of peace *(acto de conciliación)*, provided that within two months from its celebration, the complaint as to possession or ownership of the thing contested be presented in court.

1948. An express or tacit acknowledgement which the possessor may make in respect to the right of the owner also interupts possession.

1949. Against the title recorded in the Registry of property, the ordinary prescription of ownership or of real rights shall not obtain against a third person, except by virtue of another title similarly recorded, and the time shall begin to run from the date of the inscription of the second.

1950. Good faith of the possessor consists in his belief that the person from whom he received the thing was the owner of the same, and could convey the ownership thereof.

1951. The conditions of good faith, required for possession in arts. 433, 434, 435, and 436 of this Code, are equally necessary for the determination of said requirement in the prescription of ownership and of other real rights.

1952. By a just title is understood that which legally suffices to transfer the ownership or real rights, the prescription of which is in question.

1953. Title for prescription must be true and valid.

1954. A just title must be proven; it never can be presumed.

1955. Ownership of personal property is prescribed by an uninterrupted possession in good faith for a period of three years. Ownership of personal property is also prescribed by an uninterrupted possession of six years, without the necessity of any other condition.

The provisions of art. 464 of this Code shall be observed in respect to the rights of the owner to revindicate the personal things lost or of which he has been unlawfully deprived, and also in regard to those acquired at an auction, on exchanges, at fairs or markets, or from a merchant lawfully established or habitually engaged in the traffic of similar objects.

1956. Personal property stolen or robbed can not be prescribed by the persons who stole or robbed the same, nor

by their accomplices, or harborers, unless the crime or misdemeanor or their penalities and the actions to exact the civil
responsibility, arising from the crime or misdemeanor, have been
prescribed.

1957. Ownership and other real rights in respect to real
property shall be prescribed by possession for ten years as to
persons present, and by twenty years in respect to those absent,
when held in good faith and under a just title.

1958. For the effects of prescription, a person, who resides
in a foreign country or beyond the seas, shall be considered as
absent.

When said person has been present during part of the time,
and absent during another part, every two year of absence
shall be considered as one year to complete the ten years of the
time required to be present.

Absence which is not for a whole and continuous year
shall not be considered in the computation.

1959. Ownership and other real rights in respect to real
property shall also be prescribed by the uninterrumpted possession of the same for thirty years, without the necessity of
title or good faith, and without distinction of persons, absent
or present, save the exception set forth in art. 539.

1960. In the computation of the time necessary for
prescription, the following rules shall be observed :

1. The actual possessor may complete the time necessary
for prescription by adding to his time that of the person under
whom he holds rights.

2. It is presumed that the actual possessor, who has been
a possessor in former a time, has continued to be such possessor
during the time intervening, unless there is proof to the
contrary.

3. The day on which the time begins to run is considered
as a whole day but the last day should be wholly completed.

CHAPTER THIRD.

PRESCRIPTION OF ACTIONS.

Article **1961.** Actions are prescribed by the mere lapse of
the time specified by law.

1962. Real actions in respect to personal property are prescribed by the lapse of six years after the loss of possession, unless the possessor has, during a shorter term, gained the ownership in accordance with art. 1955, and with the exception of the cases of loss and public sale, and those of theft and robbery, in which cases the provision of paragraph third of said article shall rule.

1963. Real actions in respect to real property are prescribed after thirty years.

This provision is understood without prejudice to what is provided in respect to the acquisition of ownership or of real rights by prescription.

1964. Hypothecary actions are prescribed after twenty years, and those which are personal and which have no special term of prescription fixed, after fifteen years.

1965. Among co-heirs , co-owners or proprietors of adjacent tenements, the action to ask partition of the inheritance, the division of the thing held in common or of the demarkation of the adjacent properties shall not be prescribed.

1966. Actions to exact the fulfillment of the following obligations are prescribed by the lapse of five years:

1. For the payment of pensions for support.

2. For the payment of rents, whether they are derived either from rural or city tenements.

3. That of any other payments which should have been made annually or in shorter periods.

1967. Actions for the fulfillment of the following obligations shall be prescribed after the lapse of three years:

1. For the payment of judges, lawyers, registrars, notaries, with and without records, *(notarios escribanos)*, experts, agents and clerks for their honoraries and fees and the charges and disbursements made by them in the discharge of their duties or offices in the matters to which the obligations refer.

2. For payments to apothecaries for medicines which they have supplied; to professors and teachers for their salaries and stipends for the instruction which they have given, or for the exercise of their profession, art or avocation.

3. For the payment of mechanics, servants, and laborers

the amounts due for their services, and for the supplies or disbursements which they may have made concerning the same.

4. For the payment of board and habitation to innkeepers and to traders for the value of goods, sold to others who are not traders, or who being traders are engaged in a different trade.

The time for the prescription of actions, to which the three preceding paragraphs refer, shall be counted from the time the respective services have ceased to be rendered.

1968. By the lapse of one year, are prescribed:

1. Actions to recover or retain possession.

2. Actions to exact civil responsibility for contumely, or calumny, and for obligations derived from blame or negligence, set forth in art. 1902 from the time the aggrieved person knew it.

1969. The time for the prescription of all kinds of actions, when there is no special disposition providing otherwise, shall be counted from the day on which they could have been exercised.

1970. The time for the prescription of actions, the object of which is to claim the fulfillment of obligations in respect to principal with interest or rent shall run from the last payment of rent or interest.

The same shall be understood in regard to the principal of the consignative ground-rent,

In the emphyteusis, and reservative ground-rent, the time for the running of the prescription shall be counted from the last payment of the pension or rent.

1971. The period for the prescription of actions to exact the fulfillment of obligations, declared in a final judgment, shall begin from the day the judment became final.

1972. The term for the prescription of actions to exact the rendering of accounts shall run from the day on which those who should have rendered them ceased in the discharge of their duties.

That pertaining to the action for the balance of accounts, from the date on which the latter was acknowledged by agreement of the parties interested.

1973. Prescription of actions is interrupted by the exercise of the same before the courts, by extrajudicial claim of the creditor, and by any other act of acknowledgement of the debt by the debtor.

1974. Interruption of prescription of actions in joint obligations shall equally benefit or injure all the creditors or debtors.

This provision shall equally rule with regard to the heirs of the debtor in all kinds of obligations.

In obligations in severalty, when the creditor does not claim from one of the debtors more than the portion corresponding to him, the prescription shall not be interrupted for that reason, in respect to the other co-debtors.

1975. Interruption of the prescription, against the principal debtor by judicial claim of the debt, shall also be effective against his surety; but that produced by extrajudicial claims of the creditor, or private acknowledgements of the debtor, shall not injure said surety.

FINAL PROVISION.

Article **1976.** All the legal compilations, uses, and customs which constitute the common civil law in all matters which are the object of this Code are hereby abrogated and they shall remain without force or effect, either as direct obligatory laws, or as supplementary law. This provision shall not apply to the laws which have been declared in force by this Code.

TRANSIENT PROVISIONS.

Changes introduced in this Code to the injury of rights, acquired under preceding civil legislation, shall have no retroactive effect.

To apply the corresponding legislation in cases not expressly specified in this Code, the following rules shall be observed:

I. Rights arising under the legislation preceding this Code, from acts realized under its rules, shall be governed by said preceding legislation, even whem this Code regulates them in another manner, or does not recognize the same. But when such rights appear declared for the first time in this Code, they shall at once be effective, even when the facts which originated them have been accomplished under the preceding legislation, provided that they do not injure other acquired rights having the same origin.

2. Acts and contracts entered into under the *regime* of the preceding legislation, and which are valid according to the same, shall produce all their effects according to the same legislation, with the limitations set forth in these rules. Therefore, last wills, even when jointly executed; powers of attorney to execute wills and testamentary notes, executed or written before this Code was in force, shall be valid; and the clause *ad cautelam*, the trusts (*fideicomisos*) for applying the estate in accordance with the secret instructions of the testator, and any other acts, prescribed by the preceding legislation, shall be effective; but the revocation or modification of these acts or of any of the clauses contained in the same, shall not be effective, after this Code has been enforced, except by making the testament according to the same.

The provisions of this Code which sanction, with a civil penalty or deprivation of rights, acts or omissions which had no sanction in the preceding legislation, shall not be applicable to the person who, when the latter was in force, had incurred the omission or commited the act forbidden by this Code.

When the fault is also punished by the preceding legislation, the mildest provision shall be applied.

4. Actions and rights arising before this Code was in force, and not exercised, shall subsist with the extension and according to the terms acknowledged by the preceding legislation, but shall be subject, in regard to the exercise, duration, and proceedings for enforcing them, to the provisions of this Code.

When the exercise of the right or of the actions is dependent upon official proceedings, begun under the preceding legislation, and these are different from those established in this Code, the persons interested may chose either one or the other.

5. Children who have attained the age of twenty three years, when this Code becomes effective, are emancipated and not subject to the parental power, but when they continue living in the house and at the expense of their parents, the latter may

retain the usufruct, the administration, and other rights which they are enjoying in respect to the private property of their children, up to the time when the children should be freed from the parental power according to the preceding legislation.

6. A father who may have voluntarily emancipated a child, reserving to himself some rights out of his adventitious property, may continue enjoying the same up to 'the time when the son should be freed from the parental power according to the preceding legislation.

7. Fathers, mothers, and grandparents, who are exercising guardianship of their descendants, shall not withdraw the securities which they have constituted, nor be obliged to constitute them, when said sureties have not been given, nor to complete the same, when those given appear to be insufficient.

8. Guardians and curators, named under the provisions of the preceding legislation, and with subjection to the same, shall preserve their charges, subject as to the exercise of the same to the provisions of this Code.

This rule is also applicable to the possessors, and temporary administrators of the property of other persons, in those cases in which the law establishes the same.

9. Guardianships and curatorships, the definite constitution of which is pending the decision of the courts, at the time this Code becomes efective, shall be constituted according to the preceding legislation, without prejudice to the preceding rule.

10. Judges and municipal attorneys shall not of their own accord proceed to name family councils, except in regard to minors whose guardianship may not be definitely constituted, when this Code becomes effective. When the guardian or curator has already begun to exercise his charge, the family council shall not be named until one of the persons who has to form a part of the same, or the same guardian or curator existing petitions for the constitution of said council, and meanwhile the appointment of a *protutor* shall remain in suspense.

11. Proceedings for adoption , those for voluntary emancipation, those for dispensation of law, pending before the

Government or the courts, shall be continued in accordance with preceding legislation, unless the fathers or petitioners for such grace desist from these proceedings and prefer those established in this Code.

Rights to the inheritance of persons who have died, with or without a will, before this Code is in force, shall be ruled by the preceding legislation. The inheritances of those who die after that time, with or without a testement, shall be adjudicated and distributed according to this Code, but complying, in so far as the latter permits it, with the testamentary provisions. Therefore, the *legitimes*, advantages, and legacies shall be respected; but their amounts shall be reduced, when it is not possible, in any other manner, to give to each participant in the inheritance, the portion corresponding to him, according to this Code.

13. Cases, not directly comprised in the preceding provisions, shall be determined by applying the principles on which they are founded.

ADDITIONAL PROVISIONS.

1. The President of the Supreme Court and those of the Territorial Audiencias shall transmit to the Secretary of Grace and Justice, at the end of each year, a report in which, referring to the affairs of which the civil branches have taken cognizance during the same year, they may point out the deficiencies and doubts which they have met in applying this Code. They shall state, in detail in the same, the questions and points of law controverted, and the articles or omissions of the Code which have given cause for doubts to the Court.

2. The Secretary of Grace and Justice shall transmit these reports and a copy of the civil statistics of the same year to the General Commission on Codification.

3. In view of this data, of the progress made in other countries, which may be utilized in our country, and of the jurisprudence of the Supreme Court, the Commission on Codification shall formulate and transmit to the Government, every ten years, such reforms as it may be convenient to introduce.

TABLE OF CONTENTS.

CIVIL CODE.

PRELIMINARY TITLE.

BOOK FIRST.
PERSONS.

BOOK SECOND.

PROPERTY, OWNERSHIP, AND ITS MODIFICATIONS.

PRELIMINARY PROVISION.

BOOK THIRD.

DIFFERENT WAYS OF ACQUIRING OWNERSHIP.

PRELIMINARY PROVISION.

BOOK FOURTH.

Obligations and Contracts.

www.ingramcontent.com/pod-product-compliance
Lightning Source LLC
Chambersburg PA
CBHW021724110726
47902CB00005B/1338